THE FRIDAY NIGHT CLUB, A NOVEL

Jacob Nelson Lurie

ISBN: 1-4392-6247-0
ISBN-13: 9781439262474

ACKNOWLEDGEMENTS

Thanks to Susan and Uwe for guiding me to this point, to Sean, Joelle, Tatjana, and Brenda for their notes and suggestions, to Dustin, Julie, Kevin, and Phil for their kind reviews, to my mother and sister who were able to read this as fiction, and to my father for spending countless nights teaching me how to read and write.

DEDICATIONS

For Karie, Brody, and Colby, without whom I'd still be living within the realm of my own Friday Night Club.

DISCLAIMERS

Disclaimer A: This is a true story. Aside from the parts that aren't true, of which there are a few, though not as many as you would believe. The characters are *all* real people, though their names have been changed and the events do not necessarily correlate to that individual in real life. That said this is a novel, and *not* a memoir. Aside from the parts that are a memoir … of which there are many, though not as few as you would believe.

Disclaimer B: This story is about a bunch of guys being guys and shit happens to them, usually of their own design. And anyone who's ever been around a bunch of guys being guys knows for a fact that: A. Nothing gets done; B. Very little gets solved; C. Nothing makes sense until you over-analyze it years later and even then things are blurry; G. Events and conversations are often insensitive, coarse, rude, foul, jaw-dropping, and not-at-all politically correct; M. Punches are usually thrown and very few connect; Q. Alcohol is the main character, culprit, mother, lover, therapist, hero, and villain; W. None of those guys would ever trade those experiences, good or bad, for anything in the world. Not money, sex, drugs, sex, or sex. Except for sex. Any guy will trade anything for sex; And Z. We men are dumb.

Disclaimer C: Whether you know this or not, these people are your friends, your lovers, or your family. I *guarantee* that you know someone like one of these characters. I *guarantee* that person has lived a life more interesting than all of these characters combined. I *guarantee* that if you didn't know that person then, you would hate who they were. And I can *guarantee* that you love that person now.

PROLOGUE

Saturday

I want to run. Past my friends, my family ... Her ...

Flashes of the night before: colored stars, a backroom, naked flesh, Her face.

Sharply, I inhale. Beside me, Jonesy smiles, probably believing my gasp is a result from feet-numbing fear instead of gut-churning horror. I attempt to attach Her face to the naked flesh the night before. The colored stars fade into Christmas lights; the back room into a bathroom. Music — the Violent Femmes? Kisses inside my bare leg. I'm naked ...

I look out to Her. She's looking back, her half leer full of tales that could fill a *Penthouse Forum*. Or am I imagining the look? Is she squinting from the setting sun? Or is she trying not to cry because it's all about to slip past us — the potential, the wanting, the desire to say 'fuck all' and run off to the jungles of Brazil or the mountains of Argentina or some remote place where we can just be alone, just be us, just be naked, just be entwined in the passion of ...

Something happened. I know something happened. But when I close my eyes and look down at the woman kissing her way up my body everything goes white and I ...

The music starts. Not the muffled Violent Femmes, but the march ... the march of the grip, closing on the future, closing on the jungles of Brazil and the mountains of Argentina and promising a life of comfort and routine instead of sweat-down- the-back excitement. Everyone stands, including Her, and they all look back, including Her, and I can't help but follow their gazes — Her gaze — to the foot of the aisle and the bride walking toward me ... my fiancée, the future mother of my children ... Pamela ...

I want to run.

CHAPTER ONE

The Wednesday Before

Peter Carter is pissing in the corner of the hallway. We're on the second floor of a Boulder office building, plush, expensive, and the bathroom door is a foot to his right.

He says, "Sometimes a good piss is better than sex."

I'd picked him up from Denver International six hours ago, three days before my wedding, one day before my bachelor party, at 6:12 p.m. on a Wednesday, and he was already jazzed to the gills. When he first saw me — through ridiculously big sunglasses and the bill of a Colorado Avalanche ball cap low over his eyes — he skipped the offered hand and kissed me full on the lips.

He said, "Davis, my friend, seeing you up there, walking into a lifetime of pain, will bring me more pleasure than a glory-hole fuck in a Kansas gas station."

I debated asking him if he'd ever been in a Kansas gas station, but decided against it. The key to Peter was just going for the ride and not hitting the brakes.

"You're getting fucking married," Peter said. "What the fuck?"

I shrugged and pulled onto I-70 going west. Traffic was already starting to thin out from rush hour, but with all the construction these days, I wasn't holding my breath.

"Wow, things are changing around here," he said, leaning forward, peering out at the downtown landscape.

"When was the last time you were back?"

"Few years. High school reunion."

"Yeah? How did that go?"

Peter pulled out a pack of Camels and offered me one.

"I quit," I said.

"No shit?"

"Year and a half."

"Fuck." He lit up and I rolled down the back windows a bit. After a moment, he looked at me, started to ask a question, stopped, and looked away. You could always tell when Peter was thinking because he rubbed his nose as if he had a coke problem. Over the years, the tabloids have filled their copy with rampant speculation on the subject.

"I love her," I said, unsure at that moment if I really did.

He put his feet on the dashboard and said, "Shit, Davis. I've been in love a dozen times, that doesn't mean I married 'em all."

"You married three of them."

He was silent. "Yeah," he said, finally. "But you're a better man than me."

I met Peter at a party he threw eleven years ago. My —

Freshman Year

— at the University of Colorado at Boulder, his junior. I was sitting in my dorm room having phone sex with Marnie, my girlfriend of three years who was still a senior in high school down in Denver, when my roommate, Adam Jones, burst in.

"We're leaving."

"Um, busy," I said, my pants open, flag flying high.

"There are girls that can take care of that for you," he said as he tossed me my coat.

That was the last time I spoke with Marnie, but it was getting old anyway. A month earlier, I refused to go down on her because I'm all about reciprocation. We'd spoken on the phone since, but hadn't seen each other. I was glad to cut ties and roam the uncharted desert without care.

We arrived before the cops showed, but after the band started. I don't know what I was expecting, my only real basis of comparison being high school parties, and, let's face it, they aren't even in the same lot, no matter what people tell you. It's like comparing a bored-out V-8 '65 Mustang with a Yugo. They can both get you somewhere, but until you can handle the curves, the acceleration, the speed, you're just driving.

The best way I can describe this party was "three dimensional." We grow up watching movies, yearning to toga with Otto, slam dance with Gutter, or streak with Frank-The-Tank, but we never truly experience the moments because they're truncated versions of the truth. The best parts. The *SportsCenter* highlight reel.

I never caught the name of the band, but I'm sure it was Granola Death or Vegan Apathy or something apt for the town of Boulder. Regardless, they were loud. The moment we stepped in the door, sound encompassed all, leaving you to quickly obtain a master's in lip reading or find someone selling a damn good fake.

Weaving between warm bodies, I followed Adam in search of the master of the townhouse. We found him, in the kitchen, doing body shots with mostly naked girls — no, mostly naked *women* — and this was when the third dimension truly kicked in because I could smell them, feel them, hear their unspoken whispers, bathe in their wanton desires.

And then, I realized I would have to talk to them.

Thank Granola Death for being so damn loud.

"Jonesy!" Peter said to Adam Jones. Or I thought that was what he said. What followed was jumbled with unintelligible lyrics from the band and Peter kissing Jonesy full on the lips.

He looked a lot like a young Matthew McConaughey, a mop of blond covering a high forehead, on the tall side, lanky. Already you could see his trademark side leer that would melt the hearts of millions of women across the globe.

We were all introduced — no kiss from Peter, thank God, but also no kiss from the women, shitballs — and were promptly handed shots already lined up on the counter.

After the third of these sweet shots, I was introduced to Hillary. Blond, pigtails, a small John Elway practice jersey cut to cover everything I wanted to see. She smelled of peppermint. She whispered of lust. We talked, but didn't hear anything. I don't think either of us cared.

After the seventh shot, I asked Jonesy what we were drinking. Something was wrong. Seven shots in twenty minutes and I didn't feel a thing.

"Smooth, isn't it?" he said, with a crooked, boyish smile. I knew I was in trouble. I could hear him clearly. They say alcohol dulls the senses, but there's a moment between cold sobriety and the buzz where you achieve absolute clarity. Most people miss it, forget about it, or dismiss it as a figment of their imagination. It's the moment when everything bad ceases to matter, where you stop thinking and everything makes sense. Where all the questions are answered and then forgotten. I call it the Wave. It sweeps over you and every part of your being relaxes. Tension transforms into relief. And you can smell the faintest of scents (Hillary's designer conditioner), see the smallest of details (Peter's slightly chipped front tooth), and pick out the sounds among the earsplitting cacophony.

I must have made a face because Jonesy said, "What? You don't like vodka?"

Peter lined up the shots for a refill — vodka with a splash of sweet and sour. Hillary giggled at my look of horror. I could hear it, and yet Vegan Apathy was still kicking, the cops yet to arrive. I blushed. The next round of shots wasn't as smooth. I gagged.

Peter slapped me on the face and said, "Congratulations! You've just taken your first step into a larger world!"

Peter Carter. The closet geek.

Five hours later, I was horfing in the back bushes, my home and garden since I bailed when the cops showed up an hour earlier. I was sure my ears were bleeding from the sonic pounding and my stomach had detached itself in protest, relocating to my small intestine.

"There you are," Peter said. "Hillary was worried about you." He must have read my face. "Pigtails."

Ah. The memories started to return.

Jonesy spoke the truth about the party, and in my book, a man's word is his bond. I'd met him just two weeks prior, always unsure of new people, and now if he shouted, 'Thar be barmaids there!' I'd battle the elements and sail with him the wrong way around the Horn.

"Remind me to thank Jonesy for walking in on me and Marnie," I said.

"Who's Marnie?" As I started to reply, Peter said, "You know what? I don't care."

Fair enough. The less I explained, the more I concentrated on Peter's voice and the more I concentrated on Peter's voice, the less the world spun.

"Here." Peter took out a Camel from a pack and put it in my mouth. I didn't have the strength to protest. He lit it and I was soon coughing.

"You act as if you've never smoked," he said.

"Never have."

"Ah, but you're in Rome, my boy. You don't want to upset the status quo."

My lungs voiced their protest, quickly followed by my stomach. No wonder the empire fell.

As we talked, I learned that Peter was the oldest of four brothers, Catholic, not Mormon, he was quick to point out, and his parents were in the oil business.

"Which sucks because now that I'm out of the house, they start making a bundle and the three jackasses behind me ride the high life."

But he loved them, you could tell. The way he told childhood stories — inevitably someone broke a bone, got maimed, cut, bruised, or just plain embarrassed — it was evident that he would die for them in a heartbeat. As it turned out, one of those jackasses, Ian, knew Jonesy in high school and Peter made it a point of ensuring all of his brother's friends enjoyed their college life. It was oddly refreshing knowing that I could blame a faceless person for my current lot. In that moment, I understood the underlying force behind every protest in history. Blame the man, move on with life.

Peter was in his third year of a five-year plan in the film and theater program, and when I asked why he chose theater he said, "Because the chicks are hot and the guys are gay, so there's no competition. Plus, I get to act, so I play to both of my strengths."

I looked at him for clarification and he said, "Fucking women and being a fool."

Hard footsteps neared. I let gravity take over, my head rolled to the side, and I was nose to nail with red open-toed fuck-me pumps. Hillary knelt, smiled, and handed me a glass of something crimson. "Hair of the dog," she said. "Now, if you drink it, you'll get a spanking, young man."

"I think I'll leave you two alone," Peter said. But before he left, he glanced back. "Davis?"

I looked at him. After a moment, he said, "You enjoy yourself?"

I glanced at Hillary, her blond pigtails, my shirt, and realized I was wearing the small John Elway jersey. A flood of memories hit me.

"Some," I said.

He nodded, unsmiling, sage-like. "See ya next Friday."

And he did.

Wednesday

Peter started to fiddle with the radio. He settled on KBCO — Toad the Wet Sprocket, 'Fall Down' — sat back, and smiled. "This. This is what I miss from this place. Not the people. Not the friends, no offense, but the fucking radio. Best damned radio in the country."

I said, "Not the women?"

Peter's blue eyes widened, as if he'd remembered a past love. In this case, many. After a moment, he said, "Jonesy still live in Boulder?"

I changed lanes and prayed to whatever God controlling the flow of traffic that our new route be an even one. Then I thought about Peter's first time down the aisle — this to Pamela's best friend Naomi — about the last time Jonesy and Peter had spoken, and knew in my heart it wouldn't be.

I said, "When was the last time you saw him?"

Despite spending the past couple of days wondering the best way to raise the subject, I still felt like a dicknose for asking. I didn't want to destroy Peter's cheery mood, nor did

I want to delve into any realms of guilt he might have hidden away. I simply felt it best to acknowledge the stress so as to lessen a potential breakdown of any future enjoyment.

I needn't have worried. My fears were squelched as Peter slapped me upside the head with a classic demonstration of tactical obfuscation.

Peter said, "So, I fucked one of your students on the plane."

I blinked once, twice, cocked my head to the side and said, "Excuse me?"

"Vivian Miller."

"Vivian Miller?"

"You do know her, yes?"

"I do know a Vivian Miller, yes."

"So, you're telling me you know Vivian Miller."

"I thought we were talking about Jonesy."

"Jonesy knows Vivian Miller?"

"Not that I'm aware of, no."

"He should. He'd like her."

"Wait, you know Vivian Miller? My student?"

"No," he said, thoughtfully. "I don't." He was looking out at the passing houses, the passing cars, all reflected in his ridiculously big sunglasses. "But I fucked her. First-class bathroom. Those suckers are cramped."

I blinked, started to speak, stopped.

Peter said, "She says hi."

"What?"

"Vivian Miller. She says hello."

"Oh."

"Nice girl. Flexible. I never thought anyone could wrap their legs —"

"Exactly at what point did my name come up in conversation?"

"Actually," he said, "you were my in."

"I was your in?"

"Yups. She didn't fall for the usual 'I'm A Movie Star So Fuck Me' vibe I put out." He paused and for a moment, rubbed his nose in memory. "But then I saw the school logo on her t-shirt and I asked if she knew you."

"Wait, she only slept with you because —"

"She said it made her feel safe, but not too safe. Just enough to keep the mood, but take the edge off. Because I knew you, I was no longer your run-of-the-mill movie-star pervert."

"But ... you are."

Peter sighed. "I am."

After a moment, I said, "Did you ask how old she was?"

"Sorry?"

"Her age. Did you ask her how old she was?"

"Not by policy."

"You have a policy?"

"It's a loose policy."

"She's seventeen."

"She's not seventeen."

"She could have been. A lot of freshmen are underage."

Peter removed the Colorado Avalanche ball cap and scratched his mop of blond hair. "They are?"

"I was seventeen half of my freshman year."

"No."

"Yes."

"You were?"

"Sure was."

"Odd ... she didn't taste seventeen."

The key to Peter was just going for the ride and not hitting the brakes.

Twenty-eight minutes later, the three of us stood outside the bar on the ass end of Pearl Street in Boulder. Jonesy had buzzed his auburn hair since I last saw him, but he still looked the spitting image of David Bowie. Thin, pale, sour, although he was one of the most affable men you'd ever meet.

It was May, and spring is one of the best times to see the beauty of the area. But you have to be careful, or you'll get whiplash. The moment you spot a stunning college girl, you'll see another out of the corner of your eye and your natural instincts take over. I'd considered becoming a chiropractor in Boulder just for this reason.

Peter said, "They closed it?" It being the James, a frequent choice of ours because of the dollar beers they served after 10:00 p.m. "How could they close it?" Peter was still wearing the ridiculously big sunglasses and the ball cap low over his eyes, despite the lack of sun.

"Fire-safety violations," said Jonesy.

"Beer beats fire. I don't understand the problem."

"Garnished with a handful of health-code violations."

Peter arched one brow. "That's why the pretzels wiggled?" He turned around completely, as if surveying the land. "Well, shit. What else ya got?"

As we trekked, Peter ignored the unspoken tension between him and Jonesy and proceeded to give him the third degree about married life.

"How you handling it?"

"Fine."

"How many times have you cheated?"

"Zero."

"But you've thought about it, right?"

"No."

"You lie."

"I do?"

"Every man thinks of it."

"Not me."

"How many times does your wife put out in an average week?"

"None of your business."

"I bet you're like rabbits. All over the house — the kitchen, the dining room, the bathroom, the —"

"Kids room?"

"Fuck off, you don't —" Peter swung around and put his hand on Jonesy's chest, stopping him. "You have kids?"

"For five years now."

"You have a kid that's five-years-old?"

"A son."

"You have a five-year-old son?"

"And a one-year-old daughter."

"Fuck off."

"Okay."

"You're not fucking off."

"I'm not?"

"You've had a son for five years and you never told me?"

"It's not as if I've kept him locked in a box."

"That'd be cool if you did though."

Jonesy blinked, and after a moment of staring into Peter's eyes, started laughing. Hard. Bent over, hands-on-his-knees laughing until it became coughing. And Peter waited it out, smiling his crooked smile, but not in amusement, in reflection.

When Jonesy was finished, he straightened, looked at Peter, and said, "You're forgiven."

Peter looked away, shook his head. "I shouldn't be," he said. "I'm sorry I dropped out of your life."

Jonesy shrugged his thin shoulders. "You had your reasons."

"Yeah, but they weren't very good."

"They sucked, actually."

And they laughed some more.

As they walked, Peter learned that Jonesy had sold his software business just before the economy crashed and had opened up a wine shop called The Old Cork, a few blocks away. Debbie, his wife he'd met his senior year in a C++ class, was consulting from home, and together they had weathered the storm and were stronger than ever.

"You weren't in the market?" Peter asked.

"A bit. But mostly in gold."

"Gold?"

"Yeah. As the dollar drops, the value in gold rises. I bought in about seven years ago when the economy was at its peak."

"Seven years?" Peter looked down at his hand and counted off the fingers. "That would be your senior year."

"An actor and a mathematician?"

"Where'd you get the money?"

Jonesy shrugged. "Dead aunt. I never really knew her, but she seemed to think she knew me and I'll make damn sure my kids know all about her."

"Immortality through generosity," Peter said. "Shit. I lost a house and my third wife when things turned. I'm gonna fire my guy and hire you."

"You lost your wife?"

"Yeah. You seen her?"

"Read about her. Didn't you cheat on her with Rebecca What's-Her-Name from your last movie?"

"Yeah. But that was after I lost her. We've a big mountain lion problem in the hills of Cali and she likes to jog. I tried to find her, but after one, two hours, I gave her up for dead. Who knew she was out to lunch with her mom?"

"Didn't you?"

"Hey, I'll be the first to admit, I panicked. You ever see a mountain lion up close?"

"Not lately. You?"

"No. But the Discovery channel on a big-screen TV? Very persuasive."

I slowed and let them walk ahead for a bit, then pulled out my cell and called Pamela to tell her we wouldn't be home until whenever. She told me not to forget to pick up Donald and my mother in the morning.

I said, "I thought they were taking a cab."

"You don't make your parents take a cab. That's rude."

"They don't care. How many times have they said they don't want to be a burden?"

"Davis, it's your parents. They deserve —"

"I'll pick them up."

"At 7:00 a.m."

"Seven a.m."

"And be nice."

"Be nice?"

"You've been cranky of late."

"I wonder why."

"What?"

"Nothing. I'll pick them up at 7:00 a.m." I hung up before she had a chance to say anything else. Instantly I felt the tremor along that oft-traveled road between my stomach and my conscience, forcing me to think about the way I've acted to her of late, about my entire questioning of the coming events. But then my neck snapped to the side — a brunette, short skirt. Was she wearing any panties? She definitely wasn't wearing a bra — and the tremor ceased.

I said, "Beer beats fire, braless beats guilt."

I smiled and caught up with the guys.

Twenty minutes later, we were sitting at The Border Cantina with three of their fishbowl-sized-margaritas. Surrounding the chest-high table was a standing-room-only crowd, the happy hour a sight to behold. The killer prices attract the young, poor college girls, which attract the young, horny college guys, which attract the young, horny college girls. It's been likened to a feeding frenzy. No blood, but if you were a hound, you'd go crazy with the amount of pheromones in the air.

"To the Captain of the Rooftop Fuckballers, Davis Robertson," Peter said, puffing out his chest theatrically. "May his remaining days be painful and plentiful."

We clinked glasses, began to drink. That was when the ebb of the bar switched to flow, and a jock the size of a Volkswagen bus accidentally fell back into Peter, causing his ridiculously big sunglasses to slip off his face.

It was as if I were watching a slow-motion shot in an action film — the mask falling to the ground, revealing the villain to be a close, trusted friend of the hero. The sunglasses hit the table with a small splash from the condensation ring left by a marg fishbowl.

The hungry trawlers picked up the scent.

"You're Peter Carter," said a redhead, her eyes widening. A pair of blonds within earshot spun toward us, one of them spilling her beer as she knocked into the other. If they cared, I didn't notice. Because what I saw sent chills to the bone. A wordless wave of awareness — as if we were the epicenter of a hormonal quake — swept across the crowd as predators turned our way.

When I glanced to Peter, I saw an all-together different reaction. Rather than feeling the chill of excitement, as if he were about to be engulfed in ecstasy at any moment, his head was down, his shoulders slack.

16

I leaned in to ask if he was all right, and froze as I saw Peter age before my eyes. His face collapsed. Wrinkles swelled, cheeks drooped, hairline receded. For a moment, he was twenty years older and thirty years weaker. But then he took a deep breath, pulled back his shoulders, looked at me with a shine in his eye, and it was gone. He had rebuilt himself. Better ... Stronger ... More advanced. He smiled a half smile, and with a wink, a shrug, he was sucked away from the table to be devoured alive by wild hyenas.

Jonesy said, "He never changes, does he?"

I thought about the momentary look of exhaustion, knew by his comment that Jonesy hadn't seen the transformation, and was silent.

He said, "You ever wish it was you?"

I shrugged. "You all planned for tomorrow?"

Jonesy slapped me on the back. "You just try not to think of the wedding and leave the rest to me."

"That doesn't make any sense," I said.

"Doesn't it? When was the last time you slept?"

I saw Peter, smiling a wide, shit-eating smile in a throng of women, all trying to get close for an autograph, a picture, a nuzzle. I said, "I don't know. February?"

"Cold feet?"

"Hot blond beats cold feet."

"What?"

"Nothing. You see the game last night?"

"Some. The highlights. Abby made some nice saves."

"We're playing terrible. We have a team of all-stars and not a heart among them."

"They'll pull it together."

"I don't know. The Wings are looking damn good. Who knew Cujo would bounce back after the crappy beginning?"

"I still get freaked out when I don't see the human weeble-wobble behind their bench."

"No shit, right? At least then I knew who to hate."

"The Avs will pull it together. Have faith."

"They'd better."

"Or what? You gonna renounce your fanship?" he said. "Is Pammy feeling it too?"

"Nah, she hates hockey."

"That's not what I meant. I meant, is Pammy feeling —"

I said, "I know what you meant," and was surprised at the ferocity of my tone, the way I spat the words. But rather than apologize, I stared into my fishbowl, finding solace as my vision rode the crests and falls of the vast, ever-changing alien landscape.

Jonesy put his hand on my shoulder, drawing me back to reality. I looked up, saw the sorrow behind the mask of joviality in his hazel eyes, and wanted to punch him for his gall to pity me in my hour of confusion; wanted to hug him for his sympathy and understanding in my hour of bewilderment.

He said, "Is she feeling the stress of the wedding?"

"Yeah. Sure. No. Shit." I returned to my alien landscape, wondering if I could drown in the frozen goodness. I surmised that I could, but only if I tipped the fishbowl just right and squished my head to the side. But even then I'd only fit half of my face, my nose, and a portion of my mouth inside the fishbowl, and I'd most likely end up with frozen margarita down my shirt and one hell of a neck-ache.

A shout from the crowd. Jonesy and I turned to see Peter on the bar, his shirt off, the pair of blonds licking salt off of his chest before they each did a shot of tequila and took turns kissing him in lieu of sucking the lime.

I smiled, shook my head, heard Jonesy say, "You talk to Hillary lately?" and felt the time was right to flag down the waitress — a blond spiky punk-meets-goth look, athletic — and order another round of sweet, lovable, generous fishbowls.

Jonesy said, "You sure you need another one?"

"Oh, I'm gonna need a lot more with the doors you're wanting to open."

To his credit, Jonesy kept his composure, nodded. "Fair 'nuff. But if you don't answer the question, I'll ensure you don't see another drop of alcohol tonight."

I pulled my fishbowl close to my chest. "You wouldn't." Then, marveling how my speech was already beginning to slur, I said, "No. I haven't spoken to Hillary in a while. I did send her an invite, but I doubt she'll come."

"You know, I ran into her the other day. She's certified now. Has her massage-therapy shop near the North end of Crossroads."

"Good for her."

"You should stop by and see her. Get some of that tension out."

I blinked twice, sure I hadn't heard him correctly. "You're kidding." He was quiet, drinking his marg. "You're not kidding."

"Look, I'm *not* advocating cheating, but if you're going to do it —"

"I'm not going to see Hillary, okay?" I unthinkingly took a huge draw on my marg fishbowl and, in a heartbeat, a sharp pain stabbed the back of my throat. My vision tunneled, the world spun.

I don't get brain freeze. I get throat freeze that travels down my esophagus and into my stomach. What follows is usually a quick moment of nausea, akin to a hangover, a bout of vertigo, and the sensation as if someone is driving an ice pick into the base of my skull. Over the years, I've mastered the art of breathing deeply until it fades, but this one caught me off guard and I gagged.

Soon, the pain faded.

"Well," I said. "At least I'm awake now."

What Jonesy didn't know was that I had already been cheating on Pamela. What Jonesy also didn't know was that it had been with Hillary. What he did know was that I hadn't spoken to her in a while. You know how some engaged couples who have already been having sex try to abstain a month or so before the wedding? My take on it was to stop fucking around on Pamela a month before the wedding.

It was killing me.

I'd run into Hillary —

Six Years Earlier — The Renaissance Festival

— after Pamela and I started getting serious, and we'd hit it off as if we hadn't spent three years apart. She'd dropped out of college her sophomore year to pursue a career in modeling, and although I thought I'd seen her once in a phone-sex ad in the back of a *Penthouse*, I'd assumed that she'd given up the whole idea and picked up her schooling again somewhere. But apparently, she'd decided to join the wannabe twelfth-century circus.

Down in Larkspur, Colorado, Jonesy and I were tanked. Debbie and Pamela were off somewhere trying on dresses and drinking. Debbie would later buy a corset-crunching long dress with poofy arms, I forget the name of it, but she thought it made her look hot. She was right. The next day she would learn she was preggers and the dress would sit in a box in the attic yearning for the curiosity of a precocious teenage girl to stumble along.

Later that night, in bed, Pamela would rest her head on my chest, her dark brown hair still wet from the shower, and tell me: "I thought about buying a dress, I even picked one out and oh God, was it beautiful, but not practical and I hate it when I'm faced with deciding between beautiful and practical because it's like choosing between your head and your heart and you just know that later they're going to fight about it and those fights just suck because they last forever and my head starts to scream about how often would I really wear a renaissance dress and so I walked away from it, I really did, but then my heart remembered how beautiful it looked when I put it on and so I just had to return and try it on again because — and I don't know if I can stress this enough — it was so beautiful so I thought about it some more and looked around and after a long time agonizing I decided not to purchase the dress because in the end I realized that I'd only wear it once a year at the festival, but now I'm kicking myself because maybe I could have worn it on Halloween and New Year's if we have a themed New Year's, which I'd have pushed for because I'd have bought the damn dress, but what's really getting to me is that I missed a golden opportunity to be impulsive."

And I marveled that somehow Debbie had calmly waited this out.

Hillary was working the festival circuit as a busty wench, hocking beer. She played the part perfectly, her breasts nearly spilling out over the top of her dress. She laughed as she saw that I couldn't take my eyes off of them.

"It helps with the tips," she said.

"Right," I said.

"It does. The more you show, the more you make."

"Sounds like advice from a pole dancer."

"How'd you know?"

"Who do you think you're fooling, Hil?"

"I'm not fooling anyone."

"Come on. This is me. Davis."

She looked at me, her green eyes full of lust. "Okay," she said, biting her lower lip. "Maybe it also turns me on."

Fifteen minutes later we were back in her tent.

Before she took her lunch break, Hillary told me she had been seeing the sword swallower, and I'd confessed that I'd been seeing a second-year law student from Denver University. For some reason that made it better — that we were both about to cheat. We both could feel it, but didn't speak it aloud. There are things you can just tell in a look, and when you suddenly run into an ex-girlfriend, you know the signs without thought. It's like riding a bike. You look at the pedals and know they're designed for one thing. The look Hillary gave me was her pedals. Only there for one purpose. Not teasing, not promising for later. Wanting it now and only now. I returned the look without question.

"Equally yoked," she said.

I asked her what that meant.

"'Do not be yoked with unbelievers. For what do righteousness and wickedness have in common?' It's from the book of Corinthians," she said.

I asked her if she had found religion since I saw her last.

"No. But I was fucking a priest for a while in Albuquerque."

Then she took her lunch break and we went behind the festival where the tents and campers and such are crowded. And while Jonesy wondered where I went, and while Debbie and Pamela were trying on dresses, we got to it. Fast, unromantic. But something about the surroundings made it feel animalistic, hedonistic. Like it was right. Equally yoked in our wickedness. And I loved every second of it.

It was like a fix. A drug. The physical high keeping whatever emotional demons I deny possessing buried deep.

Later, as we were lying there, my pants around my ankles and her skirt up to her waist, she told me she was thinking about getting out of the festival circuit.

"It's hard though, ya know? It's like a cult. Not that they drug you or anything — though, there's plenty of anything if ya want it — but it's a lifestyle that you can't have in the real world. You can't have the free party, free sex — being here, living here, existing here is almost without responsibility — and it's a culture shock when you return. Some lifers have said it's like returning from prison. You don't know how to relate to society because you've been removed from it for so long. So you're inexorably drawn to the fringes. The dark coffee shops that aren't named Starbucks and have yet to become trendy with the high school kids. You start to remember living the life. You start to role-play with dice. You withdraw until all you have is the past."

She went on, but I stopped listening. I was role playing, wondering what it would be like to forget about all responsibility and just fall into the pit of sex and drugs. In my mind, it was something like the '60s with Woodstock and flower power and dancing in the mud and the rain. But everyone was dressed as they were at the festival. And all the women had their skirts up around their waists.

"Hillary?"

"Yeah?"

"Do you like photography?"

She glanced over, her green eyes still glazed in endorphin intoxication. "You saw that ad?"

Wednesday

The jocks ended up saving Peter, although Peter contends that he had the situation totally under control. One college girl had her hand down the front of his pants, nibbling his ear, another he was kissing and fondling, and a third had her hand down the girl's pants he was kissing and fondling. All the while, he contends, he was going to talk the drunk and jealous boyfriend out of tearing his head from his neck, placing it on a pike, lighting it on fire, and running around the streets of Boulder as if he had the Olympic torch.

It started when a jock the size of a Chevy Nova came up to the jock the size of a Volkswagen bus who ran into Peter earlier, starting the whole feeding frenzy, and said, "Dude, I think I just saw some guy in the men's room with your girl."

Jonesy and I looked at each other, took off, and narrowly beat the Jock Brigade to the lav. Guys are like that. It's the Mr. Spock philosophy in reverse: the good of the one out weighs the good of the many. It sounds dumb in theory, but in context, it makes sense to every guy and no matter how we explain it, women will never understand.

Plus, there are the perks.

Woman: "Why did you jump into the fight with the ninjas and circus midgets when you could have been maimed?"

Man: "You see this?"

Woman: "Ewww."

Man: "In a month, it'll be a scar."

Woman: "A scar? I like scars."

'Captain' Lance Murdock was dead-on when he said, as he lay in a hospital bed mentoring a troublemaking boy, "Bones heal, chicks dig scars, and the United States of America has the best doctor-to-daredevil ratio in the world."

Once we beat the jocks to the lav, we quickly slammed the door and (thank Buddha) discovered it had a lock and clicked it. We then followed the moans to the far stall and swung the door open.

24

"Hey, guys!" Peter managed through the kissing and fondling. "You want in?" He then heard the pounding. "Did you lock the door?"

"Something you should have done or you wouldn't be in this mess," I said.

"But that's just silly. I'm not going to make someone hold their water just for me." You had to hand it to Peter. Somewhere deep inside, he cared about the little people. "You sure you don't …?" He motioned to his harem and while inside I was all for it, I didn't betray a bit of my yearning.

I said, "Escaping imminent demise beats lust."

Peter said, "Since when?"

"Since we have about two minutes before the Jock Brigade either pounds down the door, or they find someone with a key and use his head to pound down the door."

A toilet flushed in another stall and out stepped a skinny, drunk college kid clearly in need of acne medicine. He gave a cursory glance toward the sink and made a beeline for the exit.

Jonesy said, "You touch that door and you'll be pissing out a straw," moving to him with speed that caused the drunk kid to fall back against the wall. Jonesy, the usually quiet family man now determined to stop all hell from breaking loose.

"And you," he said to Peter over his shoulder. "Do you ever fucking change?"

"Hey, I thought I was forgiven."

I noticed a small window over one of the stalls. "Come on, Peter. We're leaving."

I moved to open the window, but stopped when he said, "Can't. Playing a game."

First girl: "It's a good game."

Second girl: "The best."

Third girl: "Mmmmmm."

Peter said, "If any of them stops, they won't get the prize."

I said, "Prize?"

"Yeah. Me."

First girl: "It's a great prize."

Second girl: "The best."

Third girl: "Mmmmmm."

The Jock Brigade was about to storm through the door and Peter was as cool as a man named Luke.

I said, "What do they get if you lose?"

All three girls looked up in alarm. Peter calmed them with an incredulous smile and a slight shake of his head. That was all it took. They relaxed, and went back to the game.

I took a moment to consider, looked at Jonesy. Then a decision was made. As Jonesy tried to grab Peter from his three- girl bliss, I forced the window open. But Peter wouldn't budge. With the weight of the three girls added, Jonesy was hard pressed to get him standing. I jumped in to help, but stopped when we all heard a very loud 'click.'

The skinny, drunk college kid had regained his wits and unlocked the door. But when he chanced a look back, he froze again in fear.

Jonesy said, "Oh, shit."

I said, "Oh, fuck."

Peter said, "Oh, baby."

And then the Jock Brigade forced open the door, slamming the skinny, drunk college kid back into the wall and out cold.

I jumped in front of the jock the size of a Volkswagen bus, but he knocked me aside as if I were Campus Security trying to shut down a kegger. He grabbed Peter by the neck, began to haul him effortlessly to a stand, but stopped when

Peter pulled out of his kiss and calmly said, "You don't want to do this, Michael."

Michael the jock stopped and said, "How do you know my name?"

Peter nodded to one of the girls. "Celeste told me. She's told me all about you. She hasn't been able to shut up, actually."

Celeste, her hand down Peter's pants, her own pants full with another girl's hand, stopped kissing Peter's neck long enough to say, "It's true. I told him we're in love." The other girls moaned in agreement.

Michael the jock balked for a moment. That's all Peter needed. He said, "Michael, are you telling me that were you in Celeste's shoes, you wouldn't be doing the exact same thing? You wouldn't be going for it? I'm not talking about with me. I'm talking about with a woman. A hot woman. A famous woman. You're telling me that if Jennifer Garner walked in that door right now and said, 'Michael. I want you to put your hand down my pants as I kiss you,' you'd say no? You'd actually say, 'Sorry, Miss Hot Famous Woman Who I'll Probably Never See Again In My Lifetime, Let Alone Get People To Believe I Saw Her Or Had This Chance With Her, but I can't do that because my girlfriend would be upset with me?' This is a once-in-a-lifetime chance. How many times will Jennifer Garner say that to you? Once, maybe. Twice if you're me. But you're not me, so you take the chances when you have them. That's the understanding we have with each other. That's the understanding you have with Celeste. And that's what's happening here."

Michael the jock, who still held Peter by the neck, but had lost the focus to squeeze, said, "So ... Jennifer Garner is asking me —"

"To put your hand down her pants. Yeah. Hell, yeah. Celeste?"

"Mmm?" Blinking as if she had just woken from a dream.

"Tell Michael, the man you know and love, that if he had the opportunity to put his hands down Jennifer Garner's pants that you'd let him."

"Jennifer Garner?" she said.

"Yeah," Michael the jock said, his jaw muscles dancing in nervous anticipation.

"The chick from *Alias*?"

"Yeah," Michael the jock said, adding squinting to his dancing jaw muscles. As if he were the one caught with his hand down someone's pants.

"I don't know, Michael," she said.

And for a moment, I braced for the inevitable fight. But only for a moment.

"I think I'd like to have my hand down her pants, too," she said.

That was all it took. Michael the jock broke into a stupid grin, released Peter, and watched as Celeste pushed the other girl aside to shove her tongue down Peter's throat, her hand still down his pants. As she moaned, Michael the jock turned to his friends and, after a moment, they, too, broke into stupid grins and started slapping each other's hands in celebration.

"Jennifer Garner," Michael the jock bellowed. The others mimicked him as if he, in fact, just had his hand down Jennifer Garner's pants. It was amazing to watch, but at the same time, it wasn't. This was vintage Peter Carter, the man who could seemingly talk his way in and out of anything. The man who talked his way out of all math and science classes in college, and somehow talked his way into receiving the credits anyway. The man who talked his way into a pop-star-slash-actress-whose-name-rhymes-with-Randy-Door concert, talked his way backstage, and talked her out of her panties that he later sold on eBay and donated the proceeds to one of those Sally Struthers charities. No wonder he'd made millions upon millions of dollars, been married three times (and counting), and still made women of all ages swoon at the utterance of his name.

Jonesy shook his head. I shrugged. But Peter, with the stall door open and at least a dozen people watching, continued the show. Sticking to his strengths. Fucking women and playing the fool. The fool who doesn't believe rules apply to him and somehow lives a happy life without a conscience.

But there are always the critics.

As the jocks celebrated their conquering of Jennifer Garner, a man dressed in a t-shirt, jeans, sneakers, and a cowboy hat shoved his way through the crowd and, when he saw Peter and the girls, almost did a double take.

"Jennifer Garner, dude," Michael the jock said to the Urban Cowboy, holding his hand up to slap.

The Urban Cowboy ignored Michael the jock, narrowed his eyes at the sight in the stall, and said, "Gabby?"

The girl now nibbling Peter's ear, her hand down Celeste's pants, looked up fast. Stunned. Worried. And very guilty.

Peter looked up at the Urban Cowboy. "Arnie," he said in his calm, 'I'm hooking up with your girlfriend' way that only he could pull off. "You don't want to do this."

The Urban Cowboy said, "Who the fuck is Arnie?" and then lunged at Peter.

Michael the jock helped me pull the Urban Cowboy off Peter before he did too much damage. A bloodied nose, a split lip. The Bouncers took over, tossing out the Urban Cowboy, but not his girlfriend.

Despite his harem still intact, the excitement had caused Peter to lose his enjoyment. "I had it under control," he said, kicking the trashcan. "Fucking kids. I had this under control."

And with that, we left.

But not before Peter turned to the girls and said, "You girls are eighteen, right?"

An hour later, we were sitting between the narrow aisles of The Old Cork, Jonesy's thriving wine store, our backs propped up on the sturdy oak racks lined with bottles. Although Jonesy opened the shop three years ago, it had the feel of days gone by. Old world. But not American old world. European old world. "What is this?" I asked Jonesy.

"Home-grown mystery wine. Every once in a while I get a batch of mixed grapes from someone, brew 'em up, carboy it, and wait until the tannins soften. What you're drinking was bottled three years ago, five years from the carboy, eight years from scratch."

"You sound as if you actually know what you're talking about," Peter said, draining his glass and holding it to Jonesy for a refill, ignoring any lingering anger seeping his way.

"Wait," I said, doing the math. "This is eight years old?"

Jonesy smiled a toothy smile. "I considered calling it Chateau de Bathtub, but it just doesn't flow off your tongue."

I said nothing, marveling at the percolating memories. I was drinking something I'd helped to create on a whimsical moment early one Saturday afternoon during our —

Junior Year

—while we procrastinated studying for midterms. Jonesy and I had fled our apartment in search of something, anything, and had come across a used winemaking kit at a yard sale. The owner was parting with it upon discovering he didn't have the patience for the fermentation process.

We grabbed the kit, got some grapes from the local home-brew store on Pearl Street, and spent the rest of the afternoon in the kitchen and bathroom whipping it up. But after a few months, I discovered I, too, was short on patience, and Jonesy bought my half of the equipment for a week of drinks.

Wednesday

Eight years ago … Eight years ago I was a junior in college, unsure of what I wanted to do, who I wanted to be, or who I wanted to be with. Yet I felt happy doing everything at once and rolling with what came my way.

What happened? When did I change?

Jonesy said, "I've been checking it twice a year, and it finally came around about eighteen months ago."

Right about when I got engaged.

"Right about when you got engaged," Jonesy said.

And there it was. Eighteen months ago, I got a hair up my ass and proposed to Pamela. Eighteen months ago, I decided to change. I decided to be with the same woman for the rest of my life.

I took a large swig of the wine, and swallowed hard, forcing the fear of reminiscence back into my gut. I suppressed a small cough, and said, "It's good. Not too sweet."

"We got lucky," said Jonesy. "I'd say one of three batches of mystery wine turn into anything worth drinking."

"What do you do with the rest?" asked Peter. "The leftovers?"

Jonesy mimicked a magician, replaced the bottle of Chateau de Bathtub with another, unmarked bottle, and refilled Peter's glass. "Nothing but our finest for Hollywood royalty."

Peter looked at the glass, at Jonesy, back to the glass. "I fucked up again, didn't I?"

Jonesy smiled.

31

Peter shrugged and drank up.

The hush that followed began as a normal pause, but soon transformed to strained silence. We didn't need to ask what the others were thinking. We knew it, we felt it. But surely I was alone in stepping from the shore of current tensions and wading into the inky waters of discarded memory.

Before that moment, I'd chalked it up to cold feet, my wanting to run, my anxiety. But as I sat there, I felt something … What was it? Was I holding onto the past? Was I fearful of growing up? Frightened of losing my independence? Or, was it something deeper? More primal? Was it simply human nature rebelling against society's traditions? Or was it much more mundane? Was I just feeling trapped? Strapped down while a hooded figure slowly cut away an identity I had fought so hard to obtain and only recently began to understand?

As we walked back to the car, I realized I didn't want to go home. Not now. Not ever. But at the same time, I wasn't going to be 'that guy.' I wasn't going to rabbit. I wasn't going to be the guy who ruined her life, who destroyed her magical day. But where did that leave me?

Selfishness beats selflessness?

Selflessness beats selfishness?

"I need to pee," Peter said.

"My house is fifteen minutes from here," Jonesy said.

Peter stopped, rubbed his nose, and looked around. A wicked grin formed on his handsome mug. "Hey," he said. "I know this place."

He took off in a trot. Jonesy shook his head. I shrugged. We followed.

The night was starting to cool to bearable with a chance of breeze. Very quickly, the mystery wine within my system joined forces with the still powerful regime of fishbowl margaritas. Together they affixed a strobe light to my optic nerves. The bustle of Boulder fluttered as we ran onto Pearl Street, in and out of similarly buzzed college goers, narrowly missing the occasional late-night biker, the traffic crossing the pedestrian mall at the lights, the local flora and fauna.

College dropouts, feeling an existence within a world of perpetual marijuana haze and patchouli oil lathering was preferable to obtaining a higher education, were scattered about the outdoor mall, creating a veritable minefield of unwashed distaste. Couple this with uneven brickwork that whispered a comfortable, soothing history, but betrayed a malicious desire to strip the skin from your limbs or bestow upon you a subdermal hematoma, and we nearly lost Peter. Thankfully, he made enough hoots and shouts for a deaf cripple to follow his tracks.

Eventually, we found him standing outside an office building, looking in the dark windows.

"Okay," said Jonesy. "We passed a dozen places with a bathroom. What gives?"

I sat down, marveling at my lack of cardiovascular endurance.

Peter said, "Do you guys remember Archer Phillips?"

The name rang a bell.

"Tall guy, wore a duster, loved tomato sauce."

A big bell. A loud bell. A painful bell.

"My roommate. Friday Night Club."

Holy shit! How could I forget?

CHAPTER TWO

Freshman Year

"You enjoy yourself, Davis?"

I looked at Hillary, her blond pigtails, my shirt ... and realized I was wearing the small John Elway jersey. A flood of memories hit me. "Some," I said.

He nodded, unsmiling, sage-like. "See ya next Friday."

And he did.

And the next Friday.

And the Friday after that.

What started as a one-time feral happening became a string of finely tuned shindigs often possessing an astonishing lack of tune. At times, events were wild, chaotic, and mind-blowing. Other times, events were simply a handful of people sitting back, imbibing copious amounts of whatever alcohol happened to be on sale at the local Liquor Mart. But always, events promised sanctuary to victims of collegiate responsibility.

The backdrop rarely altered. *Beavis and Butthead, The Simpsons,* and the gi-normous hair stylings of *Telemundo* soap operas. The last was always a treat, for once the booze began to flow, Kathy Booth and Hillary Leakey — the only regulars who knew a lick of Spanish — acted, and then argued the validity and sanctity of their respective translations. Often, they left us marveling at their abilities to wax philosophic, while simultaneously diving into the swamp of political rhetoric and catty observation. Wagers upon the victor in each endeavor were common, forcing a decree that the house take was twenty-five percent.

And from this lone decree sprouted the Commandments ensuring that Friday Nights forever be blessed.

Commandment #1: No band or any ear-splitting music that shakes the fillings from your mouth or the neighbors from their slumber; Commandment #2: No smoking inside the apartment, thus ensuring Thomas Divan never again douses his t-shirt in lighter fluid and sets it aflame if he feels the party is lacking pizzazz; and Commandment #3:

"Let it be known," slurred Peter Carter as he addressed the Schnickered Tribe, "that the most important lesson one can glean at the University level is not 'Never … forget to check your references,' as Dr. Meredith would have you believe."

And the tribe booed the name of Dr. Meredith.

"Nor is it 'Economics is summed up as supply and demand,' as Father Sarducci has attempted to pass as truth."

And the tribe hissed the name of Father Sarducci.

"And, although many in this room will debate this, the most important lesson is not 'He who amasses the greatest number of offered credit cards, wins', as Professors Bank and Fargo will tell you, over and over, no matter how often you ask them to stop."

And the tribe cursed the names Professors Bank and Fargo.

Peter Carter said, "Do you wish to know the most important lesson at the collegiate level?

The tribe said it wanted to know.

"The most important lesson at the collegiate level is ... Always ... invite the neighbors. For even if the neighbors are the nicest of people, never wanting any trouble, they'll be filled with spite and spend countless nights plotting your eventual demise if not invited to the shindig."

And the tribe went wild.

To these three commandments, we held, only adding a fourth after 'The Miracle of the Indoor Snowstorm.'

In a testament to drunken stupidity, we rigged some floodlights to a flat part of the second story roof in order to play Midnight Rooftop Hacky Sack. It was short lived, highly dangerous, and we loved every minute of it. But it was not without wrinkles.

The first thing we (Kathy) understood (insisted upon) was the need for designated 'spotters' to warn us if we strayed near the edge of the roof.

"Head does not beat sidewalk," Kathy said, tossing a watermelon to its doom in order to silence the grumbles of protest and inebriated repudiations of physics.

Secondly, we (Jonesy) realized (whined about) the need for designated 'runners' to retrieve said Hacky Sack were it to escape our veritable wall of chaotic footwork.

"Okay, fuck that shit," said Jonesy, sucking wind.

"Look at it this way, you'll only get the Freshman Five," said Peter.

"I thought it was fifteen?"

"Not the way you're kicking that thing."

As we ironed things out, we began to create the International Rooftop Hacky Sack League, our team name, care of Peter Carter, The Rooftop Fuckballers. Alas, the occupants directly below our playing field quickly deflated our highly lucrative bubble.

A nice young Vietnamese family, who often refused our party invitations (we later realized that they spoke very little English and took our friendly invitations as deadly serious threats), finally hit the breaking point when drywall texture began to snow inconceivably from their ceiling.

To this day, I will contend that you have never witnessed raw insanity-laced anger until you have seen a tiny, slightly balding Vietnamese gentleman swell with the ferocious energy of a rabid ferret.

What he said: "You kids! You kids! No more boom boom!"

What we heard with his arms flailing, his voice screeching, and his spit hitting us with every syllable: "If you epileptic maggots don't stop this jumping crap, I'm going to strip you naked, wrap your eyelids around your knees, and kick you down the stairs!"

Commandment #4: No pissing off slightly balding Vietnamese gentleman. Punishable by shame.

Thus ended the short international reign of The Rooftop Fuckballers. But in its wake formed the almighty Friday Night Club. Peter Carter, Adam Jones, Thomas Divan, Hillary Leakey, Kathy Booth, and me, Davis Robertson.

We six lost circus performers were simply in need of an escape from the daily dullness of classes and studying. Maybe it was the unstructured nature of college life. You leave the regimented existence of high school and are tossed into the pee-in-the-sink-or-swim-in-the-pee world of higher education. And although the distractions are addicting, they're rather mind numbing. Different faces, different parties, different locations. A vast ocean filled with creatures of every size and color from the primeval predators of the moment to the amorphous blobs of endurance. But a few weeks into the school year, we six unconsciously discovered that while the wave crests could be exhilarating, the troughs caused so much emotional and mental nausea that we yearned to set foot on dry land.

To this day, Jonesy will tell you, "College was the best four years of my life because of the random, insane, crazy, fucked up, egomaniacal, boring, insecure, sober, suicidal, higher-than-a-kite people I met, befriended, drank with, partied with, swapped spit with, threw up with ... but I had it lucky ... we all had it lucky. Because even with all of that ... just knowing there was a party at Peter's Friday night with a core group of people ... enhanced it all. The Friday Night Club was the one thing I could look forward to if the week was bad. It was the dry blanket and bottle of whiskey after walking in a rain storm of shit. But ... if the week was good ... goddamn, that party was the icing on the cake. It was my home away from home. It was my sanctuary. No. It was *our* sanctuary ... *our* church."

For if it wasn't, how could you explain how —

Thomas Divan

— always arrived with a six-pack in one hand and the biggest damned bottle of tequila in the other, and he didn't even attend the university?

He was the embodiment of what we felt. Every week, he not only looked forward to Friday Night, but he *worked* for Friday Night. Worked to *worship* on Friday Night. When he spoke about his faith in its "glorious powers for healing the ill and curing the savage mental strife society places upon its citizens," you half expected him to charm a snake into submission.

Every Friday afternoon, Divan got off early from his job as a low-rung-on-the-ladder grunt at Gates Rubber Plant and trekked up from Denver on his 1983 Honda Goldwing, looking a lot like a young Steve McQueen with his thin frame, knowing smile, and fuck-it-all attitude. Upon arrival, he would let himself in (the door was oft unlocked, although Divan could pick any lock known to man), start fixing drinks, and hand them out as people arrived. We'd party, then sometime when we were passed out, he'd disappear, never to be heard from until the next Friday.

I can't recall who, but someone started calling him Divan Soze, because like the enigmatic character in *The Usual Suspects*, when he left, he was — poof! — gone.

Divan became a fixture at the parties because of —

Kathy Booth

They met at a private high school that attempted to cram Christ down your throat without mentioning him by name lest they turn off possible converts. And while Divan later explored other divinities to understand the world on a broader scale, Kathy was, perhaps, the perfect example of following authority — her parents, or her God — to the letter.

Twice a week, her mother would say, "Kathy, I want you home by 7:00 p.m., no exceptions, and I want you to call me every two hours even if you're in a class or a movie or a blah, blah, blah, if anyone offers you alcohol or diet-rat-tumor-soda or Elmer's Glue, you are to say, 'that's very kind of you, but no,' and then kick them in the blah, blah, blah, nothing with Demi Moore, Rob Lowe, or those blah, blah, blah, eggnog is Satan's plasma."

Kathy's family didn't even own a microwave oven because those might cause cancer.

"But they never use the word 'cancer,' because that's just tempting the devil," Kathy said to me one Friday night on the balcony. "Instead they use the word 'cavities'." Kathy sipped her drink, sighed, and looked out over the twinkling Boulder night. "Until the age of nine I was convinced my Aunt Betty died from gingivitis."

You'd think that Kathy would have rebelled. But no. She was a strait-laced girl who felt that the rules were in place for her protection.

On the second Thursday of Kathy's freshman year, that security was breached, and her laces were curled.

Returning from a Meg Ryan romantic-comedy without a hint of Rob Lowe, Kathy caught a whiff of an odd smell emanating from her dorm room. She unlocked her door, opened it, and discovered her roommate pressing a curling iron into her arm.

Fat and flesh sizzled. Kathy inhaled what she later described as "a bitter charcoal steak, with a seasoning of matches." She gagged, doubled over, and vomited her non-diet-rat-tumor-soda and unbuttered popcorn onto old, speckled linoleum.

At the sound, her roommate spun on her desk chair, curling iron to arm, tendrils of smoke slowly rising. And with a thin, phlegm-filled scream, she charged.

Kathy looked up, the veil of innocence unpeeling to reveal the real-world. Nothing in her mother's guidance had prepared her for a raging roommate with a fired up curling iron. Had her roommate opted for assaulting her with a devilish concoction for yuletide nausea, things might have been different.

Instinct, however, discovered a lone nugget of motherly aid. Kathy straightened and calmly said, "That's very kind of you, but no." Then she shut the door, locked it with her keys still hanging in the lock, and ran.

Later, on the phone, her mother said, "Kathy, I know this was bad, but didn't you bring this on yourself?"

Kathy was silent.

"Maybe she was curling her hair and you startled her. Or maybe you accidentally dropped her medication down the sink when you were brushing your teeth."

Silence.

"I understand the first few weeks of college can be crazy. But it's academic suicide to leave the dorms for off-campus housing."

Silence.

"You have to gut this out."

Silence.

"Kathy? Are you going to gut this out?"

Silence.

"Good girl."

And for the better part of three hours, Kathy tried to gut it out. Not until the other girls on the floor comforted her with tales in the lore of psycho roommates did she realize that her ordeal wasn't an isolated incident. When she realized that the real world wasn't something she could avoid forever.

Kathy figured she had two choices: run back to Mommy and Daddy, or break away from the womb, face the world, and find salvation elsewhere, even if it wasn't in the most ideal of conditions.

So, she decided to look up an old family friend, Peter Carter, who was more than happy to clear out his walk-in closet for her.

He said, "It won't be like home, but you'll have a lock on the door and no one owns a curling iron."

That was good enough for Kathy.

Later, much later, at —

Peter's Wedding — One Year After Graduation

— to Naomi in San Diego, after the Las Vegas trip where I learned Kathy loved me, after the Las Vegas trip where Kathy learned to hate me, I asked how she was able to do it. How she was able to handle living with someone like Peter. How she was able to put aside her faith to live with the devil.

"Peter isn't the devil," she said.

"You know what I mean."

When she turned to look at the ocean's black abyss, I saw the shadows beneath her striking brown eyes, and wondered if I had caused them.

She said, "Did you know my mother offered to buy me an apartment if I didn't move in with him?"

"She must have hated him."

"Oh, my mother loves Peter. Always will. Not a phone call goes by when she isn't asking why we aren't together."

"Then ..."

"She didn't want me living in sin. Even if it was completely platonic, to her, it was living in sin."

"And you passed on an apartment to —"

"Live in a closet, yeah. And if I had to do it over again? I wouldn't change a thing."

"Not even one?"

Silence. Strained. Long.

"How's Newman?" I asked.

And for the first time since Vegas, and the last time until the night of my rehearsal dinner, I saw Kathy's shoulders lower, her face relax, and the warmth — the innocence we had all fallen in love with — shine through.

"He's good," she said. "He's happy."

"You made the right choice."

"Did I?"

Silence. Strained. Shorter.

Her warmth was already beginning to dissipate, the tension returning. She said, "I didn't put aside my faith when I moved in with Peter. I put aside my *mother's* faith, and went in search of my own."

I learned more about Kathy in that one statement than I ever knew before. And when Divan neared, saw our silence, and slipped his arm around Kathy's shoulder to lead her away, I realized that I would never understand her any better.

On the day that Kathy moved into Peter's closet, the second Friday at Chez Carter during our —

Freshman Year

— it just so happened that Divan called to see how she was settling in. And when he heard what happened, he immediately drove up.

Some friends are like that. Gotta love them.

Upon entering Chez Carter that Friday, I stiffened in confusion when the stranger known as Thomas Divan handed me a red plastic cup.

He said, "The dog's gonna bite ya, so you might as well bite him first."

I then cringed in apprehension when the stranger known as Kathy Booth gave me a long, warm hug.

She said, "I've heard so much about you."

But when I caught a whiff of Kathy's hair — vanilla with a hint of coconut — my face relaxed into a smile. Kathy looked like a cross between Marnie, my high school girlfriend, and Debbie Harry — blond, buxom, innocent, and yet somehow very wanting. Discovering I was pitching a tent, I quickly found a place on the couch and focused on concealment.

"Davey!" said Peter, sitting on the back of the couch, watching *Telemundo* with Jonesy and Hillary (who quickly rearranged herself to sit next to me, which did not help the tent concealment). "You speak Spanish? Don't worry, neither does Divan, and he's half Mexican."

"Two thirds, thank you very much!" said Divan, nearing with a bottle of vodka, a couple of shot glasses, a packet of pink lemonade, and a bag of pink jellybeans.

Peter said, "You have got to be the hairiest two-thirds Mexican I've ever seen."

"Hairy and proud," said Divan, his sun-cracked lips breaking into a smile, revealing his perfectly straight, perfectly white teeth.

How did Peter know all this about Divan? Had they not just meet? Or was this a case of Peter's lack of political correctness?

Peter: So, you're Mexican.

Divan: Two thirds, actually.

Peter: But you're hairy.

Divan: Alas.

Peter: You don't wear Speedos, do you?

Divan: Special occasions. Bar Mitzvahs.

Peter: My sister's friend had a Bar Mitzvah. Great party.

Divan: Bat Mitzvah.

Peter: Excuse you?

Divan: Bat Mitzvah. Bar is for boys, Bat is for girls.

Peter: Who are you to be so wise in the ways of Jews?

Divan: I'm half Jewish.

Peter: Let me get this straight: You're two thirds Mexican, half Jewish, and all Wookie?

Divan: I think that about sums it up.

A blue plastic cup magically appeared in my hand not holding the red plastic cup.

Jonesy said, "You're at least a time zone behind, so catch up."

Bewildered, I said, "Thank you, Easter Bunny."

Without thinking, Divan, Hillary and Peter said, "Bock, bock!"

We laughed. We drank.

As realization dawned that my magical blue-cup drink was a foul beer and rum concoction called Reer, Divan ripped open the pink lemonade, poured it directly into the vodka, and shook it up. He then produced a deck of cards.

The game was Down 'N Dirty, known to the masses as Texas Hold 'Em. But in lieu of antes, raises, or bets, the winner of each hand decided who drank a shot of what he called, Surrender the Pink.

Divan said, "Let me 'splain. No, no, there is too much. Let me sum up." He poured a shot of the vodka mixed with pink lemonade, dropped in a pink jellybean, drank, and licked his lips theatrically. "The only rule is that if you fold, you're out."

Translation: No more game. No more camaraderie. No more club.

"So, who's in?"

I had seen movies where hardened bikers, criminals, or fools swallowed an unfired bullet with a shot of bourbon or whiskey. After two shots of Surrender the Pink, I realized they were pussies. At least they could taste the booze, thereby calculating their alcohol consumption before it hit them. For us, the pink lemonade whipped the vodka's roar to a submissive peep. To know this and continue drinking was tantamount to insanity.

After the third shot, the memories of the previous Friday Night rose up to warn of coming ills. But how could I abstain? Not only was this a bonding experience, a gelling experience, but —

"Ladies and gentlemen," Divan said, standing and smiling as if he were introducing his new bride. "I'd like to make a toast. To Kathy Booth's first sip of sin ... In her entire life."

She blushed, hesitated, shot, cringed, gagged. We gawked, encouraged, clapped, laughed, hooted.

Peer pressure at its finest.

After my second shot, I said, "This shit is way too smooth. It's Liquid Death."

Three shots later, a vote passed requiring anyone calling the shot Liquid Death to drink a shot of Liquid Death. I hate democracies. Long live the Roman Empire. My stomach grumbled in agreement. An inauspicious beginning to a hell of a night, which officially began when —

Archer Phillips

— arrived. He was two weeks late for school, as was his nature, and the occupant of the second bedroom in Chez Carter. And he was all about first impressions.

"What the fuck is this?" he said, dropping his Nike duffel bag and stepping toward us in his Nike running shoes. He reminded me of Bill Paxton in *Weird Science*. Part yuppie, mostly redneck, all full of himself. He wore his black hair long, and was clad in a gunmetal-grey trench coat, despite the temperature dwelling in the upper eighties.

Jonesy said, "This? This is Down 'N Dirty. Why don't you grab a seat and —"

"Who the fuck are you?" And then to Peter, "Who the fuck is this?"

"This? This is Jonesy."

"Who?"

"You know Jonesy. Everybody knows Jonesy."

"Yeah, whatever," said Archer. "Carter, I've had a long flight, so just get these people out of —"

Divan said, "Who's Carter?"

"The bum-fuck sitting across from you."

Divan looked at the bum-fuck sitting across from him. "That's Jonesy. You know Jonesy, don't ya?"

"Not that bum-fuck, you moron. *That* bum-fuck," Archer said, pointing at Peter. "Now, out. Everyone."

Peter said, "You sure you don't know Jonesy? You know Jonesy. You met him, remember? That time at that thing."

Archer's brow wrinkled. "Thing? What thing?"

"That thing. You stripped naked, smeared yourself in tomato sauce, and ran down the street yelling 'I'm the Flash!'"

"Dude, you're joking?" said Hillary.

"It never happened," said Archer, with a hint of uncertainty. "He's making this shit up."

"He doesn't think it happened," said Peter.

"It didn't happen."

"So, you're saying it didn't happen."

"That's exactly what I'm —"

"I have proof."

"Bullshit."

"Video."

"The hell you do."

Peter said, "What does that mean? 'The hell you do.' I mean, it sounds right, but when you stop to think about it —"

"I knew you were full of shit," said Archer, turning to pick up his bag.

"You sure you want to doubt me?"

Archer stopped, locked eyes with the now very serious Peter Carter, and said, "Fuck you."

"Whoa, doggie!" said Jonesy, holding up his hands as if to stop a herd of stampeding sorority girls. "Is he calling ya out?"

"He's not calling me out," said Peter. Then to Archer, "Are you calling me out?"

Archer said, "I think I am."

Peter said, "We need to work on the stability of your statements, Arch. Either you're calling me out, or you're not. There is no middle ground."

"I am. Damn straight I am."

Peter threw down his cards and jumped up. "You sure you want to do that? You want all these kids to see your twig and berries covered in Ragu?"

Archer narrowed his eyes. "I'm calling your bluff."

Peter paused, then shrugged and said, "Hey, it's your meat flopping around." He then disappeared into his room upstairs.

We all sat silent. A minute passed. Two minutes.

Archer said, "Okay. He's not coming back. All of you, out."

"Dude, you've had a bad day," said Divan, dropping a pink jellybean into a shot and offering it up. "Take the edge off."

Archer looked at the potion, scowled, then slapped it from Divan's hand, spilling it across Kathy, Hillary, me.

In a blink, Divan was up and in Archer's face. "What's your problem?"

"You come into my house and ask me what my problem is?"

"You heard me."

"Fuck you."

"Fuck me?"

"Yeah, fuck you."

This is a perfect illustration of how, as testosterone mixes with adrenaline and alcohol in the male body, the mind turns into Cream of Wheat. From joy and witty banter to exchanges of 'fuck you' and posturing like roosters. Next up, brought to you by Stupidity, The Male Gene, is a dumb fight.

That is, unless you grew up in a low-income family and, before you received financial aid for a hoity-toity private high school, you attended public schools where fighting was just another class period called 'the walk home.'

"So you learn how to hold your own," said Divan, many Fridays later. "After a while, the fear dissipates enough for your mind to creep back. You begin searching for ways to defuse the situation."

The theme was Bigger Than Your Head, and, as he offered his wisdom of the streets, he drank from the spout of a watering pail almost twice the size of his noggin.

"The trick, though, is not appearing as if you're defusing things, or you can appear weak. But, more often than not, the other guy wants an out as much as you do. All it takes is a sneeze or an off-the-cuff comment to alter the other guy's perception. And a moment is all doubt needs to spring into action."

In a blink, Divan was up and in Archer's face. "What's your problem?"

"You come into my house and ask me what my problem is?"

"You heard me."

"Fuck you."

"Fuck me?"

"Yeah, fuck you."

"Really? Fuck me?"

"Are you deaf?" said Archer.

"Well, okay," said Divan, unbuttoning his pants. "But go easy on me this time."

Archer's anger became confusion.

Divan unzipped his fly.

Confusion became understanding.

Divan dropped his pants.

Understanding became horror.

Archer took two steps back, his arms raised as if fending off an attack.

"What?" said Divan, standing in his Snoopy boxers, his jeans around his ankles. The moment held. Then Divan fell to the ground, holding his stomach in laughter. Soon we were all smiling. Soon we were all laughing.

"What's so funny?" said Peter, coming down the stairs, holding a video tape. We all fell silent.

Kathy said, "No shit?" Her face darkened. We barely noticed.

Peter looked at the tape, pursed his lips, and walked to the VCR. Before he popped it in, he glanced to Archer, whose face was rapidly whitening, his eyes wide and unblinking.

Silence. Then Jonesy offered an olive branch. "Dude, no worries. We all do stupid shit when drinking. Don't sweat it."

But rather than taking the obtainable way out, Archer set his jaw, swallowed, and said, "You're full of shit, Carter."

Peter shrugged, put the tape in, and hit play. A party came alive on the screen. Peter grabbed the remote, sat down on the couch. "This is too early. It happened later. Right, Arch?"

Peter pressed the fast-forward button.

The television exploded.

Archer had thrown something. We later learned it was a shot glass.

He said, "I'll pay ya for it." Then calmly, very calmly, he picked up his Nike bag, entered his room on his Nike shoes, and shut the door.

After a moment Jonesy said, "Dude, why are you living with him again?"

Peter rubbed his nose in thought. Then, shaking his head, he said, "Because no one else will."

The next year, a pair of transfer students — a redhead with a spatter of freckles on her nose, and a dirty blond with a patch of grey she called 'her skunk spot' — replaced Archer. They were philosophy students who transferred every year to whatever university *Playboy* named their top party school. An upgrade if there ever was one.

Archer Phillips became just another body on campus. Until that —

Wednesday — Three Days Before The Wedding

— night we chased Peter from the outdoor mall of Pearl Street to the office building.

As the memories flooded back, Peter pulled out a key ring and selected an ugly piece of tarnished brass. Surprisingly, no alarm sounded. Maybe it was a silent alarm. Maybe we were all gonna get pinched for breaking and entering with a valid key in hopes of ...

I said, "What are we doing, exactly?"

Peter said, "We, Sir Robinson, are knights in a distant land out for a quick bout of revenge."

"Technically," said Jonesy, "knights aren't into that whole life of revenge thing, but whatever."

As we crept through the office building, Peter explained our mission. "Archer replaced the television he blew up with the shot glass. But he stole it when he moved out."

"Dude," said Jonesy. "Ten years. Let it go."

Peter stopped, gazed at Jonesy, and said, "Have you forgiven Scientology?"

Silence. Then Jonesy said, "Fuckers."

Peter said, "A grudge is a terrible thing to waste."

The summer between my freshman and sophomore years, Peter was performing in *Titus Androgynous* at the Colorado Shakespeare Festival. One night, as the curtain fell, he ran home to catch a Denver Nuggets playoff game, only to find Archer Phillips had moved out, taking the television with him.

Now, poking his head around a hallway corner, Peter said, "The only items he left behind were a toaster oven, and a box of random shit. And while I made a valiant attempt of holding them hostage, Archer wouldn't budge." This caused Peter's rage to discover a voice, as well as arms and legs. "I proceeded to destroy every goddamn thing in that box with a ball-peen hammer."

As his rage dissipated, Peter had found a set of keys among the shards of broken shit. And after some investigation, he discovered he held the instrument of entry to the office of Archer's family business, a real-estate management and investment company.

"So, I snuck in, snaked some files, cost the company about a hundred thousand bucks."

Jonesy said, "You didn't."

"I did."

"Can you say 'over-the-top'?"

"Scientology."

"Fuckers."

Peter said, "But that wasn't the fun part. The fun part was strategically placing magazines of the homosexual persuasion around the office. A coffee table here, his father's desk there. And on each one? A true-to-life mailing label with the name and address of Archer Phillips."

"How the hell did you pull that off?" I said.

"I found a *National Geographic* in the box of shit, photocopied the mailing label and glued a copy to each new magazine."

"Dude," I said.

"Yeah. Nice, huh?"

Jonesy held up a hand and said, "And when you say magazines, you mean —"

"*Glory Hole*, *Playgirl*, and *Husbands That Suck Dick*."

I said, "There's a magazine called *Husbands That Suck Dick*?"

The only drawback was that Peter couldn't view the damage. He never saw Archer, and didn't want to risk staking out the offices. So, he resigned himself to reading the occasional article in *The Daily Camera*, Boulder's local paper, about the company losing a contract, or botching some negotiations. Despite this third-hand joy, Peter felt he never received the satisfaction he deserved.

"So, tonight?" he said. "I'm going to piss on Archer's desk."

We were all amazed the key still worked. In ten years, you'd think they would have changed the building locks. But there we were, on the fourth floor, nearing the office, and still had yet to encounter a gate we couldn't breach.

Then we arrived at the door to Phillips Real Estate Management and Construction, Inc.

The key ran home.

Peter smiled. "Dumb fucks."

His smile faded when the key wouldn't turn. With each attempt, Peter's ten-year-old smoldering rage flashed. Soon, he was in the throws of a mini-rage, consisting of a lot of silent yelling and flipping-off the door with great emphasis.

Then, he caught sight of his reflection in the small door window, and stopped. Stopped, took a deep breath, smiled.

He then turned to the corner of the hallway, a foot from the office door, unzipped his fly, and proceeded to urinate.

And I will always remember his smile. As if he had just rolled off his first lay and walked among the gods.

CHAPTER THREE

Thursday – Two Days Before The Wedding

I pick up my mother and Donald at the airport at 8:32 a.m., my head pounding, my system full of black coffee, and a McDonald's sausage McMuffin sitting in the pit of my stomach like a crying child throwing things around in the playground sandbox.

"You're late," says my mother.

"Leave the boy alone," says Donald. "Can't you see he had a busy night?"

Busy. Donald's way of saying carousing.

"What happened to your Jeep? You lose it in a poker game?" Donald's way of making a joke.

"I traded it in for an Accord."

"But you loved that Jeep," says Donald.

"I needed something practical. The Jeep was flair, but no substance."

"The Jeep was compensation," says my mother.

"Martha!"

"Oh, come on, Donald. You and I both know the Jeep was compensation for a lack of something. Just like his father. Driving around in that '65 Mustang he had to have bored-out to feel like a man. And what the hell is 'bored-out,' anyway? Your father could never answer that one, but by God, he needed it! I'm so happy you have Pamela to knock some sense into you. I bet it was her idea to get the Honda."

Ah ... this was going to be a fun drive.

"Can you roll up your window?" says Donald, as we pull into airport traffic, heading to the highway.

"It is rolled up," says my mother.

"No it isn't. I can feel a draft."

"You're imagining it."

"No, I'm not. I feel a draft. Right in my left ear. My left ear feels a draft."

"Your left ear is imagining things."

"Are you going to roll up your window, or am I going to catch hypothermia?"

"You can't catch hypothermia from an imaginary draft, Donald."

"I'm not imagining the draft. I feel it. Right in my ear. I feel a draft in my ear."

"Stop it. You're upsetting Davis. I'm sorry, Davis. Donald isn't well."

"I can hear you. Don't you think I can hear you?"

"Oh, for Christ's sake, Donald. Focus on your draft."

Donald moves to the other side of the back seat and it is quiet for at least thirty seconds. His image in the rear-view-mirror is all hair. About three inches long on top and battleship grey, it seems to have a life of its own. Always sticking out, moving in the breeze only he feels. The first time we met, I thought of Harry Hamlin holding up the severed head of Medusa to the Kraken.

"What a bleak state," says Donald. "Everything's so brown and flat."

"There's a drought," says my mother.

"In May?"

"Yes, in May. May is drought month. Everyone knows that."

"Where are you getting this? May is drought month. No wonder you're not teaching anymore."

"Oh, here it is."

"What? What did I say?"

"Donald is just upset I get to sleep in."

"I'm not upset. Who said I'm upset?"

"Donald is lashing out. He's always been a lasher. Not like your father, Davis. Your father never lashed."

"I can hear you! I'm right here!"

My mother rolls down her window a crack. Donald puts his hands to his ears. His grey hair dances.

Another thirty seconds of quiet. It feels like a lifetime of bliss.

They met eleven years ago at one of those over-fifty Club-Med type vacations where everyone is fine with the wrinkles and the surgery scars. Donald was a retired cop. My mother had just completed her twenty-eighth year teaching fourth grade. It took them all of nine minutes to begin bickering like seasoned veterans. Nine days later, they married.

My mother rolls up her window and says, "I'm not teaching because of the economy."

I click on the window locks without her noticing.

She says, "They're laying off teachers instead of hiring them. It's the government, Congress. Let's tack on a bill to build a statue of Saint Kickback in some cornfield while teachers are looking for work. You know where parents should send their kids to learn? The unemployment line. That's where all the teachers are."

Ten seconds of quiet.

"You know May is drought month. Right, Davis?"

Five seconds.

"What kind of mileage does this thing get?" asks Donald.

"Twenty-five, city."

"Wow."

"That's not wow," says my mother. "That's not even good. Angie from across the street? She has one of those Volkswagen Jettas that gets fifty miles to the gallon."

"Why do you have to do that?" says Donald.

"Do what?"

"Knock Davis down like that."

"I'm not knocking."

"You just did. You knocked his choice of cars."

"I did no such thing."

"And Angie is a liar if she says it gets fifty miles to the gallon. No car gets fifty miles to the gallon. Big Oil would never allow it."

"She's not a liar."

"She is a liar. And a harlot, too. You know how she got that fancy-schmancy cable setup of hers for free? She schlumped the cable guy, that's how. What kind of girl schlumps the cable guy to get cable? I'll tell you who. A harlot!"

"You're delusional. She gets fifty miles to the gallon. I saw the factory sticker."

"You saw the factory sticker?"

"Fifty miles a gallon."

"The actual sticker? On the window?"

"The actual sticker."

"Fifty miles a gallon … Big Oil got schlumped by the cable guy."

"Donald!"

Donald says, "What? What did I say?" as he looks in the rear view mirror and winks.

Five minutes.

I turn on the radio. KBCO — Dada, 'Dizz Knee Land.' Peter is right. No matter what city you're in, you'll never find a better radio station. The perfect mixture of whatever. It's as if they're pumping subliminal messages under their songs, telling you to believe every song is perfect, the disk jockeys are your closest friends, and you should sing along at the top of your lungs with the windows down.

Dada fades out. Big Head Todd and the Monsters fades in. 'Bittersweet.' I sit back and listen to Todd Park Mohr's gravelly vocals. I want a Camel. I want a Marlboro. I want a damn GPC. I curse silently and grit my teeth as I try not to belt out the chorus. Damn you, KBCO.

"You don't look good, Davis," says my mother. This pulls me out of my cigarette fixation. "You've looked better."

"Well," I say, "I'm under a bit of stress, Mother."

"Yes, but even with the stress, you don't look good. When was the last time you went to the doctor?"

"I'm not seeing a doctor, Mother."

"Then how are you going to get better?"

"I'm not sick."

"How do you know?"

"I'm not going to the doctor."

"The doctor will know. What's his number? I'll call him for you."

"Mother."

"You really don't look good, Davis. Something's wrong. Donald, doesn't Davis look bad? Like something's wrong?"

"Will you leave the boy alone?"

"He needs a doctor."

"He doesn't need a doctor."

"He looks bad."

"He looks like he needs a glass of hot fat and an aspirin. Or waffles. I love waffles. Do they have the Waffle House here? I love the Waffle House."

My mother says, "Why can't you ever back me up? Why can't you ever agree with me?"

"Turn up the radio, will you, Davis?"

I hold back a smile and wonder if Donald wants to sing along.

My parents divorced when I was eleven. Not a good age for it, not that any age is good for your parents divorcing, but if there ever were a bad age for it, it would be eleven. At eleven, you're mired within the confusion and awkward quagmire of seventh grade. While remembering the warm blanket of elementary school, you begin to taste the fear of the high school social labyrinth. Your instincts take over.

My instinct was to strap a bomb in the guise of a model rocket engine to some cardboard and balsa wood, and watch it blow up one hundred feet above ground. It's a guy thing. Sure, I could ready the parachute and watch it float back for another go, but when instinct told you to glue down the nose cone for some fireworks, you didn't argue.

I was in my room building an Estes Rocket when my mother entered and sat on the bed behind me.

She said, "Your father and I are getting a divorce." Simple. Your father and I are getting a divorce, now I'm going to Dizz Knee Land. "Davis, are you listening to me?"

I heard her, yet my reaction never passed the internal stage of expression because I was lining up the tail fins to the fuselage. Parents believe children ignore them when they don't immediately answer. What they forget is that children have an amazing ability to focus on something, while still absorbing the world around them. I'm not sure when we lose this unique ability, but it's shortly after flight and invisibility. Honest. Just ask any kid and he'll tell ya.

It's a shame. We learn to focus on our surroundings as we age, and forget the joy of total absorption within one task. Despite society's disdain, guys retain a modicum of this focus, and it becomes an instrument of bonding. This is why we can spend hours discussing sports, women, and the *Simpsons*.

Alternatively, women appear as if they're bonding over anything, when, in fact, it's all an excuse to gossip. Their nails, the latest Oprah, the not-yet-seen pimple three days from surfacing but is already christened Mount Zitimanjaro. Mediums for discussing how Betty Slutshername is sleeping with blah, blah, blah, her ass is huge, blah, blah, blah, chocolate.

A guy gossiping over the *Simpsons*? Rip off your penis, your membership's been revoked.

It is this retained focus that enables guys to bond over the seemingly ridiculous. Example:

"*GI Joe*, or *Star Wars*?"

"Dude, Joe."

"Good call. My sister played with *Star Wars* figures."

"She also go the glitter route?"

"Every lame-assed toy that sparkled."

"Baubles, man. Women and their fucking baubles. Wait. Are we talking Pre-Slaughter Joe, or Post-Slaughter Joe?"

"Give me some credit. The moment Sgt. Slaughter became a character, I started rooting for Cobra."

"Fuckin' Yoko Ono of the Joe Crew. I got one for ya: Scarlet or Lady Jaye?

"Scarlet, in a heartbeat."

"A heartbeat? Really?"

"I love redheads."

"But Lady Jaye? She's got spunk."

"And redheads don't?"

"Yeah, but Scarlet seems like a conservative redhead. Maybe she grew up hardcore religious, maybe she just doesn't like to experiment, I don't know. But Lady Jaye has the glint."

"The glint?"

"Yeah. When a girl's diggin' on ya, she has that glint in her eye?"

"You sure it's not a piece of glitter?"

"Baubles, man."

"Okay, I can buy the glint argument, but dude. Everyone knows the moment you get a redhead into the sack, they're wildcats."

"Yeah, but Scarlet's with straight-laced Duke. She sounds more repressed than wildcat."

"Repressed can be fun."

"Trust me. Repressed is never fun."

"Where the hell are we?"

"I don't know, I was following you."

That afternoon:

"Davis," said my mother.

"It's too hot," I said. When you're a kid, excuses come out of your ass before you know what you're doing. "It's gotta be at least 146 degrees outside and I can't play in that heat. I'm going to die, I tell you. Die!"

She said, "You're not going to die."

"How do you know? I could die. And it would be a nasty, painful death like I was marooned on a desert island by pirates and was out of water and I slowly shriveled up and my skin was all scabby and sunburned and became leather, but not the soft leather for those World War II bomber jackets, but really hard leather that bullets can bounce off of and I was later found by archeologists who thought I was an alien who crash landed on Earth but they couldn't find my spaceship so they thought I was an alien who was marooned on the desert island by alien pirates and I was out of water and I slowly shriveled up and —"

"You don't need to go outside."

"I don't?"

"No."

I eyed her, trying to guess her game, see her trick, discover her secret agenda. I gave up and went back to my rockets. I don't know how much time went by, but enough for me to forget she was there.

And then she repeated what she thought I had ignored. "Your father and I are getting a divorce."

I later realized that moment began her selfish period. When she decided to run and find herself, no matter the expense. She would later force a massive custody battle because she grew up when the woman got the house, the kids, and a nice alimony check. But I also think she fought for me because, well, she thought Pop worked for the mafia.

No joke.

He didn't. Work for the mafia, that is. But he also didn't talk about his job because he was emotionally closed off, something I have no doubt that came from the age gap. A generation removed from each other, my mother grew up in the *Stand By Me* days when you put a penny on the train tracks, while my pop grew up during The Depression when you put a penny in your pocket.

Enter the Vietnam War. When the boys went off, gender roles were clearly defined. The man worked, the woman didn't. But when the boys came home, they had to feel as well as talk about it.

Pop grew up in The Depression, enlisted in the Navy shortly after Pearl Harbor because it was the right thing to do. He was shipped off to the Pacific theater, did his thing, managed not to wet himself when the bullets flew, managed not to die.

After the war, Pop never sat still. As if the threat of society collapsing shadowed him. Law, international trade, politics, he did it all. In his late forties, he started a family, and although he tried to change with the times, he never got a handle on the social upheaval. Feeling wasn't something a man did, and the more my pop tried to adapt, the more be became the epitome of a hard-working man who kept things to himself.

There's a problem at work? Fix it. Don't concern your family. You feel weak? Fix it. Don't concern your family. The man is the foundation of the family, the rock.

My mother also attempted to adapt. But although she was all about empowerment and equality, her childhood had taught her that questions equaled problems. Smile, and just accept things as they are.

Such was their relationship. Pop never offered, my mother never asked. He left early, returned late. She knew he was a real-estate attorney, but never questioned it. It's real estate. He aided parties in buying and selling land. Simple. Normal. Very un-mafia-like.

Her view changed following a business party where she recognized some Gentlemen recently in the news for Unsavory corporate dealings. Gentlemen who later fled to Cuba to avoid paying millions of dollars in taxes and felt a communist nation was more appealing than a democratic prison.

The unpaid taxes generated in real estate were not in question. Where the money originated to purchase the real estate, was. And when my mother connected the Unsavory Gentlemen with old-time Las Vegas, the questions flew.

During his final hours, Pop said, "I felt pinned down. Under fire. With each explosion, I searched for a solution, and then, well … and then instinct took over."

I said, "You blew something up?"

He said, "Oh, there were plenty of explosions."

It's not easy to sleep when you're a hallway away from a battleground. Nothing physical, but enough verbal, mental, and emotional blasts to fill a lifetime with nightmares.

In retrospect, I think my mother wanted an excuse to leave. Never truly happy, she saw herself a husk of who she could be.

After the initial onslaughts, tempers eased. My pop swallowed hard, opened up, and tried to ease my mother's fears. But no matter how great his effort, his answers, his adaptations, my mother wanted to leave. And so, Pop made a last-ditch effort and laid it all out.

He said, "Martha, I live my life with blinders on. Life is full of unsavory people and sometimes you can't avoid them or else you'll die lonely and broke. But *interacting* with them does not mean you become one of them. A long time ago, I contemplated my view of unsavory, and I drew a line in the sand. On one side is me. On the other are the businesses of gambling, tobacco, and alcohol.

"But real estate? It's land. Land doesn't hurt anyone. Land doesn't kill anyone. Someone wants to buy land, and another one wants to sell. I make it happen. And at the end of the day, all I am is an attorney who represents parties involved in real-estate dealings. Not gambling, not tobacco, not alcohol."

She said, "But the money —"

"The money to purchase the land may come from unsavory types, who may be involved in unsavory businesses, but I don't know anything about that, and even if you wanted to tell me about it, I wouldn't listen. Because I *interact* with unsavory people, but I am *not* one of them. I don't steal, kill, or hurt anyone."

She said, "Yeah? Then what *do* you do?"

"I provide food and shelter and a future for my family."

And my mother looked at him, and drew a line. On one side of it was Pop. On the other side was the door.

Pop told me in the hours before he died. It's sad that only when your parents are near the end, we're filled with the desire to know about them. It's a guilt thing. If all were healthy and well, we wouldn't give a good goddamn. Guilt is a catch-22. If you give in to it, it'll hit you from both ends.

Thursday

"Nice of you to show up," says Pamela as we walk in. "You have fun?"

I mumble something incoherent, but stop when I notice how stunning she looks. Colorado Rockies cap, brown ponytail pulled through the hole in the back, plain white t-shirt, faded jeans, sneakers. Women don't realize how something this simple causes men to sizzle. But do I tell her? Hell no. Why? Because she's giving me that 'Stop being a child' look, prompting me to throw her the 'I'll be a damned child if I want to be a child' look, and she sighs and I smile and she rolls her eyes and we both turn from each other.

"I called you," she says.

"I had it turned off."

"You're mumbling."

"I had my phone turned off."

"Why would you do that?"

"I didn't want to wake the kids."

She cocks her head. "What kids?"

"Jonesy's kids."

"You were at Jonesy's?"

"Yeah."

"You're mumbling again."

"Yes. I was at Jonesy's."

"And you didn't think to call?"

"I … No. It didn't cross my mind."

"Good to know I'm marrying such a thoughtful man."

"You can always back out."

"Such a gesture."

"It's the little things."

"Mumbling."

"I said … I said I'm tired and I'm going to take a shower and a nap."

She begins to speak. I cut her off.

"If you do decide to reconsider marrying me, wake me up."

"I'll leave a note."

"All the better."

As I take my mother's bags to the guest room, my mother hugs Pamela and they exchange something about how men never change, or some other dumbass thing women say to each other when they don't understand the actions of men.

Pamela says, "How was the flight?"

"Crowded," says Donald. "Martha spent so much time looking for the cheapest fare that she forgot to book us leg room."

"Cheap is what got us to the wedding in the first place," says my mother.

"Well, I'm just glad you're here," says Pamela. And then she trails off as I'm moving to the other end of the house.

I plop my mother's bags in the guest room and catch a glimpse of myself in the mirror. Yep, I look like shit. No wonder Pamela is pissed.

All told, I'd managed about an hour of sleep. But it was worth it. Smoking cigars and clove cigarettes; telling war stories. The memories are so fresh, so vivid.

A five-minute shower later, I find that Pamela is off on some last-minute wedding errands, and my mother and Donald are down for a nap. I ready for my own nap, but remember Jonesy asking if Divan had e-mailed me his flight info, and plop down at the computer.

A minute passes. Nothing from Divan. But when I see that I've received an email from —

Joanna Mills

— I open it without a thought.

I've never met Joanna. Which is good, for she probably would have given Hillary a run for the Best Sex Award in the category of Other Woman in Davis' Life.

Three years ago, on a rainy Cheshire afternoon, Joanna was killing time before the pubs opened, and happened upon my *Yahoo!* profile with the Woody Allen quote: "Is sex dirty? Only if done right."

Feeling randy, she shot me a flirtatious note. We'd since exchanged many pictures — redhead, athletic, but soft — and although I often question the validity of one's online photos, hers, aside from the sexually explicit pics, have been from various weddings and family gatherings.

A year ago, Joanna's father was diagnosed with cavities. Her flirty disposition took a header, and we spoke over the phone for the first and only time. I understood what she was going through. I saw Pop fight the Big C for many years, and as much as I hated unlocking the chest of stored emotions, she needed someone. Unfortunately, upon hearing her British accent, my thoughts sprang from consoling, to bedding.

This is another example of the retained focus that enables guys to bond over the seemingly ridiculous.

"One woman, one accent, go."

"Elizabeth Hurley."

"Too easy."

"I wasn't aware obscure was a factor."

"It's not, but there's a point where the more a woman is fantasized about, the less desirable she becomes. Hurley is sorta like the slutty cheerleader for a global football team."

"Disturbing imagery. Okay, who's your pick?"

"Oh, Elizabeth Hurley. I like the easy ones."

I was hers. A beautiful redhead with a killer accent? I was browsing through tent city when I was supposed to guide her through the town of self-help.

Somehow, though, I was able to look past my desires. I told her what I went through, and how I dealt with it without cracking.

It was the first, and only time, I ever spoke about my pop's death. Not with my friends, not with Pamela. A healthy bastard, I am.

So, I took a deep breath, closed my eyes, and unlocked the chest. I told her everything I wished someone had told me. I told her that death isn't about what you're losing, but what you've already gained from knowing that person. I told her to embrace the time he had left. That she should place her life on hold, and spend as much of it with him. That she shouldn't do what I did.

"And what was that?" she said, coming out 'An woot wus that?'

Memories flashed like a grease fire and I wanted to hit something. But I didn't, because Joanna had turned to me — not her friends, not her mother, but me. And I would be damned if I'd let my self-pity interfere.

Oh, but it tried.

"What did I do? Well, I fucked up is what I did. From when my pop was diagnosed until he was almost ... until he was on his last legs, I ran away. I played, drank, and never let myself believe it was happening. Because if I thought about anything not in front of me, I'd lose control. I could only grasp where I was, whom I was with, and what I put into my body to dull and blur everything. And what makes it worse, is I knew I was doing it."

I took a breath, my throat catching, tears flowing not from sadness but self-anger.

"And only after I wasted all that time, only until the very end did I realize that *he* could have been scared of what he couldn't control. All his life he met problems head on, found solutions, and found a way. And suddenly he was not only losing, but having his nose rubbed in the dirt.

"Only at the end did I realize *he* could have been wishing to drink and play and laugh. Only then did I know *he* would never see another sunrise, another sunset, another snowflake. That <u>he</u> would never hold his grandchildren.

"That's when I shut the door on the child and opened the door for the adult. God, that sounds cheesy, but I'll tell ya, until you're in that situation, you'll never understand it. That fucking role reversal."

"But you were there," said Joanna. "In the end, when he needed comforting."

"It wasn't enough. I helped him to be strong, but it wasn't enough."

"It was brave, what you did," she said.

I laughed. "That's not brave. Brave is doing something extraordinary in the face of death or destruction or —"

"Fear?"

"Fear? Yeah, maybe. But not with me. Not then. I did nothing extraordinary. I didn't throw myself onto a grenade or pull anyone from a burning building. I ran away from the fear and that's what led me to him. It was fear that chased me from a drunken stupor so I could have one more day with him, even though he was in and out of consciousness, and I was in and out of a severe hangover."

"But you gained something, didn't you? In those talks."

"Yeah, sorta."

"Yeah, sorta?" I could almost see her face when she spoke. Smiling, making fun of me even in *her* time of need.

"I got something. I was able to fill in some of the blanks of his life that I needed filled. The gaps between the stories I already knew. But you know what happened instead? For every gap filled, a hundred more appeared.

"And you know what those gaps are like? They're like the gaps in the Theory of Evolution. Creationists always focus on the fucking gaps between discovered links in the evolutionary chain from chimps to humans, but with each new discovery, another fucking gap is created. With one filled, two remain. I can't imagine your life's work creating more gaps than filling them. That's like filling one pothole with the rubble of one you've just dug out. So, yeah. I gained something. I gained more potholes."

Not until later did I realize the role reversal that had occurred. She called me for help, but ended up helping me.

Two days later, she e-mailed me to say that she shared the most meaningful conversation with her father in her life. A part of me was happy, but a part of me didn't give a shit. Because if we hadn't spoken on the phone, I never would have opened up the chest, and never would have had to feel that loss.

After my shower, as I sit at the computer, as I force the growing haze of sleep from enveloping me, I read Joanna's email. She says she's 'racked with guilt' because she can't attend the wedding, but wishes me the best.

I smile a bit, my exhaustion taking hold. But when I read on, the haze is burned away.

Because after she says that she wishes me the best, she says, "Wait. No. I can't lie anymore. I wish you the best, but I don't. Does that make sense? It doesn't matter. What matters is that I need to be truthful and honest with myself.

"I was actually going to fly out this morning, but when I was boarding the plane, my hand wouldn't release the boarding pass. No matter how much I willed my hand to open up and let go of that flimsy piece of paper, it wouldn't."

Then the boarding pass tore in half.

"I stood there like a right idiot. Looking from my half of the pass to the ticket agent holding the other half. It was a nice go 'round. My half of the pass, the ticket agent holding the other half, reverse, repeat, scream, cry. Nothing made any sense. I thought I missed something. Then my vision began to blur and shrink. I fell to my knees, gasping for breath. People rushed to my side. Sound left me. And still, I would not let go of my half of the soddin' pass. It wasn't until thirty-minutes later, after the paramedics and security officials checked me over, did I understand what was happening.

"It was you, Davis. It was all because of you."

I reread that part once, twice. I read it aloud, hear the words, and fail to comprehend. I look away, to the keyboard, back to the computer screen. Reverse. Repeat. Scream. Cry. I read on, confusion and horror expanding.

She was terrified because in the past three years, with our emails and flirting and erotic pictures, she had fallen in love with me.

Reverse. Repeat. Scream. Cry.

It began with the phone call. Love and hate and loss and guilt were flying around her world and when I reached out to help her, all of her extreme feelings flew in my direction. I became more than just words on a page. I became real.

She figured that, after a point, she could discard the emotions raised by words on a page because they're akin to a romance novel. But when she heard my voice, heard the warmth, the kindness, the strength and security, the romance novel became reality. Something she didn't become aware of until she attempted to board the plane to attend my wedding.

She says, "Hell, had I known this was bouncing around in my head, I never would have dropped plastic on a non-refundable ticket. But once it came to me, it all fit. Everything made sense. A light came on."

The way she always looked forward to my letters. The way she read them on the computer monitor, only to print them out to read again. The way her stomach fluttered when I joked about visiting so she could show me around that wee island of hers. The way her stomach dropped when she heard I was getting married.

And so, because of her feelings, she would not allow herself to see me for the first time, for the last time, and place flesh to the pictures, the voice, the warmth.

She says, "That just wouldn't be fair to me. That wouldn't be fair to me at all."

I read this once, twice. The email is long and full of life, full of the heat of her pain and love. And after a long while I say, "Holy shit. This chick is nuts."

I rub my eyes, try to comprehend how this all happened.

"This is crazy," I say. "Capital crazy in the land of Crazytown, home of the world's largest ball of crazy."

In my state of clear thought, I decide to tell her just that. Tell her that she's crazy. That she's nuts. That she's loopy as a fruitcake. And then I'll call Customs and report she's illegally importing a highly toxic and contagious form of crazy.

I hit reply. I begin to type. I hear a soft knock at the door behind me. I turn.

There she is. Joanna the redhead. Standing there in nothing but what God has graced her with. And dear lord in heaven, she is stunning.

She nears, takes me by the hand, and pulls me to the bed. She leans over me. In a whisper, she tells me where she's going to nibble. Her accent is intoxicating. Her warm breath is exhilarating.

I pull her to me and start kissing down the side of her neck, over the top of her right breast, but then I look up and ...

It's Her. Not Joanna, but Her. I've waited for a hundred lifetimes. She's here. She's in my bed. She's pulling me near and kissing me and saying how much she loves me and wants nothing less than for me to touch her and rub her and —

I open my eyes. Pamela's are closed. My hand is up her t-shirt and cupping her right breast. With the other I've unbuttoned her jeans and the zipper is half lowered and my hand is moving down to —

I inhale so sharply it burns. I must have been sleeping when she walked in and she took my dreams of making love to *Her* as my desire to make love with *her*.

I pull away. Pamela opens her eyes in shock and wanting, and when she sees me, confusion engulfs her. We're silent a moment, unsure of what is happening, unsure if we can speak, until —

"You're right," she says. "We've waited this long, we shouldn't ruin it now."

Fuckstick. She thinks I pulled away out of respect for her. She doesn't want to have sex until the wedding — six months, rather than one — and believes I pulled away to ensure we stick to the plan.

"No," I say, then babble about how we can't give in to the passion, and other crap I know she wants to hear.

Pamela leans to me, her soft lips kiss me tenderly — first on my forehead, then my lips — with hesitation and longing, and thanks me — genuinely thanks me.

She says, "I know we've both been on edge of late and the sex thing isn't helping, but I love you and I love that you're putting up with my decision. That is an example of why I'm marrying you. Because you aren't selfish and you consider my feelings."

And then she leaves.

For a moment, I do nothing but breathe. I breathe and try not to focus on any of the thousand thoughts knocking about my head like lottery balls in the bubble.

I crawl back into bed and sleep.

I dream, but not of Joanna, not of Pamela ... not of Her ... but of running across the high school football field in a town named Crazy. It's the height of summer, the sun warming my skin feels like a comfortable nap, and I'm watching the parachute carry my Estes rocket safely to the ground. It disappears over a small hill, and when I run to the crest, I stop because the rocket has landed in the middle of the aisle for a wedding procession.

Two little girls are walking down the aisle, dropping white rose petals, covering the rocket until I can't see it anymore. The wind picks up. The flowers blow away. The rocket is gone.

Only the engine remains. Small. So small. And when it explodes I'm thrown backward and tumble down the hill. When I crawl back up, there's nothing left of the wedding site but a huge — so huge — crater.

And slowly falling from the sky are white rose petals.

CHAPTER FOUR

I met Pamela during my —

Senior Year

— at Colorado University, ten months before I cheated on her with Hillary at the Renaissance Festival, by complete happenstance. We were at the Hotel Del Coronado in San Diego for Peter's first wedding. This one was to a young secretary named Naomi he'd met at his agent's office, his first week in Los Angeles, six months prior.

At the onset, Peter was just working Naomi.

"I'd take her out, romance her. Make her feel important and all that sorta shit." We were on the side of the white-capped river, the day of his bachelor party. "It didn't hurt that she's a spitting image of a young Sela Ward, and when she agreed to dress up as a 'bama cheerleader just like young Sela in those photos?"

"I love those photos."

"How could I throw it away?"

"What was she getting out of this?"

"I'd tell her about her beauty and brains. You know, ease her insecurities."

"So, typical Peter Carter."

He nodded, shrugged. "She'd slip my headshot into the casting calls for that particular day. She couldn't get me any gigs, but hey, I got face time."

And that was all that Peter needed.

Within a month, he had a recurring role as a drug dealer on *NYPD Blue*. Within three, he had a starring role opposite Kurt Russell in a John Carpenter film. And while on shoot, he signed on to a Spielberg film with Meg Ryan and Dustin Hoffman. It was then that he proposed to Naomi.

Most people believe he married her out of obligation. To do the right thing. Horseshit. If any of those people knew the real Peter Carter, not the movie-star Peter Carter or the crass party-boy Peter Carter, they'd know the truth. The problem was the real Peter Carter rarely showed itself.

How do I know? Because for his bachelor party, the real Peter Carter insisted on whitewater rafting instead of the strip clubs. And while the real Peter Carter would vanish in three months, he would resurface seven years later at my bachelor party.

At lunch, on the riverbank, I asked him if he knew what he was doing.

"I love her," he said.

"Yeah, but it doesn't mean you have to jump in and marry her."

"I know, but — and this is gonna sound pretty gay — but it's not just that I love her, but I've fallen for her, ya know? In that dumb Shakespearian sense."

"You've fallen?"

"Hard."

"And you can't get up?"

He paused, rubbing his nose. A raft passed on the far side of the river, occupants waving and cheering, then suddenly disappeared from view. Screams echoed off the canyon walls.

Peter said, "Naomi calls dating The A.D.D. Adventure, because everyone has the attention span of one date and one fuck. No one wants to focus on someone for too long lest the fun that caught your attention in the first place lose its shine. Because if it does, they'll search for problems and they'll overanalyze and they'll fall into the trap of being a real person in a real relationship."

He picked up a rock, rolled it around in his hand, and threw it lazily into the water. He said, "She told me this on our third date. As if she was reading the blueprint to my life."

He looked at me and I knew from the innocent, boyish smile that I wasn't looking at the Peter Carter of the Friday Night Club, but the Peter Carter from the Las Vegas trip a few months earlier. The Peter Carter still reeling from the adventure, from the highs, from the lows, from staring into the barrel of a gun cocked and ready to fire.

The real Peter Carter said, "I can get up. I just don't want to."

So what happened? I think he confused his love for Naomi with the high generated by his sudden rise to fame. He equated Naomi with success, and never knew her in any other light.

That said, the real Peter Carter would tell you that Naomi was the only one he'd ever loved. He'd tell you this, secretly, if he trusted you.

I was the only one he told.

Years later at my bachelor party, in the alley behind Damon's Steakhouse where Peter confessed his betrayal, I wished he never trusted me at all.

Pamela was the maid of honor for —

Naomi

The two met in grade school in Tempe, attended the same high school and double dated to homecoming and prom all four years together, applied to the same three colleges together (Yale, Princeton, and UCLA, just because if they couldn't get the Ivy, they'd get the sun and the surf), and when Pamela got into Yale and Naomi got into UCLA, they cried together.

While Pamela relished the east-coast Indian summer, Naomi found herself caught in the UCLA undertow, and quickly realized college life was not for her. And so, three months into her freshman year at UCLA, she took a deep breath, dove off the relatively safe rock of education, and plunged into the churning ocean waters of the job market. As fate would have it, she was picked up by a small Hollywood agency trawler in need of a secretary.

A year later, that small Hollywood agency trawler was overtaken by a larger Hollywood agency pirate-brigantine, and she became an executive secretary. Two years after that, the larger Hollywood agency pirate-brigantine was overtaken by a Royal Navy frigate of Hollywood agencies, and she found herself the executive secretary for the head agent. And so, almost four years after she jumped from the rock of education, when most of her friends were about to take their own employment plunge, Naomi was debt free, making sixty-five thousand a year, and having the time of her life.

That was when Peter Carter boarded her ship.

Moments after Peter proposed at the Hollywood Observatory, Naomi called Pamela.

"Will you be my maid of honor?"

"Of course I will. Who are you marrying?"

"Peter, you silly tart!"

Two weeks later, we gathered at the Hotel Del Coronado in San Diego for a small, four-hundred-person wedding. Pictures of the event were sold to *People Magazine*. The headline: 'The New Hunk On The Block — Sold.'

To this day, when one of my students finds the pictures of me with Peter Carter and his brother Ian, they're first confused, then shocked, then amazed. In that order. Confused their soggy American history professor is friends with a couple of superstars; shocked that said professor would know any superstars; amazed that the pictures are real, and not attached to a virus infecting their computer.

But it might have all been different. Sure, I'm deluding myself when I ask: What if it were me? What if I were Peter's best man instead of just a groomsman? Because of that one degree of separation —

Ian Carter

— was in the majority of the wedding pictures. And when those pictures hit *People Magazine*, Ian Carter, Peter's younger brother, Jonesy's high school buddy two grades behind, became an overnight sensation.

One degree away.

One.

That was how close I came to maybe (close = never), possibly (dream on), perhaps (shut the fuck up already), being a superstar. That one degree changed my life forever. But not because of what *might* have happened, but because of what *did* happen. That one degree of separation from stardom and supermodels gave me something altogether different. That one degree gave me Pamela.

At the time of the wedding, Ian was a sophomore at the Colorado School of Mines for Engineering. The boy is a damned genius. It's annoying being around someone who knows everything useful and useless. He's like the freak love child of Cliff Clavin and Steven Hawking. One minute he's talking about the chemical makeup of Jupiter, and the next he's throwing out the most useless and irrelevant shit known to man.

"Did you know that it's impossible to lick your elbow?"

You want to kick him. But you don't because unless he's drinking, he doesn't thrust his ego in your face. Somehow, despite his brilliance, he's down to earth and affable. Though that makes you want to kick him even more.

"Did you know when they first started selling *Coke* in China, it was translated to read 'Bite the Wax Tadpole'?"

Just how smart is he? At seven, Ian was four grades ahead in math and science. At nine, he was interning at Lockheed Martin. At twelve, he worked summers there. And at eighteen, when Peter got hitched to a girl he had met six months earlier, Ian was on track to graduate from a five-year program in three years, begin a double PhD he planned to complete in two years, and go full time at Lockheed Martin. I'll say it again, the boy is a damned genius.

"Did you know that most toilets flush in E Flat?"

But what's really annoying is that he can be almost as charming as Peter, and just as handsome. And when you wrap your mind around that, you begin to imagine a mad scientist who has side-stepped reality and perfected the genetically impossible three-way love child of Cliff Clavin, Steven Hawking, and Brad Pitt.

It's funny. His parents aren't anything special, but the damned kids popped out as genius supermodels. Everyone assumes with those good looks they must be male bimbos. But when they open their mouths, that assumption is replaced by awe, later replaced by wanting, later replaced by naked flesh.

make sure she doesn't sober up to realize you're just a normal, everyday boob.

"Yeah?" I said. "Why Denver?"

"First-year law student. Denver University."

My eyes widened.

"What is it?" she asked.

"What? Oh, nothing."

"It's never nothing. Anyone who says it's nothing knows it's something."

I stammered, attempting to push aside the coincidence I would forever keep to myself.

I said, "It's just ... Law? Really?"

She took a moment, chose her words. "Is that so surprising?"

"Well, yeah, actually."

"Be careful. You don't want to dig a hole you can't climb out of."

"No, no, you don't understand. That's why I'm surprised."

Her brow knitted together.

I said, "Feisty plus smart equals I'm out of my league."

Rule of thumb: When a beauty reminds you of another woman, pretend to be a stammering dork.

She smiled, playfully pushed my shoulder, and as she withdrew her hand, I quickly took it in my own. Then, catching her gaze, I placed the fresh drink into her hand, and slowly kissed the inside of her wrist. Over the surf, I heard her inhale, saw her chest rise, saw her smile falter, saw her bite her lower lip.

Then, as if kicking herself for being caught off guard, she pulled back her hand and looked away, allowing the wax tadpole to calm her.

After a long moment of silence, I said, "So, why law?"

She shrugged, said, "I don't know. Ever since I saw my daddy in a courtroom, I was hooked."

"I hope he wasn't the defendant." A bad joke, but she laughed, so all was good. "What kind of law?"

"Criminal."

"The private sector?"

"For the state."

"Idealistic."

"I'm young."

"Older than me."

"Do you like older women?"

"Depends how old."

"Where do you draw the line?"

"I find it hard to get in the mood when you're looking at blue hair." Another bad joke, but this time she not only laughed, but snorted and covered her mouth quickly with her hand, only to snort again. Either I was on that night, or I needed to buy stock in Bacardi.

I said, "What made you decide on Denver?"

"Oh, you don't want to hear that."

"I asked, didn't I?"

"Okay. You want the long story or the short?"

"How long is the long?"

"When do you fly out?"

"One short version then."

Smiles. I put my tuxedo coat across her shoulders. It wasn't chilly, but I wasn't the one wearing an armless dress hiked to my knees so it wouldn't get wet.

She said, "Okay. I fell for a guy two years ago, moved in with him, accepted his proposal, and decided on Denver University because he was taking a job in the area."

"You've been engaged?"

"The short version of the story will be longer than the actual engagement, trust me. Anyway, late in the summer when we were going to move out, he started to pull away. At first I thought it was because of nerves — you know, moving and stress and the new job and the jazz. But then I found him packing a bag one afternoon."

"What kind of bag?"

"A duffel bag. Small. Like he was about to go camping for the weekend."

"The weekend you were moving."

"And so I asked 'What's up?'"

I smiled, tried not to laugh. She saw me and also smiled and playfully slapped me on the shoulder. "It's not funny."

"It's a little bit funny."

"No, it's stupid! It was a stupid thing to ask when you know the answer is going to be bad, but it came out before I thought about it."

"What did he say?"

"He said, 'I'm leaving.' I said, 'Leaving where?' He said, 'The Peace Corps.' And I felt as if he'd reached into my chest and pulled out my lungs because suddenly I couldn't breathe. He said, 'Don't worry, it won't be for long.' I asked him, 'How long is not very long?' He said, 'Two-year stint.' And I said, 'That's not long?' as I was slowly melting into this puddle of goo on the floor. He said, 'It'll go by like that.' He snapped his fingers, and closed his bag and I was about to say, 'This is a joke, right?' but then I realized he'd shaved his head like he was going into the military and it wasn't a joke. It was real. And just like that," she snapped her fingers, "he left."

"Ouch."

"Mega ouch."

"And you still decided to come to Denver?"

"Not an easy decision. But after some sleepless nights, I decided to do what I've always done."

"Press on."

"Exactly."

"Life throws you a curve and all that junk."

"You got it."

I was becoming more amazed with this woman by the second, and it wasn't the alcohol talking. She was beautiful — I've always been a sucker for long-haired brunettes with a strong jaw line and dimples — something I had seen before I'd filled the glass, but she was also smart and headstrong.

"Wow," I said.

"Yeah," she said.

We were silent for a moment. A nice, level, comfortable silence where you just enjoy being in each other's company.

I smiled. She smiled. We held each other's gaze, and then she looked away, to the dark ocean. I didn't take my eyes off of her.

Then she said, "What do you do in Boulder?"

"Senior at CU."

"Isn't graduation soon?"

"Next May."

"And then what?"

I paused, wondering how honest to be. The truth might push her into the arms of a Carter brother. Dishonesty would kill any chance of a hookup back in Denver. But this girl was more than a hookup, wasn't she? She had the hat trick of qualities, and that's hard to find. What the hell …

"I don't know. Teach somewhere. Maybe take a year off and apply to PhD programs."

"In history?"

"It's the only thing I'm good at."

"Oh, I bet that's not true."

"Ah, I never look a gift flatterer in the mouth."

"It's not flattery."

"No, really, it is. I can't act or add. And I look awful in a suit."

"You look good in a suit."

We stopped. Something was happening here, something beyond the basic flirting and teasing, and I don't think either one of us knew what it was. We smiled. Looked away. Looked back at each other.

"I mean I look awful in a three-piece suit," I said. "Everyone looks good in a tux."

"I know what you meant. I saw a picture of you at Peter's apartment."

"Wait ... What?"

"A picture."

"In Peter's apartment?"

"Yeah."

"Which one?"

"The one near the Tar Pits."

"No, which picture."

"Oh. You were all gussied up for some night on the town."

"Gussied? Did you just say —"

"Maybe."

"You did. You just said —"

"Where were you going?"

"I thought I'd tease you a bit more about your use of participles, and then we'd hang a left at —"

"In the picture."

"What?"

"In the suit. Where were you going?"

"Oh, um ... I don't remember, actually. What suit was I wearing?"

"You have more than one suit?"

"Fine point. What was Peter wearing?"

At this, she stopped, cocked her head to the side.

She said, "You know Peter's wardrobe?"

"Work with me here, young lady."

"Um, Okay. He was wearing a dark bluish, sorta greenish suit with —"

"Got it. What tie was he wearing?"

Again, she paused, this time leaning back a little as if she needed a wider view to clear something up.

She said, "Okay. He was wearing, what was he wearing? Oh, ah … dark red, solid. With a slight shimmer to —"

"They Might Be Giants. The Ogden Theater. Two years ago." And the moment I said it, I realized it was the verbal equivalent to an uppercut. No man pays attention to another man's clothing. At least, that's supposed to be the case. But it was out and the punch had landed and I could tell by the way she was looking at me with her head lowered, eyes fluttering, lips scrunched, that I had stunned her and she was trying to find her bearings.

I plowed onward with damage control. "You know how some girls have underwear of the day?"

She raised her head a bit. Her eyes stopped fluttering. "Peter has ties of the day?"

"Now that I think about it," I said, "It is kinda weird."

Success. Life was returning. She laughed a small laugh and looked away again, then back at me.

She said, "You really love him, don't you?"

"Who?"

"Peter."

"Oh, yeah. He's a great guy. What's not to love?" See. This is what women like. A sensitive guy who's not afraid to admit —

"You know, Davis? You're really easy to talk to."

Oh, shit.

"A great listener."

Oh, fuck me.

"And I can't tell you how refreshing it is that you really haven't made a move on me."

She thought I was gay. I could see her gaze darting about, not looking directly at me, and knew she was confused, even embarrassed. In my attempt to steer away from the iceberg, I had rammed straight into it.

She said, "You want to go back to the party?"

But as the ship was taking on water, I glimpsed a stray piece of flotsam nearby. Pamela was unconsciously rubbing the inside of the wrist I had kissed earlier. I needed to do something, needed to brave the icy waters, swim to the floating sanctuary, and I needed to do it fast. But I also realized that swimming to safety would not be enough. I needed to swim in such a manner that all thoughts of this shipping mishap ebbed from her mind.

And so I kissed her.

Later, we were interrupted by Divan. He had accepted the mission to locate us and drag us back to the Crown Room (the Carter family bypassing the traditional ballroom because they were huge supporters of Richard Nixon's first presidential bid and attended his first out-of-D.C. state dinner there). There, we were to mingle and imbibe heavily. Only then, could we abscond and get naked. Orders care of Naomi Carter.

Pamela said, "Did she really say that?"

"Who?" said Divan.

"Naomi. Did she really say that she wanted us to —"

Divan said, "Word for word."

It had been a harmless, throwaway line, but I've learned over the years that you never know what can trigger an emotional flood. As I put my arm around her, as I began to lead her back to the wedding, Pamela's look of shock from being interrupted kissing a near stranger transformed to great sadness.

Later, she said, "When Divan told me what Naomi had said, I felt my stomach slowly turn in on itself like ... what's something that slowly turns in on itself?"

"A piece of paper being crumpled?"

"Yeah. Like a piece of paper being crumpled. I ... I felt so closed off from Naomi. I mean, the Naomi I knew four years ago is not the Naomi who just got married. Four years ago, Naomi wouldn't have been so relaxed and nonchalant. She would have been reserved. She would have been ... I don't know ... different."

Despite the calls and visits since high school, the unthinkable happened: they had grown apart. The old Naomi had been replaced by a more carefree twin of herself, one to which Pamela felt disconnected.

With each step toward the hotel lights, I could hear her breathing increase; see her eyes glisten with wetness. I stopped and embraced her. Through the thin tuxedo shirt, the warmth of her body caused goose bumps to infect my flesh. I closed my eyes and drank in the all-encompassing shiver of anticipation.

When we parted, Pamela's eyes were still damp, but the vacant look had been replaced with a small smile of embarrassment.

I winked, saw her face flush, and raised my brow. She took a deep breath, held it, exhaled, nodded.

We hurried inside.

Nothing is better for wiping away guilt than a cocktail of dance and booze. The catch is to make sure you don't splash in a taste of thought. Such a mixture causes the drink to sour with remorse, and the result can be New Year's Day nasty.

For the remainder of the evening, I made a point of checking on Pamela, much like a doctor ensuring a concussion patient doesn't fall asleep for twenty-four hours. Every so often, I could see her slip away into reflection. It wasn't life threatening, but just the same, I wanted to deflect her thoughts so she could look upon the night with mild happiness instead of gut-wrenching anxiety.

Throughout all of this, I mingled. I flirted, without coming on. I schmoozed, without kissing ass. I did all the things a groomsman should do without taking any of the attention off the bride and groom.

I was taken aside by Peter's parents, who asked about my future. Not in a parental manner, but in a genuine, caring way.

"We wanted to express our condolences about your father's passing."

"You know, we consider you a part of our family."

"And you also know that if you need anything, don't hesitate to call on us."

I thanked them, and although they meant well, I knew they were drunk with emotion. Generosity abounds in high times. It's intoxicating, and they pass the drug out like candy. But I knew that although they meant it now, had I ever taken them up on their offer, it would have tainted the goodness of the gesture. I haven't seen them since.

I was wrangled to the dance floor by Gloria, an ex-girlfriend of Peter's from high school, who'd secretly hoped it was her in the white dress. As we danced, she buried her head in my chest. To everyone else she just looked as if we were enjoying the song. Only I knew she was crying.

I was ambushed by Kathy, who I'd been avoiding for six months because of a decision I made when we shared a bathtub in Las Vegas.

She said, "I want you to know how much you hurt me," her hand on my arm tightening with every breath.

"I know."

"Years of trust could have remained intact if you'd just picked up the phone to see how I was doing. How I was feeling."

"I know."

"Even," she all but whispered, "if it was to say it was a mistake."

And I agreed with it all, especially when she called me spineless. Because of course, I was. Why else didn't I call her? Why else had I avoided her? Why else was I nodding and agreeing while my thoughts wandered to Pamela?

I was roped into a conversation with the two youngest Carter brothers, Brad and James, over how long the marriage was going to last.

"Three months," said James.

"No way," Brad said. "Six, at least."

"You kidding? This is Peter! He doesn't give two handfuls of bile about women!"

"You're right. He'll have dumped her mid-honeymoon."

Then they both said, "What do you think, Davis?"

I stood in silence, considered my options: a) I could tell them what I really felt about the conversation, the sanctity of marriage, how good Peter and Naomi seemed together, and that they had a great future ahead of them, or, b) I could be a guy.

"I think he's going to nail the Wedding Planner later."

Tasteful to the last.

I looked over at Naomi laughing with Peter and my gut tightened in disgust. Was this what happened at weddings? People placing wagers on how long it'd last? Side wagers on how they'd break up?

Later, Naomi pulled me aside to enlighten, caution, and threaten me. She was half way through a bottle of champagne, her words slurring into each other.

"You know, Davis. That girl," she turned to look at Pamela across the room, "is a goddess. And I'm not talking about goddess in the sexual sense, I'm talking about in the spiritual sense. She is an old soul. A good, good, good person. And ya wanna know something?" She got closer to me, her voice lowering. "If it wasn't for that girl, I wouldn't be here today. For my entire life — and she doesn't know this and if you tell her I'll deny it all — but for my entire life, I've tried to be better than her. Because to her, it's effortless. Look at her over there. What do you see her doing?"

"Um, well, she's talking —"

"No, she's not talking. She never *just* talks or walks or smiles ... she glides."

"She glides?"

"She glides. Because gliding is effortless. While the rest of us are struggling to crawl, yearning to walk, she glides about on the winds of life. Look at her. Just stand here for a moment, and watch her. Watch her glide effortlessly around."

I did. And after a moment, I saw it. As if every move, every gesture, every expression, every word was seamlessly gliding about in an exquisitely fluid dance of perfection.

In that moment, I asked myself if I could love another person as Naomi loved Pamela. Unconditionally.

"Davis?" Naomi said. "If you ever hurt that girl? If she ever stops gliding because of you? I —"

"Naomi," I said, unable to look away from Pamela, "I'm not in any position to hurt your friend."

She cupped my chin and rudely brought me nose-to-nose with her. And with complete seriousness and total sobriety, she said, "But, if you ever are in that position and ever do hurt her?"

She held my gaze with a firm, unwavering glare. My testicles pulled into my body with a dull, constant throb. Every pore in my body had run dry. And then she smiled, kissed me on the cheek, and left to mingle.

Within moments, I felt hot and sweaty. After taking a moment to see Pamela wasn't concocting a sour cocktail — she was talking to Peter's parents and laughing heartily — I stepped out to the back deck overlooking the beach to get some fresh air.

I wasn't the only one.

I said, "Jonesy. You okay?"

He didn't turn to me, his gaze affixed on the inside activity. The veins on his forehead throbbed, but his face was tense with strain, not dancing with anger. He said, "Yeah. No. I haven't a clue. I was just thinking how time flies by. I mean, fucking Peter's married. Fucking married. I didn't think any of us would marry and settle down for at least ten years, and now that it's happening, I don't know, man. I don't know."

It took a moment for comprehension to hit, but when it did, it hit hard. Of all the people to feel sorry for themselves, Jonesy was the last one to come to mind. I thought about how to defuse the situation and blew it up instead.

I said, "Another one bites the dust."

His head turned to me so fast I almost recoiled. "The first one bites the dust, you mean. Not another, the *first*. And the first always gets people thinking about their own lives. 'Should I get hitched? Should I start a family?' For God's sake, we're not even twenty-two. These are supposed to be the best years of our lives."

"Hey, calm down, dude."

"We're supposed to be drinking it up, hitting the town, not fucking ... fucking *married*? No, man. That's just fucked. Fucked, fucked, fucked."

Heads began turning in our direction, and I pulled Jonesy into the shadows.

He said, "I'm sorry. I don't know what's wrong with me."

"You need a drink."

"I have a drink."

I took his glass, sniffed it, grimaced. "What the hell is this?"

"Paint thinner."

"Paint thinner?"

"It's the name of the drink."

"Cute. Let's find you something less toxic."

I began to step away, holding the drink at arm's length as if it were a smoking bomb, but stopped when Jonesy grabbed my arm with shaking hands.

He said, "What the hell is Peter thinking? Just tell me that. What is he thinking, getting married? After all the shit he's pulled? After that whole shit in Vegas?"

"He's in love."

"Horseshit." Point and counter point, care of Adam Jones.

I said, "Okay, he *says* he's in love."

"He says that to get into a chick's pants."

"Aw, who knows, Jonesy? Maybe this time it's for real."

"Peter has no real." He threw his arms up in dismay, and then thrust his hands in my face in an almost comical, overacting manner. As if paint thinner was the scientific elixir that transformed Dr. Jonesy into Captain James T. Kirk. "He lives in a permanent state of fantasy and he's taking it too far."

I said, "Don't you want him to be happy?"

"After the shit he's pulled, he doesn't get to be happy."

Ah. No matter how excited Jonesy appeared for Peter, the drink had pulled out the deeper emotion. That of betrayal.

"I'm going to get you another drink."

He said, "I have a fucking drink, Davis," and grabbed it from my hand.

I said, "Then fucking drink it and stop gushing like you're on the rag."

He looked at me in shock, my words the equivalent to a punch.

He said, "Fuck, Davis, don't you see? It's like, fuck. I feel as if it's all slipping away. I feel like the best times of our lives are already past us."

I said, "You can't be serious." But he was.

"People don't care anymore. They don't care about their friends, what they do to them ... They only care about themselves in the moment. And then they only care about what society thinks they should do. Marriage. Kids. Bills and responsibility."

"But that's the way things work. That's the next step."

"Yeah, if you're worried about being eaten by an Allosaurus or catching the bubonic plague. Once upon a time you got married and had kids at fourteen, fought the Huns, and died in your thirties. Once upon a time you got married and had kids at twenty, fought the Germans, and died in your sixties. But we're living until our nineties, and soon we'll be past one hundred. Why the hell would you choose to spend four-fifths of your life with the same person? We feel we have to settle down, but in reality we don't."

The next semester, Jonesy would meet Debbie Newsome in a C++ class at Colorado University. He would think little of their classroom flirting and subsequent dating at first, just believing the tall, athletic lass with short and spiky red hair was someone to have some fun with as school was ending and the inevitable job market loomed. But a few weeks before graduation, during a Seattle interview for a little company called Amazon.com, he had one of those moments of realization where you see your lifeline stretch from your feet into the horizon.

And when faced with the dilemma of ending the relationship with Debbie and moving away to a new city, he knew he wanted to spend his life with her.

Upon his return, at the airport, as people moved about their own lifelines to destinations unknown, he proposed. It was impulsive and void of accoutrement. On the moving escalator at Denver International Airport, at 2:15 on a Thursday afternoon, Adam Jones bent to one knee. Kids pointed, women cried, men laughed at the sheer audacity of it all. And before they hit the end of the moving escalator, Debbie was kissing him and whispering 'yes' over and over and over again.

Three months later, as I lay with Hillary at the Colorado Renaissance Festival, as Jonesy tried to find me, Debbie was trying on a dress when she felt a little light headed. She brushed off Pamela's arm of support, dismissing it as the aftereffects of food poising a week earlier. It would be two weeks before she discovered the poisoning was not of food, but of wine. Construction workers had accidentally cut the power to the neighborhood when repairing a water main and Jonesy surprised her with an apartment alive with candles and romance and the unknowing creation of their son.

A year before the power was cut, Jonesy stood at the Hotel del Coronado and said, "I just don't understand what he's thinking. I feel like he's turning his back on us."

He looked out into the ocean's black abyss, finished his paint thinner in three long pulls, and threw his glass into the night. It shattered on the concrete path on the edge of the sand.

"That's ridiculous, Jonesy."

"Is it? You can't tell me that the man who just got married is the man we went to Vegas with."

"You weren't with us, Jonesy. You didn't see what he went through."

"Oh, don't fucking give me that. He's stronger than this."

"Jonesy, you weren't there."

"This isn't how you treat friends. This isn't how you treat your brothers. You don't just leave and become a different person."

"He's right, ya know." It was Divan, nearing with one hand behind his back, his other with a lit cigar half burned down. His bow tie was loose and he looked more like the sauntering Steve McQueen whose charisma seemed too large to be contained by a rental tuxedo. "This is no way to treat your friends."

"Don't encourage him," I said.

"Oh, but I'm not encouraging. I'm simply agreeing with the fact that a brother has fallen." And with that, he brought his hand from behind his back. Goldschlager, and three shot glasses. It had become his drink of choice and, later, ours.

Jonesy brightened. I relaxed. We drank.

"To Peter," Divan said.

"To Naomi," I said.

"To Peter and Naomi," we all said.

"To those who remain," said Jonesy. We fell silent and looked at him. "To those who didn't fall in battle, and who continue to press on. For those who fight the good fight, and hope when their day comes, they'll have no regrets. And when they fall, we wish their final memories are filled with past battles and past victories and laughter and glee. And when that day comes, they declare they did it all their way, standing tall, with only one liver."

We shouted and yelled and drank and laughed.

Soon, Kathy found us and started drinking, but for another reason altogether. Her scolding glare burned tiny holes into my flesh. I considered leaving, but didn't want to give her the idea I was slinking away, afraid of her glare, her words, her belief I had betrayed her. I would not give her that satisfaction.

"Fuck all," I said into my drink. What was wrong with everyone? This was a wedding. A time to smile, dance, reflect, enjoy.

After the third shot, it happened. Jonesy gagged, coughed, and then smiled when Divan began laughing. It spread, overtaking the tension like a virus. Time passed. People gravitated toward our little group. We drifted inside. And like a shot of adrenaline, things got moving.

It's eerie how all parties hit the point when everyone is harmonious mentally and emotionally. You can try to wait for it, try to capture it, but it's elusive. Many a times I've attempted to grasp its threads, but found myself drawn into the wake of energy.

Peter and Naomi danced their dance, and the tempo had progressively risen. When we reentered, the swing portion had just begun. People moved. The herd thinned, the old and young called it a night. Then the serious fun took hold. Ties loosened. Dinner jackets and uncomfortable footwear piled up. Singles became couples. Exes and enemies put aside their pasts. It became a real wedding.

From the swing, it kicked into the '70s set, mixed with some '80s, and then to the '80s mixed with a little '70s. Everyone wordlessly agreed that age was perception. The mother of three became the sixteen-year-old with painted-on acid-washed jeans. The graying Fortune 500 CEO became the hip seventeen-year-old with the Hugo Boss jacket, colored t-shirt, and Vans.

Glancing about the room was like flashing through a high school yearbook. You could tell who wore mullets, who wore the hooded sweatshirts. Who wore legwarmers and who wore Member's Only jackets. Rather frightening, if you thought about it, which no one did lest they fall ill with acne and issues of self-esteem. But we felt it. We felt what drew us together, to the wedding, to the dance floor.

Pamela pulled me from my memories. After watching me for two songs, waiting for me to ask her to dance, she decided to ask me. Dancing with her was easy. As if we had known each other for years, rather than hours. Maybe it was the alcohol. Maybe we singles were melding into couples. I didn't care. Once we started moving with one another, the world ceased to matter.

We danced, we drank, we talked, we danced some more. And when the party broke up, we went back to my room. As we were kissing and undressing — not awkwardly, but as we were dancing, comfortably — I briefly wondered if Jonesy were right. If our best days were passing us by; if we were snack food for a rogue Allosaurus when we least expected it.

If so, I was going to make the best of them.

Physical beats emotional.

No regrets.

CHAPTER FIVE

Thursday

Bachelor Party

The limo parked in the driveway is one of those four-by-four stretch jobs that you want to ram off the road while driving fast, but is surprisingly fun when you rent one.

It's 6:32 p.m., two days before my wedding, and already my epidermis has sensed the chemical imbalance and has scurried about for new residence. This happens when alcohol infuses my nerves without the balance of sustenance. I fear at any moment that someone will scream in horror as my features begin to resemble a Picasso. Thankfully, this fear dissipates the more I drink.

Peter, Ian, and Jonesy arrived at 5:00 p.m., three wise men with gifts of Goldschlager, Captain Morgan's Spiced Rum, and Everclear. After Pamela left for her bachelorette party, we consumed a shot of each. Before she did:

Pamela: I'm going to lay down some ground rules.

Peter: Ground rules? This is his last night as a free man! You can't lay down any ground rules.

Pamela: Oh, they're not for Davis. They're for you.

Peter: I get ground rules?

Pamela: Number one: no hookers.

Peter: For me?

Pamela: For Davis.

Peter: Technically, that would be a ground rule for Davis.

Pamela: Repeat after me: No hookers, Pamela.

Peter: Hey, why are you talking to me? Jonesy is the best man.

Pamela: I'm not worried about Jonesy. I'm worried about you.

Peter: I'm touched.

Pamela: I'm worried about you hurting Davis.

Peter: I'd never hurt Davis. Davis is my friend. My friend is Davis. I'd never hurt my friend.

Pamela: I'm worried because you'd be the only one who would actually follow through with getting hookers, and so we're nipping this in the bud before you do.

Peter: Let's continue talking about you nipping my bud.

Pamela: Repeat after me: No hookers, Pamela.

Peter: Define hookers.

Pamela: Hookers. Whores. Prostitutes. Ladies of the night. Streetwalkers.

Peter: I wasn't aware that anyone used the term Streetwalkers.

Pamela: No hookers.

Peter: *Hookers*, people use.

Pamela: Focus, man-child. No hookers.

Peter: Call girls?

Pamela: No call girls.

Peter: Escorts?

Pamela:	No call girls, no escorts, no any women that you have to pay for sex.
Peter:	Well, why didn't you say so? No problem.
Pamela:	Rule number two: No sex with women of any kind.
Peter:	Now, is this another one for me, or for Davis?
Pamela:	*You* can sleep with whoever *you* want for all I care.
Peter:	That's so sweet.
Pamela:	You can go to bars, strip clubs, the eighth level of Hell, whatever. But at no point —
Peter:	The Malebolge.
Pamela:	What?
Peter:	The Malebolge. The eighth level of Hell. Arms and legs strewn about. Very messy.
Pamela:	At no point will sex be a part of the evening.
Peter:	Now Pammy, I must confess: You're starting to sound as if you don't trust me.
Pamela:	I wonder why that is.
Peter:	Pammy, are you still cross about Vegas?
Pamela:	See, you're not as dumb as you look.

Peter lit up as if she had given him a genuine compliment. She continued to lay down the ground rules: No drugs, no fights, or anything else that could get us in trouble with the law.

"Basically," she said, "use common-sense."

And, of course, Peter did no such thing.

Earlier, before Peter, Ian, and Jonesy arrived, Pamela said, "Divan called." She had swapped her jeans and t-shirt for a low-cut red top with spaghetti straps and a short black skirt, and was packing for her hotel stay after the bachelorette party.

"You were sleeping. He said something about his flight from Australia being delayed in Hawaii, so he won't be here tonight."

"Divan's in Australia?"

"No. He's in Hawaii."

"Yeah, but why was he in Australia?"

"A speaking engagement? You can ask him when he gets in."

"When did he call?"

"I already told you. When you were sleeping."

"Yeah, but what time?"

"I don't know. When were you sleeping?"

"Around noon."

"Then he called around noon."

"You were back by noon?"

"No. I got back around 2 p.m."

"So, he called at 2 p.m. then. You answered the phone, right? So he must have —"

"Does it matter?"

"Not really."

"All right then. So, who's your backup?"

"My what?"

"Your backup groomsman. In case Divan doesn't make it."

"He'll make it."

"But in case he doesn't, do you have a backup?"

"I don't know. I never really thought about it."

"Well, if worse comes to worst, you can use Donald."

"I'm *not* using Donald."

"Why not?"

"Donald is not going to be in the wedding."

"If you planned ahead, he wouldn't be."

"I'm sorry if I didn't plan for Divan to be late."

"You always plan for the unexpected. That way you're never surprised and things always go your way."

"Thank you ever so kindly for the lecture."

At this, she looked up at me with her rich brown eyes, tears threatening to slide. "Oh, hon. I'm sorry. Really. I wasn't … It wasn't meant to be a lecture." She neared, hugged me. After a moment of hesitation, I wrapped my arms around her thin shoulders.

She said, "What's wrong with us? I know this is supposed to be stressful, but I didn't count on this."

We could talk for days about what was wrong, but holding her in my arms, I decide to look past all of that.

I said, "Don't think about what's wrong. Think about what's right."

It was the type of cheesy line that causes men to gag on their popcorn when uttered in a chick-flick, but it came off my tongue with ease. She sniffled and I could feel wetness on my chest. Pamela is a strong woman, but it's amazing how the strong can crack in just the right situation.

Then she said, "Do you still want to marry me?" Her tone wasn't laced with pain or irony. Just matter of fact and honest.

Without hesitation, I said, "Of course," and meant it. I did want to marry her. Holding her, alone, in our room, I knew that I wanted to spend the rest of my life with her. I wanted to wake up next to her and go to bed next to her and never wanted to miss a day lying by her side. I wanted her to be the mother of my children. I wanted to grow old with her.

I kissed her forehead and held her tight and wondered how long it would last. An hour? Three? How long until I started to think of Hillary or Joanna or even the almighty Her? The moment Pamela walked out of the room? When she left the house?

I tightened my arms around Pamela, not wanting this moment to end. Not now, not ever. This was the only thing that made sense, and knowing it only made sense in our little world, our little bubble.

Pamela said, "I love you. You know that, right?"

I said I did. I said I loved her too. We went on like this, reassuring each other that everything was all right and that we were doing the right thing.

And then the doorbell rang and —

POP.

The real world intruded, our moment broken. We kissed. She left. I sat back on the bed, staring at the empty door, at the rug on our hardwood floors, at my feet.

In the distance I heard the boys enter, heard Pamela lay into Peter. And then something odd happened that gave me hope that I was not stepping into folly, and that maybe, just maybe, I wouldn't run. The bubble reformed. Pamela wasn't next to me, I wasn't holding her, and yet I felt it.

How long had it been? How long had it been since I last felt this for Pamela? Weeks, for sure. Months, at the least. When did it …

Thanksgiving. Five months ago. A year into our engagement. That was when it began. The strain. When I started to pull away. When the hole of fear began to grow within me and I began to fill it the only way I knew how. When I started cheating on Pamela.

Yes, an argument could be made that I'd been cheating on Pamela, off and on, for six years. That I'd betrayed our relationship, betrayed our commitment. To that I'd argue that in my mind, I'd been committed to Pamela since day one. Because if not, I would have left a long time ago.

In truth, never in my life have I believed that I would be with anyone, including Pamela, for a lifetime. A *lifetime*.

Such an encompassing mass is incomprehensible to fathom. Every day of the remainder of your life. With one person. It was something I couldn't fathom. It was like comprehending God, or the Afterlife, or Deep-Fried Snickers bars. Logic and faith are locked in a cage-match and you can only watch for so long before you're covered in a veil of philosophy and gore.

Even when I asked for Pamela's hand in marriage, it never dawned on me that I was asking her for a lifelong commitment. Stupid, yes. But in my mind, I was simply waiting for her to wake up one morning and realize I wasn't the man she wanted to spend her entire life with. Sorta like realizing she wanted a new wardrobe. A style change. She wanted a newer, hipper man.

So, when we sat down to Thanksgiving dinner and someone asked, "How long is it until the wedding?" and when another someone replied, "Five months," I freaked the fuck out. Because I realized Pamela saw me as a lifelong partner.

Outwardly, I was cool, calm. I was a Zen master of male panic and insanity. While inwardly, my stomach shrunk to the size of a snow pea. My lungs crystallized, two hunks of meat forgotten in a walk-in freezer.

Then the panic started. When lifelong suddenly meant *lifelong*. Until that dinner, I set myself into believing that whenever Pamela and I pulled apart emotionally, for even a few days, the end was near. That she was waking up from her haze of mediocrity to see the truth of who I was — a rebound. Because, really, wasn't I? Hadn't Pamela just been three months removed from an engagement to a man who ran off to the Peace Corps? Hadn't she stumbled upon me in a time of crisis? A time of emotional upheaval full of drink and dance in a fantasy world? Hadn't she simply needed someone to fall back on until she regrouped?

When we returned to Colorado after Peter's wedding, I completely expected she'd come to her senses. That the wedding had been a fun little escape, and she could now focus on her studies instead of her ex-fiancé. And, in all truth and honesty, I was fine with that. I'd had a good romp in it all. No hard feelings. In fact, all the better.

I was going into my senior year, and then, whatever. And we all know how hectic and time consuming the world of whatever can become. I needed to prepare for such a time. I needed to bathe in my resolve, soak up the strength to endure the endless days and nights of whatever. My life was quite full.

Much to my surprise, I found a message on the voice mail when Jonesy and I returned to our apartment.

"Davis, hi. It's Pamela. From the wedding, in case you forgot, though, if you forgot, we're probably going to have to do the whole introduction thing again when you call me. Anyway, I wanted to say how much I enjoyed spending time with you. I know, I should play the dumb game and wait a few days, but ya know what? I hate playing games.

"Well, not all games. I'm particularly fond of *Parcheesi*. I love saying that name. *Parcheesi*. It sounds like an Italian pasta dish. Not too spicy, not too bland. *Parcheesi*.

"I also like *Chutes and Ladders*, although I always hated the name because my cousin used to take out his ping-pong-ball gun when we played and every time anyone ever landed on a slide he shot you in the head with a ping-pong ball but he used to put the ping-pong balls in the freezer first so they'd be all icy and hard and so we put his ping-pong-ball gun in the trash compactor and started calling the game *Chutes and No Dumb Cousins Can Play*.

"The point is, I like saying *Parcheesi*, and I'm clearly not waiting the customary two days to speak to you. So, if

I haven't scared you off, call me. No, scratch that. Even if I scared you off, call me. Because I have some icy ping-pong balls with your name on them. Bye! ... Come on, say it. Just once. You know you want to. Say it. *Parcheesi.*"

Listening to her message, I was laughing so hard I couldn't sit up for a week without pain. But it was more than worth it. A headstrong girl who was willing to speak her mind even through her nervous ramblings? If you remove any thought she could be one of those psycho-stalker types with an odd form of Tourettes Syndrome, it was damn sexy.

I'd never been a fan of wishy–washy girls, probably the main reason Hillary and I never stepped to the next level. Pamela was a woman who went after what she wanted. And hell, if she wanted more fun, I was happy to oblige. I liked fun. Fun and I were good friends. Compadres. Brothers in arms.

So, two days later, I called her back.

And things were good. We saw each other often, laughed, shared washcloths and all that junk. It was great. It was fun. And, if asked, I'd even say that it was great fun.

That was, until six months later, in the week leading up to the Renaissance Festival. That's when Pamela began to pull away. And not just a quiet, 'I need time to think' pull away, but a serious, 'I need time to reevaluate what I'm doing with my life and can't see you for a while so I can think clearly' pull away.

I figured it was the end. She needed a change. I had served my purpose and she wanted someone hipper. Someone more her speed. Perhaps another attorney or someone, well, more adult.

I had been applying for history-instructor positions around the state, but mostly I was flapping in the wind of whatever. I'd felt I needed a break after college. I wasn't sure how long

I'd give myself, but would sit back and do whatever was nice and see where it took me. Pretty un-adult like, so, I understood why Pamela needed to think. It made all the sense.

Things were strained at the Renaissance Festival. Not argumentative strained, but quiet strained. Hard-to-find-conversation strained. Both knowing that we needed to address matters, but neither wanting to begin the conversation for fear of touching off a brush fire strained. And without saying it, we both knew that we weren't qualified to put out a raging beast, so we held everything in check. Silent. Incommunicado behind our walls of strain.

And then I saw Hillary, her breasts nearly popping out of her costume, and I felt that knowing desire I hadn't felt in years. That memory of the drug. That yearning for a physical fix to tamp down any emotions threatening to spill out over Pamela. So I figured, why not? Pamela's about to break up with me, so why deprive myself of a quickie with Hillary? Maybe this quickie could be parlayed into a regular thing? I was already having memories of college Hillary booty-call, and was quite comfortable if Hillary wanted to use her boot on my call whenever she wished.

I want it to be known that at no time was I upset with Pamela for the decision I thought she was about to make. I understood it completely, and in her shoes, I would have done the same thing. Sure, I would be sad that a fun thing was ending, but it had a nice run. Some good laughs. Some great sex. Some really great sex. But I wasn't going to cry about it. I wasn't going to hold on longer than necessary, thus creating undue tension that would have burned bridges. Because that's just not something a guy should do. It was something very anti-guy. And I wasn't keen to renounce my membership in the ranks.

But I also wasn't going to fall into the scorned-man trap wherein I cut all ties with Pamela and placed her on the shelf labeled: You bitch, you slut, you whore.

The high road I would take. Good times, great memories, total understanding.

And so, later that night, driving back to her apartment near Denver University in strained silence, I said, "I think we need to talk."

She agreed.

I said, "I don't know if you know this, but I very much enjoy our time we spend together and I feel that meeting you is something that has caused me to grow as a person."

She said that was very kind of me to say.

I said, "You're very special to me, do you know that?"

She was silent.

I said, "I can't imagine what life would be like had we not met. I wouldn't take away the time we shared for anything in the world."

She remained silent.

But as I was about to say that I didn't want to part ways with animosity, she said, "I think we should move in together."

This took a moment to register, for I was focused on setting the cruise control toward the remarkably un-rocky road to Singletown. A logical step, considering what I thought was happening. The task completed, I was nearly blinded by lightning, causing me to take in the surrounding terrain and realize, hey! This isn't the remarkably un-rocky road to Singletown. This looks suspiciously like the terribly dark and frightening road I've only read about in off-color Brothers Grimm fairy tales and books banned in many southern states!

I began to see images that can only be identified by trained professionals: Bedspreads designed for display but don't double as blankets; fluffy toilet-seat covers that you never sit on; bathmats that aren't towels. And then I saw the sign. My neck slapped away shivers. My bladder fought against releasing. My testicles packed their bags and waited for their new home.

Committed Relationshipburg.

It wasn't just a fairy tale.

It was real.

Pamela said, "I've been doing a lot of thinking. About how at first I wondered if this was a rebound relationship, and I didn't want to make something out of a rebound relationship if it wasn't meant to be, and so I pulled away to think about it. But every day that passed in the last week, I realized how much I love you."

Loved. Me. I remained quiet, attempting to process this stunning information.

She said, "And after I realized how much I love you, I told myself that it was silly to analyze and over analyze because we, us, together, feels right and that has to mean that it's meant to be, and I told myself to just go with it because no matter which road I analyzed down, I kept coming to the same road sign that said: How can I argue with what brought us together?"

She went on to talk about fate and karma and all that junk that had led her to Colorado, and that it had opened a doorway to, well, me. She told me that, "Each day I'm apart from you, I feel pulled toward you, and that means something and that something isn't something I'm going to deny because when you have something that special, why would you throw it away?"

The longer I remained quiet, the more she rambled on about her 'something' logic. The headstrong girl who had just put her heart on her sleeve was nervously babbling onward so she couldn't hear my silence. In that moment, I fell for her. I felt the bubble form. And although I'd misread the signs in the past few days, it didn't matter. This was real, not a passing fancy.

So I said, "Sure."

"Sure?"

"Yeah."

"Really?"

"Yeah."

And we smiled.

And we kissed.

And we made love in the car like two teenagers who didn't have any other place to express our affection even though we were right outside her apartment.

But as time passed, months, years, I found myself waiting for the other shoe to drop. Maybe because I *so* hate surprises. Well, not the surprise itself, but the way I react to them. I, well … I panic. Sad, yes. A man is supposed to stand tall and confront the unknown, not turn tail wheezing like a newly gelded eunuch.

The days passed. Weeks followed. And with each red x on the calendar, I waited for it to happen. I waited for the worst. Because anything good always comes with a catch, and I aimed to locate said catch.

Let's be perfectly clear: I did not run back to Hillary after the Renaissance Festival. The Renaissance Festival was a one-time thing. I didn't speak to Hillary for another two years. I was completely faithful to Pamela. Things were great. The usual ups and downs. The crap that everyone goes through when learning to live with one another. But I couldn't complain. We'd formed a bubble. And within that bubble, for the first time since I'd learned to bury my emotions at the Heaven and Hell party during my freshman year in college, I forsook the physical drug, took a risk, and allowed my emotions out to play. I figured, why not? Inside this bubble, our lives were immune to the crap of the outside world. Inside this bubble, I was safe.

When Jonesy's son was about a year old things took a turn. Such was my perception, and only in hindsight can we detach and become an impartial third-party. But in the moment, I began to see the joy in Pamela's eyes whenever she was around the child, and this spawned my internal questioning as to my desires to have children. Quickly, I decided *no*. Davis and kids didn't jive. Separate, they jived. A kid at arm's length? Perfecto. A kid who needed to be potty trained? Not so much.

Earlier, when the future wasn't looming on my doorstep, I was all for kids. I grew up with my pop's belief that children are the ticket to immortality. Instilling them with a part of us and they'd go into the world to represent us in a favorable fashion. But when I saw the gleam in Pamela's eye, I ran. I passed the gelded and beat feet for the hills.

In retrospect, that gleam might have been her longing for the future, but not the particular present. Her clock might have been ticking, but she would have muffled it with a towel for a few years. Neither of us was in any position to have children. Hell, I was still thinking she would leave me at some point, because I wasn't an easy guy to live with. I have my ways, and am very uncompromising. So to consider children in the now was unthinkable. Hell, even for the future. I didn't want to change my ways. I was going to be stubborn. Because at the end of the day, the one thing I could always count on was my stubbornness. It was my security blanket. My woobie.

Enter stage left: Hillary and her beautiful breasts.

I did not look her up, *but* I did inquire about her current whereabouts. Nothing overt. I was quite stealthy. And that was how I stumbled upon her. Complete overt stealth. No lie.

One evening, after I jumped online to get the number for the local Pizza Hut, the stealthy happenstance presented itself. But to prove to myself I wasn't tiptoeing out of my way to search for her, I pointedly surfed in directions completely unrelated.

I discovered a dozen D. Robertsons lived within a twenty-mile radius. I discovered twenty H. Leakeys in the Denver Metro Area, an oddity, Leakey not being a household name unless you're a paleontologist in Africa. I discovered three Pizza Huts within walking distance of my home, and that two brothers in possession of their mother's recipe founded the chain in Kansas, circa 1958. Enjoying my newfound knowledge, I pressed on.

Here, I discovered something very intriguing. The Diamond Cabaret listed a Hillary Leakey as a featured exotic dancer. This was intriguing, not because Hillary had taken her exhibitionist side to new heights, but because she felt confident to use her real name. We used to joke that she would make a great Carmen or a Rita because of her Latin blood via her biological mother — Hillary's blond hair a dye job, the carpet not matching the curtains. I found this knowledge intriguing, and began to wonder to what ends her confidence had grown.

I also discovered Hillary had a members-only web site, which I contemplated joining — for research purposes *only*, thank you Pete Townsend — but decided I should continue my search in person.

I'd like to point out that at this point I did not sleep with Hillary.

"You're not going to sleep with me?" Hillary said, sitting next to me in a secluded booth near the back of the Diamond Cabaret, her hand on my thigh.

Later, at my bachelor party, I would sit in the same booth and witness two beautiful women locking lips for my pleasure. Before my world almost collapsed. Before I was hunted down like a rabid dog. Before the police arrived.

"Nope," I said to Hillary. "I'm not going to sleep with you."

"You mean you looked me up just to talk?"

"Yeah. I guess I did."

She glanced at the floor and when she blinked, I could see a few pieces of glitter escape into the air. "Wow."

"Wow?"

She looked back to me, her brow wrinkled. "Well, yeah. This is unexpected."

"How do you mean?"

"You're just, well, we just don't have that type of relationship."

"What type of relationship?"

"The verbal kind."

"You mean we can't talk?"

"Have we ever just talked?"

"I'm sure we have. At some point, I'm sure we've sat down and had a meaningful conversation."

"No," Hillary said.

"We have. I mean, we've had to. At some point."

"We've tried, but we usually ended up fucking."

I said, "That's not true."

"It is. We fucked a lot."

"Well, yeah, but in between all the —"

"What's my middle name?"

"What?"

"What's my middle name?"

116

I struggled.

"Okay. What's my favorite color?"

I guessed.

"What's my favorite movie?"

I knew this one.

"Deep Throat."

"The Princess Bride."

"No, I recall quite vividly when you said —"

"It was a pickup line."

"No."

"I was picking you up."

"Really?"

"It worked, didn't it?"

"I had no idea."

"You never asked."

"The Princess Bride?"

"So, what do you want to talk about?"

"Um, well —"

And then she said, "You're getting married, aren't you?"

I began to talk, stumbled, attempted to regroup. "What? No, why would you think something like that?"

"It's the second-year law student, isn't it?"

"She's actually not a law student anymore."

"How proud you must be."

"Why would you think I'm getting married?"

"Because you are, aren't you?"

She removed her hand from my thigh, leaned away. Emptiness overwhelmed me. I felt that if I chose to be honest with Hillary, the door to my past would shut and lock forever. Panic began to fill the emptiness.

I said, "No, no. Why would I get married? I mean, come on. Can you see me getting married? I'm what? The last person you'd expect to marry."

A waitress in a sequined bikini top, g-string and leather chaps set down a pair of unordered drinks. Hillary smiled, thanked her silently.

"You know," Hillary said, taking a sip on the twin barrels of the ultra-thin straw, "the last person I expected to marry, got married."

"But he got divorced."

"You're getting married. Just say it."

"Why wouldn't I say it?"

"It's the law student."

"She's not a law student anymore, she's a —"

"I stopped seeing the sword swallower."

"What?"

"After you and me, you know, fucked. At the RenFair. In the tent."

I paused, trying to fend off the question rising within me. I failed. "Why did you stop seeing him?"

She said, "I don't know. I guess I figured that we would try things again." She leaned back, looking up at the ceiling fans, at the air ducts, at anything but me. When she spoke, numerous pieces of glitter danced above the small puffs of air escaping her lips. She said, "I don't know why I thought that. You never really gave me that idea, I mean, you never really said anything to give me that idea, but still. When we were together, I don't know. It felt like old times and I wanted so badly to relive them. I guess I secretly hoped that you'd call me. It felt, you know, good."

I was silent for a while, taking this all in. Then I said, "Did you have a phone?"

"What?"

I said, "In the tent. Was there a phone?"

"Um … No. I guess there wasn't."

"So, what phone did you wait by? If you were waiting for my call, where did you —"

"Do you love her?"

"What?"

She looked at me then, rolling her head to the side, her green eyes staring down her nose. She said, "The second-year law student. Do you love her?"

"She's an attorney now. Passed the bar and everything."

Hillary blinked, glitter flew.

I thought about it, felt the panic within me recede. I said, "Yeah. I do." Saying it and feeling the emotion surge within me and knowing it to be true. But then it was overtaken by the practiced and well-worn desire to bury the emotion in the drug. It was the first time I'd felt it since the Renaissance Festival, *two* years prior, that need for a physical high to stave off this thing called *real* emotion. I fought it, taking a deep drink and trying not to gag on the straight vodka.

"Well," she said, "that changes things, doesn't it?"

"What does?"

She said, "That whole thing about the sword swallower? I made it up."

"I sorta figured that."

"Yeah?"

"The phone."

"Right. In the tent. But it doesn't matter."

"Because I love her?"

"I wanted to see if you were lying."

"What?"

"When you said you weren't going to fuck me."

"You thought I was lying?"

"I thought you were playing hard to get."

"Hillary?"

119

"Yes?"

I said, "Have I ever played hard to get?"

She started to speak, stopped. And not for the first time I wondered why she was hanging on, and what she saw in me in the first place.

And after a moment, she exhaled through dark red lips and said, "I don't know. It *has* been a while since I've seen you. I mean, you walked in and it all flooded back to me. I didn't know if you had changed. If you were the same person I once knew."

"And in that time, you figured maybe I'd learned how to play hard to get?"

She said, "The way you say it makes it sound silly."

"So," I said. "Is this it?"

"Is what it?"

"That meaningful conversation we've never had."

We talked for a while, but the relaxed, easy-going dialogue I imagined never materialized. And although I knew I could step up and ride Hillary's pedals if I so choose, I exited. No lap dance. No sex.

I was still *completely* faithful to Pamela. That is, if you consider the first six months an 'open' period, which I did. I *had* to. We never had a spoken commitment until we moved in together, so in order for the bubble to remain intact, for my protected realm to exist in which I allowed my emotions to play, I had to draw the line. Our relationship began when we moved in with one another. Done and done.

So, this, too, passed. Pamela and I were fine and dandy. And after a point, I figured I'd propose. Why not? It was the thing to do. All the rage. Peter had proposed five times by this point, and three actually resulted in a wedding. Not that I'd attended the second or third, mind you.

After a nasty breakup with Naomi, Peter dashed off to Scotland for a lengthy run in *Hamlet*. While Jonesy found it annoying, I shrugged it off as typical Peter. As for Pamela, upon returning from comforting Naomi, she forbade Peter to step foot in our house. Another rule Peter later broke.

My single friends were dropping like flies and they seemed to be happy. So, I supposed, could I. Truth be told, I started to feel, well, empty when Pamela wasn't around. She could run out for some milk and I'd feel as if a part of me were missing. As if she spirited off with an arm or leg or whatever appendage one spirits off with to aid them in grabbing milk.

Thusly, four years after moving in together, Pamela and I were engaged. And it felt good. Damn good. Like I'd written the great American novel, climbed Mount Everest, or had just been invited to the Playboy Mansion for a Halloween bash. I was converted, ready to tell everyone how good this felt, to become a missionary for the cause.

Because in all honesty, I felt it. That emotion *outside* the bubble. That realm *beyond* the drug of physical gratification and outside the bubble. That truth that happily married couples gush over. What you gain versus what you give up. I felt that giddy, fulfilling comfort where you are impervious to whatever the world had to throw at you and I wasn't afraid to share it.

At least, I felt it at the beginning.

That we had a long engagement did not hurt. A year-and-a-half a lot of breathing room makes. Enough room for me to let down my guard. I didn't anticipate any surprises, any hitches, any shoes to drop.

Leading up to that damn Thanksgiving dinner where I panicked. Where that giddy, fulfilling comfort became a painful, I-just-gorged-myself-on-emotional-promise-and-I-need-to-vomit. Leading me to another search for Hillary … and leading me to cheat on Pamela.

But it didn't matter now. Now —

Thursday

— the bubble has returned. I feel for Pamela again, for us again. I will ride this out. I will be strong and nothing will stand in my way. Just hold on to the bubble, get through the wedding, and we'll head to our honeymoon, relaxation, and happiness. Yes. Things are going to work.

I smile a genuinely happy smile. And as if on cue:

"Need an ear?" It's Donald standing in the hallway, his grey hair swaying. I shrug. He says, "There's no right answer, ya know. To all your questions. There's no right answer, there's no wrong answer. If everyone just realized that, life would be so much easier."

I look at him, silent. And then he says, "Did you know there's a draft in your hallway?"

After Pamela leaves for her bachelorette party, after my mother and Donald leave for dinner, Ian cracks the gold stuff and we toast to women of ill repute. Then we toast to meeting women of ill repute. Then we toast to Peter and Ian sleeping with women of ill repute. Peter adds Jonesy and me into that toast, but we set him straight. Jonesy, as we all know, is a family man completely faithful to his wife. And I, as far as they know, am a completely faithful fiancé.

The problem, I soon discover, is that Peter insisted he be involved in the planning for the evening's activities. Meaning he took it upon himself to take the evening to the edge of decency and good taste. Meaning he will push me off into the chasm of indulgence and sin at first chance.

To this, I tell him, "I don't want to be pushed off the edge. I want this to be an evening of sanity." And when I speak the words, I stand a bit straighter, a bit prouder.

Peter sees this. Frowns. Nods. And then I see his eyes narrow just a bit, and I know that no matter my words, my desires, I'm in for a hell of a ride.

Peter's cell rings and he steps out back to talk to his agent about some haggling over an offer. A stage offer. The show is *Back To The Future, The Musical.* I laugh, but quickly realize it can work. The only problem is I had only heard him sing Meatloaf's "Paradise By the Dashboard Light," and as everyone knows, a tone-deaf monkey can sing Meatloaf and sound good.

As Peter haggles, Ian steps out to have a cigarette, leaving Jonesy and me with the shot glasses and three bottles of glory. Without toasting, we do a shot of each. We drink for the for the sake of drinking and damn, does it feel good.

"How you holdin' up?" Jonesy says.

I smile. "You gonna ask me that every time you see me?"

He takes off an imaginary pair of sunglasses and says, "Son, it's my job to make sure you don't rabbit."

"You think I'm going to run?"

"I don't know, Davis. Are you?" He's serious, but his smile is playful. I don't answer. Then he says, "You talk to Hillary?"

"Today?"

"She called me this morning."

"She called you?"

"Wanted to see me. She actually wanted to see you, but talked herself out of it."

"Yeah?"

"I asked her if she was coming to the wedding. You want to know her response?"

I already know.

He says, "You said you sent her an invitation."

I say, "Yeah, well. I figured it best if she wasn't around."

Jonesy nods, his smile gone. He looks out the back window, out at Peter and Ian. I don't want to ask. I don't want to burst the bubble. But I have to know.

I say, "What did she tell you?"

He's silent, his teeth clicking to an unheard beat. He says, "She's hurt, Davis. She understands why, but she's still hurt. A phone call would have been nice."

"That's it? That's all she said?"

He says, "Is there more?" and the way he looks at me, the calm smile, the tired eyes, I realize he knows.

I say, "No. I guess there isn't."

Every open lie, every discovered deception, hangs about us like a smoky barroom haze. Then he puts a reassuring hand on my shoulder and says, "You know, I'll support you in any decision you make, right?"

I smile, look out the back window. I say, "Thanks, man, but I think I'm gonna be okay with this."

"You sure?"

I think about the bubble, feel its presence, it's safety. "Yeah," I say. "I'm sure."

And then Peter and Ian step inside and the evening begins.

All told, we've a dozen guys packed into a stretch SUV limousine with the occasional straggler who joins for the tame outset, and the throng that joins in hopes of participating in the finale of great debauchery. But there is always Peter and Jonesy.

"Where are we headed?" I say.

"Haven't a clue," says Peter. He knocks on the divider and it rolls down a smidge. "Hey. Where we headed?"

In answer, the divider rolls back up. Everyone looks confused, but then shrugs it off. Someone puts some porn in the DVD player. Someone starts the drinks.

Soon I'm looking at the half-naked girl on the television and say, "Why is she wearing a strap-on?"

Peter says, "Because she's about to fuck that guy in the ass."

"And we're watching this, why?"

Peter says, "Dude. You're getting married. This is an instructional video. There will be a test later. Pay attention."

I look at Jonesy and he says, "What were you expecting?"

Peter lines up shots of tequila. He hands me one, but I decline and reach for the rum.

Peter says, "It's mother's milk, Davis. The good stuff."

I say, "I've had the good stuff. It's not that good."

Peter says, "Did you listen to anything your future wife said?" And then he breaks out into an imitation of Pamela. "Rule number one: Drink whatever the boys put in front of you."

Before I can stop him, he pours the contents of the shot glass into my mouth. I swallow on instinct, and immediately regret it.

Everything is black. I squeeze my eyes and clench every muscle into hypertension. Unlike the back-of-the-throat freeze the night before, my body is not attempting to deal with one source of pain. Pain is everywhere. Every nerve is on fire. Acid is seeping out of my pores, mixing with my sweat, and soaking my shirt. Bowels clenching, I dig my nails into the seat as I try not to let everything loose. And then it's gone. I pull my nails from the seat cushion and feel bits of stuffing under them.

Peter looks at me for a second, blinks, and then hands me another shot. He says, "Now that you're past the crap, have some mother's milk."

I balk.

"Come on," he says. "You don't think I'm gonna take a chance of your horfing up the good stuff, do ya?"

Twenty minutes later, the four-by-four stretch limo stops and, before I know what's going on, I have a coat thrown over my head, and am hustled inside a building. For a moment, I catch the lights of Coors Field, and hear the whistle of the train yards. Lower downtown Denver. Warehouses converted to pricey lofts, four bars to a block, and ritzy restaurants side by side with the best the nightclub scene has to offer. I'm surrounded with possibilities ...

Inside, there is no pause as events blur into one another.

Muffled laughter is followed by a muffled argument followed by a muffled shout and I'm moving forward while Peter and Jonesy jabber on about being expected as I'm woven in and out of chairs and tables and broken beer bottles and I enter doorways and exit hallways and I bump into chairs and doorjambs and I curse and protest and I'm shoved to the side and pushed backward and led from dirty bathroom tile to red carpeting with a double-diamond pattern and I hear someone shout and protest and jabber on in a rising pitch only to be quashed by a solitary voice full of strength and confidence and a hand pushes my chest while others push my back and I stumble and fall to one knee and try to pull the coat off to see what's going on but I'm lifted to my feet by hands pushing me forward and pinning my arms and I hear more shouts and the dull thud of punches and the sharp cracking of wood and I see a splintered chair leg fall at my feet while I'm pushed through a set of doors and the carpet becomes tile and then concrete and plates and glasses shatter at my feet and someone falls — Max Richards? — and blood shoots from his nose and I'm running and it's dark and I feel the concrete become tile and then carpet and I'm thrust into a chair and the coat is pulled off and ...

Calm, soothing sounds of a baby grand piano roll over me. I'm sitting at a large table in a dimly lit dining room. A menu appears in front of me. Damon's Steak House. High class. So exclusive a normal head count is a Who's Who of A-list celebrities, *Fortune 500* CEOs, and break-the-bank athletes.

I blink, look around, blink again.

Sitting at every table are naked women in various Carnival masks, casually dining with each other as if this is the most normal thing in the world.

Before I can take it all in, before I can register that I have a table of friends staring at me with shit-eating grins, Jonesy slaps me on the shoulders, leans in on one side, and says, "You don't have to do this, ya know. All you have to do is say no."

I say, "Um, I don't have to do what?"

"You don't have to turn around."

"Why are they wearing masks?"

He says, "You need a special license to be fully nude. Now focus, Davis. Focus, and know that no matter what Peter says, no matter how he says it, all you have to do is say no."

I try to turn, try to look him in the face, but he stops me.

He says, "Think about it first, Davis. You see what's around you. You see Peter's handiwork. You know to what ends he'll take you and to what extent you can be hurt. But you have the choice. You don't have to turn around. You don't have to give in. All you have to do is say no."

I say, "Jonesy, what are you talking about?" But I already know. With naked women all around me, the anticipation to see what's behind me rises fast. And that's just what Peter's counting on. He knows me. He knows that I'll kick myself for the rest of my life if I don't find out what's there, what's behind me.

My eyes dart to the sides, to the Carnival masks blue and yellow and red with glitter and feathers and deep black oversized eyes and theatrically elongated noses.

I pry my gaze from the women, from the masks, and look down at the table in front of me. The tablecloth is soft, but not silky. The silver is subdued, but not tarnished. The bachelor is intrigued, but not fanatical.

I replay Jonesy's words, his warning. I hear his voice in my head and silently move my lips as I repeat them. Over and over, like a mantra, I hear them, I speak them.

All I have to do is say no.

I tell myself that I shouldn't do it.

All I have to do is say no.

I tell myself it's going to lead to trouble and when Peter Carter is involved trouble turns into chaos.

All I have to do is say no.

I close my eyes, take a deep breath, and feel the bubble.

All I have to do is —

The bubble is with me.

All I have —

Pamela is with me.

All I —

The naked women.

Pamela is with me.

The temptation.

Pamela is with me.

Everything is all right.

Pamela is with me.

I open my eyes.

Pamela is with me.

I can do this.

Pamela is with me.

I'll be fine.

Pamela is with me.

I turn slowly, look at Jonesy, and nod. Without expression, he recedes.

With a game-show host grin, Peter advances. Peter the showman. Peter the used-car salesman.

Peter the groomsman says, "A wiser person once uttered, 'Yield to temptation; it may not pass your way again.' I do my best to live by these words, although I know they're not for everyone. I know the toll it takes on the body, on the mind, on the soul. But at the same time, I weigh the benefits against the detriments. I weigh the memories, the tales to tell, against the injuries and the nightmares. Beyond that, I consider the length of a single human life, and I weigh the enjoyment against the sorrow.

"At any time, we could go out. Hit by a rogue meteor. Run over by lemmings. Lead poisoning. The list is endless, but the point is that it could happen at any time. At any moment, you could drop. And when that happens, I don't want to look back on everything and wonder 'what if.' I don't want to look back and have any regrets.

"Because in the next life, in the afterlife, who knows what chances you'll have? Who knows what you'll be handed? What you'll have to work for? Who even knows if there's anything after this? Wouldn't that just suck? If you're on your deathbed and you're going toward the light and it's brighter and brighter and it overwhelms you and then you open your eyes and find … nothing, nada, zilch. And in that moment, wouldn't it just suck if your final thought is: What if?

129

"That's all I'm saying to you, Davis. What if? So, now you have a choice. You can see what's behind me, behind you, or you can forever ask, what if? I'll give you a moment to weigh your options."

He recedes, but his focus on the back of my head remains. Not glaring, not drilling into my brain to do harm, but I feel it just the same. Waiting. Wishing.

So too I feel Jonesy's gaze. Hoping. Praying.

But as cheesy as it sounds, I feel Pamela in my heart. And even though this is my bachelor party, even though this is supposed to be my last night of freedom, and I'm supposed to let it all loose for one last night of debauchery, I feel Pamela in my heart, and know I will not cross the line into harm, into destruction. I'll be all right. No matter what happens, I'll press onward and survive. I feel Pamela, I feel the bubble, and know above all else that I will endure whatever is set before me.

Like angel and devil, Peter and Jonesy return to either side of my face.

"Have you decided?" says the devil.

I nod.

"Are you sure?" says the angel.

I nod.

Not until later, after the alley, after the fight, after the police, do I hear the warning in Jonesy's tone.

And then I'm spinning slowly around in my chair. Slowly toward the unknown. Slowly toward the 'what if.'

And then, all at once, the bubble pops.

CHAPTER SIX

Freshman Year

Halloween in Boulder, Colorado had always been a sight to behold. Every October 31st, revelers ranging from seventeen to all-but-dead converged on the Pearl Street Mall for the holy festival known as the Mall Crawl. Included in the activities were trolling for sex, alcohol abuse while trolling for sex, climbing light poles and screaming that sex was being trolled, and, if things got out of hand, breaking storefront windows and looting when it was discovered that sex swam in different waters. Only the minority engaged in the breaking and looting, as a blind idiot could see that sex was quite plentiful. Overall, the revelers had two things in common: All wished for a good time, and all were in costume.

I stress the word 'had.' In recent years, the Boulder Police Department cracked down on the Mall Crawl. Apparently, the owners of Overpriced Imported Moroccan Shit got their panties in a wad when shards of windowpane embedded themselves in rugs woven at a jock-wanking one million points per square inch, and this year, alas, the festivities were not meant to be. Sad when the overzealous few ruin the fun for the majority. Sad when people care about textiles over a good time.

So there I was, October 31st, a Thursday, studying in my dorm room. Sure, I could have been out searching for a party, trolling for sex, but I'd been at the Mall Crawl two years prior, my only time dropping 'shrooms, and I highly doubted if anything could compete with such an experience. An hour into the drug, I decided to spend the night in search of Dracula, but instead followed a gorgeous woman in a cat suit as she hissed and meowed at me. Sober, it sounds silly. Drunk, it sounds dumb. In my mind, it was sizzling. So, believing a quest for enjoyment would inevitably fail to match past endeavors, I hunkered down in my dorm room with an American lit anthology and a box of wine.

Shortly before my first break, the door flew open. Cap'n Morgan stepped through. Rather, Cap'n Morgan if he slipped a cucumber down his skintight black pants and donned red spray-painted football shoulder pads under a poofy shirt.

"Argh," he said, hands on hips, yarn-goateed face in grinning profile.

"Argh?" I said.

His smile became a sneer. "Argh!" he said, and strode toward me with a head of steam, stopping so close his crepe-paper pirate hat poked me in the forehead. His breath smelled like fruit and vodka. He stared me down with wide, wild eyes covered in what I first thought was blue eyeliner, and learned in the months following it was permanent marker.

In a single motion, he plucked my American lit anthology and tossed it out the window. Rather, it would have gone out the window had the window been open. Instead, it plunked the glass and landed on the floor.

"Argh?" he said. We stared at the anthology, its dog-eared pages fanning open as it strained for spinal equilibrium.

"Right, 'nuff of that then." He pulled me to a stand while checking my attire as if I had recently signed on for a whaling expedition. "Hoy! You call yourself a sailor? What is this manner of dress? Are those slippers? Answer me, boy. Are those slippers?"

"How many screwdrivers have you had?"

"And bunny rabbits, nonetheless? Pathetic, just pathetic. How we can plunder and pillage when my first mate employs bunny slippers? This needs to change if you're going to pluck a heartless lass this eve. We must act fast. We must be brave. We must ..."

Two girls dressed as slutty Smurfs passed the room.

After a moment, I said, "... pluck a heartless lass?"

"What? Oh, yes. I mean aye. Aye! With much haste will we find a heartless lass!" He turned, opened my closet, and started tossing things out randomly, occasionally mumbling about what he found while shouting "plunder" and "pillage" and "Damn, I need a shoehorn for this thing."

In the end, he pitched me a spatula, an eggbeater, and a wooden cooking spoon.

I said, "Hey, I've been looking for these."

"Belay that talk, matey! Smartly now! Don them scraps and let's sally forth!"

With that he left in a flourish, following a trio of giggling cowgirls trailing the slutty Smurfs. I promptly swapped the bunny slippers for sneakers and gave chase.

After a quick stop by the Army Surplus Store, my makeshift costume was set. I would play the challenging role of, The Love Doctor. A role I took to heart, suddenly a student of method acting. And by method acting, I meant rum.

My accoutrements: A wooden spoon for paddlin', stirring drinks, and whackin' the knuckles of anyone straying near my drink; a spatula for making a sitting woman squirm, àla

Bill Murray in *Stripes;* an egg beater for … well, I'm not sure what Tom Hanks was planning to do with an eggbeater to Tawny Kitaen in his most underrated movie, *Bachelor Party*; a wide-brimmed safari hat (stolen from a Hunter S. Thompson clone we passed on the sidewalk); a pair of handcuffs; and a large, obnoxious, tinfoil badge pinned to my shirt that read: "To Serve and Pleasure."

"And no, I'm not Dr. Love," I corrected many that night. "Dr. Love is a back-alley hack infomercial guru who dolls out advice on how to pleasure your prostate for a buck a minute. I'm the real McCoy, sunshine. My exploits are shouted with pleasure from rooftop to bedroom the country over."

As we ran like hell from the Hunter S. Thompson clone, the Cap'n rebuffed my attempts to discover our destination, saying, "If ya have to ask, you're not meant to know."

That's when I employed the Lisa and Bart Simpson manner of questioning.

"Where are we going?"

"Not sayin'"

"Where are we going?"

"Not sayin'"

"Where are we going?"

"You continue them words and I'll flog ye with the cucumber in me pants!"

"Fair enough," I said. "You ever find that shoehorn?"

"Argh!"

We pressed onward.

Soon, I realized the Cap'n was right. I should have known our destination. I mean, Sunday football moves a few games to Thanksgiving Thursday, so why must the Friday Night Club only convene on Friday nights? With this in mind, Peter made an executive decision.

For one week only, The Friday Night Club was relocating to Thursday.

Which begs the question: why was I not notified?

"I have a very good reason," I later told Divan after he did no such begging. "Okay, maybe not a very good reason, but a reason that makes sense to me, and that's what matters."

Divan said, "You had me at good reason."

"Hillary's driving me nuts. She's everywhere. The door, the phone, the ladder outside my window." I shuddered and took a long pull of my coke-splashed rum. "She's the best damn sexually transmitted disease a guy could never want."

"Clearly you're employing the Hiedelschmecklepeppy belief wherein, and I quote, 'Ignoring a woman gains eternal entry into her pants.'"

"Logic clearly has no part in such truth."

"So, why head down this road of maturity?"

"I'm not ready for a full-time girl in my life — hell, it's only been two months since I spoke to Marnie."

"Who's Marnie? Ya know what? I don't care."

"Fair enough. Where was I?"

"Full-time girl."

"Right. I'm not ready for a full-time girl in my life, but, unfortunately, Hillary's ready and willing for me to be a full-time boy in hers. I mean, it's cool to see her on weekends, the occasional weeknight, but I need my space."

"Why?"

"Why do I need my space?"

"Are ya using it for anything?"

I thought for a moment before saying, "I'm sure there's something, but for the life of me, I haven't a clue."

"I know the clue."

"Classic Hiedelschmecklepeppy?"

"Classic Davis."

"Do you know me well enough to identify classic Davis?"

"You tell me. You're running away because you still feel as if you need to focus on your collegiate surroundings, and as much as you enjoy the solace of our beloved Friday Night Club, you need to keep things in perspective."

I said, "Whoa." And meant every word of it.

He said, "Put more simply: If the Friday Night Club is the concert, passing grades are the tickets."

"Damn."

"Also, and on the geeky side, you seem to really love school. So, maybe her constant presence is cramping your style."

"You are a truly frightening individual."

He sighed and said, "I know."

After the first party, Hillary was a mainstay at my dorm. I woke up, Hillary. I returned from class, Hillary. I needed to pee in the middle of the night, Hillary. After a few weeks of this, I contemplated speaking to a law professor to see if her constant presence entitled her to Squatter's Rights.

Jonesy, unlike me, didn't seem to mind. Hillary was nice eye candy, especially when she began to discover her exhibitionist fetish. But Jonesy had the luxury of popping on the headphones and tuning out, while I was stuck listening to her babble on about whatever happened to be on her mind at the time. More often than not, she babbled on about sex, which, at first, was great. Though it's funny how you tire of talking about sex when sex is the only topic to discuss. If you doubt, consider: "I like sex. I like sex a lot. How can I get more sex? I really like sex. Can we have sex?" and so on. At that current juncture of her life, Hillary hadn't quite discovered her ability to elucidate her reasoning behind her enjoyment for carnal pleasure, but I felt even if she had, conversation still would have grown stale.

She talked, she jumped me, we had sex, sex was had, repeat. But afterward, the lack of pleasure derived from conversing in the matter began to take away from the act itself. Because the world still existed. The world still demanded. After a few weeks of Hillary, I felt as if I had blinders on because objects unseen were knocking me around.

This fell into the category of surprise. With Hillary, I found myself walking into tests, presentations, and lectures completely unprepared. A stray question asked in a lecture hall full of my peers would slam me to the side. A rogue solution to a problem that counted for a quarter of my final grade would trip me down some stairs. A labyrinth of hallways, students, and out-of-order signs would confound me as I searched for a bathroom. Soon, the consequences edged beyond my patience to endure. Were I to continue along my path with Hillary, I could well have been out of college, and out of the Friday Night Club.

You probably think I was crazy. Between sex and studying, most men would choose sex. To be honest, on the outset, I was among the masses. A killer party, enough booze to down a Yeti, and a tight-bodied nymphomaniac in my bed? I had scored the hat trick of college joys known to men the world over. But in the end, I simply felt the pain of being unprepared outweighed the pleasure of sex three times a night.

The older of two adopted daughters, she never quite meshed with her father. As she spoke about her pre-college life, her old boyfriends, her first love, losing her virginity, it sounded as if Hillary associated sex with male attention. I never understood why, in the sea of college possibilities, she chose me.

"Why don't you tell her you need space?" said Jonesy one night as Hillary had run to the bathroom. "She's a big girl. She'll understand."

"I really don't think she will."

"How do you know? She's strong. She's mature."

I said, "A short memory you have. Need I remind you about my small penis?"

It was the —

Third Friday Night Club Party

— and the scent of new woman-blood filled the air. So, I welcomed them, and chatted them up. It's a guy thing. You could be married or dead and still make it a point to chat the new girls up. We know it's not going to lead to anything, but that contact, that chatter, that casual flirting sates our desires. It's what keeps us from turning a simple glance over the proverbial fence into scaling it with glee.

So, I chatted, flirted, made them feel welcome. And Hillary got pissed. Pissed, in Hillary's case, began with sulking, morphed into huffing, and transformed into excessive consuming while calling me a 'cold bastard.' She then proclaimed I was a terrible lover with a two-inch penis.

Funny when a woman feels scorned, she first attacks the penis. This is because of society's belief that bigger is better. And, understandably, if you happen to be in the fast-food line of sex, you want to super-size the penis and breasts. Small is bad, but only in certain situations. We're taught this the moment we pop out. It's an unspoken societal law of the urban jungle.

When a highly intoxicated Hillary stood on the coffee table and began her attack, the response was what you would expect. A giggle here, a stifled guffaw there. Gazes shot in my direction to see if Hillary's proclamation had struck a chord. When I rolled my eyes, Hillary's anger grew. But when she began to repeat her assertion, Divan cut her off.

"Two inches?" he said.

"Yeah," said Hillary. "Isn't that pathetic?"

Divan looked at me, shaking his head. "Two inches? Dear God, man! You're hung!" He then looked back at Hillary. "I'm lucky to hit an inch and a half, and that's with sucking in my gut."

An audible silence overtook the room but was quickly contained, beaten into submission, and locked in the crawl space.

"Oh, that's nothing," said Peter. "This Cheeto?" He took a bite and held up the remaining half. "If I'm lucky."

"Shut the fuck up, you guys," said Jonesy. "I'm so tired of hearing you guys boast about the donkey cocks you have."

"Aw, come on, Jonesy. You're at least the size of my pinky. That's huge!"

"Am not! I am so small! I'm smaller than small! This toothpick? Well endowed compared to me!"

As our penises got progressively smaller, Hillary got progressively redder. This led her to grab a bottle of tequila, step out back, and get progressively drunker.

I checked on her an hour later. Nearly passed out, clearly going to be sick. I carried her to the bathroom, held her hair, and listened to her apologize as she continued to flush the toilet so she could feel the cold spray on her face in between bouts of vomiting. The event served as a reminder to what ends she would travel if she felt slighted.

That was how I found myself hunkered down in my dorm room, isolated from the outside world. And that was how I didn't hear about the special Thursday Night Edition of the Friday Night Club — a.k.a. —

The Heaven And Hell Party

Before that night, I had never been a believer in fate. Things happened, you chose your course, done and done. Later, while I would not be a convert, I would forever question the random events that befell me. For all my hunkering, for all my self-sequestering, had powers not intervened, I never would have met Her.

The layout was simple: Upstairs, Peter's room would be Heaven, the main level would be Limbo (later Purgatory), and Archer's bedroom, just off the main level, would be Hell. A theme party is never a bad way to go, and since the Mall Crawl had fallen in battle, our shindig would fill in the gap for newcomers deciding between a normal, humdrum Halloween party and our spectacle of insanity. And while the theme wouldn't blaze any trails, most felt for a last-minute idea, pardon the pun, why the hell not?

There's a theory that claims no large event can be created without the ingredient of drama. It is the balance of things. And while we complain when the drama comes knockin', we secretly yearn for its arrival to enrich the memory.

So no one was surprised when, upon hearing the theme, Archer knew — just knew! — this was his opportunity to avenge his first party embarrassment. While he didn't voice his desires aloud, his gritting teeth, popping knuckles, and low snarls were a not-so-subtle give-away. Everyone there saw that Archer would make damn sure that Hell was the core of the party.

Peter later said, "It was nice to see, actually. He was out of his morose, fuck-the-world shell. So, after I felt the initial surge of spirited competition, I let it go. Because, fuck — a party is a party is a party. And no matter what happens, as long as people come and enjoy themselves, I'll be a pig swimming in shit."

Divan later said, "The guy had to do it on his own. Had to prove his realm of eternal afterlife was superior. To be honest, he did a pretty damn good job."

As they walked in the door, Thomas Divan, clad in a dark robe, his face dolled up in black-light paint giving him a skeleton glow when illuminated by a jerry-rigged flashlight, greeted them as Charon the ferryman. More than one partygoer voiced the comparison to the Ray Bradbury short story about the doctor who removed people's bones, leaving the host a living slug. Eeriness aside, once the booze flowed, the collective whole dismissed the haunting image and began calling him Charon Carpenter, Karen's ghostly sister.

Upon entry, Charon Carpenter handed each guest some Death Punch —

"Fresh from the River Styx!"

— each glass bubbling over with a dry-ice fog. From there, they passed into Limbo, the walls covered in stark-white crepe paper, the room illuminated with browns and yellows, giving the appearance of haunting sadness. Around the couch, a large cardboard castle, its turrets and ramparts curling and twisting in on itself, appeared as if it flowed from the walls to consume the surroundings (care of Max Richards, who would later win awards on some of Broadway's biggest shows). And rolling from the foot of the castle was a two-foot thick fog, completing the scene.

Somewhere, Dante was smiling.

Employed to counter all this glorious depression were massive amounts of food and drink, because no matter the theme, you couldn't have people entering, falling depressed, and wishing they were watching an episode of *Touched By An Angel*, or some other crapfest people watch to feel better about their stations in life.

In Limbo, people had a choice. You could enter the Gates of Hell, guarded by Cerberus the three-headed canine, the role played by a large stuffed Muppet Rolf with the heads of Gonzo and Kermit the Frog lopped from their bodies and duct-taped together, or you could take the Stairway to Heaven (groan all you want, were you there, you'd have thought it was cheesy cool, too) and enter the ethereal plane above.

The only problem was, while all signs promised a swift opening of Hell's gates (a sign on the door read 'Opening Soon'), Heaven's switchback staircase was roped off (a sign read 'Closed Indefinitely for Renovations.') A bit confusing, but many believed it was Peter's way of giving Archer his moment.

The theory was that Archer was the Jekyll and Hyde character we'd all known in life. The guy who was completely normal around you, but whose personality altered when others entered the picture.

Sure, to an extent, everyone is this way. The social butterfly who thrives on making the masses happy but is quiet in smaller groups. The shy introvert who jumps to the bar and dances with her top off without a lick of the drink. But to Archer's end, it just turned nasty. Only when others were around, did he felt threatened. And when Jekyll felt threatened, the switch was flipped and out came Hyde.

I think that Archer just wanted to be the center of attention for being Archer, much like Peter was the center of attention for being Peter. But while it came naturally to Peter, Archer had to work at it. And no matter how hard he worked, it would never be enough. Because anyone who sweats and bleeds for a goal will have unending resentment for anyone else who can achieve the same without a lick of effort.

Peter never admitted he closed off Heaven for Archer. When asked, he said, "Things aren't up to code," or "Not enough staff on duty," or "Dead hooker, nasty smell." And so people laughed, shrugged, and went along with the night. We had drink. We had food. We had fog. What more could we want?

In Limbo, as I fought to raise my alcohol levels to those of the masses, Peter said, "Where the hell have you been?" He was dressed as Fat Spider-Man, extra padding in all the wrong places, plumber's crack.

"Ah, ya know," I said.

"No chick is worth it, Davis."

"Argh!" said Jonesy, appearing from the crowd. "That's what I've been telling him! Although, I must confess, I do so enjoy them nudie shows."

"Wait, what? I thought you were sleeping," I said.

Jonesy took a huge swig of beer, which spilled over the sides of the cup and ran down his yarn beard. He belched loudly and said, "I was, Matey. But every once in a while, me eyes were opened by the light of a full moon." With that, he was off for more beer.

I said, "Fucking pirates."

Peter said, "You really thought he was sleeping?"

"Hillary's libido never gave me a chance to check."

"And the sex isn't worth putting up with her?"

I exhaled through gritted teeth, shook my head.

"Yeah," he said, putting his arm around my neck and leading me into the throng. "You need to cut ties."

I was about to ask how one cut ties from a girl with low self-esteem and a penchant for excessive drinking, when a one-hundred-and-five-pound Bill The Cat jumped on my back, hawked a cold, wet hairball into my ear, and began howling into the night.

As I grimaced and pulled a wet and wadded paper towel from my ear, I realized Bill The Cat was Kathy. I playfully tossed her the hairball.

Deftly catching it, she leaned in and began rubbing her face along my shoulder. "But Davis, it's a gift." She nibbled on my ear, purring softly, and then exhaled one long warm breath. My eyes closed in pleasure, opening only when Kathy slowly trailed the wet paper towel down my neck, along my collarbone, and across my chest. I tried to inhale, but my breath kept catching as each promise of rapture rolled over me.

Then Kathy said, "Is that beer?" She plucked the red plastic cup from my hand as if it were a fly in the air, drank the contents down in one breath, and belched loudly. "Whoa, that's some good hooch!" She then kissed me on the cheek, bounced to the floor, and was off to Charon's kitchen.

I watched her, endorphins mingling with alcohol. "Well," I said. "There's that."

"In her defense, she does have eighteen years of wanting to burn away."

"And how's that going for her?"

"Not bad. She's not jumping into bed with a guy each party, but she's certainly macking on enough to get the lay of the land. But hey — at least she's in a safe environment with people to look out for her. How many people can say that as they're exploring the wild side of themselves?"

I turned, my eyes wide in fear.

He said, "What? I can't care for someone without being shit-faced?"

"Ex-nay on the air-cay," I said. "People will get the wrong idea."

He considered, said, "Fine point," and batted away one of the two blow-up dolls floating in and above the crowd.

I turned back to the kitchen in time to witness Kathy kiss Divan. No, kiss isn't the correct word. What's a good word for jumping someone and sucking their intestines through their mouth? Ah, yes.

I turned back to the kitchen in time to witness Kathy *attack* Divan.

"Forget about coming out of her shell, she's exploded out of it." A new drink appeared in my hand and I said, "Thank you, Easter Bunny."

From the crowd, a few voices said, "Bock, bock!"

"She likes you," said Peter.

"The Easter Bunny?"

Peter nodded toward Kathy.

I said, "You sure about that?"

"You don't live in someone's closet without opening up."

I was about to ask more, but never got the chance.

The Gates of Hell opened up.

Limbo was packed. Standing room only. The room went dark. The music died. A brief moment of panic infused the masses. A deep bell rang out from behind Archer's doorway. The walls shook. We all turned. A soft light behind the bedroom door began to glow. Soft begat hard. The bell chimed again. Hard begat harsh. The bell chimed again. The panic transformed into excited tension. Light began to spill around the door. Harsh begat blinding.

To this day, I don't know how Archer did it, but he plucked an image from our collective memory of childhood as we watched *Ghostbusters* on the big screen and wanted to hide under our seats when we saw that canine head start to push through the seemingly solid doorway. It felt as if it were looking at us. At all of us. From the right, then slowly across to the left. Amazed gasps and small yips of fear emanated. The energy in the room sparked. To call it electric would be a disservice to its power.

The bell chimed again. The walls shook.

And then the doorway went up in a flash of solid red flame accompanied by white flashes all around us. Streamers and glitter rained down. Then the music kicked in. Good ol' '80s AC/DC, "Hell's Bells." A cheer went up.

After a moment of hesitation, people crossed the River Styx — an ornately painted wooden threshold that felt as if one slip and you'd fall into the watery abyss — and into the mouth of Hades.

Inside wasn't any less incredible. It was Hell incarnate. I still wonder how much Archer dropped to put on the show. Demons and ghouls and other beasties crawled through the walls and along the ceiling (I later learned it was a track system with moving rubber models). On the floor, through the thick layer of fog, hundreds of life-like snakes writhed. Short bursts of air shot across the ground, feeling as if something was crawling by your legs. Various strobes throughout the room lent realism and depth to it all. It was as if the room were alive and ready to consume you without hesitation.

But the centerpiece of the room was what left people talking. As if it had been pulled from the pit of Hell stood a massive throne of human skulls. And sitting upon it was Archer, his long hair cut and combed, a pipe in hand, a big smile that radiated from his eyes rather than his lips. He was the heathen God for every boy and man, Hugh Hefner.

This was Archer's moment.

But I didn't care. My mind was on something altogether different. My mind was on ...

Thursday — Bachelor Party

Again, I nod.

And then I'm spinning slowly around in my chair. Slowly toward the unknown that I'll withstand. Slowly toward the 'what if.'

And, all at once, the bubble pops.

She's gorgeous. A Goddess, but not in the old-soul, bow-down-to-me-and-sacrifice-something-that-is-not-a-swine-because-swine-is-dirty-so-how-about-a-bunny-?-no-wait-bunnies-are-cute-and-furry-so-how-about-just-doing-that-kiss-my-feet-thing-and-we'll-figure-out-the-rest-later sense, but in the sexual, I-will-crush-you-with-my-thighs-and-by-crush-I-mean-cause-your-eyes-to-roll-back-into-your-head-as-you-scream-out-in-pleasure sense.

Greek poets would have written tales about her, wars would have waged in her name. I see her and I'm a boy again, trying to form words with a tongue that has thickened and melted simultaneously.

Then, in a blink, it passes.

She isn't gorgeous; she doesn't break my heart.

She isn't a Goddess. She's an Imposter.

She makes my skin crawl, my chest tighten. I stand and back away as if she's covered in pus-oozing wounds festering with maggots.

Peter says, "Davis?"

He's barely audible. My heartbeat thumps hard and deep in my ears. I turn and with what feels like three giant strides I'm through the batwing doors to the kitchen, across to the back exit, and into the alley. I stumble, lurch, and vomit beside a dumpster.

I will forever remember the moment. The tequila around for another lap. The nightclub down the way playing a remixed version of Dexy's Midnight Runners, "Come On Eileen," which somehow slows and warps until it synchs with my gags and retches. The blue and yellow bumper sticker on the side of the dumpster with large black letters reading: 'Life is sexually transmitted and always fatal.'

I hear the kitchen door behind me swing open. Peter, Jonesy, the others. They're staring at me with smiles of mirth laced with worry and concern of the unknown.

Peter says, "What the fuck was that?"

With the back of my hand, I wipe the warm tequila and stomach acid from my lips. I stand.

Peter says, "I mean, for fuck's sake, Davis. What the fuck was —"

I hit him. Without thinking, I spin, swing, hear a crack. Pain from my right index finger rockets to my elbow and explodes. Peter goes down on his ass, holding his nose. I grit my teeth, curse, scream.

The nervous laughter dies. Dexy's Midnight Runners down the alley begets Soft Cell's, "Tainted Love."

Then Jonesy is in front of me, his hand on my chest, holding me back in case I'm of the mind to strike Peter again. He's also taking charge, pushing everyone inside, telling them to break open some vodka and get the girls drinking and the music kicking.

The kitchen door opens, holds, closes.

I close my eyes, breathe deeply. The scent of bleach and waste fills my lungs.

With each thump of my heart I feel the pulse in my hand.

Peter says, "What the fuck was that for?" Except with the blood filling his nose, it comes out as, 'at da uck us at or?'

I open my eyes to discover he isn't surprised I hit him.

"You're a bastard," I say.

He scrunches one eye, and says, "Probably. But you know what? You'll remember this night now. I may be a bastard, but if it weren't for me —"

"I would have remembered it before."

"No," he says, standing as he holds his nose and spits blood. "You wouldn't have. It would have turned into a dream. Each day that passed, the details would have become more fuzzy until you'd call me up one day and say, 'Dude, I had this great dream the other night about strippers and —'"

I hit him again, just to shut him up. I hit him with my left hand as he's already off balance and this time he sprawls to the ground.

"Why?" I say.

"Why did I get you a stripper?"

"Why did you tell her to dress like that?"

"Pretty hot, huh?" he says, popping up, smiling as if this is all a big game.

I say, "You did it to get a reaction out of me."

"Fuck that." ('cuk at.') He rubs his jaw.

I say, "You can't just let people be happy, can you? You have to find a way to manipulate them, to warp their happiness until it's dark and sad and it's all because you can't let anyone around you feel —"

He hits me. I'm so wrapped up in trying to keep things straight and ensure that Peter doesn't confuse me with his mental misdirection that I don't see his fist flying until I'm on one knee, facing the dumpster. The wave of pain travels from my jaw to my brain. I feel my vomit soak into my pants.

Peter says, "We all square now?" Peter, pulling a line from his ass like we were on a movie set.

The next thing I know, I've tackled him into the alley wall and we're actually in a full-fledged fight. It's not a fight like we see in the movies, but a scrambling, not-having-a-fucking-clue-what-we're-doing fight. Peter will later tell stories about how we were like two hockey enforcers pounding it out, the crowd roaring its approval, Jonesy being the lone referee waiting for us to wear ourselves out.

In truth, it's rather pathetic. It's more wrestling and rolling around as we try and gain a foothold of stability and a grasp of target. At one point, I throw broken bags of garbage at him. At another point, he lifts me into the dumpster and drops me in.

Only when I'm out of the dumpster and have Peter to the ground, do I stop. The Imposter is here. The Imposter and her amazing legs. I look up at her, and ...

Freshman Year — The Heaven and Hell Party

Hillary arrived shortly after Hell opened for business. She dressed as a busty wench, a precursor for larger venues. I wasn't aware that she'd arrived for another hour, something for which I regret and thank the gods, but neither for the reasons one may think.

When the gates of Hell flashed into nothingness, I understood what it felt like to be alive. And an hour later, I understood what it felt like to die.

Flash. Cheers. All eyes turned to Hell.

Mine turned to Her.

She was a young Carla Gugino. The soft Carla, from *Miami Rhapsody*, not the hard Carla from *Karen Cisco* or *Sin City*. She was dressed as Rachel, the brunette bombshell replicant from *Blade Runner*. A dark blue, 1940's-style dress, cut to the knees, shoulder pads, and that immediately recognizable high collar. A faux fur coat, high heels and, the best part, her hair piled on top of her head — I've always been a sucker for long-haired brunettes with a strong jaw line and dimples — making her the perfect image of a film *noir* femme fatale.

My attraction extended beyond looks. We all know about that lightning bolt that strikes so infrequently and when it does, we feel the surge of it for days, months, years. And when it hits, it seems to reorganize your atoms until your surroundings fit like a shoe so comfortable that you can walk forever without getting sore.

But later, when it's gone, it hurts. It hurts where flesh meets soul.

Had I known the pain this woman would cause me later in life, I never would have approached Her.

No, that's a lie. I would have. Because I'm a man, and men are gluttons. Had I known of the pain, it would have only served as a slap to the bullshit 'male undertaking a challenge' side of me. Either way I'd have fallen for her.

And either way, I was fucked.

She entered. I watched.

The music shifted from AC/DC, "Hells Bells" to the Violent Femmes, "Blister in the Sun." She was greeted by Charon. She jumped in fright. She laughed. She was handed a drink. Charon left her to greet another. She looked around, uneasy, as if she didn't know anyone at the party. She began to enter. She hesitated.

I moved.

I told myself that I would be her ambassador to the party. I told myself a hundred dumb things a man tells himself before he approaches a beautiful woman. I told myself this was the biggest moment of my life. I told myself I would be just what she wanted. Her rock. Her savior.

Sure, grounded in reality, I knew it was just another moment. I knew it didn't deserve a buildup, that no earth would be shattered. All the same, each step toward her caused my toes to tingle. I just had to nail the first impression. It was the only thing that counted, and I wasn't going to screw it up. No, I wasn't going to *fuck* it up.

That was how I met Her. The woman of my past fantasies. The woman who would haunt my future dreams. The woman I would measure all other women against.

I moved toward Her.

I took in a lungful of courage.

I said hello.

The moment never matches the anticipation. Reality isn't planned. It's like the climax in a Stephen King novel that's been building for the past five hundred goddamned pages and never feels complete. As if the moment were so close to being big, but reality stepped in. Maybe that's why King is so popular — placing authenticity in the big moments. Telling us reality is more frightening than fiction.

I said hello, and we were off. Nothing suave, nothing cheesy. Nothing about being the Love Doctor and could I flip her. Just hello. I actually fumbled the delivery, sounding a bit softer than I should have, a bit less secure, but it was all right. We made do.

I said, "Hello, I'm Davis."

She cocked her head, one ear closer to me, and said, "What?"

Ah, yes. It was the stuff born of romantic-comedies and gonzo pornography.

I said, "What do you mean, what?"

She said, "I mean, what did you say?"

"What did I say when?"

"Just now."

"When I came up to you?"

"Yeah," she said, wrinkling her brow.

"I introduced myself."

"Right. And what did you say?"

"My exact wording?"

"To the letter."

"Um … Hi?"

She waited for a moment, and then said, "Yeah?"

"Oh, um … I'm Davis?"

"Oh," she said, brightening into a smile. "That makes much more sense."

"What did you think I said?"

"Oh, it doesn't matter."

"Oh, I think it does."

"Really, it doesn't matter."

I said, "Okay, see? Now you're just being rude," but smiling a little to show I was playing.

She said, "Ha!" and pushed me lightly.

I said, "You're keeping secrets."

"I am not keeping secrets."

"See this? This is me begging to differ."

"Beg all you want, but I do not, nor have I ever kept secrets."

"Ever?"

"Never ever. I'm awful at secrets, just ask, they'll all tell ya."

"Can I ask them now?"

"If you don't trust me."

"Are we at that point?"

She said, "No time like the present," and took a long drink from her red plastic cup. I followed suit. In a moment of self-consciousness, I realized that watching someone take a drink is like watching someone yawn.

I said, "Well, that's good then, because secrets don't make friends."

Looking into the crowd, at the blowup doll bouncing near, she said, "And how do I know I want to be your friend?"

"Oh, but you do."

"Oh, but I do?"

I said, "Trust me," and she looked at me.

"I don't know. You're sorta pushy," she said as she pushed me again, lightly, allowing me to sway back just a bit so her hand would linger on my shoulder.

I said, "Pushy is good."

"But secrets aren't?"

"Oh, now look at what you did."

"What did I do?"

"You brought it back up. Why did you have to bring it back up? It doesn't like it when it's brought up. It's shy."

"It understands. I needed to gain the upper hand."

"It's not over yet."

She said, "Wait. Listen."

"What?"

"You hear that? That sound? That's the sound of it being over."

I started to speak, considered my words, and then said, "Isn't there another way we can settle this?"

She thought for a moment, pursing her ruby-red lips, looking me up and down. "What did you have in mind? And if you say Jell-O wrestling —"

"I was going to suggest thumb wrestling, but if you prefer Jell-O, I'm game."

"You any good?"

"Only in grape, I don't know why."

"Thumb wrestling, young man."

"Grade-school champion. First through third."

"Impressive."

"So, you going to tell me what you think I said, or am I going to have to bring out the big thumbs?"

Her mouth fell open, her eyes closed. She said, "That was awful."

"You're starting to laugh."

"I am not starting to laugh."

"Then your lips are running away from your teeth."

"Wow, that's even more awful."

"Then why are you laughing?"

"Because it was so awful."

"Are those tears?"

"Tears shed because it was so painfully awful."

"We've learned something today: Puns are your friends."

"They most certainly are not. Now you're never going to know my secrets."

"If you don't tell me, I'll bother you all night long."

"Is that what you're doing?"

"I don't know. Is that what I'm doing?"

She started to reply, started to continue this banter fueled by nervous lust, but fell silent when I put my hand on hers. And when the tips of my fingers lightly brushed the back of her hand, time hiccupped.

I took the now empty red cup from her hand and replaced it with my not-so-empty red cup.

Silence. Smiles.

She said, "I'm Heather."

I said, "Nice to meet you, Heather. I'm wondering if you can help me."

"I can certainly try," she said, not taking her eyes from mine.

I said, "Who am I?"

She cocked her head slightly, ran her tongue along the bottom of her upper teeth — not in an 'I want you' way, but in an unconscious, 'I'm trying to figure out what to make of you' way — and peered into my eyes, studying me.

I was naked before her. Not just flesh, but essence and soul. Panic rose within me. I tried to pull back my hand, but she held firm, as if breaking the connection would cause her assessment irreparable damage.

After a few heartbeats, she laughed.

"Silly boy," she said. "You're Hyman Davis."

The panic ceased. I was in love.

Her name was Heather. And I was right. She didn't know anyone at the party, yet. Yet, because she was early.

"But now," she said, "I know you."

And that was how it went. Everything else ceased to matter. Our conversation paused when it was our turn to enter Hell. We jumped at all the right spots. She grasped my arm and pulled close when frightened. And after we took a three-cent tour, we escaped to the balcony. Only then did I notice her heavy breathing.

I said, "Are you okay?"

"Yeah, just, wow. I had no idea how claustrophobic I was until I came out here."

"Is that code for get the hell away from me?"

She laughed and put her hand on my arm. She didn't remove it.

The bubble formed. It was my first sighting of the rare and elusive creature, but it was enough for me to spot it were our paths ever to cross again. It was short, but sweet to the point of addiction. At the time, I couldn't explain what I saw, what I felt, though I knew we both saw it, both felt it. In the years following, I've learned it goes by many names. And every time I've attempted to explain it I sound like a coffee-house poofta trying to describe love and pain. No matter the description, it just sounds wrong. So, instead, I'll explain what it wasn't.

It wasn't cold. It wasn't harsh. It wasn't strained. It wasn't gut wrenching. It wasn't, in fact, as if we'd just met. And for just an instant, I wondered about all that crap about reincarnation and feeling perfectly comfortable with someone within a minute of meeting.

With all the things it wasn't, the thing it very much was, was smooth. Not me, smooth. Us, smooth. A satisfying smooth. Like ice cream that reaches the perfect temperature and slips down your throat betraying just a hint of chill.

As if it were meant to be.

On the balcony, seconds expanded into minutes that ballooned into lifetimes.

About forty minutes into the conversation, I said, "That's just crazy."

She said, "I know, I know. But I wanted to know what it felt like."

"But you were fourteen. You were just a girl."

"I don't think age matters in this case."

"That still doesn't mean you're not crazy."

She said, "Look, I had to know, ya know? I had to figure out for myself if I'd enjoy it."

"And so you just jumped right on in?"

"With both feet."

"You? Crazy."

She said, "What would you have done?" turning toward me with only her eyes.

I said, "I would have waited."

"Why?"

"Because at fourteen, I wasn't ready. I wasn't even close to ready. I was light-years from ready."

"You mean you weren't mature enough to deal with it?"

I exhaled audibly and said, "Hell, when you put it that way, I can't say that I'm mature enough now."

She turned to me, body as well as eyes, and said, "This is the way I see it: Seventy-five-percent of students change their majors at least once, so I figured I'd beat myself to the indecision and explore the field of law early."

"Whoa, now you're getting nasty," I said.

"I felt it was time to bring out the heavy artillery."

"But dropping percentages borders on dropping nukes."

"You're right. I jumped the gun."

"We'll just say that this was a test."

157

"So, I'm like France?"

"Yup. You went against the better judgment of the world and decided to test that sucker anyway."

"Got your attention though, didn't it?"

"So why this attraction to law?"

"I don't know," she said.

"Yeah you do."

Her eyes narrowed over a leering, playful half-smile. "You calling me a liar?"

"I'm just saying that you don't strike me as the type of girl who's going to go into something without knowing why you're going into it."

"I'm that transparent?"

"Or I'm that good."

"Whoa, ladies and gents, an ego bomb has just been dropped."

"More like a shot across the bow," I said. "And you haven't answered my question."

"I love obscure laws, what can I say?"

"You love obscure laws?"

"The ones that make absolutely no sense at all. The ones that boggle the mind."

"Lob one up."

"Okay. In Oklahoma, it's illegal to whale hunt without a permit."

"You're joking."

"Your mind is boggling right now. I can see it."

"And because of this you fell in love with law?"

"You have to follow your attractions. Want another? In Liverpool, it's legal for a woman to go topless if she's the sales clerk in a tropical fish store."

"I've always wanted an aquarium," I said. "Wait. You got this job at fourteen?"

"Paralegal's assistant. Friend of the family."

"But at fourteen? You should have been into — what are girls into when they're fourteen?"

"Boys."

"And yet you were attracted to obscure laws."

"Oh, I liked boys too." She turned away, looking out at the Boulder night. "The paralegal I was assisting was cuter than sin."

"Is sin that cute?"

She smiled at a memory. "You ever seen him?"

"Can't say that I have."

"You'd switch sides."

"Uh, no."

She turned back to me. "You don't know that."

"I know enough to know that I wouldn't switch sides."

"But he's really, really cute."

"He could be the hottest thing since toast and I still wouldn't switch sides."

"I detect some homophobia."

"Ah, see, that's where you're wrong. I'm not homophobic. I simply know that when I look at a guy I see a guy, but when I look at a woman, I see heaven."

"All women?"

"Well, there are different levels of heaven."

"I never read that volume of Dante's work."

"Very obscure," I said.

"So where am I?"

"What?"

"In heaven. What level of heaven am I in?"

"You don't want to know."

"I don't?"

"It's, well, it's up in the air."

"What? Why?"

"Many reasons."

"Give 'em to me."

"Um, okay, well, there's your insatiable love for *ABBA*."

"I told you that in confidence, and you're holding that against me?" she said, lightly pushing me, and then allowing her touch to linger. We moved closer.

"I'm just saying it's one of the things."

"That's so arbitrary."

"Well, *yeah*."

We held there for a while, suddenly both aware of how close we were, but neither wanting to break away. "Okay, what else?"

"Bob Barker."

"That's. Not. Fair."

"You have to admit, it's weird."

"I was young, I didn't know what I was doing."

"Nevertheless. A crush on Bob Barker at ten is not normal."

"I knew I shouldn't have told you that secret until you asked me out."

"Ask you out?"

"Yeah. And what's taking you so long?"

"How do you know I'm going to ask you out?"

"Come on. You know, I know."

"How do you know I haven't done it already?"

"You haven't," she said.

"I may have. Maybe you missed it."

"I've been paying attention."

"Not the whole time."

"Come on! A guy walks up to me and tells me his name is Hymen Davis? I'm hooked!"

"If I knew it was that easy."

"You'd have jumped right on in, huh?"

"Both feet."

"Then what's stopping you now?"

I said, "Not a thing," as we moved closer to each other and smiled that smile before you first kiss someone and —

Hillary came out onto the balcony, singing along with whatever song was playing at the time. We both turned to her. The bubble popped. And we were enveloped in a cloud of strain and frustration that would forever exist between us. All because of what happened next.

CHAPTER SEVEN

Hillary saw us, smiled big, neared, and said, "There you are!" She stepped outside, nearly spilling her drink as she tripped on the hem of her dress. She caught herself, but even if she didn't, Heather was already there to help. I was marveling at the speed she moved to Hillary, when it occurred to me she had already been approaching before Hillary tripped. As if they knew each other. When they hugged, I realized I wasn't the one Hillary had been addressing.

She said, "How long have you been here?"

"About an hour," said Heather, who then turned to me, causing me to squirm. "Has it been an hour already?"

I nodded, and laughed a half-hearted laugh that would have betrayed my uneasiness, had anyone been paying attention.

"Wow, you look beautiful," Heather said.

"Thanks. I just threw it together."

"Bullshit," said Heather. "How long have you been working on it?"

"You like?"

"You need to make me one and we'll hit the Renaissance Festival."

"Hey, there's an idea," said Hillary. "I've never been." And then she looked to me.

Inwardly, I cringed, expecting a repeat of the scorned-woman routine. I needn't have worried. Hillary was happy. Genuinely happy.

"Davis!" she said, nearing me, hugging me. "I can't thank you enough."

I muttered something about it being no big deal.

"Are you kidding? With this bunch? I don't trust them with me, let alone my little sister."

And there it was.

Thursday — The Bachelor Party

Only when I'm out of the dumpster and have Peter to the ground, do I stop. The Imposter is here. The Imposter and her amazing legs. I look up at her, and ...

Peter sucker punches me in the temple. My world closes in. I've never had a concussion, but I've had enough head rushes to instinctively tighten my abs to avoid the momentary blackout.

Peter rolls me to my back and starts patting my cheeks. "Don't you pass out on me, you fucking baby!" ('on't oo ass ou on ee ...')

Then Jonesy is there. "You stupid moron!"

"Don't call him a moron," says Peter.

"I'm not. I'm calling you a moron!"

"Why am I — He's the moron who started it!"

"You sound like my kids. Have you grown up at all?"

"He threw the first punch!"

"You're making my point for me."

"But he did!"

"You really want to do this?"

"Do what?"

"Look around you, Peter."

"I don't know what you're —"

"Can you honestly say that if you hadn't abandoned your friends we would be here today?"

"Are you *shitting* me? Since when do I have this sort of influence over anyone?"

"God, you're pathetic. If you wouldn't have gotten married in the first place, Davis wouldn't have met Pamela."

"I did good! They're getting married! I did good!"

"Don't give me that. You've fucked it up for him before and you're doing it now."

"I'm not fucking it up now. I'm trying to give him some fun."

"The problem is that your definition of fun is fucking it all up! If you want to be there for someone as a friend, fucking be there for them as a friend! But don't be this cocky over-the-top asshole who's living vicariously through other people's happiness! Davis met Pamela though you, fine. Let them be happy. But don't go starting fights in back alleys because someone else has the chance of being happy!"

"I defended myself."

"Oh, *come on*. You knew what his reaction was going to be when you planned this thing."

"I didn't know he was going to punch me."

"The thought never crossed your mind?"

"Never."

"Horseshit."

"Seriously. I thought I'd talk him out of it."

"So it *did* cross your mind."

"That's my life, dude. After a point, I have to talk everyone out of hitting me."

All of this as I'm slipping in and out of the black hole.

The Imposter steps near, her head covering the alley light, creating a halo effect around her brunette, femme-fatal features, and I realize I was mistaken. She is beautiful.

I say, "Heather?"

Freshman Year — The Heaven and Hell Party

It didn't hit Heather until later, but not much later. We were on the balcony, the girls catching up. I began to pull aside when Hillary stopped Heather in mid sentence, turned to me and said, "Have you been avoiding me?"

It caught me off guard, and I must have shown it.

"I'm just kidding, Davis." Then to Heather, "He's so serious all the time."

"Yeah?" said Heather. "I hadn't noticed." She gave me a wink that Hillary missed because she was moving toward me, saying, "So, you gonna just stand there, or are you gonna flip me?"

I blinked, and when she caressed the spatula hanging from my belt, I managed a weak laugh. I said, "Behave yourself, young lady."

Her brow arched, and as she slid her hand down the front of my pants, squeezing lightly, yet knowledgably, she said, "How's this for behaving?" With her other hand, she cupped the back of my head and pulled me into a kiss.

I inhaled sharply, attempted to mumble a protest through Hillary's tongue, but stopped when my gaze fell on Heather. She stood rigid, her head cocked to the side, her brow knitted. She was confused and shocked and all at once angry. Then her features softened as understanding arrived.

After a long moment, Hillary broke the kiss, our breath still mingling, and said, "What did you say?"

When I didn't respond, she withdrew, saw me looking behind her, and began to turn. My panic flushed. My future flashed before me full of chaos, wrath, and scorn. Heather's eyes widened and I realized her future had flashed as well.

We moved as one. Wanting to stop time, wishing to change the path toward our fate, we reached out to Hillary.

Then, from inside, bedlam erupted.

The Stairway to Heaven opened up.

As Heather and Hillary turned to the townhouse, I closed my eyes and thanked the heavens for intervening. For sending down a guardian angel to step in and stop the madness. For placing upon this earth the being that would save the day.

Fat Spider-Man had come to the rescue.

Although not as grand as Archer's display, it was more than moving. Apparently, over the last hour or so, the occasional hot college-girl had approached Peter and he'd pointed her upstairs And not your everyday hot college-girl, but girls who had grown past that awkward stage and into their own. Girls who knew they were hot but were confident, not cocky. Girls who could melt your spine and fan your libido with just a walk and a wiggle.

No one thought much of it. They were just some good-looking girls in various costumes talking to Peter. A normal, everyday occurrence. Nothing to see here, people. Move along, move along.

Peter counted on this assumption and used it to his advantage. Obfuscation. Confusion and redirection. Chisel yet another title onto Peter's headstone: Magician.

Although people had not forgotten about the ethereal realm above, the flowing alcohol and the opening of Hell had successfully redirected their attention. So when Peter excused himself to go up the switchback stairs, through the loft, and into his bedroom, everyone just thought 'Peter's getting lucky.'

Normal. Everyday. Obfuscation.

Time passed. No one noticed when the upstairs lights dimmed, or when a dark mass began to lower from the ceiling. But when the lights and the music were cut, their attention was abducted.

A spotlight mounted behind the twisted castle popped on and struck the dark mass still lowering from the ceiling. Light flashed everywhere at once. Eyes adjusted. People peered up at the lopsided papier-mâché disco ball, and then they looked beyond. The upstairs lights rose, the spotlight dimmed. A figure stepped to the loft railing.

Peter Carter, no longer Fat Spider-Man, stood in flowing white robes, his bedroom behind him, a dark curtain in the doorway. When he raised his arms, the chatter ceased.

"My children," he said, softly, but everyone could hear him. "I … I am ashamed. I am ashamed because you have fallen prey to the golden idol. You have become idolaters and have lost your path." He paused and looked around, solemn. "But worry not, my children. Like Moses, I will lead you to the Promised Land."

The spotlights cut off, and on either side of him, silk screens, one in blue, the other in red …

Thursday — The Bachelor Party

The Imposter steps near, her head covering the alley light, creating a halo effect around her brunette, femme-fatal features, and I realize I was mistaken. She is beautiful.

I say, "Heather?"

My vision blurs. Colors swim in and out of darkness, gelling together, borders coalescing. Blacks darken reds that stain whites that dilute blues …

The Imposter frowns, begins to speak, but her head pops up in synch with Jonesy's and Peter's. A siren rolls once, echoes in the alley, and then falls silent.

I blink, breathe. The nausea ebbs when understanding dawns.

The police exit their cruiser, their dull footfalls echoing in the alley. Flashlights shine. I squint, and as I look aside, I see that surprise has overcome both Peter and Jonesy.

Silence permeates the alley.

Then the Imposter speaks. "Hello, boys. Here for the party?"

I cringe.

Officer One looks me over, and then speaks into his shoulder-clipped radio requesting an ambulance.

"No, no," I say, trying to sit up. "I'm fine." Everyone turns to me. Except for Peter. He's frozen, his mouth slightly open, looking completely out of his element. Leave it to Peter to shut the fuck up at the worst possible time.

"What's going on here?" It's Officer Two. Casual. Confident. Almost playful. He's tossing down the gauntlet, challenging us to give him a story. To tell him we aren't doing anything, honest.

Now it'll happen. Now Peter will speak and confuse and step up to the challenge and become the legend who can talk his way out of anything. Step up, introduce himself, and spin some yarn about aliens from Planet X in search of young, nubile women, not unlike Jennifer Garner or Randy Door, and we felt it our duty as Americans, as citizens of Earth, to fight them as God intended — fist to tentacle — and so we did.

But he's silent. No yarn. No aliens. Not a peep.

The Imposter helps me stand. My world begins to spin. I close my eyes for a moment, waiting for the bout to pass, and when I open my eyes, something interesting happens.

I'm not me. I'm not Davis Robertson, rather, I'm someone *inside* Davis Robertson's body, a third party operating the controls. That's the only way I can explain my actions, my thoughts, what's pulled from the depths of my ass.

"You see the guys?" I say.

The officers look to each other and say, "What guys?"

I say, "The fuck you mean, 'What guys?' The guys who jumped us." I sit on an overturned produce crate. The

Imposter puts a handkerchief she's pulled from God knows where to my bleeding lip.

Officer Two says, "You may want to rethink your tone."

"You're right," I say. "I have no right to be pissed off that we just got the shit beat out of us by two guys who probably ran past you as you were two of the three blind mice."

"We didn't see any guys," Officer Two says as Officer One looks back down the alley.

"Jesus Christ," I say. "You guys are like Clydesdales. Looking big and impressive, but always wearing fucking blinders so you miss what really happens in —"

Jonesy puts a hand on my shoulder.

"Oh, don't defend them, Jonesy! We're jumped when we come out for air, and now we're the problem? Fuck that! Fuck all of that!"

One and Two size up the situation, and when Two begins to ask the question I know he's going to ask, I cut him off.

"I.D.? Sure, why the fuck not?" I pull my wallet from my pocket, my broken finger screaming but the entity at the controls ignoring it, and toss it to One, all in one motion. In my mind's eye, it's fluid. Jonesy later tells me I'm right.

One opens the wallet, says, "Davis Robertson?"

"Yup," I say. "History professor at Denver University, Libra. I'm right-handed, but can use my left in a pinch. This is Adam Jones, business owner, Leo, father of two. This is ..." I look at the Imposter and she gives her name (not Heather) on cue, "And this is Peter Carter. Perhaps you've heard of him from such films as *Getting My Ass Kicked*, and *Two Cops Scratching Their Balls*, and my personal favorite, *The Fucking Guys Who Did This Are Running* —"

"You're Peter Carter?" says Two.

After a moment, Peter blinks a few times, and then says, "Would you boys kindly point those flashlights elsewhere?"

169

The flashlights pull away, and …

Freshman Year — The Heaven and Hell Party

He paused and looked around, solemn. "But worry not, my children. Like Moses, I will lead you to the Promised Land."

The spotlights cut off, and on either side of him, silk screens, one in blue, the other in red …

The colors began to shimmer, then waiver as the music — the KLF melding into 808 State mixing into Energy 52 — started slow, but quickly began to thump. Then, we saw the hot college girls Peter had sent upstairs.

They were pole dancers. Professionals, I later learned. Peter had clandestinely removed his bedroom door, replaced it with a black-as-night velvet curtain, and installed two poles on either side of the entrance.

"My flock," he said, his voice loud and clear over the still rising beats. "Rise above the quagmire of filth in which you wade." He snapped his fingers. Christmas lights along the stairway popped on, rolling as if they were on a runway and directing everyone to the top of the stairs. There, behind a closed gate and a podium, stood Peter holding a parchment and a feather quill. On the front of the podium, a sign read: 'Saint Peter Is In.'

With each member of his flock, he questioned their greatest sin. He discussed it, weighed its value against the good spawned from such admission, and pondered how large it would appear if dwarfed by another, greater sin.

"Because through that curtain?" he said. "Such a sin may reside."

Understanding dawned on the masses. Only two girls danced outside Peter's bedroom. And, although the counts varied, at least seven girls had been directed upstairs. Imaginations rooted and spread throughout the party.

Everything and anything could happen beyond that black-as-night velvet curtain.

"The question is," said Peter, "will you embrace the sin, or turn away?"

Some turned away. Most didn't. Ethics and philosophy aside, entrance was rather easy. Each man was to make out with a woman, and each woman was to make out with another woman, or Peter, or both. But every soul who gained entry made a promise to go forward with a mind open to possibility.

As the evening progressed, so grew the legend of Peter Carter. Because he wasn't only Fat Spider-Man, he wasn't only Saint Peter, he was the Almighty Oz. What secrets did he possess? What bullshit had he conjured? You never knew with Peter, so people always returned. It could be a room chest high with plastic balls in which people groped, licked, and copulated anonymously. It could be a slip-and-slide down the stairs into an inflatable pool. It could be a glowing lava lamp. No matter the effect, the results were always the same — people talked. They'd enter with dreams of tromping throughout the forests of their wildest imaginations, and they'd leave with fulfillment on levels they often could not comprehend.

It was Peter's personal psychological and social experiment. He once said, "You know what it's like? It's like giving people a pill they think is a drug, but is really a Tic-Tac. Because they think their mind is embarking on a journey, they make it so. But it's all a big joke. Because, goddamn, people take life way too seriously."

The lava lamp? People considered it deep. For him, it was laziness. A last-minute thing. Focus on the lamp and expand. They did. He laughed.

So, what was behind the black-as-night velvet curtain that night in Heaven? I never found out. I only heard the stories, the tales. Not one of them was the same. Some felt energized by their futures. Some felt cleansed by their pasts. All of them felt incredible. And not a one of them knew how Peter did it.

I never felt the power of Heaven. After Hillary squealed in delight, kissed me quickly, and made her way to the pole dancers, I returned to the balcony. Heather followed.

"You don't want to enjoy the fun?" I said, my back against the railing, looking down at my drink.

She was silent, then, "I don't think anything can salvage this evening. Do you?"

I smiled, but not in joy.

She neared the railing, leaned on it, and shivered.

We talked, but everything had become serious. Everything had become strained. We talked about who we were. What we were. What we were denying ourselves. We talked about what was important. Our friends. Our families. Our pasts. Our futures. It was still smooth, but the edges were frayed. Neither of us wished reality to enter our lives; both yearning to feel that connection again. The bubble. The drug.

She said, "Have you been avoiding her? My sister?"

My *sister*. "Not as far as she knows," I said.

She nodded as if this didn't surprise her. "She's always gotten attached quickly," she said.

"But not you?" I smiled.

She looked at me and laughed. It helped lessen the strain, but not by much.

Heather was a year younger than Hillary and a senior in high school. The party was a last-minute decision after an argument with a friend created a Halloween void. The *Blade Runner* costume was Hillary's, circa two years earlier.

"So," she said. "You're the one she's been talking about."

We were silent for a long while. Cheers in the night. Laughter in the party.

I said, "You want another drink?"

She gazed into the darkness. After a few heartbeats, I shrugged, and began to move toward the door when she put a hand on my arm. I stopped, looked at her, saw the lines of sorrow, the lines of angst, the soft shimmering, the tears.

She said, "I can't hurt my sister. You know how she is, and I can't do that to her."

I nodded, said nothing. We just looked at each other, neither wanting to blink, both wanting the bubble to reform.

"You felt it though, didn't you?" she said.

I gazed at my feet, to the party, into her eyes sparkling with the reflection of the Boulder night. I said, "I still do."

After a moment, she said, "Yeah."

Her hand squeezed my arm, relaxed, squeezed again. Without thinking, I began to lean toward her. Our heads began to tilt, our chests tightened, our breath caught, our eyes —

"Wow, did you guys see me up there?"

We turned. Hillary was in the doorway, beaming like a streetlight. "The girls said I was a natural." Then she saw our nearness, our pain. She frowned in confusion. "What's going on?"

Silence.

Then, "Davis was just going in to find you. I stopped him, asked if he'd get me another drink." Heather handed me her red cup, and when I took it, our fingers brushed. I looked down and saw the cup wasn't quite empty, not quite full. I left.

Although I fully intended to return, it was another year and a half before I saw Heather again.

In the kitchen, as Charon refilled the cups, he said, "You look like you've been shot."

"I wish."

"Hillary?"

"Sorta."

"The other one?"

"Sisters," I said.

"No shit?"

"No shit."

He paused, as if he felt we needed a moment to switch gears. "I saw you with her. You didn't look like yourself."

"How did I look?"

"You looked happy."

"I don't normally look happy?"

"Not that kind of happy."

"Yeah, well. You won't be seeing it for a while."

"Just break it off. Date the other one," he said.

"You're kidding."

"Hillary's a big girl. She'll get over it."

"Women don't work like that."

"Yeah? And who are you to be so wise in the ways of women?"

"I'm not. If I was, I wouldn't have been shot."

I exited the kitchen, and began to weave toward the balcony when all hell broke loose.

Jekyll-Archer had smiled when Peter opened up Heaven, but once he saw the pole dancers, he knew his moment had passed. But he tried. He struggled, but tried to be the nice guy, to stop the transformation, to keep Hyde-Archer at bay.

He grinned a little too big, laughed a little too loud. He waited in line with the rest of the throng, trying to be a guest at his own party. But after a point, he couldn't take being second best.

Jekyll-Archer excused himself, retreated back into Hell, and tried to be a gracious loser. But his mind kept wrapping around the same old problem: Peter had cheated. Peter always cheated.

It was the pole dancers. How could he compete with that? It was akin to hitting on some girls at a concert only to have the band give them backstage passes. But Peter wasn't a band. He was a mortal. And he had to pay.

Hyde-Archer began by cutting the power cord to the stairway Christmas lights, but people were too intoxicated to notice. He then cranked the music in Hell — The Rolling Stones, "Sympathy for the Devil" — so loud it rattled fillings, but people only raised their voices to compensate. So, in the end, he did the only thing he felt was left.

He pulled out his paintball gun and blew the papier-mâché disco ball all over the room.

No one noticed Hugh Hefner standing at the gates of Hell with a large black and silver gun. It's amazing what people miss when they're in their own little worlds. He stood there for at least thirty seconds, Jekyll fighting with Hyde for control over Archer. To no surprise, Jekyll lost.

People screamed when red paint and glitter began spattering down. From there, it was a chain reaction of infectious panic. Each scream only added to the belief that someone was maiming another.

It's a miracle no one was trampled. One hundred schnickered college kids running at top speed into a doorway bottleneck is a sure sign of disaster. Alas, the only casualty was Cerberus, the three-headed guardian of Hell. Gonzo's head had torn free, never to be found. We later toasted our comrade.

The dust settled. Only a handful of us remained. Hillary had run off, protecting her sister. I didn't see them leave, but I certainly felt it. In one moment, I stood as a rock in a river, the flow moving around me as I searched for Heather. The next, I felt a rush of emptiness as if my chest had spilled to the floor. My legs buckled, my feet lost traction. The surge toward the doorway picked me up, held me, and then it felt as if a vacuum were sucking me to the floor. I saw heads, shoulders, elbows, hips, knees —

Charon saved me. He saw me go down, reached in, and pulled me into the kitchen. My lip was bleeding, as was my ear. Charon handed me a glass of something that caused me to tingle all over, but did not push away the still overwhelming hollowness. As realization slowly hit that Heather was not returning, I began to wish I'd been trampled.

After the exodus, those of us who remained glowered at Archer in disbelief. To this, he smiled big, shouldered the paintball gun, entered his room, and shut the gate to Hell. We all looked at each other. The music stopped from his room. Then the power in the entire townhouse went dead. After a few moments of silence, Peter said, "The breakers are in his room."

In the darkness, someone cursed.

From then on, we never gave Archer a thought. He cut the power? We turned on flashlights. He locked the doors? We climbed through a window. He stole our rum? We kicked down his door and duct taped him to his toilet. In short, we approached every problem as if it were an everyday annoyance, like the summer's heat or the night's darkness. Find a quick solution and return to the fun. After a point, he stopped trying. He became just another person at the party.

As we waited for the police to arrive, we constructed stories to explain the mass exodus, the blood-curdling cries, and the phoned-in tales of rampant psychopaths wielding unique kitchen utensils with very sharp points.

They never showed. Leave it to the police to answer our prayers the one time we prepared for their arrival.

At half past 1:00, we were zombies in search of fresh brains. We all felt the need to end things on a note less shrill, but without much enthusiasm, direction was beyond our grasp.

Then Kathy guided us to the land of the living.

Over the years, her mother had included a candle for every occasion that warranted a gift. But, as always with her mother, nothing was offered without a catch.

"I give these to you, my daughter, out of love, compassion, and trust. But, always know that under no circumstances, can you use them."

"Then, why —"

"They're for an emergency."

"So, I can only light them if —"

"You can never light them. Under no circumstances can you bring wick to flame. These are emergency candles."

"For emergencies?"

"For emergencies."

"So, I can light them if I'm —"

"Kathy, you're not listening to me."

Kathy considered her mother's words for all of a shrug. Within minutes, the loft became a heavenly sight.

Peter turned on a battery-powered clock radio — KBCO, Blues Traveler, "Run-Around." Time passed. Tensions receded. Until the sun rose, the five of us, the guy Kathy was snogging in her closet when Archer slew the party, some guy who had wandered in after hearing the screams, and the pole dancers, consumed heavily and engaged in a vigorous game of strip poker, and when there was no more stripping to be had, sexual-act-poker.

It should have been a perfect mix: Strippers, alcohol, a deck of cards. But even as we all disrobed, imbibed, and paired up, even as Megan, one of the pole dancers, gave me a lap dance and much, much more, I couldn't excise Heather from my mind.

At random times, I would experience the shock of that lightning bolt. I would close my eyes and feel Heather's hand on my arm squeezing, relaxing, squeezing. Then I would open my eyes and see Megan on my lap, feel her squeezing, relaxing, squeezing. The cycle reminded me that I was supposed to follow the male mantras of free love, multiple-partner, and never-make-close-ties-to-a-chick. That I was a man and men are supposed to be creatures of overwhelming temptation, shameless excuses, and no remorse. That I was supposed to grow a pair.

That night, I learned that emotions are more powerful than the mind, more powerful than the libido, more powerful than sanity. I learned that I wear my heart on my sleeve, and when I drink, I flaunt it like a cheap whore flaunting her sagging flesh. I learned that if I were ever going to remove the pain, the emptiness I was feeling for Heather, I had to become that creature.

And so, by candlelight, with a pole-dancer's head in my lap, I grew a pair. And I began to learn the art of burying my emotions with physical gratification.

Many years later, I learned another bore witness to my transformation. That night at the party, Peter Carter saw it all. He always saw it all. Sometimes through his eyes, often through the eyes of others when he charmed them out of whatever secrets they held. In this case it was, in a moment of weakness and alcohol, Heather.

He told me all of this, later. The night of my bachelor party. After the police left and …

Thursday — The Bachelor Party

After a moment, Peter blinks a few times, and then says, "Would you boys kindly point those flashlights elsewhere?"

The flashlights pull away. Peter talks, spins his yarns, confuses, enthralls. Within minutes, there's an all-points bulletin for three non-descript guys wearing hooded sweatshirts and ski masks. It's May, so the chances of anyone wearing such apparel are slim to none, and if someone is, he should probably be hauled away for troubling stupidity.

Just as the officers are leaving, tensions threaten to flare up again when Ian Carter blows out of the back door saying, "I just heard you punched my brother like a fucking coward?"

He moves at me fast. I blink, prepare for the punch I know is coming, and decide this time I'll remain lying where I fall. Then Peter's in front of me, holding Ian back, telling him to be cool and to shut up.

Ian doesn't listen. He says, "Peter sets this shit up for you and this is how you treat him? You ungrateful son-of-a —"

Peter hits Ian. Not hard, just enough to silence him.

The officers look to one another, then to Peter, who says, "My brother's a bit retarded. An autoerotic asphyxiation accident. Very sad."

After the officers leave, Jonesy leads Ian back into Damon's and the Imposter goes in search of an ice pack. Peter and I are alone. We're silent for a while, staring each other down, two guys who both know they're in the wrong but neither wanting to admit it.

Peter breaks. He sighs deeply, looks down the alley, at his feet. He pulls two cigars from his pocket, clips the end off each with a small cigar razor, and hands me one. As we light them up, I wonder what men did before the cultivation of tobacco when they wanted to signify the discovery of common ground.

I look past the Zippo's flame, the puffed smoke, and see a vacant look in Peter's eyes. I wonder if one of my puny blows knocked something loose inside his head. The future flashes: One heartbeat, two, Peter collapses. I try to catch him, fail. I kneel, begin CPR, and curse every television show for making it look so easy. Then the crowd is there and I'm pushed aside. Sirens wail. EMTs place Peter on a stretcher as they continue to pump his chest. They lift him to the ambulance, shut the doors and roll away toward the hospital. I see them pull the paddles out, charge them, and attempt to shock his heart back to beating. I'm alone. On my knees, watching the blue and red lights on the alley walls fade away.

The Zippo clinks, the flash ends. A chill runs over my soul and I know that we're not leaving any time soon. The Imposter returns with the ice.

Peter Carter begins to talk.

He says, "I saw you with Heather the night of The Heaven and Hell party." He looks down, slowly exhaling a mouthful of smoke, the light from the backdoor giving it depth. "You were out on the patio talking, getting close. I knew who she was because Hillary asked me to look out for her. And … And when I saw you two, I wanted to tell you who she was, what you were stepping into, what to expect. But then I saw …" he emits a silent laugh, hollow, but full of effort, his chest and shoulders moving with it, "I saw how happy she made you, and I couldn't. I tried. I made it to the patio doorway but, was about to step out and —

(and burst that oh-so-addictive bubble)

"— then Heather put her hand on your arm, and … And I just couldn't."

He's pacing now, slowly, half in and out of the light. With each step, I hear the soft scraping of leather to rock to asphalt. He says, "Later, I told myself. I'll tell him later. After the party. Let him have some more fun. Let him enjoy this. Let him feel this."

When he pauses, I realize something: this isn't the actor, or even the misdirection Peter Carter. He's raw, as if he's been flayed open and his life is spilling to our feet. He doesn't look at me when he speaks. Not at me, not at the Imposter holding the ice to my face and allowing me to lean back into her warmth. But we hear every spoken word because we're meant to hear them. *I'm* meant to hear them.

He says, "I forgot about it until I saw you upstairs with Megan. That's when I knew that you knew they were sisters … Because if you didn't, you never would have allowed Megan to go down on you. All I had to do was look in your eyes. You were empty. You had a hot-assed blond working on you and you were empty."

He's nearly whispering. Every so often, a car alarm, a drunken shout, an ambulance's wail, intrudes. Each time he pauses, waits it out. Because we're an audience, but not an Audience. We aren't detached as if watching a movie. It's the real Peter Carter, but at the same time, it's not. It's the Almighty Oz behind his black-as-night velvet curtain, but at the same time, it's not.

He says, "What was there to say? 'Oh, yeah, Davis. I meant to tell you about the whole sister thing. Save you the trouble.' And sure, I could have asked how you were holdin' up, if you wanted to get things off your chest, but I'm not that guy.

"It was your thing to deal with, and if you wanted to bitch to me, you would. But you didn't. You talked to Jonesy, to Divan. Never to me. But hey," he's louder now, voice cracking, "I'm Peter Carter, the great fucking friend everyone loves, who's always there to make people forget about their shit! God forbid if we tell him anything!

"But ya know what? In the end? I knew every fucking thing that was happening with everyone, and I wasn't going to be a fucking girl and get upset that I wasn't let in."

He stops to catch his breath, to cough. When he continues, he's back to the cracking near-whisper. He says, "If there was a reason someone didn't want to tell me about something, I fucking respected it. Even if there wasn't a reason, I fucking respected it. But I knew. I wasn't there to fix things, I was there to put a band-aid on things. Parties, women, booze. Not a cure. A cover.

"It was a year and a half later when Heather talked to me about it. My junior year, your sophomore. It was just after your weekend with Hillary and her friends in Winter Park —

(just before Hillary dropped out of school to follow her urges to take her clothes off in as many settings as she could)

"— and from what I heard, wow, dude." He looks at me with a crooked, shit-eating leer, his hands open at his sides. For a moment, the Friday Night Club Peter Carter is fired up, a glowing force in the alley illuminating everything within sight. "That big sex fest sounded impressive, even for my standards."

He holds this for a moment, looking at me, waiting for me to say something about how crazy things were and how much I enjoyed it, waiting for me to toss more wood into his fire to keep it stoked.

But I don't. His smile slowly ebbs, the light fading to an ember of its former self. He resumes pacing.

"I found it odd that Heather came to me. She said she didn't have anyone to turn to for advice, for guidance, for a soundboard. I didn't understand why until later."

He pauses, brings his hand to his forehead, then turns on me quickly and says, "Did you know she didn't want to go on the trip? She only relented to make Hillary happy. Hillary who just wanted to make sure her little sister's college experience was a good one. A loving fucking sister. How could Heather say no? Even though she knew you were going to be there, how could she say no?

"It took her two shots of vodka and a paper bag to put a smile on when you walked through that lodge door. And yet, there she —

(she was glowing and looking perfect and I wanted to go to her right then and there and forget about everything and everyone)

"— was, prepared for it. She put on the mask, the happy smile, as if nothing had happened. Did you know she didn't participate in any of the sex that weekend? A little kissing, a little fondling. She drew a line. But she saw that you didn't. She saw that you could lock away your feelings for her —"

(all I did was feel for her)

"— and have at it. Dear God, man! She was right in front of you! Drinking from a bottle of vodka, she watched you fuck her sister all night long! Not ten feet away. How the fuck you didn't see her watching, I haven't a clue. But ya know what? A part of me was impressed. A part of me said, 'Holy shit. Davis is compartmentalizing and enjoying life even if things in life aren't perfect.' Not many people can do that shit, and it's a survival technique that has saved my ass more than once.

"So, when Heather returned from the trip, she came to see me. She said I was the bridge between Hillary and you, and she felt I was the guy who would understand. The guy who, and I'll never forget these words, 'may aid her in understanding what she was feeling,' because it was all new to her and she was terrified."

Then Peter tells me why she came to see him. Why she came to talk to him about this instead of someone else. And when he speaks, I realize that I've gone numb. The anger is there, but it's encased within a cold tomb.

Not a cold cure. A cold cover.

Despite this, I know what he's about to tell me and I can feel the heat of the anger rise up.

He says, "Heather tried to lock away her feelings, to be an adult and face reality without the heartthrobs of a child. But when you walked through the door, the lock sprung and those emotions popped out like a fucking jack-in-the-box. They startled her, scared her, and caused her to want to run both to and away from you.

"That's when she grabbed the vodka again and just started drinking. She watched you two, the emotions welling up inside of her, and even then, she couldn't stop feeling for you. Your dick was inside her sister, and she still loved you.

"So, she came to me for help. Help to understand. Help to get strong. Help to learn how to turn off the emotions.

"'How do you do it?' she asked. 'How are you able to keep everything inside and locked away?' I told her that she didn't want to know. She insisted she did. She told me that this was tearing her up and she 'needed to find something that would stop it all.' How could I say no?

"I told her how I did it. She was quiet for a long time. She pondered, wondering if it would work, wanting it to work, because anything was better than what she was feeling. She said, 'I want to try.' I told her, 'No.' And then she said, 'You don't have a choice in the matter.'"

And then she jumped him.

I want to kill Peter Carter. I want to take his head and drive it into the asphalt and see his blood and brains and soul spattered over the ground and the walls and the fucking bumper sticker on the dumpster and I want to scream out that it was me, a lowly history professor who took him down, who killed him, who ended his reign of terror upon the world.

But I don't. Not because of a fear of societal retribution or physical pain in familial revenge, but because I know that no matter how much I don't want to believe Heather came to him, talked to him, bedded him, I see absolutely no reason for him to lie to me. Because everything he told her, about the way he lives his life, about the way he deals with his emotions, is the God's awful truth. He confuses the emotions and redirects them. He cons them.

And Heather said, why the fuck not?

To his credit, he tells me that he told her no. In the alley, tears streaming down his face, he tells me that he put up a fight.

He says, "I mean, shit. Even as she was undressing me — *she* was undressing *me* for Christ's sake — I was trying to pull away. It was one of the hardest fucking things I've ever done, but I was determined not to let it happen. Anyone else, fucking bring it on. But, this was the girl Davis loved. This was the girl who loved him. And I couldn't bring myself to touch this girl. Even if she was attacking me for God's sake ... but then she unbuttoned her shirt and slipped off her bra and I saw her —"

"Bastard," says the Imposter. "You fucking bastard."

Peter looks at her, blinking, as if trying to figure out when she arrived.

She says, "You're a lying ... cocksucking ... bastard!" She stands, advances on Peter, wanting to lay into him. But as her face reddens, her will to yell fades, and she's left looking at him with sad, angry eyes. She laughs a small laugh and shakes her head. Then she turns, kisses me on the cheek, and whispers, "I'll be inside, waiting for you."

The way she says it, I know I can get anything I want from her that night. And the way she softly brushes her lips against my ear causes me to want to take her up on the offer.

Then she is gone. Inside. Leaving only me and Peter in the alley. And then it's only Peter in the alley.

I've entered Damon's without a word to him.

CHAPTER EIGHT

People are fucked up. They react to things in a way you'll never expect or comprehend. Take our return to the restaurant. One might think they'd react with concern or apprehension after they see the blood, smelled the garbage. Maybe that'd put a damper on the evening. 'Sorry, gents. Flesh and drink are one thing, but police and fists cross the line. Enjoy the clink, and we'll see you at the wedding.'

But no.

We step back into Damon's and they cheer as if we're war heroes returning from a grueling campaign on the front. We manage to smile. We manage to laugh. We manage to look past the pain and resume enjoying the night. But none of it changes the fact that I'll run Peter over with an ice-cream truck if the chance presents itself.

It's like Mardi Gras, except all of the women are already naked and no one has to worry about the cops telling them to keep things moving. Music, beads, confetti, flesh, booze, a disco ball, floor thumping ... Damon's has been transformed into a naked nightclub for us and only us.

I swap out my garbage-stained shirt for a waiter's coat, and quickly get to drinking. I learn the Imposter is a few months shy of a paramedic degree, dancing to supplement her income. She splints up my finger with some packing tape and two spoons, and bandages Peter's swollen, shamed, but unbroken nose with a Maxi pad.

The questions come. We tell them what they want to hear. Mostly Peter does. The stories he spins are a bit larger than life, but they do the job.

A cover, not a cure.

We put on the masks as if we're still the best of friends. We talk to each other, laugh with each other. But if you look closely, you'd guess Peter was just some guy who happened upon the bachelor party. Amazing how years can be erased in moments.

Jonesy says, "How's the finger?"

"Terrible. It's my pickin' finger."

"At least you have another."

"It's not the same. I have to think about it now. The positioning, the angle. Before, it was second nature. Like meeting an old friend. But now ..."

"You consider hiring a professional?"

"Sure, but what happens when I heal? A professional nose picker to self picking?"

"So, you'll suffer then?"

I sigh. "Alas."

He nods toward the Imposter. "Maybe you spoil yourself for one night."

We're silent, looking at the Imposter nearby, her dark brown hair released from the confines of the up-do, now framing her face.

"You get things settled?" Jonesy says.

His tone catches me off guard. I blink, glance down, and then my eyes widen as memories fall into place like pieces of a puzzle.

I look at Jonesy, say, "You knew?"

He nods in a manner that tells me that he has known all along. I want to crack his fucking nose for his deception.

Jonesy sees the anger rise within my cold tomb and says, "Would it have helped? Would it have changed things?"

"And you're the one to decide this for me?"

"If I'd told you, then you'd never have gone to Peter's wedding, you'd never have met Pamela, and you wouldn't be getting married in two days."

"Amazing gift of foresight, Adam. You only use this power for good?"

Silence again.

Then he says, "The day I found out, your pop went into the hospital."

I think back to my junior year, to the day I got the page that my pop had taken a turn for the worse. "The James?"

Jonesy nods. "St. Patrick's Day."

I say, "Fuck me."

Junior Year — St. Patrick's Day

It was a Sunday morning when my pop started feeling bad. His stomach was tight, he said. Probably just something he ate, he said. I think you should get it checked out, I said. And, on Wednesday, after three days of enduring the pain, he did.

At 3:00 that afternoon, we knew it had returned. He'd been in remission for nine months, but cancer is the nasty uncle who always shows up at your door with a crack-whore nineteen-year-old wife looking for a place to crash.

St. Patrick's Day was an all-day affair at The James. One-dollar green beer. One-dollar shots of Irish whiskey. Women wearing green bikini tops got half-price drinks. Girls wearing a green thong drank free.

But this St. Patrick's Day wasn't just a holiday, it was a pre-sendoff. Peter was graduating in a month and already packing his bags for Los Angeles. The end of an era. Many a shot was toasted. Many a woman absconded with Peter for their fifteen minutes of goodbye.

The turnout was extraordinary. That night, The James cleared more money than ever before. Not yet a movie star and the masses were already shelling out the dough to see him.

I missed most of it.

I began carrying a pager after my pop's first round with the disease, and it buzzed on the waning side of noon. I set my third beer on the bar, drove to Rose Medical Center in Denver, and spent the next fifteen hours in the hospital room as they ran test after test after test after …

"What are you doing here?" he said.

"Funny," I said.

"I try, but it just gets harder and harder every day."

"So, what god did you piss off this time?"

"Don't know. All of them, I think." Most of his dark red hair was already gone from the chemo, the only remaining tuft sat at the front of his head. To keep his (my) spirits up, I used to put a pink ribbon in it when he was sleeping and wait to see how long before he noticed. He said, "Is that beer I smell?"

"I'm here, aren't I?"

"The last thing I need on my mind as I go out is that you died coming to see me off."

"Fuck off, old man. You're not going anywhere."

"I must have screwed up somewhere, if my son tells me to fuck off as I lay dying." After a moment of silence, he said. "Oh, come on. Don't clam up on me now."

I said, "It's back, isn't it?"

"Look, I don't want you to worry."

"Don't tell me not to worry. Don't ever tell me not to —"

"Then can you at least hide it better? You're sorta freaking me out here."

I managed a weak smile. "I must have screwed up somewhere, if my father starts to say 'freaking out'."

"Better. Much better. Keep that up."

"Sir, yes, sir. So, how bad is it?"

"Eh. You know cancer. It's like the mafia. Never satisfied with just —"

"Pop."

"It's bad."

"How bad?"

"Stomach, intestines ..."

"Operable?"

"I'm not sure there's much left to operate on."

"What about chemo? There has to be something. What about trials? We can get you into a study that is cutting edge and ... Why are you laughing?"

"Because, because I can. Because it's never ending, and it's only going to delay things, and, my lord, it feels good. So damn good." He sighed, took a deep breath, held it, sighed again. "Ya know? I love this feeling. Because finally, when I know there's nothing that can be done, I feel relief. I feel lighter than I have in five years. Five years. Wow! The slowest five years of my life. Every day, looking forward to a good day. Not wanting to go to sleep each night because I didn't want to wake up to a bad day. I never told you this — never told anyone this — but those bad days ... There were points when I didn't think I could go on. I never really considered the alternative, but I came so damn close at times. The pain. The nausea. But now ... Now that I know I can't fight anymore ..."

I said, "You're not giving up on me."

"Don't look at me that way, Davis. I'm still your father."

"You're certainly not acting like —"

"Have you known me to give up on anything before in my life, young man?"

I paused, said, "First time for everything."

He sighed again, this time without a smile. He said, "Yes. Yes, there is, and if it means I don't have to go though another five years of wanting it to be over, then I'll gladly do it."

"Stop being so fucking selfish!"

He looked up at me from that fucking hospital bed, and for the first time I allowed myself to see what he looked like now, instead of what I remember him looking like before the shit-storm hit Casa Robertson. He was a crust of his former self. Skin covered in liver spots drooping over itself, once athletic shoulders now folds of flesh hanging from bone. I marveled that his frail and shrunken body could support the weight of his head. But all that ... all that I could deal with. What I couldn't take was the look of pain in his deep brown eyes. A weighty pain. A full pain. A pain that cuts through the layers and betrays the secrets of your soul.

I froze. I understood. I nodded. I held his hand. We talked. We cried.

Seven hours later, Peter Carter was dancing on the bar with Kathy. Adam Jones was making out with some random girl in the ladies room. Thomas Divan was collecting money he just made in a foosball game. I was crying my eyes out in the hospital bathroom. And my pop was having a stroke.

He died the following morning.

An hour after the stroke, Peter found Jonesy in the ladies room and said, "We need to talk."

Jonesy said, "Okay, later."

"No okay later. Okay, now."

"Later."

"Now."

Jonesy pulled his tongue from the redhead, turned to Peter, said, "Now?"

Peter nodded.

"A little bit busy?"

Peter shook his head.

"A more convenient time?"

Peter said, "If I don't tell you this now, my head will explode and you and the girl will be covered in bits of skull, scalp, and grey matter."

The girl and Jonesy looked at each other and agreed that Peter had destroyed the mood. She left.

"So," said Jonesy, trying to act nonchalant as he sat on the toilet in the ladies room. "What gives?"

Peter lit a cigarette with shaking fingers. "I fucked up."

Jonesy was on his feet and alert. "Where are they? How many? Did they see you come in here?"

He was moving to the door when Peter said, "I slept with Heather."

Jonesy looked back at him. "When?"

"About a year ago."

"About a year ago?"

"Give or take a few months."

"Jesus!"

"I think he knows."

"Jesus?"

"Him too."

Jonesy said, "Fuck, fuck, fuck, fuck! What the hell were you thinking?"

"I wasn't."

"Apparently!"

"No, I mean, I wasn't thinking at all about it. She jumped me."

"Who do you think you're talking to?"

"Seriously, Jonesy. She wanted to know how I kept myself emotionally removed from reality."

"And you showed her."

"No, I told her. I told her how I did it, and she jumped me."

Jonesy reached out and slapped Peter upside his head. "You fucking jackass!"

Peter closed his eyes and said, "I know. I know."

"I don't think you do. Davis is barely hanging on right now."

"So, he does know?"

Jonesy stopped pacing and balked. "You're kidding me, right? Do you even know where he is? Do you even know he's gone?"

"He's gone?"

Then Jonesy told him where I was.

"Aw, shit," Peter said.

"Yeah, 'Aw, shit' is right. You're a real fucking piece of work. Ya know that?"

Peter said, "Look, I know I fucked up, but I didn't know a thing about his dad."

"Not today, but you knew. You knew he was sick. You knew he was struggling."

"And I helped by keeping his mind busy."

"By fucking Heather?"

"She. Jumped. Me."

"Tell that to someone who doesn't know you!"

Peter looked at —

Thursday — Bachelor Party

"— me and I knew he was telling the truth," Jonesy says, "I knew he didn't plan it. And I knew he truly felt sorry. I know that doesn't mean much, and it shouldn't mean much, but it's something that I knew he felt and it's something you need to know."

I'm quiet, watching the party in front of me, but not seeing it.

He says, "And when we heard about your dad ..."

I nod then, not wanting to talk. I'm still pissed off at Peter for fucking Heather and at Jonesy for knowing all these years and never telling me. But what really chaps me is I can see why Jonesy didn't tell me. Because were I in his shoes, I would have done the same thing. And I fucking hate myself for it.

And then I realize something.

"Wait," I say. "He told you on St Patrick's Day?"

He nods. Soon, I understand. My eyes widen.

Jonesy says, "And now you know."

I say, "Fuck me."

He says, "Things happened so fast between St. Patrick's Day and his wedding that I just lost it. Peter was being a hypocritical asshole for saying he's found the 'one' and then getting married six months after almost killing you in Vegas and a year after fucking Heather."

I say, "And all this time you've been pissed at him?"

"This surprises you?"

"Well, sort of. I just didn't think it had anything to do with me."

He shrugs. "You're my brother."

"And the Allosaurus?"

"Oh, I'm still pissed at the Allosaurus."

Jonesy continues to talk, but I don't hear him. I'm mentally sorting and reorganizing lest the looming mounds of crap topple, sending my rage into action.

As I do this, I drink. I take a bottle of whatever is closest and drink. I become *that* guy.

Things begin to accelerate. The world cuts to time-and-a-half speed. The more I drink, the faster the world rushes.

What a great way to flee reality.

Fast Forward — First Gear

The Imposter makes sure I have the time of my life. Not only is she all over me, but she makes it a point of making sure all the other girls act accordingly. In contrast, she tells every girl that Peter slept with the love of my life — most assume the love of my life is my fiancée — and she ensures they cut Peter off.

As the girls rub, grab, nibble, and lick me, they marvel I'm not beating Peter to a bloody pulp. Peter plays along, smiles, acts as if he doesn't notice his shunning. Peter Carter, banished to the backseat of our pathetic short bus.

Ian comes up, swaggering not from attitude but from drink. He says, "Hey, yo dude. I'm sorry, man, dude. You know, shit, man. I'm sorry. For earlier. I'm sorry, dude."

I say, "Ian, there isn't anything to apologize for."

"Yeah, dude, I know. But Peter made me come over."

Jonesy apologizes, too.

I say, "For what?"

"For not stopping Peter."

I hug Jonesy and give him the bottle I'm holding. He drinks. We nod.

"Fuck it," I say. "It's only life."

"Fuck it," he says.

Fast Forward — Second Gear

We're moving to the stretch SUV limo. As I fight the exiting throng, attempting to grab as many bottles as possible, I ask why we're leaving.

"The contract's over," someone says.

"Over?" I say. "What time is it?"

"Ten."

Ten. It's only *10:00*.

I clutch the bottles to my chest as a chill engulfs me. I say, "Someone's going to die tonight."

Someone replies, "Only if we're doing things right."

We load into the limo, and I realize the Imposter is serious about easing my pain with her tonic of endless lust and flesh. I find this disturbing since she tells Peter to shove his money up his ass. She's doing this on her own time.

This turns me off.

Were she on the clock, I'd be comfortable. But as she's a mere mortal, I'm a bit spooked. This falls into the category of wanting what you can't get, and not wanting what's offered. The jewel dulls when it's presented in gift rather than taken in guile.

Everyone's been there. Everyone's been in a relationship where you wonder where the magic went, the lust ran, the desire to connect vanished. When you no longer have to work for it, you lose your focus on the chase, the adventure, the anticipation and, in the end, the dance. Because I know I *can* get whatever I want from the Imposter, I want nothing to do with her.

To further complicate matters, I realize I'm bored with the strippers because I *can't* get them. They're just flesh-colored eye-candy. When you're sixteen, eye-candy is great. It's new and fun and real, and being teased is great because you don't yet understand how annoying and painful it can be.

Five years later, when you can enter a strip club whenever you want, you bore of shelling out money to get hot and bothered. You begin to wish you stayed home and whipped it out to porn. With porn, there may be no connection, no smell, no touch, but you also have no teasing, and no empty wallet.

This is how I become bored at my own bachelor party. I still have fun, drinking and laughing. But I tire of the Imposter's advances, and I tire of the surrounding flesh. How pathetic am I?

Our next destination is the high-class Gentlemen's Club, The Diamond Cabaret. Outside, his arm around my shoulders, Jonesy says, "For my friend Davis? The best Denver has to offer!"

He has no idea that until three months ago, Hillary danced here as she finished massage-therapy school. Yet, he chooses the one place that connects me to her, to my single life, to my running from Pamela.

Coincidence blows.

Fast Forward — Third Gear

Shots.

Laughter.

Lap dances.

The bartender, a short woman with a cross around her neck who looks as if she belongs on the cover of a muscle-car mag, looks at me and says, "Do I know you?"

I attempt to place her blurry features within the context of my life, and shake my head. She shrugs, I shrug. She smiles, I smile. She goes back to slinging drinks, I go back to ogling women.

Fast Forward — Forth Gear

Shots.

I'm brought on stage and five strippers rub their breasts all over me.

Fast Forward — Downshift To Third

I run to the bathroom to pee and realize that I need to empty my stomach if I'm going to keep the night going. I understand the Romans more than I ever will again.

Fast Forward — Forth Gear

There's a point in every bachelor party when you question why you're sacrificing the single life, why you're allowing yourself to be trapped and cornered.

For me, this happens in reverse. For me, this point is filled with a love for Pamela that I haven't felt in years.

I blame this on the Imposter and the strippers. They've created the middle ground between a lack of challenge and unattainable flesh, and my emotions need to affix to something. This something happens to be Pamela.

The bubble forms during the second song in a set of three paid for by Max Richards. I'm in the same back booth I sat in when I told Hillary we weren't going to sleep together. The stripper's named Val. Not her real name, changed for her protection. Like she's a secret agent. Nothing about her is the truth. Not her name, not her background, not her body. Well, maybe her body. But she's in the minority. I know this. She knows this. We both know that the other knows this. We both know the other doesn't care. Because when the bubble forms and I'm talking about Pamela, Val the Stripper finds it refreshing that I'm not trying to paw her non-surgically enhanced wares.

She also finds it refreshing that I'm here with the Imposter because to everyone but me, she's a Goddess. For some reason, it makes me safe. A guy alone in a strip club? You haven't a clue if he's a creep who cleans up really nice or just a really nice guy. But a guy with a Goddess on his arm says you're safe, or you have lots of money. Because a Goddess wouldn't hang around with just any guy. A woman this beautiful can take her pick of the litter.

I tell Val my name is Sean. If she can be a secret agent, why can't I? The Imposter doesn't contradict me. She smiles, but not at me. She smiles at Val in a way that lets me know she swings both ways, and suddenly the middle ground looks more appealing. I quickly realize that in order for Val the Stripper and the Imposter to hook up, in order for me to join in this perfect bachelor party fantasy, I have to keep talking about Pamela.

Life is fucked up.

Fast Forward — Fifth Gear

For the third song, Val the Stripper dances for the Imposter. When the fourth starts, I learn the next nine are already covered.

I love my friends.

Val dances for me, rubs her naked flesh in all the right places. I babble about Pamela. Val grinds back into my crotch.

Then we enter the surreal.

Val: So, Sean ... What do you love about her the most?

Me: That she puts up with me. I'm not an easy guy to put up with.

Val: Everyone thinks they're hard to put up with.

Me: No, really. I'm set in my ways, and somehow, she's able to look past them and still care for me.

Val: Impressive.

Me: I mean, in the past six months, I'm sure I've freaked her out. I've been distant, combative.

Val: Sounds like a happy home.

Me: And yet she's still there.

Val: This, too, shall pass.

Me: What?

Val: This, too, shall pass. King Solomon wanted a ring of magical power. One that made happy men sad and sad men happy. He knew such a ring didn't exist, but he wanted to show up his minister, I don't remember the reason, and sent him out to find this ring. The minister searched all around and finally asked an old merchant if he'd ever heard of such a ring. The merchant thought about it, then took a basic ring, engraved something inside, and gave it to the minister. The minister returned to Solomon, and gave him the ring. Solomon's face lit up in excitement. "You found it!" he said. Then he read the engraving. His excitement faded into depression. It read: This, too, shall pass.

Me: Why again are you a stripper?

Val: Why does anyone do what they do? Because they enjoy it? Because they need to do it? Because it's all they can do?

Me: What's your reason?

Val: Life is too short to discard the things you've always wondered about.

Me: You're taking your clothes off because you wanted to know what it was like?

Val: Good a reason as any.

And her hand presses into my crotch, squeezes, releases.

Leave it to me to find the one biblical scholar who moonlights as an exotic dancer.

Fast Forward — Redlining

Whatever is happening, all three of us could feel it. This, too, shall pass. But we can hold onto it for a while. See where it takes us.

We're in the shadows. Visible, but only in form, only in outline. Val and the Imposter are on either side of me, both rubbing against me, both beginning to fondle each other.

I'm watching, a bit wide-eyed, like a kid opening his dad's *Playboy* for the first time. Both girls giggle at my ogling, but neither stops. No, instead, it just pushes them to skirt the line, tease it, and then cross into the unknown.

Val leans into me, reaches past, and pulls the Imposter into a long, passionate kiss. Then they break to kiss me. One of them begins unbuttoning my shirt while the other kisses down my neck and chest. Val crawls between the Imposter and me. She faces us, straddling my left leg and the Imposter's right. Our outlines entwine. As she continues kissing the Imposter, Val unbuckles my belt, unbuttons my pants. A warm hand reaches past the waistband of my boxers. Val whispers something about a secluded back room with a couch. I smile in anticipation. The Imposter doesn't wait. She pulls Val off me, into a kiss, a neck bite. She slips her hand between Val's legs.

And then Ian fucks it all up.

The guys think I'm getting lucky. Not sex, but maybe my last morally legal hand job before I say, 'I Do.' But Ian wants facts, not assumptions. When he nears, he's so focused on what Val and the Imposter *aren't* doing to me, that he completely misses what they *are* doing to each other.

I make a mental note to kick him in the schnutz later.

Ian says, "What do you think you're doing?"

I don't look up at him when I say, "Ian, leave, now." When he doesn't respond, I repeat myself. Only then do I look up and see he's staring at Val with contempt in his eyes, his lip curled.

With the nonchalance of a monarch, Val pulls away from the Imposter and says, "Go."

And the way she says it, with such confidence and raw power, Ian's sneer drops and he actually leaves.

Val smiles wickedly, begins kissing the Imposter again, begins sliding her hand past my unbuckled belt and unbuttoned pants.

I close my eyes, inhale deeply, and hear Ian say, "What the fuck did you say to me?"

This time, Val takes a different approach. She turns, bats her long eyelashes at him, and says with a slight pout, "I'm sorry. Did you want something?"

Ian says, "Yeah, I want to know what the fuck you're *not* doing to my friend here."

Like a cat in a sunbeam, Val reaches up and stretches, her tight body twisting seductively, and says, "Why, Ian. We're just talking. What do you think you're doing?" Part biblical scholar, part exotic dancer, all attitude.

Ian says, "I'm here to make sure you do your job."

She pulls into another stretch, this time her left breast is inches from my face and says, "I don't think you're aware of what you're about to do."

"Oh, I know I am."

I'm about to say something when Val ends her stretching and puts her hand on my crotch. Not on my arm. Not on my leg. On the bulge in my pants. I don't say a word.

"No," she says to Ian, no longer pouting. "If you knew what you were about to do, you'd have thought about what would happen to you if you did what you're about to do and you'd have realized that by doing what you want to do would be acting without thinking thereby doing what you know you don't want to do but thinking you're doing what you want to do when you really know you don't want to do it."

Ian's chin is almost on his chest, his gaze still on her, and at any moment he's surely going to start drooling like an idiot. But Val doesn't stop. "So, what I would suggest is you rethink doing what you think you know you want to do before you act on what you want to do because when you think about what you're about to do you'll realize that you don't want to do whatever it is you were planning on doing in the first place."

Ian blinks a few times, then raises his finger, but pauses as he's unsure if he wishes to make the point he thinks he was sure he was going to make.

But, in proof positive that the alcohol in the male veins trumps all wisdom ever born in the male mind, he plows through every verbal and cerebral barricade Val the Stripper has constructed and says, "First off, if you don't want to do your job … In conclusion … Davis? We're finding you a different girl."

As he pulls me to a stand, I say, "Ian, you don't know what you're —"

"Davis?" Says Val, her forehead wrinkling.

Ian looks at me. I curse, look at Val, and say, "I'm sorry, I was never cut out for this Secret Agent gig. Hi, I'm Davis." I hold out my hand, but she isn't paying attention.

She says, "Your name isn't Sean?" Her confusion becomes anger. Her brow wrinkles, the muscles in her jaw begin to dance. She says, "Holy shit," as if her sudden revelation was in front of her all along. "I can't believe I didn't see it before."

"See what before?" I glance to the Imposter. She, too, feels the tension, the confusion.

Then Val pops to a stand and says, "You've got to leave."

Ian says, "Now, hold on there. You can't just take your money and —"

"I'm not joking," Val says to me. "You need to get out of here now, before they find out."

She's pulling me, trying to be nonchalant, trying to keep things low key, but the louder Ian protests, the more people turn in our direction.

Val says, "This is bad, this is really bad."

I say, "Please define this term, really bad."

Then a voice behind us says, "Well, fuck my lord with a dildo. I knew I'd seen you before." It's the Stripper Bartender with the cross around her neck. And she isn't smiling. "You're Davis Robertson. You're the one who fucked over Hillary."

Crash

What happens next catches me completely off guard because with my *extremely* blurred, *extremely* intoxicated, *extremely* inaccurate vision I'm now seeing double, triple, even …

The Blond with the rose tattoo on her ankle looks at me as the patron she's grinding says, "Don't stop, baby."

The Redhead with the ridiculously fake breasts nearly trips as she passes, catches herself, and then shoots daggers in my direction.

The Dishwater Blond with hair past her ass seems to materialize in front of me and says, "You soulless bastard."

In this moment, I realize the Stripper Bartender with the cross around her neck is an agent for a God of Wrath and Vengeance. It's the only way I can see why she hasn't been smote by heavenly flame, that whole 'lord being fucked with a dildo' tending to piss off the Almighty. But not with the Stripper Bartender. She's been sent to punish me, Davis Robertson. Unreligious heathen who has probably committed every sin aside from murder, but there were nights when I nearly drank myself to death and I'm sure that's close enough for government work.

Yes, in this moment, I'm sure I'm going to die.

CHAPTER NINE

Friday Morning - Denver County Jail

I walk to the phone, at 3:32 a.m., my shoulders on fire from alcohol and tension. I'm fucked, and not in a good way. In a way where one wonders what hole one should dig, what gun to put to one's head, what finger to pull the trigger.

I'm not going to be able to talk my way out of this one. I'm not going to be able to put on a smile and charm my way to normalcy. Normalcy. I laugh. It's *finally* hitting me that my life wasn't normal before all the shit went down, and it's going down faster than a woman who's just received diamonds when she wanted pearls and expected nothing.

But what really starts to jab at me is that I'd thought my life was actually ordinary. My struggles. My excuses. My fucking around. I had truly believed that my actions and justifications were run-of-the-mill.

Now, confronted with the possibility of everything falling apart, I realize how close I've been to exposure, to everything collapsing. I realize how brazen I've become. Confidence begat cockiness which begat chaos. And the worst part is that Pamela will be hurt. For some ungodly reason, I never before considered her feelings. Now, faced with her discovering everything, I know that my actions will possibly destroy her.

Another time, another place, she may have been able to handle it. Sure, she'd have been hurt but she'd have been able to dive into her work and deal with it on her own time. But there's the wedding, the guests, the eyes of the world that will most certainly push her past any ability to forgive. Cheating is one thing, but to find out two days before your wedding? And to find out in the manner in which it all played out?

Later, at —

The Denver Diner

— on the corner of Colfax and Speer, after Donald bails us out, Peter in a Denver Police Department ball cap and a pair of Denver Police Department gold-rimmed sunglasses, we exchange notes. Well, the others do. I sit back and stew as they tell their stories. What happened to each of them in those small rooms without windows but each with a big fucking mirror that causes your skin to crawl inside your stomach to escape the attention. That's what the interrogation room does. It turns people into living Stephen King ghouls.

Jonesy's Tale

"Just start anywhere," said the cop.

"The beginning?"

"Sure. The beginning of the fight."

"I didn't see the beginning of the fight."

"What did you see?"

"I only saw what happened after."

"Then start from there."

"All right. I was sitting in a chair, talking to Max Richards about his latest project. Peter was going to —"

"Peter Carter?"

"Yeah. He was making sure that Max was attached to the musical he's about to sign. *Back to the Future*."

"The movie?"

"No, the musical. Broadway. New York City. The whole bit. I was talking to Max about it when it seemed as if all of the women in the club were looking at the same thing."

"At Davis Robertson."

"I turned just after the bartender hit him."

"So you didn't see *her* hit *him*."

"Not the punch, but I saw the blood."

Peter's Tale

"So, you saw it all?" said the cop.

"Hell, yeah. I saw the whole fucking thing. She hit Davis. He recoiled. And then I saw the strippers move toward him."

Jonesy's Tale

"It was eerie. Suddenly the place was filled with strippers, all looking at Davis."

"How many, would you say?"

"Twenty-five, maybe."

"That's not possible."

"You saw it."

"I don't believe that twenty-five strippers went for your friend."

"You calling me a liar?"

"I didn't say that."

"Then what are you saying?"

"There were only eleven girls on the clock."

"Well, shit. Maybe they split like single-celled organisms, I don't know. All I know is that they came from everywhere and went for Davis."

"And that's when you went to help Mr. Robertson?"

"No. That's when the bouncer ran past me and I kicked an empty chair in his way."

Peter's Tale

"I don't know how long it took me to get to Davis. It seemed like a second. I'm sure it took longer, but in the moment, I swear, I felt like I was Wally West."

"Wally West?"

"Yeah. The Flash. But no tomato sauce."

"What?"

"Nevermind. I started to run, had to jump over the bouncer who rolled to the ground in front of me, and then I was there, between Davis and the bartender."

"And that's when you tackled her?"

"Yup. She was in mid swing with her second punch when I tackled her."

Ian's tale

"It was like — BOOM! Lightning fast! Peter hit her, they hit the ground. And then Peter stood, saw Davis, and he smiled."

Jonesy's Tale

"But not like a human smiles. It was like a dog smiling when it brings a newspaper to its master. As if he were saying, 'I did good, right?'"

Peter's Tale

"I mean ... fuck ... he's my brother. He's the only one who gives me unconditional support. Everyone else has an opinion and isn't afraid to voice it. But Davis is always by my side, even when he's pissed at me. So when I saw him get socked in the face by a psycho stripper, I just reacted."

Through My Eyes

In this moment, I realized the Stripper Bartender with the cross around her neck was an agent for a God of Wrath and Vengeance. It was the only way I could see why she hadn't been smote by heavenly flame, that whole 'lord being fucked with a dildo' tending to piss off the Almighty. But not this time. Not with the Stripper Bartender. She'd been sent to punish me, Davis Robertson. Unreligious heathen who had probably committed every sin aside from murder, but there were nights when I nearly drank myself to death and was sure that was close enough for government work.

Yes, in this moment, I was sure I was going to die.

Instead, I was punched.

The Stripper Bartender punched me square in the nose. With the pain, time continued to slow almost supernaturally. I processed the events around me.

The bouncer on the other side of the room, his head popping up, knowing something was wrong and searching for it.

Jonesy and Max Richards about twenty feet away, their necks snapping toward us when the punch echoed in a lull between songs.

Ian, next to me, stunned as he attempted to comprehend what he'd just witnessed.

As I wiped blood off my face, the second blow landed.

Not a punch, but something just as powerful.

As I wiped blood from my nose, the Imposter said, "Who's Hillary?"

The Imposter. The one woman in the evening who had stood by my side, no matter how many times I had pushed her away.

Reality kicked in. The Imposter was still dressed as Heather from the Halloween Party. When she spoke, it was Heather speaking. When she looked at me, it was Heather looking at me with anger and pain and a growing desire to wrap my scrotum over my head.

She asked. The strippers answered. They told her how I screwed Hillary over, led her on all these years, toyed with her emotions, and a bunch of other shit that I didn't think was true until I heard it aloud.

After it was done, the Imposter looked at me and said, "You and Peter deserve each other."

Then the strippers begin to approach en masse. That was when I almost wet myself because the moment was turning from a surreal vision to an unreal nightmare.

As Val tugged my arm, as Jonesy kicked a chair into the bouncer's path, as the Bartender Stripper pulled back to strike a second time, Peter ran from the side, punched the Bartender Stripper in the jaw, and tackled her to the ground.

The punch was what everyone leaves out of their statements to the police. Maybe by accident — maybe they didn't see it, for it happened so fast — but it did happen. Peter punched the Bartender Stripper in mid tackle, and had I blinked, I would have missed it completely.

Peter stood, smiled at me like an eight-year-old boy playing in the sandbox, and began to toss me a trademark Peter Carter line.

But nothing came out. Instead, his eyes softened, his brow wrinkled, and in the middle of chaos, he looked as if about to cry.

And I couldn't help but forgive him. Just like that.

I nodded, smiled.

He said, "Yeah?"

I said, "Yeah."

Then he was gang tackled by every stripper in the joint.

Peter's Tale

"It was surreal on Daliesque levels. I mean, shit. All these hot women wearing next to nothing on top of me? That they were pissed off just made it that much more exciting. The only thing missing was the hot baby oil and the melting elephants."

Ian's Tale

"There was grabbing, clawing, clothing flying everywhere … What I would have given for some hot baby oil."

Jonesy's Tale

"It began as pure tension, pure hatred. And I have no doubt these girls wanted to hurt Davis. But when Peter jumped into the mix, it took on a different air."

The Blond Stripper's Tale

"We jumped onto Peter Carter on instinct, but when we touched him … All throughout high school, it was him and Tom Cruise. I had pictures of them on my wall and dreamed about them in class. So when he took Jasmine down, we wanted to stand up for our own, ya know? But that all changed when we touched him … All I wanted was some hot baby oil."

Jonesy's Tale

"I ran up, started pulling the women off Peter, but then I saw the raw sexuality in their eyes …"

Ian's Tale

"It's just not fair … I've seen women melt at one smile from him, one wink, and that was in high school, before he honed his power. Can you imagine growing up with that shit? And I had to follow in that fucker's shoes? It's not fucking fair."

Through My Eyes

As we retreated, Val pulling me, my gaze turned to a gaggle of strippers not involved in the pileup. I recoiled as their anger, their hatred, so concentrated, so raw, locked onto me like heat-seeking missiles ready to fire at the twitch of a finger.

The finger twitched. They moved as one and I felt as if trapped in a George Romero film, but instead of a shopping mall, we were in a strip club, and mindless strippers played the roles of the brain-eating zombies.

Idly, I wondered if Peter would option the movie rights.

Jonesy's Tale

"I saw Davis disappear into a doorway and about six strippers gave chase. I grabbed Max Richards and we followed."

Through My Eyes

Through a door. Into a dressing room. Down a hallway. We neared an exit. Strippers cut off our escape. We retreated. Back to the dressing room. We barred the door.

I said, "What the hell is going on?" knowing how dumb and cliché I sounded, but still wanting to know.

Val said, "What did you expect? For three years, girls have been coming in and out of this place. And each of them, at some point or another, has heard of you and Hillary."

"You're fucking kidding me."

"You did a number on her, Davis."

"Hey, wait a second here," I said, mentality backpedaling away from the insanity. "Hillary's a big girl. She didn't have to be with me if she didn't want to."

Val stopped moving a couch against the door, looked at me, and said, "When you're in love, age is meaningless."

So there it was. The fucking L word.

Peter's Tale

"I was totally and completely dominated."

Ian's Tale

"Just a smile and they drop to their knees? It took me years to learn half of what he can do naturally, and even then, I fuck it up more often than not. It's just not fair."

Peter's Tale

"I was living every man's fantasy. In all my years in Hollywood, never had this happened to me. This was unplanned. This was animalistic. This … This was … I'm sorry, this is all rather emotional for me."

Jonesy's Tale

"The strippers were pounding on a locked door, but it wasn't normal pounding. It sounded like they were hitting the door with iron fists and the door was buckling with every blow. And then they all turned toward us. And I swear their eyes were glowing with white fire."

Through My Eyes

I stopped, looked at Val, and ignored the pounding on the door.

"In love? You've got to be kidding me," I repeated, not knowing what else to say.

"Okay. I'm kidding you."

"You're not kidding me."

"What do you want me to tell you, Davis? That these girls went nuts and wanted to rip out your lungs because your friend was rude? Past the cattiness, these girls bond. They care about each other. They become a family. And when one of them is scorned, we're all scorned."

I thought about saying this was all blown out of proportion, that I didn't deserve what was happening. Instead, I followed Val's gaze to a dressing table in the corner of the room.

Although smaller than the others, I could tell it was the one most in use. Some of the dressing tables were almost bare, with only a purse and some makeup. Some had pictures taped to the mirror, some had old bottles of hair gel and glitter lotion turned upside down to get the last remaining drops. The table in the corner had a history. A life.

And, it had pictures. Pictures of Hillary with me, on the ski trip, at the Friday Night Club. Other places and times that I didn't recognize, knowing that they weren't important enough to hold a memory for me, but they obviously were to her.

"I thought she quit," I said in a whisper.

Val told me about how every year, like clockwork, Hillary came back to dance.

She said, "This is her home away from home. No matter how long she's away, she's welcomed with love and open arms. She's the one who knows the business, the one who we all go to for advice, the big sister we've never had who will drop everything if we need help. She's been here the longest of all of us. She's the foundation of our family."

I plucked a photo from the mirror and attempted to place it in my past; to understand what this girl saw in me to make her hold on. After a while, I turned to Val and said, "Why aren't you trying to kill me like the others?"

Val shrugged. "Because I got to know you before I knew who you were. And I saw that there's a side to you that does care. Even though you're just a frightened little boy afraid to grow up. Even though you're just a coward."

And then the door burst open.

Jonesy's Tale

"One hissed, 'Leave.' I don't think I'd ever been so scared. But Max, God bless him, he was like Van Helsing advancing on Dracula's women — stone faced, strong. And they backed down. The strippers saw his resolve and parted, letting us get to the door. That's when we all heard a muffled explosion on the other side of the door. And then we heard the shouts."

Through My Eyes

The phone at the police station was warm and damp from ear and hand sweat. Its previous user had been crying like a television evangelist begging his parishioners for forgiveness after being caught with three hookers, a ball gag, and a strap-on dildo. I forced down a gag as I wiped it on my shirt.

But it was probably a good thing. The wet phone. The gagging. It forced me back into the present. It gave me time to think about my one phone call.

Three and a half hours after the Diamond Cabaret, three and a half hours after we were cuffed and hauled to the Denver County Jail, Donald, driving in his slippers, pajamas, and bathrobe, was quiet. He was quiet when he got the phone call an hour earlier. He was quiet when he dressed. And when my mother asked where he was going at 4:00 a.m., he said quietly, "I need salmon."

As we drove away from the Denver Police Station in my Honda Accord, Donald said, "I'm not going to ask what happened." But it was in his tone. The question. The desire to know why four drunk and bruised men needed to be bailed out. Subtle, almost imperceptible. If I didn't know he was a retired police officer, I probably would have missed it.

Peter said, "I attacked a stripper." Offering this tidbit as if it were the most normal thing in the world. Attacked a stripper. That was how everyone ends their evening. A hot bath, classical music, tackling a topless dancer, warm milk, bed.

I closed my eyes, wanting to be anywhere else but here. Wanting it to all go away. I took a deep breath, gathered my wits. This too shall pass. Just ride it out, and this too —

"Yeah," said Ian. "You really cracked her."

The Denver Diner

— on Speer and Colfax is at the tail end of bar rush. Getting a table was easy. Getting the boys to shut up isn't. This is just another war story for them to elaborate and expand upon. By the end of the wedding, the strippers will probably be wielding razor-sharp vibrators as they chase us down.

What follows is a typical late-night eating binge by four still-drunk jackasses, and one stone-sober Donald. What isn't typical is my lack of chatter. All joy has been sapped from my bachelor party, and not even gloriously greasy 5:00 a.m. chicken-fried steak and eggs can help. It does ease the throb in my temples, but not in my veins, not in my heart.

About halfway though the meal, others begin to notice my silence, but rather than address the looming pachyderm, they dance around the tree-trunk legs. Eventually, the tales trickle to a drip; the boys fall quiet. We all know how the night's events are going to threaten my wedding, and they clearly see the stress upon me.

And then Donald speaks.

I'm surprised he's waited this long. "Silence," he often says, "is a breeding ground for mistrust." Probably a throwback from his cop days. He's mellowed significantly in his years since the force, but old habits linger. He isn't upset, but uncomfortable. Only later did I consider he might have been concerned about me.

"Well," he says, taking a sip from his coffee, no cream, no sugar, "it sounds as if you have some good stories to file away."

I look at him, anger billowing from my bloodshot eyes, and prepare to lay into him, to ask him how he can't see how fucked I am, to ask how he can be so blind.

Then he says, "You're just lucky she threw the first punch."

And there it is.

No charges were filed. In my attempt to figure a way out of the whole mess, I had assumed that we'd been charged with assault or drunken disorderly, or whatever it was we did.

Donald says, "After the police took your stories, they reviewed the surveillance tapes and discovered you didn't instigate the brawl."

We're in the clear. I'm in the clear. Apparently, I'd even been given the option of pressing charges against the Bartender Stripper, but had muttered that I just wanted to go home. Apparently, I'd muttered that quite a bit.

The tension begins to release from my shoulders. My head stops spinning. The ache in my jaw softens. I smile. I laugh. A crazy laugh, I'm sure, but all the anxiety is just flowing out in a maniacal, insane stream that causes more than a few patrons of the Denver Diner to look in our direction and then signal for their checks as if they're in a movie.

I stop when Donald puts a hand on my shoulder. Comforting. Fatherly. He says, "For every big problem, there are many small problems waiting to get out. Are you sure you really want to get married?"

Blunt, direct, to the point. All my questions, all my fears. God bless Donald.

I think for a moment, think of Pamela, allowing the bubble to reform, and when it does, I know that I do want to get married. I know that I want to put all of this behind me and start anew. With someone who supports me. With someone who loves me. With Pamela. I tell Donald as much.

He nods and says, "You dodged a huge bullet tonight, but there are still rounds in the chamber. You're smarter than this, Davis. You're better than this."

It's the first time since my pop died that I feel as if he's with me.

We leave the Denver Dinner with a sense of one door closing and another opening. A great adventure, but one to lock away for a long, long time.

Were we in the right frame of mind, were we not so giddy from the drink and the excitement, we may have realized the truth of the matter. There was no way I would get out of this alive.

As we drive, the sun rudely knocking its arrival on my eyelids, I realize something I had missed in all of the brooding and recounting of the chaos.

Donald's gunmetal grey hair is combed perfectly.

CHAPTER TEN

Friday – One Day Before The Wedding

In the shower, as the sun begins to push the whores and the homeless back into the gloom, I'm struck with a form of hyper clarity I haven't felt since the morning my pop died.

I had been driving home after sobering from a night of drink and smoke, and everything I saw seemed to leap out at me. The colors of the flowers were more brilliant; each blade of grass was distinguishable from the masses; every person I saw seemed to glow with an essence, an aura. It's in such times, as we dance between the tangible and the ethereal, when we obtain a sense of a higher power.

Now, in the shower, the hyper clarity hits me as I stare at the lines of grout between the tiles. I run my finger over it, feeling the unevenness, and suddenly it isn't grout I'm feeling but a vast mountain range that becomes stretching cities. And I wonder if there's a being in a little shower in a little house in a little city smiling a happy smile because he's been given a second chance, a pardon, a new life. I catch myself as I start to black out and realize warm water and a lack of sleep may not be a good mix. Still wet, I stumble to the bed.

I wake up with Pamela's hand on my face.

"What happened?" Her brunette hair is damp and she's wearing a light grey Denver University Hockey t-shirt and a pair of my plaid boxers.

"I fell down some stairs," I say, smiling.

"Yeah? Tyler Durden tell you to say that?"

"There is no Tyler, only Zuul."

"You know how sexy you are when you mix movie references?"

"Zuul likey the sexy."

"Just tell Zuul to come up with a better story or people will think I abuse you."

"Zuul likey the abuse."

"Perv."

We kiss. She spoons up to me, my arms enveloping her smaller frame. I take a deep breath of her freshly washed hair, and fall asleep again. When I wake, I'm warm and happy and refreshed and ready to take on the wedding rehearsal and the rehearsal dinner and whatever crap that's flung my way.

As it turns out, the —

Wedding Rehearsal

— is fast, painless, and non-eventful. It's like one of those pocket communities that you see being built in a neighborhood of crap. We smile, enjoy ourselves, joke. It truly feels as if the past is behind me.

The only thing that strikes me as odd is Peter. He, well … he isn't Peter. He isn't over the top. He isn't the jokester. He isn't the fool. Instead, he's quiet. I consider asking if he's okay, but I am so focused on Pamela that I forget. She's glowing. No, she's gliding. Getting married definitely agrees with her.

The —

Rehearsal Dinner

— on the other hand, is anything but painless. Time subscribes to judicious balance. While it was my trusted friend the night previous, tonight it's building a solid foundation for uncertainty and nervous apprehension with bloated ticks of the clock.

The banquet hall is a bog of tension and stress. Within ten minutes, I discover the source. *The Rocky Mountain News* headline: 'Actor Peter Carter Involved in Fight at Local Strip Club.'

But what's really creating a buzz is a quote from one of the strippers, which reads: "None of this would have happened if the bachelor hadn't (expletive) over our sister." It describes their sister being a dancer who is highly respected in the exotic-dancer community. It describes her as blond, buxom, kind to everyone who crosses her path, and engaged in an off-and-on again relationship with the bachelor "who (expletive) with her heart and (expletive) on it."

I read. I reread. I'm socked by fear again and again and have to remind myself to breathe. I need to talk to Pamela.

The problem is that Pamela appears oblivious to the strain, talking and laughing with the forty or so guests gathered. Family, close friends, out-of-town guests. The most noticeable absences are Divan, his flight yet to arrive, and Kathy, who never responded to my written and phoned invitations. But Pamela's family is there, and for them, she acts as if she hasn't a care in the world.

For a moment, I allow hope to fend off fear. But hope is vastly outnumbered, and I soon discover the contest is far from fair. Pamela has read the paper. I know by the way she's always moving, always talking. She appears effortless, but there's a drive to her motion, like a hot coal underfoot.

I approach her. Everyone watching, I near her and she smiles and jumps up and kisses me with glee, and when she hugs me she says in a whisper, "Later."

Any other time, I would believe everything is going to be okay. Her enthusiasm is infectious and by all accounts, genuine. But something's off. It takes a moment of identity, but then it's clear. Pamela is wearing her attorney mask. She's wooing the judge and jury to her side with her smile. With her eyes, she's arguing that her client is innocent of all charges. With her aura, she's requesting that the case be dismissed so everyone can resume their lives.

She's very good at her job, and soon her actions dispel the rising tide of stress within the crowd. Unfortunately, they also loosen the lips of many. People once remiss to discuss the taboo begin talking, making comments. Allowing any remaining tension to regroup, fortify, and come out firing.

Pamela's aunt mutters the first shot. She says with a mouthful of glazed carrots, "I always knew something like this would happen. Poor, Pammy. She can do so much better."

"Excuse me?" says my mother.

"Oh, no need to apologize, dearie. It's not your fault."

"Do you have any idea what you're saying right now?"

"I know that you're attempting to apologize for your son's actions. But it's okay. You can't control him."

"I wasn't —"

"Although I suppose it can be attributed to poor child rearing."

My mother stands. She reaches for Pamela's aunt's short and spiky white hair. She's stopped by the still-quick reflexes of Donald. He pulls her away as she says, "No one questions the way I raised my son."

I watch, from afar, and breathe a sigh of relief that the fire is extinguished before it spreads. But across the room, another ember is burning. Jonesy and his wife Debbie are swatting away inquiries as to what really happened last night.

"Was there really a fight?"

"Did Davis really get attacked by a roomful of strippers?"

"Is it true that Davis was sleeping with a dancer?"

And all of them followed by, "It's okay. You can tell me. I'm a friend."

Jonesy later tells me the chart-topping question came from Ian's Icelandic supermodel bed-buddy with legs insured for five million each. "Did Peter really beat a girl with a giant fake penis so she would stop biting his leg?"

As the night wears on, I feel cold stares when my back is turned, and I see polite smiles and raised wine glasses when I'm facing people. Each whisper echoes in my head, louder and louder and I soon want to run. Not from Pamela, but from everyone else.

I move to the exit, wishing some fresh air, and Divan, his travel bag on his shoulder, a suitcase wheeling behind him, stops me.

He says, "Don't leave on my account." We embrace, and he immediately cuts through the small talk. "Shit finally caught up to ya?"

"You have no idea."

He looks around the room, at the eyes on my back, and his weathered smile breaks out in pure amusement. "Oh, I have a good idea."

"Good to see someone's enjoying this."

"I just spent seven hours on an airplane with a screaming child and an Olsen-twins' movie playing on loop. I need this."

"It's yours."

He drops his bag, pulls a flask from his pocket, and hands it to me. "I shouldn't do this, seeing as you had all the fun without me."

I drink, relishing the burn as it stifles the echoes.

I say, "Where have you been?"

"Finding myself."

"Any success?"

He shrugs and I see looseness in his shoulders, as if he's been relieved of some lifelong weight. He says, "Some. The search was fun."

"The money?"

"It's amazing what people will pay to get motivated."

"You charge by the hour?"

"Is there any other way?" He then nods to the guests. "How much do they know?"

"Enough to know that I'm a fuckrag."

"You're not a fuckrag. You're a douche, but not a fuckrag."

"There's a difference?"

His brow lifts. "Literally?"

"They know enough to hate me."

"But they don't know the truth."

"The truth is probably worse," I say.

"I don't know about that, but you'd better find a quick story to tell."

I'm about to ask why, but see him looking over my shoulder and I turn and see Pamela's father — a smaller man with a wildly thick head of brown and silver hair that makes him resemble Joe Pesci with a dying Chia Pet on his head — stand and start to weave his way between the tables toward me. It's his half scowl, half grin that causes him to look intimidating. The left side of his face is slightly upturned in a snarl as if he smells something rotten, causing everyone who sees it to believe they're causing the smell and begin to sweat. He'd been an attorney for fifteen years and when he became bored and wanted a new challenge, he moved into the state school system and spent the last twelve years as a high school principal.

The snarl is second nature to him. Enough for people to drop loads in their shorts at even a glance in their direction.

As he nears, the room noticeably hushes. It's the main event that everyone's waiting for, but not really knowing when it's going to happen. The moment he starts toward me, though, interference is run, as if it were planned. If I wasn't so terrified, I'd think it almost comical.

First it's Ian Carter and Max Richards. But they're only able to slow Pamela's father down as they block his passage while loudly conversing about the parquet flooring.

Next is Donald, God bless him, as he attempts to open dialogue, father to stepfather. But he's politely rebuffed with a quick handshake, a pat on the shoulder, and a, "In a second."

The last line of defense is, of course, Peter Carter.

Earlier, when recalling the night previous, I noticed details I neglected to process as Peter recounted his tale at the Denver Diner. So focused on my misery, I missed the lack of edge to his voice. That flow of confidence. That thing that makes Peter Carter, well, Peter Carter.

Instead, his voice was less secure, wavy. As if someone had frayed the string that held Peter together. Now, for the first time since I saw him after Vegas, I realize that Peter Carter is uncertain.

When he sees Pamela's father nearing me, Peter gets the same look in his eye that he did at the Diamond Cabaret. Part of me fears he's going to leap into a flying tackle. The rest of me prays he will. It'll be just enough distraction for me to get to the car and on my way to Mexico before anyone notices my absence.

Alas, I don't get a chance to run.

Just as Peter moves to block Pamela's father, he glances up at me and stops. He turns Goth white. But he's not looking at me. He's looking past me.

I turn.

It's Naomi, Pamela's maid of honor, just getting into town because of scheduling conflicts. In the years since Peter left her, she'd risen through the ranks of Hollywood. While she isn't the most influential woman behind the scenes, she's in the top five. Many have speculated the fuel to her ambition is Peter's success. That she wants to rise to a point where she can hamstring his career. In reality, Naomi simply hardened once Peter left.

Success affords her a great many things, but pulling away as she once did is not one of them. And yet she's here. And she's beautiful.

But even her radiance doesn't stop Pamela's father. No. He's immune.

Peter is not. He's frozen, open mouthed. Star struck. Pamela's father passes Peter without a glance. Then, he's in front of me.

"Mr. Robertson?" He's quiet, calm, unenergetic, but not lazy. He once told me that he identified with John Wayne in speech. Talk softly and slowly and people will quake in their boots.

"Sir?" It's all I can say. My mouth is dry. Here I am, twenty-eight years old, frightened like a kid caught cursing in class.

He says, "I don't know what happened, but I know what I read." He falls silent, breathing evenly, knowing what he's going to say before he says it. He's not looking at me, but <u>in</u>

me and I know this is how his gaze would feel if he wielded x-ray vision. His tan eyes are knives, cutting away my layers until he's studying the acids churning in my stomach, my turmoil, my soul. I'd have wet my pants had I not already sweated myself dry.

He puts a hand on my shoulder, squeezes hard, and says, "Why don't you tell me the truth about last night. Why don't you put this talk to rest."

And then he's leading me outside, past Divan, past Naomi.

And then we stop. Because Jonesy is up and addressing the room. Jonesy, the last person I'd have thought to come to the rescue.

"I guess it's as good a time as ever to start." All gazes turned from me to him. Many reluctant, many angry. "When Davis asked me to be his best man, my only reservation was the speech. I'm awful with them. Beyond awful. I say this because I'm high on Elmer's glue, which gave me the confidence to speak in the first place. It's no excuse, but it's one that needed to be out in the air, and I think that's what we need to do here, talk about the air."

He breathes deeply, and there's determination in his eyes as if he's about to run into a burning building. But he's also remarkably calm. Loose. The hand that's not holding his beer accents his words in peaceful gestures rather than hard punctuations and for a moment I remember that same hand shaking in anger and frustration at Peter's wedding years earlier.

"I look out at all of you here, today, and I feel tension. No one likes tension, least of all me. That's what's led me to glue. A vile addiction, but we're not here to talk about me. We're here to talk about Pamela and Davis, two wonderful people, who have their faults but at the core of everything are nearly perfect for each other. I know this because I think I've had the privilege of being the only one to see both sides of the relationship since moment one.

"Davis, as you may or may not know, has been my best friend since freshman year and he tells me just about everything. What you may not know — what even Davis doesn't know — is that Pamela also tells me just about everything. What does that mean? Well, it clearly means I should have charged therapy rates because I know way too much about them. I know that Pamela can't stand it when Davis makes pig noises in his sleep, which, she claims, is worse than a lumberjack with a chainsaw on your bedpost. I know that Davis can't stand it when Pamela has to go into court, because the house is filled with the smells of instant coffee and he gets nauseated, turns green, and looks something like Kermit the Frog. But what I also know about these two is that they're not perfect, but they fit like two pieces to a puzzle, nearly seamless, but with the occasional frayed edges.

"So why aren't they perfect? Because the puzzle isn't complete. They're only two pieces to the big picture, and it's the rest of us that need to fill in that picture. And I'll be the first to say that I've failed in doing that for them. I've been so focused on my own two pieces that I failed with the surrounding pieces. I failed my two friends."

He looks down, purses his lips as he thinks, and when he looks up, he wipes away a tear.

"Three years ago, my wife and I separated. Things were ... well, they were complicated, but the result was that we were so focused on the frayed edges of our pieces that we didn't understand the fit. We didn't even see the fit. But Davis and Pamela did. They were two pieces who are connected to our two pieces, and they realized how they were invested in our lives, how responsible each of us is for each other. They helped my wife and me take a step back and realize what we were doing to each other. They helped us realize how good we fit together.

"Davis, Pamela, I want to be the first one to tell you that I failed in my responsibility to help you two, but it won't happen again. So my wedding gift to you two is this: my friendship, my responsibility, my love. I urge the rest of you to ask what these two have meant to your lives, and I hope that you'll aid me in holding these two people up in times of need, so they can see how close to perfect they connect."

Silence follows, filling the room. I hold my breath.

Debbie, Jonesy's wife, ends the silence by starting to clap. I'm not sure you're supposed to clap at the end of a best man's speech, but it happens. She starts clapping, and for a while, she's the only one. But then, of all people, Pamela stands up and starts clapping. She stands and walks up to Jonesy with tears in her eyes and she embraces him. And that does it.

It's so strangely reminiscent of an '80s film that I half expect Jon Cryer to step from the ether and take the microphone from Jonesy. Those who are on the fence fall off and start clapping. A few don't. Pamela's aunt looks as if her head is going to implode right there.

And then, there's Peter.

The moment Jonesy began, all eyes went to him. Even Pamela's father turned away from me to listen. The only person who didn't look was Peter. His gaze was on Naomi. And throughout the speech, it never left. In contrast, she never looked at him. Not until people were clapping and Pamela was embracing Jonesy. That's when she looked at Peter.

That's when she says, "I've been granted a restraining order for less."

And for the first time since the alley, Peter Carter genuinely laughs.

After Pamela hugs Jonesy, she comes over, disengages her father's hand from my shoulder with a flick of her wrist and embraces me. My sight never leaves her father. I try, but I'm trapped under his visual evisceration and the pressure to look away is more painful then remaining on him. But I'm not thinking about him. I'm thinking about Pamela. Thinking that maybe she's being genuine and, if so, I'm thanking her for understanding. Hoping that even if she doesn't know the full picture, she understands that we're all human and we all fail at times. Praying that she knows *I'm* human, and that *I* fail at times.

She pulls me away. Away from her father. Away to the table. Some smile. Others glare. There's still tension, but it's bearable. And I eat it up as if everything is all right.

Later, outside, Pamela hugs me again. We're alone. The night air is cool. The breeze is slight.

I say, "Do you want to talk about things?"

She pulls back, looks down, at my shoes, at the ground, at the uncertainty, nods, and looks back at me without lifting her head. "But not right now. Right now, I want to focus on the good."

We're silent again. We look into each other's eyes. Not like young lovers, but like jaded adults with a lot of baggage.

And then she slaps me.

She says, "You've made me look like a joke." She then gets into her car and drives away. I watch her, silent. I want to run after her and tell her everything that I'm thinking, even though I know it won't do a damn bit of good. But I don't. She drives away, and I have no idea where we stand.

Voices from the shadows catch my attention. Upon closer inspection, the voices become figures. Peter and Naomi. Somehow, I pull myself from my misery, duck behind the cars, and move toward them.

I'm not the only one. Divan and Jonesy are hiding behind a pickup. We all smile and attempt not to giggle like schoolchildren.

Naomi says, "But you slept with her."

Peter says, "I didn't mean to."

"What? You just fell?"

"No, I mean it wasn't my intention when she walked in the door."

"Sure it was. You've meant everything you've done in your life."

"I don't expect people to believe me."

"That's big of you. So, you're going to stick to your guns on this one? That it just sorta happened?"

"It's the truth."

"The truth like it just sorta happened that you slept with your assistant in Toronto?"

"That was different."

"But you meant to do it."

"Sorta."

"Well, what is it? You did or you didn't?"

"I didn't mean to sleep with Heather."

"But you meant to sleep with the whore in Toronto?"

"She wasn't a whore."

"Right. She was just a star-struck girl who looked up at you with star-struck eyes and you just had to fuck her. I don't blame Davis for hitting you."

"I deserved more."

"You're damn right you did. With your track record, you should have your penis taken away until you know how to use it."

"I seem to remember you not having any complaints."

"I'm out of here."

"What? Come on. Don't walk away."

"I'm not going to stand here and have you insult me."

"How did I insult you?"

"You use that smile and that wink and you think that I don't know what you're trying to do?"

"I wasn't trying to do anything. I was reliving memories … I … I was remembering the last time —"

"The last time what? That we had sex? That you saw me naked? What last time in that twisted little fucking brain of yours are you —"

"The last time I was happy."

"Are you fucking with me? You're not, are you? Holy shit. You're serious."

"When did you start cursing?"

"The day I read in the paper that you fucked me over. Suddenly it was easy. Became second nature."

"I'm sorry that I caused that."

"That's rich. Of all the things you apologize for, it's for your influence on my vocabulary."

"I'm sorry for the rest too."

"I didn't come here to be patronized."

"If I'm patronizing, I'm truly sorry."

"When the hell did you learn that word?"

"I'm learning a lot about myself this trip."

"I don't know if I can continue this."

"Continue what?"

"This. Talking to you when you're like this."

"Why's that?"

"Why? Because I've spent six years with your face on my toilet paper."

"I deserve that."

"Stop. Stop being so remorseful. … Okay, say something. Remorse is better than this … Are you acting now?"

"I wish. I'd understand what the hell is happening to me if I were."

"You can't tell me that telling Davis had this much effect on you."

"The thing that frightens me is I think he did. For the first time ... for the first time I saw in someone's eyes what I did to them ... someone I really cared for ... someone I loved and who was always there for me, and I don't know if I can forget that."

"Fuck you."

"What?"

"Which part did you miss?"

"No, you don't under —"

"That wasn't the first time you saw that, you egomaniacal jackass. You've seen it your whole life. The only difference is that this time it was one of your inner circle. Your famous Friday Night Club. The only difference is that this wasn't ... this wasn't a fucking *girl*. I'm not saying what you're feeling isn't genuine, but for fuck's sake, Peter, it's not ... it's not the first time you should have felt this. You should have ... fuck, you should have felt it with me."

And then she leaves.

Walks away.

Leaving Peter to fill in the rest.

Less than an hour later, we're in Peter's suite at the —

Downtown Denver Hotel Monaco

— and the paltry offerings of the minibar will just not do. We debate a course of action, and within moments Ian and Max Richards leave in search of greater libations. We tell them we can call for room service, but they say they want a quest, something to put focus in their lives at that moment.

Gotta love the simplicity of men.

That leaves Divan, Peter, Jonesy, and me sitting in silence. Everything's in shambles. But one man's chaos is another man's foundation. I may have lost my fiancée, Peter may have lost his sense of self, but Divan and Jonesy have regained their old drinking buddies. And drink we do.

As we drink, we talk about nothing in particular. There are dull breaks in the conversation when we near a topic that'll poke holes in the dam. We all know that one question, one apology, one bad joke will rupture the foundation and we'll be swept away by a torrid current to God knows where. So we steer the conversation to the comfortable — sports, women without last names, our past adventures. We settle on laughing at a *Simpsons* rerun on the television, and turn up the volume to drown out the racket caused by some moronic jackasses pounding on a doorway across the hall.

I try Pamela's cell. She doesn't answer. I don't expect her to, but I continue to try.

After we polish off the minibar, and with no sign of Ian and Max Richards, we decide a quest of our own is required. A quest to find the first group who went out on a quest. It's our civic duty to back them up. Families are at stake. Loved ones who will miss them greatly. This quest will be a rescue mission.

It ends the moment we exit the room. Ian Carter and Max Richards are hammering on the door across the hallway.

"Open the fucking door, you pansy asses!" says Max Richards.

"Maybe they went out," says Ian.

"They didn't go out. They're in there. Wallowing in their shit! Open the damn door!"

Max continues to bang, and that's when I see someone leaning against the hallway wall, hidden from my point of view. I poke my head out and thank the minibar for my lack of surprise. Were I sober, the wind would have been knocked from my lungs. But not this time. This time, I'm a rock.

After a moment:

"Hi, Davis," she says.

"Hi, Kathy," I say.

The past runs over me like an ice-cream truck.

CHAPTER ELEVEN

The last time I saw Kathy was seven years ago, my senior Year, at Peter's and Naomi's wedding in San Diego. She was drinking hard, feeling sorry for herself, and burning tiny holes into my flesh with her eyes. Not daggers. She wasn't trying to kill. She was trying to get my attention. Make me feel her pain. Make me talk about what happened in Vegas.

It didn't happen. We didn't speak again until we saw each other in the hallway the night before my wedding.

I'd tried, though. In the past year I called, I e-mailed. I attempted to rebuild the frame of the doorway I'd burned down so we could step through and close the past. But she never responded to any of my attempts. Not sure I blame her. Seven years removed from the situation tends to shed another light on the happenings. As time softened my outlook on my own actions, it had apparently hardened Kathy's view. Again, not sure I blame her. Only with the benefit of hindsight did I realize how badly I'd fucked her over.

Junior Year

I was sitting in my room, the shades drawn, my vision blurring as I concentrated on focusing on absolutely nothing, when the door opened. Peter, Jonesy, Divan, Kathy. Somber, sad, serious, solemn. I loved them all.

My pop had died a week before, and after the shock and the adrenaline had worn off, I'd crawled back to my bed in Boulder. Three days later, I'd barely moved other than out of sheer necessity, which included shuffling to the bathroom, showering, and stripping the bed of the sheets and using a sleeping bag after I sweated a week's worth of alcohol into K-Mart's finest. But as my eyes drew in the four blurry forms entering my room, I had the suspicion that things were about to change.

None of us knew what we were in for. An impromptu road trip to escape our ills resulted in … I wouldn't say a loss of innocence, because I believe that's a false term. As if innocence is lost like your virginity. Pop! All gone. This isn't the case.

We're born innocent. It's when you understand consequence that things become less black and white. Innocence and consequence are linked. You lose innocence when you learn you can't disregard consequence. This has varying degrees. Grey areas. So, instead of a loss of innocence, I call this whole thing being kicked in the balls. Only through the pain of consequence can you lose innocence.

The road trip was also an acknowledgement of the foundation of our friendship. A foundation we all assumed was solid, but if we removed the sanctuary of the Friday Night Club from the college environment and placed it into the context of the 'real world,' our footing was cracked and hollow.

Thirty-four hours after they pulled me from the bed, we were going —

West On Interstate 15

— and seeing the Las Vegas lights burn their image into our memory. You never forget the first time you see Las Vegas at night. The adult Dizz Knee Land never fails to bring a happy tear to my eye.

It was six months before Peter's and Naomi's wedding at the Hotel Del Coronado in San Diego, a month before Peter graduated Colorado University, a month and a day before he left to find fame and fortune in Los Angeles, and the perfect time to dip our feet into decadence and debauchery.

Our mode of transportation was a 1975 Elaganza II. A big red and white GMC motor home that looked like a stretched Tylenol on wheels. The title in the glove box had the Elaganza registered to Thomas Divan's grandparents, who lived in Eastern Kansas, but for the last decade the beast had resided in the side yard of the house Divan once called home.

Two weeks earlier, on a whim, Divan decided to see what the sucker had going for it and was surprised that it started up with only two coughs and a wheeze. Even the battery sparked. It defied all logic, but he wasn't going to question a gift from the gods. Instead, he went about cleaning and tuning. And as we headed over the hill, Divan was behind the wheel and smiling like a banshee. For a moment, I thought I could see Las Vegas reflected in his perfect teeth.

After they'd pulled me from my bed and threatened to hose me down if I didn't shower, they all but tossed me into the already idling red and white Tylenol curbside. Within a minute, they'd popped a beer and put it in my hand. Within ten, we'd picked up three girls I knew in passing from the Friday Night Club parties. Within an hour, we were playing truth or dare and one of the three girls was kissing down my bare chest. I don't remember her name, but I know she looked like a young Christie Brinkley from her *Sports Illustrated* days, had a sexy Texas drawl, and could tie a cherry stem into a double knot with her tongue. By the time we crossed into Utah, we were all calling her Cherry.

This was just before the cop pulled us over.

"Holy shit!" said Jonesy. "We're being chased by E.T!" He had dropped acid for the first time in his life two hours earlier and had been plastered to the windshield ever since, wearing 3-D glasses, watching every car pass by as if they were strippers on a catwalk. As we followed his gaze, we saw the approaching police lights in the side mirror of the Tylenol.

"Awww, shit," said Divan, driving the beast. "Can someone please lock Elliot in the bathroom until this is over?"

I cringed. The Tylenol looked as if it were Sin on Wheels. Open and empty beer cans, rum and tequila bottles all around, women's shirts and bras strewn about, and a bag of weed with a water bong sitting in the corner of the couch. We weren't driving to Sin City, we were adding to it.

Kathy led Jonesy into the bathroom and locked the door. Divan pulled the red and white beast to the side of the road and killed the engine. It was all happening so fast, I didn't have time to panic. I just looked out the back and watched as the cop exited his car and walked up the passenger side of the vehicle.

He was slow. Painfully slow, as only a cop can get away with. With each step, my heartbeat doubled until it thumped like a solo for Miami Sound Machine.

When the cop reached the side window, my heart stopped. Cut out completely. I was surely going to pass out, but then I caught a glimpse of the Tylenol's cabin, and did a double take. All evidence of booze and drugs were gone. The girls looked as if they'd just stepped out of church.

Ah, they were professionals.

The cop knocked on the side window. Cherry rolled it down.

"Howdy, officer," she said, batting those Christie Brinkley eyelashes and flashing that Christie Brinkley smile. "Surely we weren't speeding."

"You've got a broken tail light."

Divan said, "The fuck I do," and exited the driver's side door.

The cop said to Divan, "Stay in the vehicle, son," as Cherry searched the glove box for the registration.

As was Divan's way when told to do something, he ignored it completely and went to the rear of the red and white beast.

The cop said, "I told you to stay in the vehicle," and met Divan at the taillight.

Divan said, "Peter, turn the key."

The cop looked back at the cab of the Tylenol. "You turn that key, and I'll cuff you faster than —"

The side door popped open and Cherry and her two friends bounced out.

"Ladies, get back into the —"

"The bathroom's broken," said Cherry. Her friends giggled the affirmation of this fact. "And we really have to go." Said in the Texas drawl as she was already unzipping her pants in front of him.

The cop balked. Peter turned the key, engaging the electrical system of the Tylenol. Sure enough, no taillight.

Divan said, "Mother of piss," and slammed the side of the vehicle. The taillight popped on. Divan broke into a huge smile and pointed at it. "Aw, shucks. All it needed was a little lovin'."

But the cop wasn't looking at the taillight. Not at Cherry and her unzipped pants, not at Cherry's friends squatting by the side of the road, and not at Divan pointing to the red and white Tylenol. He was looking at the Kansas license plate illuminated in red by the now working taillight.

The tags had expired a decade earlier.

Inside, I knocked on the bathroom door and when it opened, saw Jonesy sitting on the toilet closely examining a flashlight keychain with an emerald green bulb. Kathy, sitting on his lap to make sure he wouldn't move, was drinking the second of a four-pack of wine coolers.

She nodded outside and said, "How are things?"

"Eh. Could be worse."

"But they could be better?"

Jonesy put the emerald green bulb up his nose and said, "Green smells like chili."

Kathy said, "So I take it he's not coming in?"

"He's too busy writing tickets and ogling the girls."

"At least they're good for something."

I smiled. "Do I detect a hint of jealousy?"

She looked away, turning red. "I'm not jealous. It's just that they only seem to come around for one reason, ya know?"

"It's a good reason."

"I guess."

"Think of it this way, if they had a better reason to come around, then you wouldn't have us all to yourself." At this she smiled. She then opened her mouth to say something, but Jonesy cut her off.

"Green burns! Green burns!" We covered his mouth and took the keychain flashlight from his nose. After a moment he calmed down. We took our hands off his mouth and he said, "Kathy is so soft." He was running his hands lightly over her face. "Davis, feel."

Before I could protest, he grabbed my fingers and ran them over Kathy's face.

"Yeah, soft," I said, and was going to pull my hand back when Kathy looked up at me with wide brown eyes. I saw her lips part just a bit and a buzz ran down my spine, hit my loins and lingered. There was a fire behind her eyes, and as she inhaled, it grew brighter.

This quiet girl who had exploded out of her shell in the years since she found refuge in Peter's closet was looking at me as if she were about to erupt like a volcano. But not in anger. This fire would erupt in passion.

It simultaneously turned me on and pushed me away. It turned me on because it was directed at me and I just wanted a lick of the flame, that emotion. But it pushed me away because there was a purity to it. It wasn't polluted with the sludge that infests past emotions. It was lustful and oh so innocently perfect that I knew I wasn't the person who should taste the fire, lest I extinguish it.

I drew back, and in a blink, Kathy's fire turned to fear. She said, "Why are you —?"

Jonesy said, "Where are you going? She's so smooooth."

I clicked open the latch, fell from the bathroom, hit the hallway wall, and slammed the door. I stood there, staring at the doorway, seeing nothing but the pain and hurt on Kathy's face.

I squeezed my eyes shut, wanting to erase the image, but it only deepened, etching itself in my memory forever. I cursed, already regretting my actions. Later, in the hotel room, I would curse again. If not for that indelible image burned into memory, if not for the accompanying feelings of lust and regret for closing that damn door, what happened later in the glorious marble bathroom tub might have been averted.

In the end, we got a warning. As the cop wrote out the citation, all the while fending off the girls and ignoring Peter's attempts of persuasion, Divan's curiosity got the better of him. He moved to the side of the police car and poked his head through the passenger window.

"Get away from there," said the cop.

Divan, unmoving, said, "That's a hell of a system."

The cop looked up from his ticket pad, blinked a few times in thought, then very stiffly and officially walked over to the driver's side. He leaned in, turned the key engaging the electrical system and, completely deadpan, cranked on the stereo. The girls and Peter recoiled from the sound — Ministry, "Jesus Built My Hot Rod." But Divan didn't flinch. Instead, he smiled.

The cop said, "And this isn't even halfway up." And then he smiled.

Divan and the cop talked stereos. They talked cars. They popped the hood of the police cruiser and admired. All that was missing were beers in their hands, a barbecue smoking in the backyard, and a backyard.

A state and a half later, we hit the city limits, followed the RV Parking signs to the —

Circus Circus, Hotel and Casino

— and took the last spot they had. The clock read 3:39 a.m., but none of us cared. We were jacked and wanting to play. After attempting to find someone to pay for overnight parking, we gave up and fed our desires. Alas, Jonesy had hit the wall and was three steps from dead. We left him asleep in the back bedroom with a note taped to his forehead reading 'Abducted by aliens. Back before dawn.'

And then we fed.

Blackjack has a way of eating up time like a whale shark snacking on krill. Huge chunks of your life suddenly disappear, and when you look down at your chips, it's as if nothing has changed. Five dollars up. Five dollars down.

Unless you're in it for winning, you learn to ride it as long as possible while getting hammered for free. That was a pact we all made. No matter how much we imbibed, we wouldn't get cocky with our bets. It sounds dumb, but we were relatively poor college students who wanted our fun to last as long as we could.

The time leaps allowed me to dismiss the incident in the Tylenol's bathroom as an overreaction. After the first hour, Kathy and I were smiling as if nothing had ever happened. We laughed. We flirted. Hell, everyone laughed and flirted. I'm sure many an observer believed we were going to retire at any moment for a big orgy in the nearest room we could procure.

"How you holdin' up?" said Divan as we walked past the dueling pirate ships outside —

Treasure Island Hotel and Casino

We'd been casino hopping and were nearing our breaking point. But none of us wanted to pack it in. We were having just too much damn fun.

"Tired," I said.

"You know what I mean." Good ol' Divan. Cut straight to the point.

I said, "Haven't really thought about it, to be honest. I mean, how fast can you go through the stages?"

"Stages?"

"Yeah. Anger, acceptance, denial, drunk, dead. I think I'm still in denial."

"The stages are bullshit. Life isn't stages. People have created the stages to understand themselves, but all it does is generate more shit for us to think about, and the more shit we think about the less we deal with what's important."

"You're saying dealing with my father's death isn't important?"

He shook his head and hooked his thumbs in the pockets of his jeans. "No, I'm saying that it's only important when you're ready to tackle that project. When you can tear it apart and rebuild it with a greater understanding of yourself.

"Dude, you're not broken, you've just got a leaky hose. Simple. In the meantime, you continue to ride. You continue to enjoy the road. And when you're ready to fix that leaky hose, you'll fix it."

"I'm a little frightened that you've been paying attention to my leaky hose." I looked at the girls waiting for us at the entrance to the casino and thought about Cherry kissing her way down my bare chest; thought about Kathy's fuck-me eyes still causing my groin to tingle. I said, "It's all just running away though, isn't it?"

"That's the cynic talking. The opportunist will tell you that you ride the road because it's there."

I laughed softly. "You sound like Peter."

"No. Peter doesn't respect the road. He hurts the road. Skid marks, potholes. He doesn't think about the other vehicles. He doesn't care about what he leaves in his dust. Peter takes for the sole reason of taking. He's very simple. He takes, runs, and never looks back.

"What Peter doesn't understand is that you can never run from your problems, because they're a part of you. They travel with you. When you accept that, you respect the road. And when you respect the road, you can avoid major obstacles and major overhauls. Along the way, you enjoy the scenery, you enjoy the wind, and you enjoy moving forward instead of breaking down by the side of the road."

I looked at him. "Who are you to be so wise in the ways of death?"

He smiled. "I thought we were talking about bikes."

I looked down, then back at the girls. "Just go with it?"

"More or less. Go with it, enjoy the road, don't make potholes. You'll know when you need to deal with things."

"I think I get ya."

"Yeah?"

"Yeah."

Not until the night of my rehearsal dinner, as I'm sitting in the —

Downtown Denver Hotel Monaco

— with Divan, Peter, and Jonesy, do I realize I don't get it. Don't get it at all. Divan was talking about going with the flow of the world around us. Enjoying the elements, the things we take for granted. Instead, I realize I've melded Divan's philosophy with Peter's. Going with the flow, biding your time, and justifying your actions with denial and false innocence.

There, in the hotel room, as we watch the *Simpsons*, I close my eyes and, like a video fast forwarding, speed through my life; from that moment outside Treasure Island to the Hotel Monaco, stopping only in the key moments when I had to make a hard choice. And in every one of those moments, I realize that instead of digging deep within myself to find the answers, find the correct direction to ride, I copped out and searched for Peter's or Divan's voice. All this time, they were my excuse. My excuse for fucking Hillary at the Renaissance Festival. My excuse for —

Circus Circus Hotel and Casino

"What are you thinking about?" said Kathy.

We were walking through the banks of the slot machines, heading back to our red and white Elaganza. Earlier, in Treasure Island, Cherry followed me into the men's room and jumped me. In the last stall, she was loud and uncaring and I was silent and close to numb. I let her have her way with me, allowing the physical to bury the emotional, even for a short while. By that time I was practiced. I was a master at the art.

After the bathroom, Cherry had given me the cold shoulder. Not acting ashamed, but done with me. She was moving on to Divan. Making her rounds. It was fun, though. I didn't regret it.

But the moment she stopped paying attention to me, Kathy was there. Smiling. Flirting. And for a moment, I wondered why, wondered what she saw in me, what made me worth it.

At some point she started walking closer to me. At some point I put my arm around her shoulder. At some point she put her arm around my waist.

"I'm not thinking about anything," I said. I lied.

She called me on it with a wink and a smile and a squeeze and a tingle. She said, "Bullshit. At any given time we're thinking about something. Anyone who says they aren't is brain dead."

I smiled. "Is that a compliment?"

"I don't know. Is it?" She looked at me with a sideways leer and the fire rose again in her eyes. This time, I didn't run away.

Kathy told me that I'd missed her signs for the past few months. She'd drop hints, make subtle suggestions, all but came out and said she wanted me. I'm sure had I been in a better state of mind, I would have caught them. Factor in my mental disposition with regards to my pop, and all bets were off. But she said she took that into consideration and didn't push. The last thing she wanted was to feel as if she were taking advantage of me in a poor time.

Why a week after my pop died did not fall into this category, I haven't a clue. Maybe it was because we weren't in Boulder, and so we were removed from reality. Or maybe it was the allure of Vegas, which jump-starts libidos and clouds judgments.

As we stepped outside and stopped to watch the sunrise, she kissed me.

I said, "Why did you do that?"

She said, "It's something I've wanted to do it since I first met you."

"Really?"

"Yeah, but Hillary was always in the picture." We watched the sunrise, kissed some more. Then she said, "You ever think about us?"

"Us?"

"Yeah. The two of us together."

I didn't lie to her, but I didn't tell her the whole truth. "Of course. You're cute, fun, smart. I'd be crazy if I didn't wonder."

What I didn't tell her was that these thoughts always ended with us jumping into bed. It's a guy thing. A guy doesn't think about the future. Not about kids, bills, old age. A guy thinks in the moment. It's not until the relationship gains a foundation does the future take root — once we know we'll never tire of waking up to the same face every morning.

Kathy took my answer as an open door. I didn't do anything to close it. She looked so damn happy in that moment and I didn't want to change that. Earlier in the Tylenol, she looked like a child who just discovered the toy she coveted had sold out. Sorry, here's a rain check. We'll call you when it comes into stock. And now, Kathy was finally getting that call.

The others saw it happening, but didn't do anything to stop it. Not that they should have. I was a big boy. I knew what I was doing. And even though they might have seen disaster in the future, they were just happy to see me smiling.

Happy that I wasn't lying in bed, staring unfocused at the ceiling. Happy that my mind wasn't on my pop.

I wasn't thinking about consequence. I wasn't thinking beyond the moment. I thought I was riding the road and enjoying what came my way. Little did I know I was going to get kicked in the balls and damn near wreck out on the side of the road.

All and all, if you remove Cherry and me fucking in the ladies room at Treasure Island, the night was rather mild. Some booze. Some gambling. Some food. The latter allowed our lack of sleep to catch up. So, after we all watched the daybreak, after Kathy and I kissed, we headed back to the Tylenol to sleep the day away.

The only problem was that the Tylenol wasn't there.

CHAPTER TWELVE

At first, they didn't know what we were talking about.

"We don't know what you're talking about."

All because they had no registry of our vehicle.

"We have no registry of your vehicle."

The Circus Circus RV parking staff was on a power trip and they were doing a good job of pissing us off.

"You're pissing us off, you fucking wankers, you know that?" Cherry said.

You had to love what Vegas brings out in a person.

First it was the lot attendant, then it was the lot assistant manager, then it was the lot manager, and finally it was the Lot Supervising Manager. With Divan, Kathy, and the girls knocking on RVs and asking questions, Peter and I were inside talking to the Lot Supervising Manager. He resembled a bald Robert De Niro with the girth of Captain Kangaroo and eyebrows clearly cultivated for future comb-over purposes.

Peter said, "What do you mean you don't know what happened?"

"You should have registered your vehicle with us, when you arrived," said the Lot Supervising Manager.

"You were closed."

"It happens at least once a day."

"So, by your acknowledgement, there wasn't any way for us to register."

"I acknowledge no such thing."

"How do you propose we should have registered our vehicle?"

"You should have waited until we opened."

"And that was?"

"Three hours ago."

"You've been here for three hours?"

"That's when we opened, yes."

"And did you see our vehicle when you opened?"

"I don't acknowledge that I know if I did."

"How can you not know? You either did, or you didn't."

"I don't acknowledge seeing your vehicle, and I don't acknowledge not seeing your vehicle."

"You don't acknowledge much, do you?"

"It's not my job to acknowledge."

"What would your superiors say about you allowing a vehicle to walk off your lot?"

"I assure you, it didn't walk."

"You can assure, but you can't acknowledge?"

"I don't acknowledge that I can assure anything."

"But you just did."

"I don't acknowledge that."

"You assured me that a vehicle did not walk off your lot."

"I assure you that no such thing took place."

"How can you assure when you don't acknowledge seeing it in the first place?"

"I can assure you that I acknowledge your vehicle didn't walk."

"Ah. Then by that assured acknowledgment, you inadvertently acknowledge that you saw our vehicle on the lot."

Silence.

"I may acknowledge to have seen your vehicle on the lot."

"Now we're getting somewhere!"

"I don't acknowledge that we are, no."

Standing next to Peter, I watched this verbal sparring for more than ten minutes. A long ten minutes. The line behind us grew. The clock behind the Lot Supervising Manger slowed. Then my anxiety kicked in.

I said, "Listen —"

"I've got this one, Davis," said Peter.

"I don't acknowledge that you —"

I slammed my hand on the counter. "Listen!"

Everyone stopped. They looked at me. I took a deep breath.

I said, "We want to know what happened to our Elaganza right now, and if you don't give us every scrap of information you possess, I'll have the cops down here within five minutes and I'll be damn sure you'll be telling them everything you know."

The Lot Supervising Manager opened his mouth to —

I said, "Say it. I fucking dare you say it. In front of all these people, say that you don't acknowledge that I'll have the cops down here and they'll be probing your ass with a microscope for the information you're holding back on us."

Sweat popped out on his forehead. His head began jerking back and forth subtly. He resembled a fat, balding chicken. Then he said it. "I don't acknowledge that —"

"Kidnapping."

The jerking stopped. "Kidnapping?"

I smiled, not happy at our lot, but happy that we'd finally gotten his attention.

He swallowed hard, and said, "I don't —"

"A man was asleep in that Elaganga."

And there it was.

He said, "I knocked."

"He was in the back."

"We used a blow horn."

"He was passed out."

He swallowed again. The sweat began beading down his face. "You're bluffing."

I smiled even bigger, blinked a few times.

He said, "That Elaganza was empty."

I reached over the counter and said, "May I use your phone?"

He grabbed the phone, hugged it to his chest, and took a step backward. When his head began jerking again, I realized he was thinking, possibly playing out his options, his future. Then his face fell. His eyebrows drooped. His wiped sweat from his bald head.

Peter said, "You really used a blow horn?"

A few ticks shy of an hour, we were at the ass end of Vegas approaching —

Ike's Junk Yard

As the Circus Circus minivan pulled through the gates, we were greeted by a maze of partly crushed cars, stacked at least twenty feet high. I wasn't sure how far the labyrinth stretched, but could make out three car-stacked towers about forty yards in the distance, each a good thirty feet high. Upon the nearest, a lawn chair sat beneath a wide-brimmed patio umbrella.

My mind flashed to the maze of debris in *The Wastelands*, the third novel in Stephen King's masterpiece saga, *The Dark Tower*. Whenever my eye caught a glint of sunlight off of rusted metal or broken glass, I half expected a crazed mutant with oozing radiation sores to jump out.

Divan said, "If the bones of Freddy Kruger step from the trunk of one of those cars, I'm finding God."

We laughed a nervous laugh.

Kathy said, "Who's Freddy Kruger?"

And we laughed even harder.

I made my way to a small tin shack off to the side, followed by Peter, Divan, Kathy, and the Lot Supervising Manager. To avoid any potential lawsuit, Circus Circus comped us a one-thousand-dollar-a-night luxury suite. The sooner we got Jonesy and the Tylenol, the sooner we would be able to join Cherry and her friends in luxury.

A pile of crushed beer cans sat next to the splintered, plywood doorway. A handwritten sign that looked as if a child using magic markers had colored it read: 'Open.'

Truth be told, it really did look as if we'd stepped onto a movie set. We could easily imagine Freddy Kruger's discarded bones to step from a half-smashed Buick or Olds, or for Dan Aykroyd in a purple wig to be running past with inner-city pimps in chase, or —

"Chopper, sic balls!" It was Kathy. We stopped, looked at her. She said, "Come on. *Stand By Me*? Even I know that one."

We looked at each other, shrugged.

Divan said, "But ... we are standing by you."

Kathy said, "No, the movie."

I said, "What movie?"

Kathy said, "*Stand By Me.*"

Peter said, "Does it have to be you?"

Kathy said, "What?"

Divan said, "I'd like to stand by Davis."

Peter said, "Already there."

I said, "I'd like to stand by me too."

Peter said, "Dude, already there."

Divan said, "What if I stand on the other —"

Kathy unexpectedly ran toward us, arms open wide, fingers curled in claws at waist level, the beginning of a howl in her lungs. Instinctively, we drew back, hands dropping for protection.

About a foot away from us, Kathy stopped, smiled big. She then proceeded to punch each of us twice in the shoulder while humming The Chordettes, "Lollipop."

We collectively shook our heads and groaned.

During our drive, we discovered that it wasn't Circus Circus' policy to tow unregistered RVs from the lot for the first thirty-six hours. It was Vegas, after all, and the siren call of the slots and tables and flesh could cloud anyone's better judgment. An imposed penalty, yes. But the lack of towing fees and impound charges could be better lost beneath the big top.

No, it was the executive decision of the Lot Supervising Manager to tow the Tylenol. One look at the beast and he felt the owners were freeloaders who would skip town before settling the bill. Peter pointed out that decisions such as this would keep him from being an executive in the future.

The Lot Supervising Manager didn't say another word until a slight breeze picked up, opening the door of the shack a bit. That's when a ragged junkyard dog bounded out at us.

The Lot Supervising Manager said, "Holy mother of Carly Simon!" as he hid behind Divan, an elephant hiding behind a telephone pole.

The ragged dog growled low and deep, but did not bark. It was moving too fast to bark. Two quick leaps and it was there, right in front of us, growling and snapping and —

— skidding to a stop at Kathy's feet where it dropped a knotted-rope toy?

The growling ceased. The dog smiled, revealed teeth stained with a lack of care, and began wagging its tail. It looked at the knotted rope, at Kathy, back at the rope. It barked once, sat, its tail swishing in the dirt like a windshield wiper fighting a never-ending battle.

For a moment Kathy balked, blinked. And then she melted. She dropped to the ground, sitting in front of the mangy cur and began rubbing its matted ears. When she began cooing to it as if it were a baby, the mutt bypassed falling to its stomach and awkwardly flopped to its back. Were it the calculated act of a cunning canine, it worked. Kathy began rubbing its belly with both hands. Within mere moments, the mutt cuddled in her lap, dirt and grime mingling with fresh and unsullied.

In unison, Peter, Divan, and I pulled our gazes from the rub-fest and looked back at the Lot Supervising Manager.

He said, "What?" as he stepped from Divan, attempting to straighten his spine.

We shook our heads and entered the shack. It was empty. In fact, other than Newman, the junkyard dog, the place was eerily absent of life. No bugs, no rats, nothing. Not alive, that is.

Bloodstains covered the junkyard. Small stains here, larger stains there. Again, our imaginations kicked in and soon the stains spread together, grew, flooded. Because after a point, bloodstains are bloodstains are bloodstains. Our minds immediately concluded that a dastardly endeavor ensued moments before our gazes fell upon the scene.

Divan theorized that Ike spent his off time shooting whatever moved with a .22. His theory was backed up with the discovery of many, many, many bullet holes in the vehicle carcasses and shell casings littering the ground. When we discovered larger bullet holes and larger shell casings, we started to spook.

What if Ike returned and thought us to be trespassers? Surely he'd see the Circus Circus van out front and put two and two together, right? At that point, rational thought took an uppercut and went down for the count. Our fears, coupled with sleep deprivation causing us to see movement from the corners of our vision, created a nasty fuel of panic.

We hightailed back to the van, Newman the dog in tow, stopping only to decide the fate of our expedition. Leave a note? None of us felt safe leaving any information that may lead Ike the gun-wielding maniac to us. So what then? We all looked over at the Lot Supervising Manager.

He saw our eyes and knew what we were thinking. "No," he said. "No fucking way I'm staying here."

"Okay," Peter said. "If you really want to play it that way." He turned to Kathy. "We're leaving. Let the dog out."

"No." Without hesitation. We all looked at her, surprised. "I'm not leaving him here."

Divan said, "Come on, Kathy. He's got a home."

She said, "You call this a home? You saw the bullet holes. You saw the beer cans. I'm not leaving Newman here to be Ike's next target."

Peter said, "He's happy. Look at him. He's one happy dog. He's loved. We can't take him away from his home."

I debated jumping into the dispute, but thought better of it. I wasn't about to come between a girl and her dog. And whether or not Divan or Peter knew it, Newman was now Kathy's dog. Newman, his tongue out the side of his mouth, panting in bliss as Kathy rubbed the back of his ears, wasn't objecting.

Were Kathy bringing a new dog home to her husband or live-in boyfriend, one would be inclined to accept the slobber factory as a two-year moratorium of Baby Fever. But Newman was less an adoption in the heat of Baby Fever, and more an adoption in the heat of connecting and nurturing another soul. It's very much the precursor to Baby Fever, and is a sign all men should be told about lest their lives be unexpectedly turned inside out.

Holding Newman close, Kathy said, "Look at him? For Christ's sake, Peter, he hasn't gotten a bath in at least a year. He has mats in his mats, his teeth are probably permanently stained, and you can see most of his ribs. He's only happy because he doesn't know any better. That's not a life, and I'm not going to let him go back to that."

"Kathy —"

"No. End of story. You leave him, you leave me. And even then we're walking out together."

Silence. Neither Peter nor Divan knew what to say. It wasn't as if she were speaking selfishly, although with love, there's always an underlying river of strength that feeds the moment. This may have been the first time we saw Kathy's passion rise to the forefront; the same fire I'd seen simmering in her eyes toward me back in the RV.

This moment would serve as a turning point in Kathy's life. It wasn't a loss of innocence, or a kick in the balls. The passion allowed Kathy to find new direction. Not only would she find herself, but she would find her future.

Ike may have been upset with the loss of Newman, but the happiness of hundreds upon hundreds of dogs that found homes would make up for that. After returning to Colorado University, Kathy quickly altered her course load to focus on nonprofit management. She added an extra year to her collegiate career, but her sense of fulfillment trumped student loans and a steady paycheck.

After a moment of consideration, Peter threw his hands up. "Fine," he said, turning to the Lot Supervising Manager.

"Now, you have a choice. You wait here for Ike to return and find out what happened to our Tylenol, or you —"

"Tylenol?"

"Our Elaganza. Our RV you towed."

"Oh."

"So you either wait here, or you drive back with us and you explain all of this to the police."

The Lot Supervising Manager shook his bald head violently, causing his neck to jiggle.

He said, "I'm not staying. You saw what he's like. He'll hurt me."

"Don't worry. You'll only be alone for a half hour. We'll send the van back for you."

At this, the driver, silent up until now, looked in the rear view mirror and said, "Like hell you will."

Peter said, "You're going to leave this man to his death?"

"Find someone else for your suicide mission. I'm just a driver."

Kathy said, "Let's just call the police."

"No!" said the Lot Supervising Manager.

Kathy said, "Jonesy is in the back of that thing. Who knows where it is at the moment. For all we know, this Ike person could have found him and —"

"She's got a point," said Divan. "What if he wakes up?"

"He's passed out," said the Lot Supervising Manager. "You said he's passed out."

"But he could wake up," said Peter. "With all the jostling and the bumping, yeah, Kathy's right. We should call the police and get them looking for the Tylenol."

"Come on," said the Lot Supervising Manager. "He'll be back. Any moment. Let's wait."

Peter said, "Or Jonesy could already be one of these bloodstains." He was calm, collected, and clearly working the Lot Supervising Manager. But his argument did possess a question of truth. Maybe not with Jonesy winding up as a bloodstain somewhere, but his well-being was in question. What if he did wake up? What if Ike did have a temper? Or a gun? Or a temper and a gun?

I said, "We call the police."

Everyone looked at me.

I said, "End of discussion. This is Jonesy. I don't give a fuck about the Tylenol."

The Lot Supervising Attendant burst into tears.

As it turned out, we didn't need to call the police. For when we arrived back at the —

Circus Circus Hotel and Casino

— we found Jonesy sitting on the sidewalk, twenty feet from where the Tylenol had been parked. He was asleep, his head in his hands, his elbows resting on his knees. We approached him. We nudged him. He woke up with a start.

"Whoa, hey!" he said. Then he recognized us. "You're all fuckers."

And then he told us what happened.

Jonesy's Vegas Tale

"I woke up and it was dark. I saw the note, laughed even though it wasn't fucking funny, and went to use the bathroom. I didn't notice the Tylenol was moving. I figured, hey, my vision's blurred because I just woke up, and I'm stumbling over everything because my body's still pissed about the drug. It all seemed to make sense."

He spoke in a calm, logical manner as if he were relating the events of a church raffle. But he was staring off into space, his eyes unfocused. He never even blinked.

"It wasn't until I made it to the kitchen, made myself a ham sandwich, and sat down to eat it that I noticed that the front end of the Elaganza was on the back of a tow truck and we were moving down the highway. That's when I threw up in the sink.

"I started hyperventilating. My vision blurred even more. I fell to my knees and figured I'd had a complete break from reality. I'd heard stories of this shit happening. You drop acid and hours later you experience total isolation. Anxiety rises and you freak the fuck out. I threw up again, and as these stories were popping around my mind, I realized I was still tripping."

He wasn't tripping, of course. Peter had known it was Jonesy's first experience with the drug, so he gave Jonesy a half a tab rather than a full hit. Jonesy didn't know this, but, in the end, believing he was still overtaken by the chemicals may have saved his life. To this day, he'll swear he had a bad trip.

After he accepted he was tripping, he forced himself to calm down. It was easy because he wasn't tripping. This all was really happening and he was justifying it any way he could. His mind didn't know he was no longer under the effects of the drug, but his body did.

A mind is a terrible thing to waste.

"After I calmed myself down, I told myself that everything was fine. I just had to ride it out. Simple. I could do it. So, I walked to the window and took in the scenery. We'd pulled off the highway and were slowing down. Good, I thought. A good time to take in the surroundings. Find my friends. Maybe make this a spiritual journey.

"We stopped for a light. I stepped out of the RV, and waved goodbye as the tow truck pulled away. I'll see it again,

I thought. It really hasn't gone anywhere. This is just all in my imagination. Ride it out."

He paused, squinted in pain, placed the palm of his hand to his forehead as if applying pressure to avert a major rupture. We calmly waited, Kathy running her nails over his back to soothe him, Newman licking his hand. After a moment, he took a deep breath and continued.

"I saw a structure in the distance flashing with lights, believed that it was the Stratosphere, and started walking toward it. Why not? It's really not as far as it seems. Go there, come back. Simple. Ride it out. See what there was to see.

"But the more I walked, the farther the Stratosphere appeared. I thought, what the fuck? My mind must be fucking with me. The drug must be fucking with me. What was I going to do? And then I had it. I knew how to fix the problem. I'd outsmart my mind. Confuse the drug. So I started running, thinking if I didn't look at the Stratosphere, my mind couldn't judge the distance, and so it couldn't fuck with me anymore.

"It was dark, and the only thing I could see were things illuminated under the streetlights. It was like blinking as I was running down the street. Parked cars, darkness, parked cars without tires, darkness, parked cars with people sleeping in them, darkness.

"I was like Forest fucking Gump, man. I just ran. The sun rose. The streetlights went dark. And I just ran. After a while, I looked up and the Stratosphere seemed to get bigger. That's when things around me started to move. Come alive. Come toward me. Come after me. Suddenly I'm dodging cars pulling out of their driveways. I'm dodging big men throwing trash cans around. I'm dodging kids on bikes who are shouting, chasing, and throwing newspapers at me.

"That's when I realized I not only had to outsmart my mind and the drug, but I had to outsmart my surroundings. Because I was running down the strip, and not in some neighborhood. There weren't any houses. There weren't any paperboys or street side trashcans. So I stopped, and started running after the kids on the bikes.

"But they kept throwing newspapers at me. So I caught a few in mid-air and threw them right back. And ya know what? I got one of the fuckers. Right in the back of the head. Laid him out rolling. I smiled, shouted at them, and resumed my trek to the Stratosphere.

"Then one of the newspaper-throwing mother fuckers came from behind me and clipped my knees with his bag. I remember falling and hitting my head on the sidewalk. Then things started to go black. I heard laughter and a bike ride off. I tried to sit up, but my limbs weren't moving. The darkness began to overtake me. But just before it did, I heard car brakes squeal to a stop and worried voices."

His tone didn't rise, rather, it lowered to a near whisper.

"I don't know how long I was out, but I woke up smelling some terrible, awful, horrid smell and feeling the mother of all big fucking headaches. I opened my eyes. And I was in a soup kitchen.

"I waited for the soup kitchen to fade into anything more pleasant, and when it didn't, I began to look around. And I saw that I was surrounded by dozens of transients and a terrible, awful, horrid smell was the feet of one of the transients on the back of my seat.

"I recoiled forward, hit my head on the seat in front of me, nearly blacked out again. But when my vision began to clear this time, I observed that the transients weren't just normal, homeless transients, they were junkie transients. I could see the track marks on their arms and the glaze in their eyes.

"That's when I realized every one of the transients was facing me, looking at me. I began to recoil, but then it all hit me. It all made sense. They all faced the same direction because the seats faced the same direction. We were in a small movie theater.

"As I started to take it all in, the lights dimmed and a beam flashed from one end of the room, I saw something appear on the screen ... stars ... space ... what looked like a planet ...

"Then a voice boomed and my head started to spin. And even though I covered my ears, I heard the voice say: 'Man can recover to himself some of the happiness. Some of the sincerity, some of the love and kindness in which he was created. We have the answers to human suffering, and they are available to everyone ...'

"The pain was excruciating and I wanted to start yelling: 'For God's sake, why are you doing this to me?' ... And then I saw the name appear on the screen ... And I screamed."

Kathy held Jonesy as he looked down at his feet, small trails of tears cutting into the dirt on his face.

"I ran over them to get out. I stepped on seats. I stepped on people. They tried to stop me, but I hit the door and I just ran and ran until I got here."

We were all silent as we digested his tale.

Then Divan softly said, "What was the name?"

Jonesy opened his mouth to speak, choked up, recovered, and said, "L. ... L. Ron Hubbard. It was the worst acid trip ever."

And then he burst into tears.

Before we retreated to the room, we gave the Lot Supervising Manager an ultimatum: get our RV back within ten hours or we call the police. No ifs, ands, or buts. He blubbered, balked, attempted to grow a backbone, failed.

He would get the Tylenol back. In the meantime, we'd sleep it all off and wake up in the morning as if nothing had ever happened.

When we entered the insanely large one-bedroom luxury suite, I realized we were all together for the first time since pulling into Vegas. It felt refreshing and comforting. As if our escape from the tension and stress would finally come to fruition.

We woke up Cherry and the other two girls, inquired to the reasoning behind their nakedness, learned our luggage was in the Tylenol, and that the hotel was laundering their clothes. Doing nothing to avert our gazes, we promptly called down for bathrobes and laundry service.

Before the bathrobes arrived, we put Jonesy in the giant porn-sized super-king bed between the very naked Cherry and one of her very naked friends. He was asleep within a minute, although he woke up a few hours later to discover he was being molested.

Peter climbed into bed too, spooned the girl not sliding up to Jonesy, and started kissing her neck, her shoulder, more. Divan's exhaustion triumphed over his libido, and within moments of laying claim to one of two huge couches in the living room, he was sawing away.

Kathy and I decided to give Newman a bath.

My initial feeling was that the bathroom must double as a bomb shelter. But instead of concrete, it was marble. And remarkably, it looked as if it had been carved from one huge block. You'd think it would feel claustrophobic, yet it betrayed a sense of soothing, as if by entering, you received a sensual massage while inhaling the unscented fragrance of calm.

It was huge. It had wings. The husband's wing, the wife's wing, and a door separating the two. No wonder so many wealthy marriages end in divorce. Style dictates they separate when happy, and they soon dissolve into their respective worlds, their respective wings, and just never open the door.

Newman was filthy. I'd judged him as an indistinguishable mutt, but as the designer shampoo washed away the neglect, I realized he was a light brown lab with a chow's black tongue. At first he freaked. We put him in the massive Jacuzzi tub, he started to buck, and soon small Newman dog prints were all over the bathroom. Kathy and I didn't care. We were laughing as we chased Newman. It felt damn good.

Later, Newman was happily curled up in the corner, half on the cool marble floor, and half on a pile of wet and dry towels. Next to his head was a dinner plate licked clean. Steak. Tender. Large. Newman was definitely making up for lost time.

Kathy and I sat in silence, watching him sleep. I made a mental note to thank everyone for dragging me out of my room. Instilling an innocent creature with happiness helped ease my pain, although I suspected I would forget the sensation when we returned to Boulder.

Kathy and I were holding hands, leaning up against the wall, when she said, "Where do you see yourself in five years?" Our fingers caressed fingers. Our chills ran over chills.

I said, "Five years? Shit, I don't know."

"Think about it for a minute."

I did. In that minute I saw myself with a hundred different futures. I didn't have the heart to tell her not a one was with her. So I shook my head and said, "I can't think. I'm sorry."

She said, "Been a crazy day, huh?"

"Crazy week. Crazy month." Suddenly, I was tired. So tired that I couldn't keep my eyes open and I felt myself slipping away.

Kathy kissed me. The fire and the electricity coursing though her veins jolted me awake. I pulled back in reflex.

But when I saw the lust and wanting in her eyes, saw her lick her lips subtly, unconsciously, saw her chest hitch as desire tensed her muscles, I moved in to kiss her. Half awake, half asleep, confused with the passion I felt, certain of the passion she felt, we lay on the floor of the bathroom.

After a while, I watched as Kathy cleaned out the tub and filled it. We were covered in wet Newman hair and wet Newman dirt. Anticipation danced along my nerves. Why had I pulled away from her in the RV? Why was I afraid of this? It was comfortable. It was right.

The tub cleaned, Kathy looked at me, the flames licking at her boundaries, ready to flare up, ready to consume her desires. She stood, and with a smile that betrayed her complete lack of inhibition, she allowed her robe to slip from her shoulders. Then, ever so slowly, she stepped into the rising water.

I would have fainted were I not already on the floor. Kathy was beautiful. She was stunning. She was magnificently curved in all the right places and tight in all the rest. And she shined.

She said, "Are you going to join me?"

I opened my mouth to speak, realized my tongue was mush, and nodded. She smiled in genuine humor as I stumbled to a stand and neared.

As I was about to step into the tub, she said, "You may want to take off the bathrobe first."

CHAPTER THIRTEEN

Eight hours later, Kathy wouldn't look at me. When Divan, Peter, and I exited the luxury suite, Kathy was wrapped in a bathrobe, her knees tucked to her chest, her arms hugging them. She was looking out the window, down at the evening Las Vegas Strip traffic. Newman was asleep at her feet.

She didn't look at me. Didn't speak to me. She was pissed because I tried to do the right thing.

The Lot Supervising Manager had called us thirty minutes earlier to tell us that he'd found the Tylenol. It was behind a strip club on the other side of town. It was still hooked up to the wrecker. No one knew why.

If the others noticed Kathy's displeasure with me, they didn't acknowledge it. When Divan asked if she wanted to join us, she said she was tired and would prefer to stay with Newman.

Jonesy stayed behind as well. He was still in bed with the trio of girls, all sleeping for short bursts until one woke and decided it was time to molest another. He'd had enough terror in the past twenty-four hours, and considering we didn't know what to expect with Ike, we didn't bother to interrupt them. That's what Vegas was about. Breaking the rules and being rewarded. Jonesy earned it. Good times.

As night fell, the Circus Circus mini-van pulled to a stop a block away from the strip club. It took us a good minute to comprehend what we were looking at.

The Drink 'N' Cooch

— was one of those nondescript enterprises that deferred to the basics to gain its clientele. Definitely not one of your classier establishments. And yet, the place was packed. Vehicles filled the dirt and gravel parking lot in a haphazard manner, as if the cars were thrown into park wherever they rolled to a stop.

"'This is as far as I go," said the driver. The Lot Supervising Manager, now off duty and dressed in black clothing, a black knit cap, with black shoe polish on his face, shot the driver a look of absolute fear.

The driver said, "Fine. I'll be down the block. Fifteen minutes. Any longer, and I'm gone."

Fair 'nuff. We nodded our thanks and exited.

The original plan was simple: Find Ike, tell him that the Lot Supervising Manager had made a mistake, have the Lot Supervising Manager pay for the tow, and get the Tylenol. To no one's surprise, the simple plan ran into a complicated wall.

The Lot Supervising Manager came clean. He was Ike's brother-in-law. Ike had loaned him some money to pay off a gambling debt, but he blew the money on a basketball game and a night of debauchery. For this, Ike broke both of his pinkie toes. He would have broken more, had his wife, the Lot Supervising Manager's sister, not intervened. Somehow, she talked Ike into loaning the Lot Supervising Manager even more money, repaid by tows from the Circus Circus lot.

At the onset, the tows were frequent. But when hotel guest-complaints gained the attention of the police, frequent became occasional. That's when Ike threatened to tie the Lot Supervising Manager's intestines into a bow tie if he wasn't paid soon.

After the driver left us on the curb, the Lot Supervising Manager ran to the parking lot and ducked between some cars. We watched, shook our heads, then looked at one another in the way guys do when they haven't a clue how to proceed.

After a moment of silence, I said, "This is crazy."

Divan said, "Yup."

I said, "Let's just call the police."

Peter said, "Where's your sense of adventure?"

I said, "Bloodstains beat adventure."

And Peter said, "But quick-and-easy beats bloodstains."

We began our search. Behind the club, we saw it. Our Tylenol. On the back of a wrecker. Looking ready to be strapped to a rocket and fired across the bow of a pirate ship.

"Sweetness," said Divan, walking up to the beast and caressing the side as if it were a horse. "How I've missed thee."

"Right," said Peter, turning to me. "Let's do it."

"Do what?" I said.

"It."

"It?"

"Glad we're on the same page. Whistle if you see Ike."

"I can't whistle."

"You can't whistle?"

"I can't whistle."

"Well, if you see Ike, pretend."

Peter began undoing the safety chains. Divan began to jimmy the lock of the wrecker because we couldn't lower the Tylenol to the ground without power. I went in search of the

Lot Supervising Manager. I found him hiding behind a lime green Gremlin and said, "Okay. Point him out to me."

"Who?"

"Ike."

"No!"

"I need to know who to watch out for."

He began to whine as if I were asking him to call Mike Tyson a pussfag. "But you have your RV, just like we agreed."

I cursed silently, knowing if I raised my voice, I'd drive the blubbering fool further into his pit of gutless tears. "Look, until we're driving away, you're still responsible for this mess."

He started to back away, shaking his baldhead, uncaring about the spit that flew from the sides of his blubbery lips.

I took a deep breath, put on the most disarming smile I could muster, and said, "Do you want me to go in there and find him myself?"

He was about to blubber out a quick response, but was cut off.

"Hey!" said a voice near the club. I turned, and knew it was Ike the moment my gaze fell upon him. He was staggering, a beer in one hand, his focus on Divan trying to pick the lock of the wrecker. A girl who couldn't have been more than sixteen though her makeup added ten years, trailed a foot behind him. She wore black cowboy boots, a leopard print mini-skirt, and an old *Playboy* tee torn down the front, exposing her ample cleavage.

Ike said, "What the fuck do you think you're doing?"

I ducked behind a Volvo.

Ike was built like a red-brick outhouse. That was, if a redbrick outhouse wore coveralls and a hat that read, no shit? 'Don't tread on me.' It looked as if he was negotiating an invisible obstacle course on the open path toward the Tylenol.

He said, "Get the fuck away from my truck!"

I considered my options, saw their potential flash before me, and made a decision. Finding a hand-sized rock in the dirt and gravel parking lot, I moved in behind Ike.

As Ike neared, a smiling Peter stepped from the Tylenol to greet him. Ike reached inside his coveralls. I pulled my arm back to strike. Peter's eyes widened in fear. I began to swing. Peter jumped past Ike and tackled me.

Before I knew it, I was on my stomach and my hands were bound with — what were those? Were those handcuffs?

Peter said, "Ha! Finally got you, you fucker!" Peter pulled me to a stand.

I said, "What the fuck, man?"

Peter said, "What the fuck? You wanna know what the fuck? I'll tell you what the fuck. You're done. It's over. We've got ya red handed." Peter turned to Ike. "I thank you, sir. We couldn't have done this without you."

He pushed me past Ike, toward Divan. He said, "Wow. That was harrowing, wasn't it?"

Divan said, "Sure was," as he continued to work on the lock of the wrecker as if nothing had happened.

Peter said, "Um, Bob?"

Divan looked over his shoulder at him, brows raised.

Peter pointed to Ike. "I'm guessing this is the owner of the vehicle."

Divan's face brightened as if he just learned the test was negative. "Yeah? Beautiful!" He stopped trying to jimmy the lock and shook Ike's hand vigorously. "You, sir, have made my life so much easier."

Ike blinked and said, "I have?"

"That you have. That you have. Wow. You have no idea how hard it is to jimmy doors these days. Do you know how hard it is to jimmy doors these days?"

"Um ..."

"It's damn hard, is what it is. And you know what would make this so much easier?"

"Um ... the key?"

Divan said, "Yes, yes. The key, Ike. The key would be wonderful."

Peter said, "Splendid."

"Wonderfully splendid. Thank you, Ike. Can I call you Ike?"

"How ... How do know my name?"

With this, Divan smiled. "It's on your chest, Ike."

Ike looked down, and sure enough, saw his name stitched to his coveralls.

"Now, Ike," said Peter. "This would go much faster if you would kindly comply with Bob's request for your keys."

"My keys?"

"Yes, Ike. To open your door. To your truck."

"Why do you need to get into my —"

"Look, Ike," Peter said, "we can either do this the easy way, or the hard way. Right now, you're complying with a Las Vegas Police Department investigation into —"

The Sixteen-Year-Old said, "You guys are cops?" This seemed to sober Ike a bit, although he was still swaying, his whored-up kickstand holding him steady.

Peter looked to Divan, confused. "You didn't —"

Divan said, "I thought you did?"

"How could I? I was apprehending this fucker."

"And I was trying to obtain the evidence."

"Let's not do this again," said Peter.

"Do what?"

"This."

"Oh, what?" said Divan. "Are you going to start that 'You're belittling me' rant?"

"This is exactly what I'm talking about. You just can't leave well enough alone, can you?"

"Stop."

"I didn't do anything."

"I said stop." As Divan threw his hands in the air, Peter took a deep breath and turned to Ike. "On behalf of me and my *partner*," spitting 'partner' at Divan, "and the LVPD, I'd like to apologize for not identifying ourselves sooner."

"Um ..."

"Don't worry, it won't happen again. Now, Ike, the keys?"

Ike swayed back and forth slowly, blinked a few times, absently scratched his belly, and said, "You guys are cops?"

Peter sighed. "We just went though this, Ike."

"If you guys are cops, then where are your badges?" said the Sixteen-Year-Old, raising one makeup-caked brow.

Peter blinked a second, and then looked back at Divan. "I didn't ...?"

"No, you didn't."

"Fuck. This investigation is killing me. I'm forgetting everything." Then Peter reached into his pocket and pulled out a badge. An honest to goodness LVPD badge. I blinked in disbelief. The Sixteen-Year-Old blinked in disbelief. Ike staggered, then blinked in disbelief.

"Ike?" said Peter, holding out his hand. "Your keys?"

Very hesitantly, Ike gave them to Peter who tossed them to Divan. For the next two minutes, Ike didn't utter a sound. It was frightening. He was silent, but his expressions had cycled from confusion, to anger, to fury, to resignation, to compliance, repeat. As the Tylenol lowered to the ground, Peter filled in all the blanks.

He said, "We've been investigating a ring of RV thieves for the past six months. What they do is they steal the RVs, smuggle them into Mexico, and then sell them to illegal immigrants who want to pose as a good ol' American family just returning from a trip south of the border."

The Sixteen-Year-Old said, "He's lying. No one smuggles RVs *into* Mexico." All proud of herself, thin arms crossed, bony hip out to the side.

Peter looked at her, and said, "If it's done right, no one's the wiser. That's why it's called smuggling." He turned back to Ike. "We caught whiff of it when we were snipe hunting in Nogales."

"Snipe hunting?" said the Sixteen-Year-Old.

"Snipe is what we call the carrier pigeons the drug runners use to smuggle in their load. We were shooting the fuckers down when we saw a lone RV cross the border, unload a dozen illegals in a Burger King parking lot, and headed back over. It was dumb luck, really. But it led us here." The Tylenol was unhooked and while Divan entered through the side door, Peter patted her side. "Yeah. Led us here to this fuckrag." He pushed me into the side of the Tylenol. Hard. I fell to the ground, my lip bleeding. "All in all, a good day's work."

Despite my pain, pride, and bleeding lip, it all looked good. Until Peter was shaking Ike's hand in thanks. That's when the Lot Supervising Manager ran up saying, "You're not leaving without me, are you?"

Ike looked at the Lot Supervising Manager, back at Peter, still holding his hand, and then smiled. "You say you're a cop?"

Without missing a beat, Peter said, "LVPD, Ike. Your brother-in-law was instrumental in our investigation that led us to —"

Ike said, "If you're a cop, then where's your gun?"

"Gun?" Peter looked from Ike, to me, and back again. "We're dealing with RV smugglers, Ike. How many RV smugglers do you know who carry guns?"

Ike looked from Peter, to the Lot Supervising Manager, and then to the ground. After a moment of consideration, he unzipped his coveralls and pulled out a handgun that would put Clint Eastwood to shame.

Peter, unfazed, said, "Now, I'd be worried if you were an RV smuggler. But Ike? You're not an RV smuggler. You're a tow-truck driver. And a damn good one at that. I'm going to put in a good word for you with the boys at the station. Put you in contact with traffic. Get you a contract with the city. How does that —"

Ike swung the gun across Peter's face. Peter fell to the ground, his chin bleeding open. I moved toward Ike but was still cuffed and couldn't block his calloused backhand. He slapped me aside. I fell to my knees, the side of my head striking the Tylenol.

Darkness began to rise. I saw Ike move to Peter, pick him up, and hit him with a closed fist. I fought the gloom.

As Ike was about to hit Peter a third time, I kicked out hard, connecting with Ike's left knee. He let out a howl. But he didn't drop Peter. I didn't get in another kick. Instead, the whored-up Sixteen-Year-Old started kicking me in the ribs. I shrunk away, not only fighting the darkness, but her wicked pointy cowboy boots.

I heard Ike say, "You think you can fuck with me?"

He hit Peter.

"You think you can come in and steal my load?"

He hit Peter.

"You think you can break into my rig and insult me with these lies?"

He hit Peter.

"You think you can make me look like a fool in front of my girl?"

Ike gripped the handle of his gun and swung the barrel across Peter's jaw. A loud crack filled my ears. The whored-up Sixteen-Year-Old stopped kicking me, turned, eyes wide, her anger transforming into animalistic awe and fascination. She said, "Ike?" And when Ike turned to her, she said, "Are you gonna shoot him?"

Ike blinked, half of his scowl becoming a smile. "Should I?"

A moment of primal lust flashed between them. The whored-up Sixteen-Year-Old rolled her shoulders back, thrust her small breasts out, and I could see her nipples harden under the old torn and stretched *Playboy* tee. She said, "I think you should. I think you should shoot him."

"Yeah? You want me to shoot him?"

"Yeah. I want you to blow his fucking head off."

Ike spat in the dust and gravel parking lot without taking his eyes from his whore, nodded, turned to Peter. "Well, you heard the girl."

He cocked the gun.

"This is what happens to fuckers who lie to me and try to steal my rig."

I focused on his hand holding the gun; saw his finger move toward the trigger.

Time slowed.

I felt utterly helpless and lost.

I screamed.

I screamed in rage.

I screamed in pain.

But most of all, I screamed like a scared little fucking girl because I was about to see my best friend's head blown off in front of me and I was handcuffed and helpless and couldn't do a fucking thing about it and so I screamed and yelled and pleaded and I prayed and closed my eyes.

The gun fired.

I screamed some more. I cried. I gave into the darkness. I began to fall. I felt weightless. Black rushed over me. I was tumbling into the maw of resolution and acceptance.

And then I felt hands grab me. Grip under my arms, fingers digging deep, pulling me to a stand and tearing a hole in the wall of darkness. A blinding light of confusion flowed inward.

I opened my eyes. My vision became a strobe of half images void of color. I heard nothing beyond my shallow breathing and rapid heartbeat. A form moved from me to the discarded form of Peter Carter lying on the ground. I swayed, started to fall back, felt the cold exterior of the Tylenol, leaned. The form lifted Peter's body to a stand, then released him. Peter's body began to slump to the ground. And then it held, suspended in mid collapse, a limp puppet on loose strings. And then Peter's body straightened. And I saw Peter raise his head and look around.

Peter was bleeding but very much alive. My internal joy cried fiercely. The blinding light of confusion pulled me from the folds of accepting darkness.

An internal switch flipped.

Sound rushed in.

Time coalesced.

Divan grabbed me by the front of the shirt, pulled me to Peter, and then pushed both of us through the side door of the Tylenol. We slumped, sprawled, collapsed. He climbed over us and past us and was in the driver's seat where he started up the beast.

As he put her in reverse and sped backward, I managed to disentangle myself from Peter, roll to my back, and sit up. The side door was open, swaying back and forth with the jerking movement of the Tylenol. Through it, I saw the whored-up Sixteen-Year-Old kneeling over the unmoving form of Ike, lying face down in the dirt and gravel parking lot.

Next to his head lay a hand-sized rock with a bloodstain on it.

We hit the street. We skidded to a stop. The engine roared with a flood of fuel. We jerked forward. The door slammed shut. The last thing I saw was the neon sign reading 'Drink N' Cooch.' Behind it, a billboard read "Vegas, good times."

The drive back to the —

Circus Circus Hotel and Casino

— flashed without time. At one moment, we were being tossed around the Tylenol, the next we were at the hotel. And then Divan was out and headed to the room to get everyone and everything together. Peter and I sat in the Tylenol in silence.

Peter's chin was still bleeding. Divan had given him the shirt Cherry had discarded on the drive out, and it was soaked. Amazingly, he would barely get a scar from it.

We sat. We blinked. We stared at the walls.

And then Peter said, "Wow."

I wanted to laugh. To just let it all out, to stifle the pain with bellyaching hoots. But I didn't. The urge died.

Peter said, "Wow. I almost fucking died."

All I could manage was, "Yup."

Again, the moment was ripe for laughter. But no. Insanity continued to dance.

"Wow."

I nodded, wordlessly.

Then Peter said, "Do the Nuggets play tonight?"

Good question. I said as much.

He said, "It doesn't matter, though. Bickerstaff is killing that team."

Silence.

Then, "I fucking hate that guy. How does he get off trading away the big man?"

I said, "The big man wanted to go."

"He didn't before Bernie came. He was a Nugget for life before Bernie came."

Silence.

More silence.

I shifted my weight, and pain in my wrists shot up my arms and into my shoulders. I grimaced, said, "A little help?"

Peter blinked, nodded. As he pulled the key from his pocket and removed my shackles, he said, "You fucking saved my life, man."

I blinked, balked, said, "I did what to who now?"

"I was fucking Bill Paxton. Game over, man. Game over. But you distracted him. You distracted Ike long enough for Divan to hit the fucker. I was fucking dead. I was so fucking dead."

I attempted to comprehend the words he kept repeating. But before I could express my confusion, he started crying. The only time I've ever known Peter Carter to cry. Four years later, his mother would die of a heart attack. Peter didn't cry. A month later, his father had slipped into a depression so deep he ended his life with sleeping pills. Peter didn't cry. But here, in the beast, in the Circus Circus parking lot, he cried.

And through his tears, he kept mumbling, "You did it, man. You did it."

Later, I learned what I did. What I said. But even then, I didn't believe it. I still don't. What I said was dumb. Moronic. It made no sense why I should have said what I said at the time I said it, and I can't for the life of me figure out how it came to mind.

It was Jonesy who pried it out of us. Pried it out of Divan, really. Everyone who wasn't there was so juiced about it that Jonesy just … needed … to … know.

And so Divan told it as he drove us out of Sin City.

Divan's Vegas Tale

"I was just about to start up the Tylenol when I saw the Lot Supervising Manager running up. Immediately, I knew there was no way we'd make a clean break. Then I saw the smile on Ike's face, heard him ask to see our guns, and I knew things were about to get bloody.

"I knew Ike had a gun under his coveralls, because when he approached us, I saw the bulge, the shape. But because I was so wrapped up in the ruse, the story, I disregarded the gun altogether. Everything was happening so damn fast … So, when I saw Ike reach into his coveralls, I remembered, and I just reacted.

"When Ike began to unzip his coveralls, I exited the driver's side door. And when I heard the crack of Ike's gun slamming into Peter's face, I began rounding the back of the Tylenol. I knew the side door was open and that it would partially block Ike's view of me coming. But I had to be careful, because if I was seen, that was it, over, done. So, when I rounded the back, I slowed, even though I knew that every second was precious."

He paused for a moment, thinking, reliving. No one spoke. No one prodded. Only the sound of the engine and the wind whipping by could be heard.

"When I made it to the side door, I heard Ike cock the gun ... And for a second, I thought it was over ... I thought we were all done ... That's when Davis saved us all. That's when he said what he said, screamed what he screamed, and gave me the time I needed. An extra second to pick up a rock, for Ike to turn toward Davis, away from the door ... And when I saw him turn, heard him ask what the hell Davis was talking about, I rushed the last few steps and slammed the rock into the side of his fucking head.

"That's when the gun went off ... One moment it was under Peter's chin, ready to ... The next it was to the side as Ike was falling to the ground, already knocked out. But his finger was still on the trigger. It flexed. The gun fired.

"Without that extra moment, we wouldn't be here talking."

Until Divan's recounting, I didn't know Ike turned toward me; didn't remember he spoke to me. I was just like Jonesy. Just like Kathy. Just like the girls. I was an audience member, at the edge of my seat, my ass sweating, hearing for the first time what happened in those moments when I was on the ground, my hands cuffed behind me, screaming like a fucking child.

And then Jonesy turned to me with amazement and said, "Well?"

I looked at him, saw the others turn to me.

"What did you say?" He wanted to know. They all wanted to know.

A part of me was grateful Divan didn't include what I said, because I didn't want to know myself. I didn't want those blanks to be filled in because that would mean I was there and it was all real and I did fall apart and Peter did almost have his head blown off.

And so I said, "I don't know."

"Come on," said Jonesy. "What was it?"

His eagerness was so infectious I actually tried to remember. But my memory was all screaming and crying and I said quietly, "Seriously. I don't know. I don't remember saying anything."

Jonesy turned to Divan who was driving the Tylenol out of Las Vegas, away from Ike, away from our adventure and back to Boulder. Jonesy turned, and so did everyone else.

Panic sucked the air from my lungs. I turned to Divan to tell him to shut his fucking mouth because it didn't happen and he was a fucking liar and he was making all of this up and, and ... and ... and ...

And I didn't speak. Because I was just like the others. I was on the edge of my seat with my ass sweating and I wanted to know. Goddamnit, I wanted to know.

And Divan told us.

And I remembered.

Vegas Through My Eyes

Ike spat in the dust and gravel parking lot without taking his eyes from his whore, nodded, turned to Peter. "Well, you heard the girl."

He cocked the gun.

"This is what happens to fuckers who lie to me and try to steal my rig."

I focused on his hand holding the gun; saw his finger move toward the trigger.

Time slowed.

I felt utterly helpless and lost.

I screamed.

I screamed in rage.

I screamed in pain.

But most of all, I screamed like a scared little fucking girl because I was about to see my best friend's head blown off in front of me and I was handcuffed and helpless and couldn't do a fucking thing about it and so I screamed and yelled and pleaded and I prayed and closed my eyes.

And I screamed out, "Who would you rather fuck, Scarlet or Lady Jaye?"

And Ike stopped to look at me, confusion short circuiting his defenses of comprehension. Because the question was so out of the blue, so asinine, so from fuck knows where, that it captured Ike's focus. He had to know. He had to take a moment from killing Peter to open his mouth in confusion, turn to me and say, "What the fuck are you talking about?"

And that was when Divan hit him in the head with the rock.

And the gun fired ... and I screamed some more ... and I cried ... and I still don't believe any of it.

The rest of the drive was uneventful. We ate, we slept. There was talk, but nothing of consequence. Jonesy was pissed that he wasn't there. He heard the words, but didn't feel the depth of emotion within the situation, didn't understand the reality of being involved. He was an armchair quarterback. What would he have done had he been there? How would he have reacted?

Of course, in his mind, he wouldn't have clammed up. He wouldn't have been hurt. And he certainly wouldn't have been screaming and crying when faced with death.

At our first gas stop, Divan pulled me outside to see how I was doing.

I said, "Good, considering." Then, "No, I'm not. This is fucked. Fucked, fucked — Did I really say that?"

He said, "You don't remember?"

I shook my head.

He said, "Isn't it amazing how the mind works?"

And then I remembered something he once told me. I quoted it before I even knew I was speaking. "'All it takes is a sneeze or an off-the-cuff comment to alter the other guy's perception.'"

Divan smiled. "Or asking if you'd rather fuck Scarlet or Lady Jaye." And then he studied my face. The strain, the exhaustion, the disbelief. "You didn't do anything wrong. You know that, right?"

I began to tell him of course I knew that. I wasn't the one who pistol-whipped Peter. I wasn't the one who put the gun to his head. But I didn't. Because I *had* done something wrong. I *should* have done something more than screaming. Something more than crying and screaming.

I looked away, shame welling inside. Getting my ass kicked by a child almost cost Peter his life. I may have distracted Ike for a second, but I should have done something more. Anything more.

Divan suggested I clean the windows, clear my head. A breeze picked up, and when it ruffled my hair, my scalp burned from the earlier bruising. Time passed.

After paying, Divan returned and he said, "Ya know? We should have called the cops. Oh, well. No harm, no foul."

I balked, said, "Peter was almost killed."

Divan ran a hand through his hair, a knowing smile broadening on his weathered face. "Yeah. But he wasn't." He took a deep breath, looked around. "Feels good to be alive, doesn't it?"

He climbed inside the beast, but before he disappeared, he turned to me and said, "For the record? Lady Jaye. She had that glint in her eye."

On the drive back, I tried not to think about what happened, but every time I looked at Peter, I saw the gun in his face. I saw Ike. I wanted to talk about it. I wanted to ask him what was going through his head. He didn't utter a word the entire trip. It was fitting. Kathy wasn't talking to me, Peter wasn't talking to anyone, and Jonesy was trying to get everyone to talk. And then I realized something that made me chuckle silently at the absurdity of it all.

I wasn't thinking about my pop.

Three days after we returned, I stopped by —

Chez Carter

— with a bottle of Jack. Peter wasn't the same, it was obvious: The darkness under his eyes, his slow, pausing speech confused by the barrage of thoughts, his staring at the turned-off television. He looked as if his emotions had walked away from a three-alarm fire and his body was finally acknowledging the pain. His shoulders slumped forward; he struggled to keep his eyes open. Every time he moved, he grimaced in pain, and yet he couldn't sit still on the couch.

And then he refused the bottle of Jack.

I set the unopened bottle on the coffee table and sat in the recliner next to the couch.

Peter rubbed his nose, looked down at the coffee table. "Do ya want one?"

I said, "One what?"

"A drink."

"I don't know."

"You can have one if you want."

"Yeah?"

"Yeah. Shit, yeah."

I said, "You know? I'm all right."

He blinked a few times. "Yeah?"

"Yeah."

He shifted on the couch from one side to the other, finally settling on propping his feet on the edge of the coffee table, his knees bent. He said, "You're okay, right? I mean, you're not offended."

"Offended? By what?"

"Me drinking, you know. The Jack."

"But you're not. Drinking the Jack."

"Because I appreciate the effort."

"Are *you* sure you don't want a drink?"

Silence. Peter shifted to the side and crossed his legs under him.

He smiled a bit too big, laughed a bit loud. I wondered if he was baked. He said, "You see the *Simpsons* last night?"

I didn't. I said as much.

"The Stonecutters. It's probably my favorite."

"Really?"

"Well." He looked at the television, rubbed his nose. "I'm torn. I mean, it is a great episode, but if I had to chose, it would be between the Monorail and the Streetcar. I mean, how can you argue with the Ayn Rand School for Tots?"

I said, "It's really so hard to choose."

Peter shifted so he could stretch his back over the end of the couch.

Then he said, "You want to know what I saw in that moment before death?" Matter of fact. No change in tone, no facial expression. He said, "Nothing. I saw absolutely nothing. And the more I think about that, the more it pisses me off."

Silence.

He said, "Because all our lives, we're told that there's going to be a fucking white light and that tunnel. And it's not as if this is some sort of wives' tale, or primeval myth or ancient folklore passed down for generations by blind eunuchs on the mountain top who only speak Sumerian. This is knowledge that we hear every fucking year of our lives from some lucky bastard who dies and comes back and brags about it to the papers. And damnit, I'm not happy about it." He rubbed his nose, not in thought but because it was wet. He said, "Do you understand what I'm saying?"

His eyes were darting all around, and he punctuated his words with sharp slashes, claws, fists.

He said, "We govern our life by rules. Rules that form when we're young and are built on our trials, our errors, our mommies, and our daddies. And I fucking *know* that every so often life fires a fucking cannonball and blows a fucking monster-ass hole in one of those rules and we're left to decide: Are we going to continue living with a damaged rule that can collapse, toppling everything built on top of it? Or are we going to tear it all down through understanding and examination even though it'll be painful and time consuming, but may save us from harm in the long run? Are we going to be chickenshits and ignore? Or are we going to be fucking men and own up to our weaknesses and change what fucking needs to be changed?"

He looked at me, eyes red and full of tears that never fell. He said, "Tell me, Davis. What the fuck am I? Am I a chickenshit, or a fucking man? Because everything is crashing down and I don't have a fucking clue what I'm going to do."

And with that, Peter grabbed the bottle of Jack, ripped off the cap, and started drinking.

I stopped him. Not at first, but after a while, I stopped him from finishing the bottle. He consumed enough to calm down, breathe deep, shudder. We sat back, staring at the turned-off television.

Silent, we agreed not to talk. It was a marvelous non-conversation, one I'll never forget. We knew the choices we could make, what paths we could walk, and to what toll those paths would expose us. We also knew that voicing our choices would acknowledge their existence and make them real. Like the Boogyman or Beetlejuice or Barbara Streisand. So we sat. And we consumed. And after a while we popped on the television and watched whatever the fuck was on.

And it felt good.

What wasn't spoken explained everything. The knowledge of what had transpired, what Peter had just told me, could never reach outside ears. If word got out, it would excise an already crumbling foundation and our club, our sanctuary, would cease to exist.

It would also carve a large chunk from Peter's aura, his rep. If anyone discovered Peter had been emotionally kicked in the balls and was questioning everything upon which he had constructed his existence …

Peter left for California a few days later. I wouldn't see him for another six months when he chose white-water rafting instead of an imbibe-and-get-naked night with strippers and whores. When he started to tear down and rebuild.

As it turned out, Peter's wedding to Naomi would be our collective kick to the balls. A kick that began with our Las Vegas adventure.

Jonesy would feel his death hold on college existence slipping, forcing a gutter mucking self-examination that would lead him to Debbie.

I would meet Pamela, would embrace the art of misdirection, and would learn the art of sidestepping the unpleasant or unwanted.

Divan would understand his tether to our band had all but frayed, and it was time for him to roam the wilderness in search of his path.

Reality would show us all that who we were in our college lives did not translate into who society wished us to be.

Some of us would decide to embrace self-examination and understanding, while others would chose to tread in knowing ignorance.

As for Kathy, she would finally understand that no matter how much you try to protect yourself from the real world, those closest to you deal the harshest of blows.

CHAPTER FOURTEEN

Friday

Downtown Denver Hotel Monaco

Max continues to bang, and that's when I see someone leaning against the hallway wall, hidden from my point of view. I poke my head out and I thank the minibar for my lack of surprise. Were I sober, the wind would have been knocked from my lungs. But not this time. This time, I'm a rock.

After a moment:

"Hi, Davis," she says.

"Hi, Kathy," I say.

The past runs over me like an ice-cream truck.

Without a word, Kathy and I exit. Down the hallway, the elevator, the hotel lobby. The hotel pool is one of those five-foot shallow concrete blights, although the decorative lighting gives the appearance of great depth. We're alone.

It's painful. Not the silence, but figuring out how to end it. Everything that comes to mind just seems so second grade. Stumbling and jumbled. I start and stop a dozen times without uttering a sound. She looks at me, her head cocked, a thin half smile, and I can tell that she still understands me perfectly. What I'm trying to do. What I'm trying to say. It's odd how she can still do that. Understand me perfectly except for those few moments when the fire spills from her soul.

She says, "I got your invite."

"Yeah?"

"It was nice. Pretty."

"Yeah, well … That was all Pamela."

"I know. There's no way you would have chosen that color."

She laughs and I can tell she's disgusted with herself. Disgusted for allowing herself to be here. To feel it again. The confusion. The pain.

So I say, "How have you been?" It helps, but not much. Her warm brown eyes once filled with innocence are now arctic. They question my intentions, the hidden meaning behind my words. She blinks, and when I see the sparkling reflection in her eyes, it feels as if an ice pick pierces one of my lungs, tensing my body in shock, allowing the air to escape. Because I *know* I did this to her. I took that innocent, fun girl and infused her with hues of jade.

Kathy takes a deep breath, straightens ever so slightly, and I realize that she can see beyond my stony exterior. She sees my pain. And it strengthens her.

"How have I been?" she says. "Well, shit, Davis. I've been great. Thanks for asking. Really."

"Look, Kathy, I —"

"No, Davis. I've been good. Really good." Though her words are sharp, I see a truth to them. She is good. Jaded, angry, but good. Because her life has purpose. Direction to channel that burning passion. What would she have been like if we hadn't shared Vegas? If I hadn't hurt her? Would she have been able to become this no-nonsense activist who didn't take any shit? Not from anyone. Not from me. Especially me.

I don't speak. A part of me wants to, though. A part of me wants to scream at her for her lashing out at me after eight years. As if we haven't grown up. I want to scream and hit back harder, to hurt her, to strike her so she not only shuts up but won't even consider attacking me again … but I don't. I just stand there. Letting her do her thing. Because I deserve it, don't I? Don't I deserve it all?

She continues. She rants, yells. And after she's done, I stand there, noiseless.

And then I say, "It's good to see you, Kathy." And I mean it. And the silence that follows tells me she knows it. Then she laughs. Not genuine. It's laced with everything that's been festering inside her, just wanting to burst forth. But it's still a laugh. It still feels good.

I say, "Are you coming tomorrow?"

"No."

I nod. "I'm sorry, Kathy."

The moment my words hit the air, Kathy's cold, frozen exterior melts. Her shoulders lower, her face relaxes, and the warmth — the innocence that we had all fallen in love with — shines through. Not completely. She's not happy. Not angry. Just … sated.

And then she says in a voice that is still mostly the old Kathy, "You know what I've figured out in the past eight years? That people don't apologize because they're really sorry for what they've done. They apologize because they want to feel better about themselves. They've looked back on the past and realize where they fucked up, and they just wait for that chance to put it right by apologizing, when in reality, it doesn't do a damn thing because the hurt has been there for so long that it won't ever go away. And that the sorry isn't there to fix the hurt, but to wash your hands of it all."

And I've done this to her. A catch of a man I am.

She says, "But, still. I want to know. What are you apologizing for, Davis? What has eight years of reflection told you about what happened and what you did?"

"Does it matter?" I say.

She looks away, closes her eyes, and grimaces as she reaches for the doorway that will open the past. She says, "No." And then she opens her eyes, looks at me, and says softly and full of strength, "But you're going to tell me anyway."

She yanks the door open.

And I tell her.

Vegas Through My Eyes

The tub cleaned, Kathy looked at me, the flames licking at her boundaries, ready to flare up, ready to consume her desires. She stood, and with a smile that betrayed her complete lack of inhibition, she allowed her robe to slip from her shoulders. Then, ever so slowly, she stepped into the rising water.

I would have fainted were I not already on the floor. Kathy was beautiful. She was stunning. She was magnificently curved in all the right places and tight in all the rest. And she shined.

She said, "Are you going to join me?"

I opened my mouth to speak, realized my tongue was mush, and nodded. She smiled in genuine humor as I stumbled to a stand and neared.

As I was about to step into the tub, she said, "You may want to take off the bathrobe first."

I did. Muddy, naked, I stepped into the tub and to her. We sat there, looking at each other, the steam rising. I was smiling like a schoolboy who had braved the walk across the gym floor to dance, but suddenly realized he didn't know how to dance, or walk, or even talk. And Kathy was smiling like a confident girl who knew what she wanted, knew who she was dealing with, and was willing to allow me to take the awkward steps toward it all.

And then I moved. It was faster than it should have been. Maybe I slipped in the tub, or maybe my anticipation was driving nerves to fire out of control. I kissed her too hard and we bumped teeth, smashed lips. Awkward silence spread across the room, replaced by nervous laughter.

I said, "I don't know why I'm acting this way, why I'm nervous." And when I said it, her eyes widened and all inhibition disappeared. She straightened, softly bit her lower lip. She moved toward me and we kissed again. This time there wasn't any teeth bumping, lips smashing. And it was perfect.

Until she spoke.

We kissed. We caressed. We nibbled and petted. And it built. We both staved it off, but we knew that it was about to hit the point of no return where we wouldn't be able to walk away and laugh it off later as a moment of 'what if.'

She said, "Do you have any protection?"

I nodded, began to pull away to look for my pants, for my wallet. But as I did, Kathy gripped my arm tight, pulled me to her, and kissed me ever so softly, ever so gently. Then she kissed down my neck and up to my ear. And between nibbles and kisses and amazing rushes of endorphins, she said in a whisper, "I've never done this before."

I panicked.

Because all this didn't fit into the framework of denial and compartmentalization I had set up in my life. This was not a case of embracing the drug of physical desire in order to bury away emotions. This was different. This was …

It took me a while to piece together what happened next, but with time and a lot of drink, I managed to do it. It wasn't pretty.

Kathy spoke. Told me she was a virgin. The wind left my lungs and I gasped. She stopped kissing, stopped nibbling, pulled back a bit and said, "Are you all right?"

I muttered something.

She said, "I'm sorry, I didn't hear you."

I pulled back from her. She held onto me. I flung her arm off me, tried to stand, slipped. I fell on the lip of the marble tub, my ribs taking the brunt of the force.

Kathy went to my side. Kind. Caring. Loving. I didn't think of the pain. All I could think was that I didn't want this. That I didn't want to be the first. That I didn't want *that* responsibility.

As I struggled to run, she struggled to calm me.

She said, "Davis, please. Don't be mad at me, don't run. It's just that I — I love you. And this isn't a spur-of-the-moment decision. I've thought and I've prayed about this for a long time and I asked myself, 'Is this what I really want? Is this what really I need?' And every day I wake up I have the same answers. Yes, this is what I want. Yes, this is what I need. And yes, I do love you and I know when I look into your eyes and your heart and your smile that you love me too and that this is what you want so don't be frightened or scared or mad because this shouldn't be a big deal, it's just something I wanted you to know because this is something that I wanted to share with you because it's special to me and because I want to give it to you means so much to me."

And in that moment, for maybe the length of a breath, I was in love with her too. But then I exhaled. Because the bottom line was, I didn't want to be *that* guy. Not only her first, but the one she would hate forever.

I knew in my soul that as much as I cared for her, as much as I loved her in friendship or beyond, that I was in no state of mind to make this decision. I knew that whatever decisions we made would be within a realm of insulation. And that once we returned to Boulder, our choices could have nasty consequences.

In the past week, my pop had died, we'd skipped to Vegas, I'd fucked Cherry in the bathroom stall, we'd lost Jonesy and the Tylenol, we'd consumed more than our fair share of booze, and I was able to swallow it all. It was a roller coaster, and although I felt nauseated from the sudden dips and the heavy G-force of the hairpin turns, the insulation of drink and environment kept me going.

But then Kathy told me I would be her first. Reality kicked in. Cracks formed in the insulation. And I panicked because if this were real, then everything was real.

Pressure built behind my eyes. Bile churned in my stomach. Everything hit me all at once with the force of a charging rhino and I needed to get out. I needed to run. I needed to be somewhere far away from Kathy, away from reality.

Kathy saw me slip and land and she moved to my side asking was I all right. I flung her arm aside, stood, and grabbed my pants as I made my way from the tub to the door and into the hallway.

Before the door swung shut, I turned. A part of me was screaming to stop running, to talk to this girl who had opened herself with the faith of goodness and trust. This girl who wanted to *help* me, wanted to *love* me.

I turned, saw her as she knelt in the tub, her hands gripping the lip so tightly they almost blended with the white marble. Her mouth was slightly open, her brow wrinkled in confusion. She watched me outside the door, wondering if I would stop and come back and make it all better and, and, and …

… and then the door shut. I closed my eyes, breathed in the cool air of the air conditioning. Goose bumps rose on my arms. My skin tightened and my penis shrank. The colder I got, the faster the insulation enveloped me.

I heard the door handle to the bathroom jiggle, and ran to the nearest place I could hide. And when I was safe, in the darkness of the walk-in closet, I put my back to the door and slept.

We didn't speak until Peter's wedding six months later.

Friday

Downtown Denver Hotel Monaco

I tell Kathy all of this. I tell her what I should have told her that night, and after I'm done, after taking a deep breath, I apologize to her. Over and over I apologize. Because only then do I fully understand how much I hurt her. I start to cry. She starts to cry. We hold each other and all I can do is apologize.

But as I do, a second understanding fades into the first. Were I to go back and do it all over, were I given another chance to sleep with Kathy, to take her virginity, to take the friendship to the next level, I'd still run. Because beyond Vegas, there wasn't a future for us.

I stop crying, stop blubbering. I tell her this.

And she waits for me to me to say that although I wouldn't have slept with her, I would have stopped that door from shutting, I would have returned to her side and explained my reasoning. But I don't. I don't tell her any of that, because had I to do it over, even if I could avoid hurting her, I wouldn't change a thing. Because of all the things I could change about my past, this was low on the list. In comparison to Pamela, Hillary, or Heather, Kathy was low on the list.

I don't tell her all of these things. I break our embrace, step back. And she punches me.

I spin, fall. And then I'm in the pool and unable to breathe and my panic rises and I'm struggling to move, to swim, to stand, but discovering that my limbs are unresponsive, the panic spikes, then all but disappears as the warmth of the sun-heated water infuses my body with a balm of relaxation and comfort and I begin to let go, begin to meld into the inevitable, begin to ...

Kathy pulls me out, of course. Just wades into the shallow end, flips me over, and tows me out. A little coughing, a little spitting up water, but no mouth-to-mouth, no drama. Which, as I gaze up at her, I realize sorta pisses her off. As if I've robbed her of this, too. As if my life being in true jeopardy would have balanced the scales.

And I'm about to ask her why this matters to her so much, why, after all these years, she still gives a damn about me. But I don't. Because she shakes her head, stands, and says, "Davis, you're just as clueless as ever. All these years, all this time, you've been thinking with your dick and assuming that if you fuck something up, it's because you either fucked someone or you didn't. But ya know what? I didn't care that you didn't sleep with me. I didn't care that you left me in that bathtub. Yes, it damn well fucking hurt, but I got over it. I got past it. Because I valued our friendship enough to do that. But what's sad, is that you didn't. And as you were talking, as you were telling me what went on in that warehouse of boxed away shit between your ears, I kept waiting for the part when you grew the fuck up. When you realized what was important — even if it was in that hallway when you saw me, or in the pool, or even ... But you're still doing it. You're still living in this little bubble of yours, and you refuse to join the real people in the real world. Hell of a fucking apology, Davis. Hell of a fucking apology."

And she leaves.

I'm reminded of Marnie, my high school girlfriend. I'd last spoken to her when she hung up on me, my freshman year at Colorado University. Back before the Friday Night Club. Back before everything. It's the finality of it all. The slap. The hang-up. They're my two moments with women that ended completely.

I ascend the hotel stairs, bypassing the elevator to give myself some more time to think before I'm back with the boys. Around floor five, I realize that Kathy was right. And I wonder what life would have been like had I returned to that bathroom, had I treated her as I treat Peter or Divan or Jonesy — as someone *worth* transcending the issues and the crap and the drama. As someone *worth* valuing as a true friend.

But then I realize that there wasn't any way I could have done that. *Now*, maybe. But not *then*. And when I go further along this line of thought, I realize that had we patched things up, had we remained friends, then I'd never be here. I'd never have Pamela. I'd never be stepping from the safety of my little bubble (oh, if Kathy knew the irony of her words), and I'd never be joining the real people in the real world.

Around floor seven, a part of me wonders if I should have lied to Kathy and told her everything she wanted to hear? But then 'should' becomes 'could' when I realize I don't have the ability to lie right now even if I wished. Forty-eight hours ago, I could have spun a fantastical yarn and we probably would have ended up in bed. But now, faced with all the lies in the past, all the delusions I've had with myself, I grasp that

I can't lie anymore. That I have to face reality. That I have to face honesty and my sins of the past.

And this scares the shit out of me.

It also causes me to wonder if I've undergone a true transformation or if this is just another justification of my selfishness. Am I hiding behind the honesty when in reality I'm just frightened of intimacy? Is that such a bad thing? I'm finally being honest with myself, and in turn, with others. Sure, I'm the bad man, but I'm not obfuscating anymore. I'm not redirecting people's attention away from me. I'm open and honest to whatever end it'll lead me.

Then I think of Pamela and Hillary and feel the burn of Kathy's slap. What if I'm honest with Pamela? Would that be selfish? Or is it selfish to hold everything back?

Selfishness beats selflessness?

Selflessness beats selfishness?

Amazing. I'm nearing my thirties and questioning the same things as a ten-year-old. How to act in a given situation. How to be a better person.

But there's a difference, isn't there? Kids don't openly question these things. They learn about them through trial and error. They comprehend pleasure and pain through years of experience.

Is this the lesson I'm learning now? Am I learning how to identify these situations as they come up? Am I entering the puberty of my twenties where the rules don't change, but my understanding of them does? Will this lead me to be the man who marries Pamela and doesn't flee?

The suite door is open, but only silence spills into the hallway. No talking, no laughing, no *Simpsons*.

A note taped to the mirror reads 'Warm beer + no ice = pain.'

I chuckle and wonder how long they've been gone. Then it hits me: I'm alone. The night before my wedding, and I'm alone.

The depression nearly forces me to my knees; the anxiety sucks the air from my lungs. I flee, stumbling, to the balcony.

The suite is high enough for me to inhale the cityscape, for my mind and emotions to run wild. I allow them. Like dogs running in an open field, they run and run until it seems as if they can't run anymore and still they run.

Time has no boundaries. My life condenses. Twenty-eight years smash together in a singular dance between sun and moon. I am but an observer, watching it all within a matter of minutes, seconds.

A five-year-old Davis sits with a seventeen-year-old Davis who plays cards with a thirteen-year-old Davis who sneaks shots from his pop's liquor cabinet with a twenty-six-year-old Davis who is keenly aware that he is a participant and observer and godlike idol in his mind's eye, and he screams with the coming insanity because all he wants to do is make it stop so he can try and find some logic, some understanding, and still the singular dance continues.

I close my eyes and slump in exhaustion. When I open them, through blurred and swimming vision, I see drops of blood dripping from my lip. Kathy's slap must have reopened a cut. Over the balcony to the parking lot where they strike the hood of a car eight floors below, I watch them. Every drop, drop, drop. And a part of me wishes I am the one releasing my grip on everything I know and allowing myself to flow into the realm of the beyond. Such a dimension must be superior to insanity, has to be better than the wave of panic and nausea and gut-wrenching depression and lung-burning screaming. Doesn't it?

My blood clots. My breathing slows. My mind returns. Tired, but it's there. Barely.

I'm still. To move in body may risk another dislodging of the mind and emotion. I wish to be here, to be now, to exist in the moment.

My vision returns from its blurred sanctuary. I hear the city. And I slowly come to understand that I'm not alone. For the first time since my pop died, I feel as though I can do it. That I can exist without everyone I know. Without Peter. Without Jonesy. But most importantly, without the girls onto whom I've grasped whenever the panic and anxiety rise up within me. I don't need Kathy or Hillary or Heather or ...

The heat of desire rises within my chest. I'm not afraid. I'm not afraid to discuss the uncertainty of future or commitment. I'm not afraid to experience the joys and disappointments. I'm not afraid to step forward without holding onto the tethers of my past.

I'm alone, and although I have any number of options to remedy this, I look to only one. I want to speak to Pamela. No. I want to *see* Pamela. I want to see her, hold her in my arms, bury my head in her neck, smell her hair, close my eyes, and feel her.

And it returns. Not the bubble, but that giddy, fulfilling comfort that exists in the realm *beyond* the drug of physical gratification.

I've figured it all out. I've turned the corner and cast off the moorings of my past with the understanding of who I was, who I am, and who I'm going to be. I will become a faithful person. I will become a good person. No, not a good person. A good man. Because of Pamela. It's all because of Pamela.

I need to tell her all of this. And I will. I will tell her what a fool I've been. I will tell her that I'm still a fool. And I know in my heart that she will understand what I now understand: that there is hope for a self-observant fool. It's progress. It's growing up.

I turn, enter the room, and take the first steps toward the man I'm going to become. But as I near the exit, my focus is jolted. Music blares from the bathroom, five feet to the left of the door.

For a moment, I discount the music, the jolting. I refocus, find my path, and begin to depart. Then I recognize the plucks of the bass guitar. I stop, my curiosity piqued. I can't place it. It … it sounds familiar, but … the Violent Femmes? My mind can't quite figure it out. I hold, listening, and then the music is gone. No, not gone, just turned down.

I say, "Peter?"

Nothing. The door to the bathroom is slightly ajar, and from the inside light, I can see the shadow of someone crossing the tile floor. There's a small squeak of metal on metal, and then the sound of water rushes through pipes and into the porcelain tub.

That's when I see the t-shirt on the floor near the bathroom doorway. Not just a t-shirt, a baby tee. One a bar girl would wear without a bra when she needed a boost of self-esteem.

I struggle. I reach for the exit, grasp the latch, but my vision never strays from the baby tee. And that's what tips my focus. I haven't forgotten about Pamela or my future with her, but I have to know.

I near the bathroom and lightly push open the door. I stop when I see a flesh-colored reflection in the mirror, already hazy from the rising steam. Christmas lights are strung up around the vanity mirror, the prints of nondescript landscapes, the globe light above.

I cast a line into the waters of memory. The lights have caused the surface to ripple with an image attached to an emotion. Something bites, jerks, pulls the line so hard that I'm yanked off my feet and into the ether. I'm weightless, effortlessly being pulled into a state of comfort and bliss and orgasmic ecstasy. I tighten my grip on the line, on the emotion, and hold on with all my strength.

I swing the door open, slowly, but completely. And the moment the wood separates from the pads of my fingers, my stomach drops out. First in surprise, then in anger, then back to surprise.

It's the Imposter. She's naked, bending at the waist to test the water, now flipping the shower on and letting the steaming streams hit her outstretched hand. And she's stunning.

Then I remember the strip club and my attraction disappears, returns, disappears, and I say, "You've got a lot of fucking nerve."

She turns to me, looking over her beautiful shoulder, smiling with her lips and fucking me with her eyes. My anger blooms and I say, "Seriously. Get the fuck out."

But her smile doesn't fade. Instead, she cocks her head to the side, stands, turns toward me, and shows me her gorgeous, unabashed nakedness.

She says, "You feel it?"

Oh, God.

She says, "You feel it, don't you?"

Oh, dear God.

And I say, "I still do."

And she says, "Yeah."

And then Heather is moving to me and kissing me and I'm kissing her and my hands touch her naked flesh and my arms envelope her and oh, God, oh sweet Lord in Heaven how I've dreamed of this moment.

CHAPTER FIFTEEN

Then

I saw him, nodded, walked to the stone bench next to him and sat. In the distance, the jingle of an ice-cream truck rolled along.

I took a deep breath, held it, exhaled. I looked at him and all plans on how to begin the conversation disappeared.

I said, "Um ... Hey."

He said, "Whoa, look who shows up!"

"I know, I know."

"You know how long it's been?"

"I know, I know."

"Really?"

"No."

"A while. A long while."

I said, "Yeah. Sorry about that."

"You should be. Christ, you should be."

"Yeah, well ... Things have been busy."

"An old excuse with more years than truth."

"When did you get so proverbial?"

"The years do that. You're looking good."

"Yeah, well ..."

"You've met a girl."

I said, "What?"

"You finally put aside the running around and decided to settle down, eh?"

"Yeah, about that ..."

"You don't think settling is a good thing?"

"Never seemed to suit you."

"I was a fool."

I said, "Was?"

"I've grown."

"Full of yourself, apparently."

"Is that why you came here? To insult me?"

"I thought we were just playin'."

"We are. You need to lighten up. Who is she?"

I said, "Her name is Pamela."

"Sweet name."

"It's nice."

"No, literally. It means 'all sweetness'."

"Really?"

"Where did ya meet this Sweetie?"

"At a wedding."

"Who got married?"

"Peter."

"Peter Carter?"

"Yeah."

"Wow. I've been out of the loop. Who did he marry?"

I said, "A girl he met in California. Naomi."

"That's a good name. Biblical."

"She seems like a good girl."

"Then why is she with Peter?"

"She's not."

"It's over already?"

"A while ago, actually."

"Ah, young love. So, what does she do?"

"Naomi?"

"Pamela."

I said, "Oh. She's an attorney."

"You landed a shark?"

"I didn't land anything."

"But you're gonna marry her."

"Who said anything about marriage?"

"Come on, Davis."

"Okay. I'm going to ask her to marry me, but I didn't land her."

"Semantics. So, you're marrying a shark, eh?"

I said, "Attorney. And she hasn't said yes, yet."

"What kind of a shark is she?"

"Does it matter?"

"I'm just making conversation."

I said, "This is happening a bit fast."

"What? Can't bring yourself to open up?"

"I shouldn't have come here."

"Where are you going?"

"Away."

"Wait. Come back. I'm sorry."

"What?"

"It's bad form to joke about your future wife. I'm sorry."

I said, "Yeah. Okay."

"So ... why now?"

"What?"

"Why are you getting married?"

"For the last time, she hasn't said —"

"But she will, right? You wouldn't be considering this if you didn't think she'd gush and cry and say yes, right?"

"I guess so, yeah."

"So, then, what is it about Pamela that you couldn't find in the others?"

I said, "I don't know."

"Good answer."

"No, I mean I really don't know. I just know I like it and I'm not sure if I want to live without it."

"You're not sure?"

"Yeah."

"Pardon me for saying this, but —"

I said, "I know."

"If you're going to marry the girl, you should —"

"I know!"

"Why are you here, Davis?"

"I thought that was obvious."

"Very little is obvious to me these days. Enlighten me."

"I ... I don't really have anyone to confide in."

"And you chose me?"

"Maybe I shouldn't have."

"No, I'm flattered. But you have to forgive me for being skeptical ... So ... what did you want to confide?"

I said, "It doesn't really work like that."

"Sorry, I'm new at this."

"It's ... Just be quiet and let me talk."

"Okay. Whenever you're ready just hit me with —"

"Will you shut up for a moment? Shit. I don't know where to begin."

"Why not start with why you want to get married."

I said, "I think I love her."

"We're back at this again?"

"Okay. I do love her. But there's a part of me that, you know, doesn't know if I want to give up the rest."

"The rest?"

"Yeah. The others. I'm trying to understand if I can love one person but still want —"

"Wouldn't Jonesy be better for this?"

I said, "He's involved with his wife and —"

"You don't trust him."

"Not when it comes to this, no."

"Why?"

"Because I can't."

"Is opening yourself up that bad?"

"This question coming from you?"

"Good point. But you have to have someone, right?"

I said, "I have you."

"Okay. Let's do this then. Why are you so afraid of commitment?"

"Just cut through the garbage, why don't ya?"

"It's getting cold out here. You bring a jacket?"

"You see a jacket?"

"Then, before you get hypothermia ... Why are you so afraid of commitment?"

"I just ... If I do this, if I step forward and commit myself and something goes wrong ..."

"So you're worried about picking up the pieces?"

I said, "And getting back to my life, yeah."

"Davis, if you marry, you can't do it thinking about the 'what if' ... You have to truly believe that being married to Pamela *will* be your life."

"But if it ends ..."

"You can't go into a game thinking you're gonna lose."

"But a game has an ending."

"So does life."

I said, "... Yeah."

"Davis, you know you love this girl. It's obvious when you talk about her and I'm sure it's obvious when you tell her."

Now

She says, "I love you, Davis. I've always loved you."

Then

I said, "I tell her all the time."

"Yeah, you tell her, and I'm sure you tell everyone else, but do you tell yourself? When you're alone, do you believe that you love her?"

Now

She says, "Tell me you love me. I want to hear it."

Then

I said, "Yeah. I do."

"Then you don't need to be talking to me or anyone. You just need to tell yourself that. And you need to remind yourself of it when you're tempted."

Now

She says, "Spend the night with me. Take a shower with me."

Then

"You need to ask yourself what you're going to gain if you marry this girl."

Now

She says, "It'll be what we've always dreamed. And then, you can decide what you want."

Then

"And you have to ask yourself what you're going to lose if you don't."

Now

She says, "Because I can't let you get married without knowing what it could be like with me."

Then

"Because you're right."

Now

She says, "I love you, Davis."

Then

"You didn't land her."

Now

She says, "I love you and I tried to stay away, but God, Davis."

Then

"She landed you."

Now

She says, "I've dreamed of this moment with you."

Then

"And a girl who can land you can get the pick of the store, but she saw that not only did you look good, not only were you in style, not only were you in demand ... but that you fit."

Now

She says, "I've dreamed of this moment, and I had to know what it felt like."

Then

"And a woman knows a lot about how things fit. And that's something that you have to trust."

Now

She says, "I had to know what it felt to kiss you, to touch you ..."

Then

I said, "How do I trust that she fits me?"

Now

She says, "... To have you inside me ..."

Then

"Oh, you'll know. It'll hit you when you least expect it."

Now

Heather says, "... To have you —"

I say, "Wait."

And when she keeps kissing me, sliding my pants down with one hand, making my mast rise with the other. I push her back. It's one of the hardest things I've ever done and I'm sure that few things in the future will match it. But I do it because I wasn't feeling it. Not the passionate desire for the physical drug, not my unbridled emotion running amuck. I was remembering something, something fucking powerful, but I wasn't feeling it.

So I push her back and I say, "Wait."

"For what?" she says, blinking in shock.

"I ... Why are you here?"

"What?"

"Why are you —"

She says, "I heard you the first time."

"Then why —"

"Isn't it obvious?"

"Yes. No. I mean, why now? Why are you here now? Right this moment?"

She says, "Have you been listening to anything I've ... I'm here because I couldn't stop thinking about you."

"When did that start?"

"What?"

"It doesn't matter. I ... I can't believe I'm going to say this, but ... but you need to go."

"Davis? What's the matter?"

"I'm getting married tomorrow."

She cozies up to me. "I know. That's why I'm here."

"No ... No." I push her back again, holding her at arms' length. Afraid to let her go for fear she'll come near me again; afraid because I'm not sure if I'd be able to push her away again. I say, "I can't be fucking around, Heather. I can't be doing this."

"Oh, but you could last night?" Stung, crossing her arms across her naked breasts.

I say, "Nothing happened last night."

"You don't need to lie to me, Davis."

"Nothing happened last night. But even if it did, which it didn't, I can't do this now."

"You mean you can't do this with *me* now."

"Not with you. Not with anyone."

"Fuck, Davis." She pulls from my grip but doesn't move. Not toward me. Not away. "Don't you want this?"

I think about it. "Yeah. I do."

She blinks, brow wrinkled in confusion.

I say, "Heather. I want you, but I can't have you."

"But I'm here. I'm right *here*. I'm standing right in front of you. I'm standing here *naked*, right in front of you."

"That's not what I mean."

"Davis," she says, her voice is softer now. Silkier. It's a side of her I've never seen. She's a siren. A flash of the eyes. A crooked smile. And the song she's singing is intoxicating. A lesser man would have fallen for her charms. A lesser man would have taken her in his arms in a moment. A lesser man would have been devoured.

I am that lesser man.

But I'm also a lesser man in love with a figment of the past, not the woman before me. The woman before me resembles the figment in physical form only. And while she's still beyond any conjured fantasy, my longing stops there. Because my figment would never come to me like this.

As she sings her siren's song, the spell I'm under shatters. And she sees this in my eyes. She sees I'm not in love with her anymore. She sees that I'm not in love with who she's become.

"Well," she says. "That's it then, isn't it?"

I pull a towel off the wall, hand it to her. A part of me wants to wrap it around her, to touch her, but I don't. That part of me is also shattered. The child within me has let go of the past. But the real reason why I don't wrap the towel around Heather? The real reason I don't touch her?

When I look at Heather, all I think about is Pamela. My fiancée. The woman I love.

I tell Heather as much. This time, I'm not slapped. This time, the girl leaves without a sound.

I wait for a moment, two, then move to stop her. I need to know something.

She's in the bedroom, dressing fast.

I say, "Heather?"

She doesn't respond. I reach out to her, touch her shoulder. She shudders, nearly crumbles. And when she speaks, my love for her returns like a hurricane lashing a beach.

"I thought … I thought that this was what you wanted. That this was what you liked."

I say, "What are you talking about?" But I already know the answer.

She says, "When Hillary told me you were getting married … she told me it was my last chance." She turns to me, her eyes wet, her cheap mascara running down her cheeks. "She knew, Davis. She knew from the moment she saw us outside on the balcony. She trusted us not to do anything, and because we didn't, her faith that you two would eventually end up together remained intact. But when you ended things with her, when you decided to give her up for Pamela, her faith disappeared.

"Instead of wallowing in self-pity, she thought about me. Because she knew how I still felt ... my pathetic attempts over the years to be crafty when I asked about you ... she knew. So, when you ended things with her, she realized that while she had all these memories to comfort her, I had very few.

"She said that this was my last chance to find out if we're meant to be together. She told me it was okay, that although she loves you more than you will ever know, she could no longer stand in the way of us taking a chance."

Heather's eyes never leave mine. This is her way of asking for forgiveness. Not begging. She has too much pride to beg.

She says, "But she also knew that no matter how much I *wanted* to go to you, I *couldn't*. Because I'm not that woman. I'm not like my sister. I could never adopt the nature of what it takes to be like her. And that's when we realized that instead of me trying to *be* like her, I had to *become* her."

With each tear, I realize that while she isn't begging *me* for forgiveness, she's begging *her pride* for forgiveness. For as much as Heather loves her sister and accepts her unconditionally, locking away her pride is the only way she can allow herself to become what she feels her sister chose to embody.

She says, "Hillary didn't want me to always wonder, to always regret. And when I continued to say no, she broke down and explained it to me in a way that caused us to become closer than we ever had before.

"We've never really shared anything. Our parents, but not our blood, not our heritage. But now, we can openly share something we both love and cherish. We can share our feelings for you, Davis. But while I have the part of you that she always wanted — your heart, your emotions — she has the part of you that I always wanted — your touch, your caress, your kiss."

And I begin to understand. Heather would never have compromised her sense of self were it not for me. To be with me, she discarded not only her clothing, but her integrity, her honor.

"She explained this to me, and we cried and we held each other … and I decided then to do it. I decided to become her so I could know what it felt like to have both sides of you. Then, I would bring that to her. I would share it with her.

"But we both knew it had to be me coming to you, but I had to *become her* to have a shot."

I stand there, listening, wanting to hold her and tell her that I'm not worth this, that I'm not worth all the pain, that I'm sorry for pretending I am. But I don't say a word, because it won't make a damn bit of difference. I've done this to her and there's nothing I can do to undo it.

But I can listen. I can listen, and I can begin to respect her. I can begin to respect them.

She says, "It was fun, actually, at first. We were girls again playing dress up. I was the little sister accepted into her world. But when I came here, it wasn't fun anymore. It was … it felt …"

She struggles. I let her. I'll insult her if I interrupt.

"Coming here was going against everything I am. It tore me up inside, but I also felt that burn because I was giving in to desire."

Her lower lip begins to quaver; her voice begins to catch.

"When you walked in that bathroom and realized it was me, I saw the way you reacted. I saw that raw desire of temptation, and it was overwhelming. I loved it. I wanted more. I began to consider things I'd never in my life considered. I wanted you to run away with me, from your wedding, and *be* with me and only me. And you know what? I would have done it."

She looks down, to the side, smiling in disgust and amazement as she comes to understand the power of the moment.

She says, "Wow. That's power." Then she lifts her chin and again we're locked into each other. "I would have done it, and I wouldn't have looked back. And even now, I'd consider it. If you asked me right now, this moment, I'd come so close to saying yes just to see again the way you looked at me in the bathroom."

She stops, her breathing labored. Her once silent tears are given depth and voice. The sobs begin to come.

She says, "Earlier, when you stopped me, when you pushed me away, I wanted you more and more and fuck all I was going to fight for it. And then I saw you look at me with disappointment and shame and a total loss of love … That was a slap across my face … A slap full of everything I've become … and now … I don't know how I can stop being her … I don't know how to go back to being the girl you fell in love with."

She crumbles then. She crumbles and I catch her and I hold her and we both cry. No words are spoken. Nothing needs to be said. We know what we were, what we've become. We know that we're so tempted by the other it's overwhelming. And so we hold each other in the moment, until we have the strength to carry on.

As we do, I push back her hair and kiss her forehead. She looks up at me and she's the girl I fell for eight years ago who cocked her head slightly, ran her tongue along the bottom of her upper teeth — not in an 'I want you' way, but in an unconscious, 'I'm trying to figure out what to make of you' way — and peered into my eyes, studying me.

I'm naked before her. Not just flesh, but essence and soul. Panic rises within me. I try to pull back, but she holds firm, as if breaking the connection will cause her assessment irreparable damage.

We kiss.

It's slow. It's tender. It's long. It's perfect.

We surge with emotions and our future flashes before us. We run off together and elope. Away from everyone and everything we know. We start a new life for ourselves in a small town far, far away. And we love each other, and we lead a simple life. And then she's pregnant and she gives birth to our son, who we name after my pop, and then a daughter we name after her grandmother, and we're the perfect happy family. And the kids grow, and we laugh, and we play in the backyard, and we continue to love each other, our family. And then our kids are grown and off on their own and we have the house to ourselves again and we're children again, chasing each other around the house, making love in every room, on every piece of furniture. And then we're chasing our grandkids around the house as our kids laugh and love, and it's complete perfection.

And then we part. And open our eyes. And we both realize we want to turn the fantasy into reality. To run off and become those people, those loving people, those future grandparents of laughter and perfection.

But we know it's just a fantasy, because life isn't perfect. It takes time and energy and we'd just end up disappointing ourselves. Instead, we nod in acceptance. We share a knowing smile. We stand and hold each other close as we stare into each other's souls like love-struck teenagers after a first, perfect date with a lifetime of possibilities ahead of us. And we part, not saying a word. We end as we began ... with perfection.

After she leaves, I stand in the doorway, enjoying the intoxicating bloom within me, when I notice something odd and wonderful. As I'm soaking in the fantasy, it isn't Heather within the bubble, it's Pamela. Everything else is the same — the love, the laughter, the same endless joy. But it's coupled with stupid fights every couple endures; with laughter when we realize how ridiculous it all is; with the drag-out screaming matches ending when you both crack and cry and hug and promise to listen to each other and to not become the monsters you just let out.

Fantasy melds with reality. Perfection couples with imperfection. Born is understanding. A life full of depth, full of shades and textures, is a life worth tasting. And it's a life I can feel and grasp and never release because it's attainable.

And it's what I want. I want the understanding with Pamela. I want this life with Pamela.

My Pamela.

Peter, Divan, and Jonesy walk in.

Peter points to the hallway and says, "Was that who I think it was?"

I nod, close my eyes, not wanting to let this feeling go.

He says, "You didn't ..."

I open my eyes, shake my head.

"Where's Kathy?" says Divan.

I shrug, say nothing.

Divan's eyes widen. "You passed them *both* up? You're a better man than I."

"No," I say. "I'm not."

Silence. Divan's surprise softens to admiration. A smile of approval appears on Jonesy's mug. And Peter ... Peter shakes his head in disbelief, and gazes at me with a smile so big and crooked and genuine that I know nothing between us will ever be the same.

For the first time since Jonesy interrupted my having phone sex with Marnie and took me to Peter Carter's party, I feel as if I'm not the Davis of the Friday Night Club. I feel as if I'm a better man.

Peter says, "Congratulations, Davis." He hands me the bottle of rum, already a fifth gone. "You've taken your first step to a larger world."

Peter Carter, the closet geek.

Then

I looked away, then back down. There was so much more to say, but nothing came out. It was probably for the better. Save it for later. Don't force it.

"Well, I'm out of here," I said. "I'm … I'm gonna propose to her soon. Probably this weekend. I'll let ya know how it goes, okay?"

I paused, taking one last look at the small granite headstone, then walked away.

CHAPTER SIXTEEN

It was Peter who told Kathy and Heather where we were staying.

He says, "Dude, I told them before the bachelor party, before the fight. And ya know, with all the shit that went down after, I completely forgot I even did it. I mean, fuck. How dumb is that shit?"

Divan says, "On a scale of one to ten?"

Jonesy says, "Or is this a 'what's dumber than dumb?' moment?"

"I'm sorry dude," Peter says. "It was reprehensible of me."

"Reprehensible?" Divan says, "Can he do that? Just make up words?"

Jonesy says, "He's an actor. He fills silence with nothing."

Peter's about to tell me why he called Kathy and Heather in the first place when I say, "It's okay."

"No," he says. "It wasn't."

"Yeah, it was. Whatever your reason, no matter how you saw it play out in your mind, it was needed."

"I guess ... I guess it ended up being your final test."

"No. As cheesy as it sounds, my final test has yet to come, and I don't have a clue how I'm going to pass."

That's when I tell them my plan. And as I stand, ready to enact my plan, Divan says, "Do you even know where she is?"

I shrug. "I expect she's at the hotel."

And when Jonesy says, "She's not at the hotel," we all look at him.

He says, "I heard the girls talking about a hotel slash spa where they could get pampered without leaving their room."

Divan says, "But you don't have any idea where this hotel slash spa is, do ya?"

Jonesy shakes his head.

I ponder, and then start to dial my cell. I say, "I'll call her mother. She'll know."

Divan says, "But will she tell you slash help you?"

I never find out. The moment I hit send, Peter grabs the phone from my hand and throws it out the balcony doorway, all without spilling his drink.

I say, "What the fuck?"

"How many times have you tried to call Pamela tonight?"

"I wasn't —"

"Eight times," he says.

Jonesy says, "I counted ten."

Divan says, "It's six actually. He checked his voice mail four times, so technically they don't count."

Peter says, "It's not going to happen tonight. Face that fact."

"Face that fact?" I say. "Do you have any idea what I'm about to lose?"

"Yeah," he says. "I do." And when he puts his hand on my shoulder and flashes his boyish smile I realize that I'm not looking at the movie-star Peter Carter, or Peter Carter of the Friday Night Club, but the Peter Carter who was reeling from our Las Vegas adventure.

But then it's gone, and there's sadness behind the mask of the Peter Carter that the world has fallen in love with. He says, "You don't know where she is now, but you know where she's going to be."

I look at all of them. And they all wear the same look: Raw determination, mixed with youthful enthusiasm. They know what Peter's suggesting. And they all want in.

"No," I say. "For once in my life, I need to do this on my own."

I'm halfway to the door when Jonesy says, "Fuck you, Davis."

I turn to him. We all turn to him.

"Yeah, you heard me. Fuck you. You think that you're going to just walk away from everything that we've been a part of? You think it's that easy? Well, fuck you!"

He's spilling his beer with his wild gestures. Divan plucks it deftly from his grip.

Jonesy says, "We're your fucking friends, goddammit. And we're not going to fucking let you leave this goddamned room to do this without us. And you want to know why? Do you want to fucking know *why*? Because we're not just your fucking friends, we're your brothers. Haven't you learned anything?"

He begins to rant about the past, about what we've been through. Some of it makes sense. Most of it is just a Faulknerian stream-of-consciousness mess that leaves us marveling. In the end, it came down to this:

"If you walk out that door and don't accept our help, you'll be tossing our friendship aside. Because if this is the most important moment in your life, then we're damn well going to help you with it because we aren't going to let you fail."

He stops, breathes. Divan hands him his beer. He drinks.

After a moment, Divan says, "What my esteemed colleague is attempting to convey, is that we love ya, man. And whether or not you want it, our backs and our shoulders are yours."

Peter smiles, tips his bottle my way.

I sigh, shake my head, and say, "Well, fuck my lord with a dildo. How can I say no to that?"

The plan we come up is flawless. We map it out to perfection. We weigh the pros and cons, hear the reasons I shouldn't do what I'm about to do, and go ahead with it anyway.

And so it's hatched. They'll run interference. The wild card will be Pamela's mother. As a last-ditch fix, I call my mother from Peter's cell and tell her what we're going to do.

She says, "You wake me up at — what time is it?"

In the background, Donald says, "Past his curfew."

My mother says, "Oh, my God, Davis? You wake me up at the crack of past your curfew to tell me this?"

"I need to do it, Mother."

"But why now? You'll have a long flight to St. Croix and plenty of time on —"

"Mother ..."

"Okay, okay. I'll help out, I'll help out."

In the background, Donald says, "Help out? Help out with what?"

"Nothing, Donald."

"What's that kid doing now?"

"Donald ..."

"Don't 'Donald' me! I know when something's about to go down. I can feel it in my bones."

"Yeah, yeah. Your bones. Always about your bones."

"Just because you retire, doesn't mean you can't feel it."

"Davis, Donald wants to help."

"You never lose what it takes to be a cop. It's in your blood!"

I close my eyes, smile, love them all.

Fast Forward

It's just past 3:00 p.m. on —

Saturday

— when we pull up to the country club. It feels asleep. The parking lot is mostly empty. The occasional golf cart skirts about. The flags hang limp above the rooftop spires.

This changes the moment I step to the asphalt. The breeze picks up. Leaves blow across the lawn. Birds take flight. Life twitches in the great monster, as if our arrival is an alarm blaring.

We watch. The four of us, side by side in our tuxedos. Jonesy, Divan, Peter, me. Silent. Calm. Cool. Terrified. We look at each other, shake hands, hug. As if we may never see each other again.

And then they're off. Jonesy, Divan, Peter. Determined. Firm. Unwavering. I stand at the car, watching them move in unison, almost lockstep. Then, as they near the Country Club, they split off to separate entrances and disappear. I'm reminded of the scene in *Silverado* when the heroes ride into town for the final showdown. Dust kicking behind their mounts, a once bustling town now silent and empty as it waits out the coming fight, the coming storm.

I hold my breath, count to fifty, start to the main entrance. With each step, I attempt to figure out what I'm going to say.

With each step, I attempt to figure out what I'm not going to say.

I reach the double doors, grasp the handle, take a deep breath, enter.

My vision darkens and before my eyes adjust, I nearly collide with the caterer. She smiles at me, a tight, insane smile, and I swear that I can see her hair grey before my eyes. And then she's off without a word.

I move on toward the hallway leading to the dressing room. Clinks of plates and glasses trickle to me. Wheels from a metal cart roll over tiled floor, thumping over each grouted rut. With each step I hear things that aren't there. A laugh behind me. A door slamming to my side. With each, I spin, search, find nothing, continue.

Realizing I have yet to hear a spoken word since my arrival, I contemplate breaking the silence. The thought causes the hairs on my neck to rise, as if I would welcome the spirits of chaos.

Down a hallway, turn a corner. The entrance to the bride's dressing room is two doors down on my right. As I approach, it opens just a bit and I'm attacked by a cacophony. Yells, arguments, curses. I freeze. Everything from my waist down goes numb.

Beyond the chaos is my goal.

The doorway to Pamela.

I swallow a hard, dry swallow and feel it rub all the way down. And before I can think about it, before I can talk my way out of it, I move to the door and pull it open.

Sound balloons, enveloping me.

I step into the assaulting noise and visionary bedlam.

To call it chaos would be extreme, but mixed with the thoughts inside my head, it's far beyond. To my right, just inside the door, are Jonesy and Bridesmaid #3, a childhood friend of Pamela's she just had to have in the wedding party although they hadn't spoken for over a decade.

Bridesmaid #3 is screaming at Jonesy for taking her purse, while he's claiming quite emphatically and femininely, that the purse is his, even though it's small and white with cherries all over it, and doesn't it match his eyes?

Behind them, Divan has Bridesmaid #2, Pamela's cousin, in stitches. He's whispering a play-by-play of the events, changing ears as he changes characters from Howard Cosell to John Madden to Harry Carrey, while tossing in some Katherine Hepburn, Spencer Tracy, and Elmer Fudd for garnish.

To their left is the doorway to Pamela's dressing room. I move.

To my right, screaming in tones that could shatter weak glass, my mother is deep into Round Two with Pamela's mother as they verbally destroy each other, their respective families, their political affiliations, and their manner of dress, paying close attention to their shoes. Physically, my mother is holding Pamela's mother at bay as she's desperately trying to pull Donald off Pamela's father.

It's Donald, bless his heart, who takes the cake in the events. I can't help but marvel at his utter enthusiasm in subduing Pamela's father. And I really mean subdue.

Later, my mother tells me that he felt awful that he failed to stop Pamela's father at the rehearsal dinner. She tells me that he didn't sleep all night, had quite a bit to drink, and kept saying, "I'm nothing but a pantywaist, a pathetic little pantywaist."

To his credit, he's anything but.

I smile as he pins Pamela's father face first over the guest book table, pulls a pair of handcuffs from his belt, and screams, "Who's a panty waste now, bitch?"

And his gunmetal grey hair moves with all of it.

Directly in front of my target, I see a calm sight, but as I near, I can taste the tension as if someone tossed moldy, wet grass onto a campfire. Peter and Naomi are nearly in whispers, exchanging barbs as if they are trapped in a black and white Screwball Comedy.

A large part of me wants to sit back and just watch, listen, absorb. But I don't. Because this is all done for me. To clear a pathway. To allow safe passage into the lion's den. I pass it all, reach my target, and enter the bride's dressing room.

I enter, shut the door behind me, and promptly Gerald Ford into a stumble off of the one-step landing. Rolling to the ground, I become entangled with discarded hair curlers, torn pantyhose, and a hot-pink feather boa.

On the other side of the small room, Pamela says, "Hi, Davis."

I pause, say, "Hi."

"What's that noise?"

"Noise?"

"Outside. Naomi went to check on it."

"Ah. Problems with the catering." I stand and begin to brush off the flotsam.

She says, "What are you doing?"

"I'm covering my eyes."

"Why?"

"... I can't see you."

"Not if you're covering your eyes."

"No, I mean, I'm not supposed to see you."

"Where did you get an idea like that?"

"Um ... tradition?"

She says, "Tradition told you that you can't see me?"

"We rapped outside. Nice guy."

"Tradition's a guy?"

"I didn't ask, he didn't tell."

"But he told you not to see me?"

"Why do you have a feather boa?"

She says, "Since when have we ever listened to tradition?"

"Um … when it's bad luck?"

"Davis?"

"Pamela?"

"Look at me."

I do. She's stunning, even without the dress. Her long, brown hair is held up and back with a simple white ribbon, exposing her soft, creamy neck that I want to kiss right then and there.

I'm nearly overwhelmed with the desire to throw her over my shoulder and run off to a small wooden church somewhere in the middle of Mexico, far away from all the drama and the history and the fucking emotional baggage.

She says, "See. No bursting into flames. No cursing the marriage to doom. All is good."

"Yeah, about that. We need to —"

"We are talking."

"No, I mean talk."

"Can you hand me the lip liner?"

I do.

"The other lip liner."

I hand her something else.

"Why are you doing your own makeup?"

"Because I want to." She stands, gets the lip liner, says, "We'll have the rest of our life to talk. Right now, I have a wedding to get ready for."

"This is important," I say.

She sighs. "Go ahead, then. Talk."

She applies the makeup like a surgeon. Deft and to the point. As if someone's life is on the line.

"Um ... Okay." I'm not sure how I'm going to begin, so I go with the easiest. "How are you feeling?"

She says, "You're right. This was important."

"I meant, how are you feeling? After last night."

"Oh, that."

"Yeah, that."

"I'm over it."

"I'm sorry?"

"I'm not. But I was tired. I was hurt. I slapped you. Now we've got an insane day ahead of us and I don't have the time or the energy or the desire to talk about it anymore. It's over."

"But it's not over."

"Sure it is. Public humiliation only goes as far as you allow it." She's not looking at me, not showing any emotional change at all. The surgeon is still at work, and it seems as if nothing is going to break her focus. She says, "In the end, Hillary was just a skeleton from your college days that scared a lot of people. At least, I'm assuming it was Hillary who felt slighted that you left her."

"Um, yeah. It was."

"But, it was a long time ago. I think the past should be left in the past, don't you?"

Aw, shit. She's leaving me an out. Do I tell her? Do I tell her that it wasn't just the college days? That it was after college and then just a few months ago?

I think about the possibilities, what damage they could cause, and after some consideration, say, "It was more than the college days."

"Oh?" No hint of reaction at all.

I say, "It was off and on until a few months ago."

Again, no reaction.

I say, "There is ... you have a right to be upset."

"Oh, I know."

"Then you're still upset."

"No. I'm over it. Did I already say that part?"

"Um ... yeah."

"Is it over now?"

"Yeah."

"Are you sure?"

"Absolutely."

"Then we'll talk about this after the wedding. Now, did —"

"Wait. That's it?"

"Yup. That's it. Now, did you pick up your tux?"

"I'm wearing my tux."

She snaps her fingers. "Jonesy did. He already told me that. I really need to write this stuff down."

"Pamela."

"Yes?"

"Don't you think we need to talk about this?"

"Priorities, Davis. I'm preparing to step into a hurricane." She's applying eye liner, or something else that goes around the eyes.

I say, "I think if you knew everything, you'd be upset."

"Oh?"

"Yeah."

"And you're sure this can't wait until —"

"I'm sorry."

"For what?"

"For everything."

"You're forgiven."

"I don't think you're taking this seriously."

"Are we done?"

I'm losing her. I'm losing her attention and I need to do something to get her to focus on what I'm saying, to get her to focus on what I need to say. I need to wake her up. To push her. Instead, I push too hard and she topples to the ground.

I say, "I saw Hillary's sister last night. I saw Heather."

Silence. Then she says, "Oh?" The surgeon just hit her first snag in the operation and is now thinking of an alternative course of action. The way she begins to fidget with the lid on a makeup jar, I can tell she's attempting to recall memories attached to the emotions when you hear someone's name. For Hillary, it's the vision of an old girlfriend whom she'd never met. For Heather, it's the one that got away.

Pamela learned about Heather from Jonesy, one evening after a baseball game, all of us drinking at the Wynkoop Brewery in Lower Downtown Denver. He had casually recounted a memory, and no one thought anything of it. Later that night, she asked me about Heather. I told her the truth, not seeing the harm. Heather was a past love. Not a big deal. But Pamela created an emotional attachment to the name, as she did with any other woman in my past.

And now, fidgeting with the lid on a makeup jar, she recalls that attachment.

She says, "And how is Heather?"

"She's good."

"Good. I'm glad she's good. That's nice to hear."

Shit. Shit, crap, shit. She's preparing to dive back into the operation. She faltered, showed a flash of emotion, and now she's cooling fast. I can't let that happen.

She says, "Is she coming to the —"

"She told me she loved me."

Silence.

"Oh?"

I wait.

She takes a breath, exhales slowly, and says, "And what did you say? When she said she loved you."

Here it is. "I told her that I loved her, too."

Silence.

"Oh?"

"But I told her I couldn't be with her. Because I wanted to be with you."

Silence.

"Oh?"

Now, I scream at myself. You have her! Now is the time to tell her everything! I say, "Can you put the makeup down?"

"I can't. In case you forgot, we're —"

"Getting married, I know. But I don't know if you know the guy you're marrying."

"Of course I do, silly." She stands, kisses me on the cheek, smiles, and goes over to another mirror, another table. "I'm marrying the guy who said 'no' to Heather last night."

"I did ... you are ... Why do you have two makeup tables?"

"Clutter. I don't like it."

"Right. I knew that."

"See? You knew that. You know me. I know you. We're getting married. Done."

Her tone moves me from calm to frustration. She's overly chipper. But behind it, she's still cold. Sterile. I force myself to take a deep breath. Force myself to understand what she's going through, what must be going through her mind. My stomach grinds into itself and I start to feel sick.

I walk to her, slowly pull her hands from her face. She doesn't look at me. Instead, she looks at herself in the mirror. As if her reflection is her counsel and is telling her to relax. To not get upset. To not run from me.

She looks down, then at me. She says, "Why are you doing this?"

"Because I think we —"

"Of all the times we can talk, why are you doing this now?"

Her focus has been broken from the surgery, but she isn't running yet. Instead, she's upset that someone dared to interrupt.

She says, "Do you know how much planning this has taken? How much time I've invested? This is our wedding day, and now, hours before, you want to talk? Such ... bad ... timing."

"I disagree."

Then softly, as if it takes all the breath from her lungs, she says, "I don't give a fuck what you think."

I balk. Who is this?

She says, "Do you ever not think about yourself? Do you ever look beyond your own little world and see how you affect those around you? There are two hundred people coming to this wedding, Davis. In two hours, two hundred people are going to be outside, watching that sunset, watching us get married under it, and because you suddenly found yourself, because you said 'no' to a girl, you think it's the most important thing in the world and you decide to barge in here and share it with me? You're like a dog that has a fresh kill and prances around showing it off to —"

"I haven't told you everything yet."

This gets her.

She says, "There's more?"

I nod slowly, letting her take it all in.

She swallows, looks away, back at herself in the mirror, and says, "Leave."

"Pamela ..."

She looks back at me. "Not now, Davis!"

She stands, goes to the first mirror, sits, and begins applying her makeup fast. Not caring what she's doing. Not thinking about what she's doing.

I say, "I think you need to —"

She spins and throws a bottle of something at me. I duck. It sails over my head and strikes a mirror. The glass spiders, but doesn't fall. Instead, cracks web from the point of impact and create more metaphors than we can stomach.

Then she stands, takes three steps toward me, forcing me to take two back, and stops. And I can see fire and anger in her eyes. She's the surgeon wielding the knife, ready to lash out at any moment. She says, "Tell me." Her lower lip is trembling. "You've got three minutes. Tell me whatever it is you want to say."

I balk again, having no idea where to begin. And all that comes out is, "This isn't fair." I inwardly cringe.

She says, "You're damn right it isn't fair." She storms past me, to the bathroom, to another sterile room of comfort, but doesn't shut the door. There, she sits on the toilet. I can see her legs. I can hear her peeing and recall the first time she felt comfortable enough to pee while I was taking a shower. I realized then it was a sure sign of comfort. When you can pee in front of someone. But now it isn't comfort. It's disdain.

"Damn, it," she says. "Why do you have to do this now?"

I wait. Until she finishes. Until she flushes. I can hear her washing her hands and, after, I can hear the water running as she stands in the bathroom and sobs. Finally. It has gotten to her.

I want to go to her. I want to tell her to forget that I'm here, forget that I'd come, forget it all and just go back in time and just think about her day. Think about her wedding. Think about all she's planned ... but I don't.

"Pamela."

"I can't ... There is so much pressure ... I ..." She struggles. And the more she does, the more I hate myself. Finally, it's me who cracks.

I say, "You're right. I've been selfish. I should have thought about what you were going through, what you *are* going through."

"They're looking at me."

"Who is?"

"Everyone. They're all looking at me and ... It's so hard to think when they're all looking at me and I'm ... I'm trying to think, to be logical. It's so hard."

"Pamela."

"And you'd think I could handle it. I'm ... I'm a fucking lawyer. I step into these courtrooms and go after huge corporations and force them to their knees in front of ... but I've never had all those eyes upon *me*, the *me* outside of the courtroom. I've never had everyone watch as *my* personal life is put on trial."

With every word, with every pause, she cuts another hole in my body. The surgeon is trying to salvage her mind, her soul, and the only way she can do that is to destroy the person who put her in harm's way.

Then, without realizing it, she goes in for the kill.

She says, "Do you love me?"

I say, "Yes, of course I do." Without hesitation. But I know the full extent of what I've done to her. I've caused her to question herself. Caused her to question the faith she not only put in others, but in herself. And when that faith in yourself is questioned, it leaves a huge wound that ends up being an aching scar, if it ever heals at all.

She says, "But you love Heather, too. That's what you wanted to talk to me about?"

"No, that's not what I wanted. Heather is in the past. She's not here. You're here. That's what I wanted to talk about."

"You wanted to talk about me being here?" Confusion has crept into her voice. Confusion, mixed with mistrust.

"Yes. Well, no." I plug forward, wanting to clear things up. To make them better. To put them behind us. "I wanted to tell you what I've realized. That in the past few days, I realized how much I love you."

"And you realized this ..."

"Yes."

"... in the past few days?"

"Yes."

"When did you stop loving me before?"

"I didn't. I never did. What I realized is that I'm not scared anymore. Not scared to marry you. Not scared to —"

"You were scared to marry me?

I pause. "I was scared to marry anyone."

"And you came in here to tell me that?"

"Yes."

"That you weren't scared to marry me anymore."

"Yes. That's why I needed to talk to you."

She pauses. Then, "And if you had to do it all over again, if you could have Heather in all the ways you've always wanted, who would you choose?"

And with that question, Pamela succeeds in what the booze, the cops, the strippers, the crazy tow-truck drivers wielding guns and, worst of all, me, couldn't do. With that question, Pamela causes my heart to stop.

My vision blurs as my head gets smoky. I sit down, hard, not realizing what's happened until I see Pamela, true to form, rush to my side and kneel.

I mutter something, not sure what I say, but it sends Pamela to the bathroom to get a glass of water. It's cold. My head clears a bit.

She says, "When was the last time you ate?"

I try to think about it and come up blank.

"Here." She puts a cookie in my hand. "Eat this." And when I don't, she breaks off a piece and puts it into my mouth. It helps. The smoke starts to dissipate.

"Holy shit, Davis. You look like you saw a ghost."

Without thinking, I say, "I did."

"What?"

I think about it then. What I'd said. What it meant. "I did."

"I'm going to call a doctor." She turns to the phone but I take her arm and lightly hold her there.

She turns back to me. "You're hallucinating from low blood sugar and, probably, dehydration. This is what happens when you drink for three —"

"I'm not hallucinating, and I'm not crazy. I know I didn't see a ghost, but ... I did ..."

"You're not making any sense, Davis."

"I know, but ..." I try to tell her what I'm thinking, but it's hitting me fast. I start to speak, stop, then resume when I decide I need to get it out or I'll overload. "You asked who I'd choose."

"Look, don't worry about that. Just clear your head and eat the cookie and —"

"I'd choose you."

"That's great, but eat the cookie and drink the —"

"Pamela ..." I take her hands in mine and squeeze. Not hard, not soft. Just enough to get her attention to know I'm not out of my mind. "I'd choose you. I'd choose you over anyone who came my way."

She studies my face, my intentions, and thinks long and hard. "Why? And don't just say that 'you love me' crap, because that only goes so far, if ya can't back it up."

Without thinking, I say, "Because when you fall down, I want to be the first one to help you up. And when you smile, I want to be the first one to see it. And when you —"

She slaps me then. Hard. And it's the first hit in the past three days that clears my head instead of clouds it.

She says, "Stop it with the sobby Hallmark shit." She isn't angry, but she isn't happy, either. She's still to the point and professional. The surgeon has returned. "Just ... just tell me, in Davis terms."

I think for a minute, then say, "Because when I think past my life with the Friday Night Club, all I see is a life with you."

The moment I say it I know it's the truth. It feels good to speak the truth. It feels good to look forward instead of behind. And it feels good to be honest.

She takes this in, composed, unspeaking. Then, "I don't know, Davis. I ... There's a part of me that wants to trust you, but it's a small part, because the greater part, the one where I place my faith in those around me, is telling me to run.

"All this time I figured you were slipping into yourself because you were nervous — like you do when you're going to give a big presentation at the university, but in the end, you'd break out of that shell and woo everyone with your confidence and your charm and your laughter — and so I didn't put much thought into you ... into you cheating.

"That word is tossed around too much — cheating. A better word would be betrayal. You betrayed me with Hillary, but, in all honesty, that part of me which is telling me to run? It's because of Heather. I truly believe you sleep with someone else because of a lack of control, an immature grasp of your primal urges, but you give your heart to someone, you love someone, because of a choice, a choice to open yourself up and trust that they won't hurt you, that they won't betray you.

"But that choice is also thrown around way too lightly these days, and instead of it being sacred, instead of it being placed in the heavens with the rest of the godly beings, it's rolling around with the rest of the filth that we mortals create.

"And so you come here and tell me that you realize how much you love me, and that you chose me over all others, and I can't begin to fathom how dirty I feel after that love was rolling around with the rest of your dirt."

She stands, sniffles. She walks to the bathroom door, and only then does she look at me. She says, "I don't know, Davis. I just don't know."

And then she shuts the door.

CHAPTER SEVENTEEN

Divan can't quite get it.

"That's what she said?"

"Yup," I say. "That's what she said."

"Yeah, I don't get it."

Peter says, "What's not to get? The girl's hurt. I would have been worried if she just accepted everything without a problem."

I look at him. We all look at him.

He says, "If she accepted it without a snit, then she'd be denying her emotions on the matter. Them's the seeds of a bad blowup in the future."

Divan says, "Did you just say 'snit'?"

Jonesy says, "'Them's the seeds?' Who talks like that?"

We're sitting outdoors, to the side of the guest chairs, near a small Romanesque fountain that seems terribly out of place at the edge of a country-club golf course. Above us, the branches of a tall pine tree stretch at least a dozen feet, creating an air of comfort. We're huddled too close together in the warm evening air, knowing that this could be the last moment we'll all be together with this mindset, this understanding of what crossroads we've traversed.

Once upon a time, four men in need of sanctuary while we fought and stumbled through a world that demanded more of us than we thought we could deliver, fell upon the Friday Night Club. Now, those same four men leave the sanctuary walls with the understanding that it was not the world they were fighting, but themselves.

Adam Jones had given in to this fact long before the rest of us. The happy family man, who for a few brief hours relived the memories of what was the glory of the hunt and the youth and the uncaring mischief without consequence, only to return to his wife and children and business and maturity. And although we will meet on weekends and holidays and hockey games where we'll curse our slowing metabolism as we drink light beer and diet soda and lament on how fast his children are growing and how age isn't as kind as it once was, we'd both know that such is a life more fulfilling and glorious than a thousand Friday Night Clubs. That such a life is a sanctuary in need of no name.

Thomas Divan is taking off in the morning. Europe, he says. On his never-ending quest to find whatever the hell he's looking for and supplementing it with motivational speaking along the way. I can picture him there, traveling on his old 1983 Honda Goldwing that he refuses to voyage without, still looking like Steve McQueen with the air of fuck it all. I once asked him how he could afford to go to all of these places, to do all of these things. He said, "If you really want to do something, you find a way."

He's discovered what he always felt but refused to acknowledge: that he is a sanctuary unto himself. And he will travel the world until he discovers the perfect place to settle down. "And there," he said, "I'll open a bar. Or a brothel. Depending on the tax breaks."

And Peter Carter...

Earlier, as we were dressing, I asked, "How did it go with Naomi?"

Divan laughed and said, "Don't ask."

"That bad?"

"You saw them. What do you think happened?"

"Yeah. It didn't look good."

"It looked awful."

"Was it really that bad?"

Peter shrugged.

Divan said, "At one point, I thought she was going to rear back and tear his throat out like a wild —"

"We're getting back together," said Peter.

We all looked at him.

He said, "Well, not together, but we're going to … try things out again. See where it takes us."

"Exclusively?" Jonesy said, brow raised.

Peter nodded. He looked tired, but he also looked more alive than I'd seen him in years. That boyish smile was firmly affixed on his face and although the lines around his eyes betrayed many a trial and error, there was a glow of hope emanating from within.

He said, "We weren't fighting as much as discussing."

Divan said, "That was one heated discussion."

"We had to get some things straight."

"You mean, she had to make sure *you* had some things straight."

"I don't know if it'll work out, but what the hell, ya know? I mean, shit, ya know?"

We all knew what he meant, what he was feeling. It was inevitable.

And that's when I asked, "What the hell did we do to deserve them? Pamela and Debbie and Naomi?"

(and Kathy and Heather and Hillary and, and, and …)

"All these years," I said, "dealing with our—"

Divan said, "Insecurities?"

Jonesy said, "Immaturity?"

Peter said, "Complete and total inability to grow the fuck up?"

I smiled. "I mean, who the fuck do they think we are to waste all this time on us?"

We were all silent for a long moment, then a voice behind us said, "Smoke and mirrors."

We all turned, stared at Donald.

"That's all it is. Intentional, unintentional. The survival of our species is based on nothing but smoke and mirrors. The attachments we make, the fears we cling to, the hopes we channel through others ... in the end, when you try to figure it all out, you discover a complete lack of tangibility to it all. It's sad, in a way, but at the same time, it's pretty damn amazing."

We all blinked at him. I wanted to ask him how long he'd been there, how much he'd heard, but the brain cells I had not maimed in the last few days were trying to process his words.

I wasn't alone. The silence stretched.

That's when Jonesy scrunched up his face and said, "No offense, sir, but I'm calling bullshit."

Donald blew a sigh of relief, smiled and said, "I was wondering how long it would take. I think I strained something trying to keep a straight face."

In the stupid grins and laughter that followed, I'm pretty sure we all felt it.

The generational gap closing, if only for a moment.

Now, sitting here, under the arms of the tall pine, I watch as people fill in the empty seats. All of them face a small wooden archway covered in fresh, blooming flowers. Behind the arch spreads a vast, lush par-5 fairway.

I haven't heard word one from Pamela, but as we're supposed to be married within the next fifteen minutes, I begin to believe all to be well. Surely she'd have told me if she were walking away, wouldn't she?

"Wouldn't she?" I say.

No one responds. It isn't the first time I've asked the question in the past two hours.

Two hours earlier, I exited the dressing room and all chaos abruptly ceased. Amid the questions, the boys drew me away. Later, after a shot or three of rum and a morsel of kitchen scrounging, I told them everything. When I was done, they all agreed that it took balls to do what I did, that I was fucking insane for doing it, and that they would unconditionally support me to the end.

To that, I said, "So, what now? I mean, really. What happens now?"

"Proceed as normal," they said.

And we did.

And we do.

And now, the Justice of the Peace nears, and smiles. We stand, shake hands with each other. Divan and Peter hug me and walk toward wherever the wedding party is gathering. I take a deep breath and —

My cell phone buzzes.

Early that morning, after we had formulated our battle plan, we found my phone chirping away on two feet of newly laid sod next to sixty feet of concrete and cars. Our awe quickly dissipated when we discovered the face of the flip-phone was cracked and void of picture.

"Eh," Divan said. "Caller ID is overrated anyway."

Next to the Justice of the Peace, I pull the phone from my tuxedo pocket and stare at it, my heart thumping loudly.

"Well," says Jonesy. "You have to know."

I nod, hesitate, flip the phone open, and close my eyes.

"Davis? It's Joanna."

I blink, laugh a hard, mind-clearing laugh.

"I hope I caught you in time. I wanted to talk about us before you got —"

I open my fingers. The phone slips, falls, and lands on the decorative cobblestone at my feet.

And then I gently, but quite firmly, snap its flip-top spine as if snuffing a cigarette.

Jonesy blinks, looks at me, to the phone, back to me. "So, we're still good?"

I sigh, smile, and say, "No. We're better than good."

Jonesy nods to the patiently waiting Justice of the Peace. We follow him along the side of the guests. Pictures snap. Eyes weep. Tissues dab.

We move to the front. I look upon everyone. My stomach begins to tighten. And then it hits me.

I'm here. I'm getting married. I'm not running. I'm fucking here. And I smile.

My shoulders lower. My jaw relaxes. I'm fucking here and I love it.

And then I see Heather in the crowd, seated near the back, and like a roaring beast from the depths of depravity and excuse and justification, the desire for one more fix for that physical attachment to my past without lasting emotion latches onto my core, freezing me in place and punching the air from my lungs and lathering me in a cold sweat and —

— suddenly I don't know what the hell I'm doing, but I know I want to run. Past my friends, my family … Her …

Flashes of the night before: colored stars, a backroom, naked flesh, Her face.

Sharply, I inhale. Beside me, Jonesy smiles, probably believing my gasp is a result from feet-numbing fear instead of gut-churning horror. I attempt to attach Her face to the naked flesh the night before. The colored stars fade into Christmas lights; the back room into a bathroom. Music — the Violent Femmes? Kisses inside my bare leg. I'm naked ...

I look out to Her. She's looking back, her half leer full of tales that could fill a *Penthouse Forum*. Or am I imagining the look? Is she squinting from the setting sun? Or is she trying not to cry because it's all about to slip past us — the potential, the wanting, the desire to say 'fuck all' and run off to the jungles of Brazil or the mountains of Argentina or some remote place where we can just be alone, just be us, just be naked, just be entwined in —

And then I see her face. I see Pamela. My Pamela.

And I breathe. And I move. And I smile.

She's gliding toward me, next to me. And I forget about Her. Because Her isn't Heather. Her is Pamela. The physical and the emotional and as cheesy and cliché as it sounds, the *reason* for my being alive.

And for a moment I wonder how I never saw this before.

I take Her offered hand, escort Her to the Justice of the Peace, and when I turn to Her and smile, I ...

Pamela doesn't know yet. I see it in her eyes that she's still struggling. Outwardly she appears fine, and by all accounts, this is going to be your typical 'I Do' wedding, with kisses and food and drink and dancing. But I know Pamela ... and I can read her ... and behind that façade, I can see her struggle even to smile as she looks at me ...

So I become strong. Solid. I show her who I've become. I'm the Davis Robertson she wants to marry. I'm a good man, a loyal man. But most of all, above it all, I'm not frightened, and I'm truly, very truly, wanting to marry her.

And so when it's time, I say 'I Do.' I feel the perfection in the moment. I know we're beginning a new life together.

And she feels it too, doesn't she? I said it. I said, 'I Do,' and meant it. But ... but she's still struggling. I see it in her eyes. She's still worried. She's still worried that I may not be the man for her, and I see the tension rise in her as the moment nears where she'll have to decide what she wants to do, and the moment is now and I suddenly find God and Buddah and Allah and Zeus and I'm praying to them all for this to be right and for us to be happy and I know my prayers are going to be answered because this is the right thing for both of us and we're meant to be together and now Pamela opens her mouth to speak.

The End

ABOUT THE AUTHOR

Jake Lurie received an MA in Screenwriting from Chapman University in 2002 and a BA in English from the University of Denver in 2000. Since then, he has completed four screenplays, several emails, and half a shopping list. He is currently working on his third novel, as his second novel was an awful disaster involving overwhelming frustration and a pathetic lack of motivation.

Made in the USA
Charleston, SC
18 January 2010